# A Dedication to...

I dedicate *Too Far Gone* to my loving wife,
Kaleigh Hackett. When the world of Tatora was just an
obscure thought in my mind, she was the one to provide
encouragement and advice along the way. She also told
me how difficult it would be to write an entire book, let
alone a series, so, of course, "Challenge Accepted!" As I
progressed with book one, *So Far Gone*, she was (and has
remained) a big part of the process. I somehow convinced
her to edit my work (pro-bono I might add), but soon it
became apparent that she had her own awesome input for
the Tatoran world. I'm proud to say that book two *Gone
But Not Forgotten*, the novella *Lorthredo & Montaug: A
Brother's Tale*, and book three *Too Far Gone*, were joint
efforts. They wouldn't be the stories they are today
without her inspiring contributions.

# Too Far Gone

## By

## J. Wright & K. Hackett

# About the Author

Jonathon Wright began writing *The Jaxon Grey Chronicles* in 2012, and the series now includes three books, a short story, and a novella, with more on the way. *So Far Gone* is the first book in this expanding series, and was self-published in May of 2015. In addition, he also has plans to write a Revolutionary War era novel based in and around his hometown.

Jonathon was born in New Jersey and raised in the rural town of Montague. He graduated from Sussex County Technical School's Engineering program in 2010, and then went on to receive a Bachelor's Degree in Criminal Justice from Johnson & Wales University in 2013.

Currently, Mr. Wright resides just outside of Rhode Island's capital, where he lives with his wife/co-author, Kaleigh, and their two cats, Stevie Wonder and Dolly Parton. During the week he works full-time for The Providence Center managing a residential program that assists individuals with mental health and substance use issues, while on the weekends he spends his time at Crossroads RI working to end homelessness.

# Table of Contents

## Part One

# Part Two

# Too Far Gone

# Part One

# Too Far Gone

# Prologue

Time wore on as Ryane continued to read Jaxon's second journal, locked away in her sealed off room on the Scynthian planet. She had nothing else to do to occupy her time, so she read fast, waiting for Orric's return.

She had read all about Jaxon's journey, starting with his disappearance from Earth, his ordeal in the Pit of the Gyx, his meeting with a telepathic tree-being, and later his escape from Aanthora. Next came his arduous journey across the Tatoran continent, where he found himself battling pirates, traversing underground waterways, and befriending Ishmae, High Chieftain of the Sapphire clan. She had recently finished reading about Jaxon's trek north, across the frozen tundra, where he and his group had finally made contact with Demtrius' people, the Dotarans.

Here she had taken a short break, interrupted by Orric. Once he had left the room, using his device that could open portals in solid walls, she thought hard about how she might escape. Nothing practical came to mind. *How many sci-fi movies have I seen with Jaxon?* she thought. *There must be something useful from at least one of them.*

Two human servants entered her room, a male and a female. They carried in her food and water, smiling at her but not saying a word.

*Maybe I can befriend them*, she thought. Perhaps it could lead to extra food and water, or special privileges. It could potentially help her to figure a way out of this place. She had no way of knowing for sure, but she knew doing something was better than doing nothing.

"Thank you," Ryane said to them. "How are you doing today?"

Neither servant replied, just widened their smiles, gently placing her meal near her.

"Do you eat the same food?" Ryane asked.

Both servants gave simultaneous nods, and then walked toward the portal.

"It's delicious," Ryane replied. "Is it always the same?"

The servants just smiled over their shoulders and continued to walk out. The portal snapped shut right behind them, and Ryane was alone once again.

*Maybe next time,* she thought, reaching for the food dish. She finished her meal in no time, using her hands since she wasn't afforded any utensils. With no napkins either, she licked her fingers clean and wiped them dry on her pants.

*Time for more reading.*

# Chapter One
# Where We Left Off

Life can be incredibly irritating at times. So much so, we tend to lose sight of what's really important and what our goals should be. For me, my biggest goal at the moment is getting back to Earth; getting back to you. Life sure is testing me, though.

It would have been easier to just give up and start anew here on Tatora; but I persevered, overcoming every obstacle with the help of my friends. Just when things seemed to finally be falling into place, and just when I thought I'd really make some headway on getting home, life hit me again. I had finally made it to the Dotarans, along with my Dotaran friend, Demtrius, our human ally, Mya, and our Scynthian companions, Nadina and Pharon. We had travelled through a bleak and frigid landscape, and at last had made contact with Demtrius' people, only to be immediately captured and incarcerated. The Dotarans apparently didn't trust us, not even Demtrius, one of their own. Now we were left to wait for their judgment.

But like my late father used to say, "Such is life." Things will happen or not happen, and most of the time there isn't much we can do about it. I am getting a bit ahead of myself though. Let me just pick up where I left off.

\*       \*       \*       \*       \*

"Demtrius?" asked one of the Dotarans skeptically, not believing his own eyes. He looked just like his two companions, and they all looked eerily similar to Demtrius. "Is it really you?"

"Yes, it is I," Demtrius replied. "I have finally

returned."

"This is wonderful," said the Dotaran. "We saw your signal from above, but none of us could believe it was actually you. Where have you been all these months? We thought you had been killed when your ship went down."

"I will tell you all that has transpired in due time," said Demtrius, "but, for now, we are all terribly cold and hungry, and are in much need of a warm night's sleep."

"Of course," said the Dotaran. "You must be exhausted from your journey."

The Dotaran then turned to the rest of us. He reached for a small compact computer that he wore on his back, as did his two companions. He pulled it forth and I watched him press a single button. Without warning, I was instantly frozen in place, completely incapable of making any movements, not even to speak. It was just like in the cave on Earth, right before I came to Tatora.

"There is no need for that, Delfwig," Demtrius protested.

"We can't take any chances," said Delfwig. "You, of all people, should understand, especially with the Scynthians."

Demtrius went to argue, but thought better of it. Then, when he regained his calm, he said, "I do understand, better than most I would say, but I have spent a great deal of time with these people. They are my friends. I would trust any one of them with my life, even the Scynthians."

A shared look of disgust crossed the Dotarans' faces.

"The four of them are our allies, not our enemies," Demtrius told them. "I vouch for them all."

"That is fine, but we still must follow protocol," said Delfwig. "Nothing personal."

"Very well," said Demtrius, knowing he was at a disadvantage. "I expect a judgment to be made and their release authorized post haste."

"If it be the will of the Captain's Council," Delfwig replied.

"Captain's Council?" asked Demtrius incredulously.

"Much has changed since your disappearance," said Delfwig, "but, as you said, there will be time for that later. For now, welcome home."

"Thank you," said Demtrius. "It's great to see you again, Delfwig."

"You as well," Delfwig replied, offering a slight smile. "Please join me in my cabin later for a drink."

"I would like that," said Demtrius.

They had, of course, been speaking in Dotaran, so I was the only other person able to understand them. It mattered little, however, as Pharon, Mya, Nadina, and I were completely immobilized by the strange Dotaran devices.

Demtrius turned to me. "I'm sorry, but we will sort this all out at the Aramis." He then started following the Dotarans back toward the iceberg.

Delfwig touched a few buttons on his compact computer, and the four of us static prisoners were lifted off of the ground, completely at the will of the Dotarans. We floated there for a second, and were then drawn forward, following Demtrius, Delfwig, and the other two Dotarans as they smoothly ascended to the top of the iceberg where their flyers were stationed.

Suddenly, though I was completely immobile, I felt Thiesel's incoming presence. He came slithering up the side of the iceberg, lunging right for us. Delfwig quickly but calmly removed the compact computer from his back and pressed another button. Thiesel came to an abrupt stop just feet from us, frozen in place just as I was. I could sense his confusion and consternation. And then I began to sense his pain. I tried to scream out for Delfwig to stop whatever he was doing to Thiesel, but it was impossible to utter even a sound.

"Strange for such a beast to be this far north," said Delfwig. "Don't worry; this will only take a moment."

He went to press another button, but Demtrius jumped in front of him and reached for the compact computer. Delfwig pulled away from him, confused by Demtrius' actions.

"Please, do not kill him," Demtrius beseeched.

"Why not?" Delfwig asked, considerably bemused.

"He is a pet of sorts, and loyal to the male human," Demtrius explained quickly. "We call him Thiesel, and he has been a reliable ally in our endeavors."

"Interesting," said Delfwig, as he pressed another button on his compact computer, instantly alleviating much of Thiesel's panic. "We will release it once we are safely in the air."

"Thank you," said Demtrius.

Mya, Nadina, Pharon, and I were then placed in the rear compartment of the larger flyer, while Demtrius and Delfwig sat at the controls in the front of the ship. We were separated by a thick pane of glass-like material that rose from the floor, effectively cutting us off from the cock-pit. The moment the ship was powered on, I was finally able to move my body again.

"Demtrius has gone back on his word," Pharon said immediately. "I knew we shouldn't have trusted him."

"He's done nothing of the sort," I replied. I was stretching my arms and legs, relieved that I had control over them again. "Everything will be sorted out once we get to the Aramis."

To be honest, I wasn't even angry with our apparent incarceration. In fact, if I had been in their position, I probably would have done something similar. Indeed, they had little reason to trust us yet. That simple reasoning failed to satisfy Pharon, however, and he continued to complain for most of the remaining flight. I'm not sure if Demtrius and Delfwig could hear him through the glass-like pane, but I thought it'd be better if they didn't.

Now that I could move about freely again, I turned to look out through one of the ship's small, circular windows. The sight of the frozen sea was much more pleasing from this vantage point. I was almost shocked, though, when I saw Thiesel scurrying after us on the ice below, following the shadow of our ship. He moved with incredible speed as he tried to keep pace with our shadow, but eventually we lost sight of him as we sped off high above the ice. I was sad to see him fade away in the distance, but something in me knew I'd see him again.

# Chapter Two
# New Leadership

It was a short flight to the Aramis, which lay hidden on a large, low lying island covered with snow and sporadic clusters of what looked like evergreen trees. Our sleek vessel zipped through the sky at incredible speeds, with the ship's mattertron providing a comfortable, non-turbulent flight. If we had possessed one of these ships at the start of our quest, then we could have made it to the Aramis from Aanthora in just a matter of hours. It was frustrating to think of, considering all we had been through to get here. Life is a journey though, and no one ever said it was going to be pleasant.

Before making it to the Aramis, we flew over a short mountain range, beyond which was a frozen lake. At the far end of this lake was the ship, sunk mostly beneath the icy surface, and covered in layer upon layer of compacted snow. The only visible parts of the craft were its main entrance at its side and a landing platform on the top. Aside from that, the ship might as well have been a large hillside on the landscape, concealed as it was.

Delfwig maneuvered our ship toward the landing platform, followed in suit by the two smaller ships that accompanied us. The entire platform then descended as one massive elevator, and we were brought to a lower flight deck on the interior of the ship. Here, I saw dozens of other teardrop-shaped ships of various sizes, as well as ground vehicles and what appeared to be construction equipment, all assembled in clusters organized by size and type.

The platform our flyer was on suddenly rotated and shifted away from the opening, bringing us off to a vacant side of the flight deck.

Demtrius and Delfwig unbuckled their belts and exited

the vessel, but the rest of us were left behind the pane of glass-like material.

"I knew they wouldn't trust us," Pharon commented for about the fifth time since we had boarded the flyer. "We'll be prisoners now, but at least Dotaran prisoners are kept warm and fed."

He seemed resigned to our apparent fate; all of us were, in fact. It was far better than running for our lives from the numerous Tatorans that wanted our heads, or staying out in the frigid cold as we had been. Still, I didn't like to be at the mercy of others, and I had found myself in that position far too often on this world.

Three new Dotarans entered our flyer, and one of them was carrying the same type of small computer that Delfwig had used. He pressed a button and, before we even had time to object, the four of us were frozen in place again, absolutely immobile. He then turned about and walked away, and we floated after him as we had done with Delfwig.

I guessed the small computer must have been some kind of mattertron; only instead of creating a space between matter to move through unimpeded, it trapped us between the matter, confining us in intangible chains. I would have admired it more if I hadn't been its prisoner.

We moved quickly throughout the ship, hovering just inches off the floor as we were led down hallway after hallway and up several elevators. On the floor was always a series of different colored lines leading in dozens of directions. We seemed to follow the orange line, which eventually took us to a locked room guarded by a pair of crewmen. The guards stepped to the side as they saw our approach, and the door was opened, revealing a vaulted corridor filled with cells of varying sizes recessed into the walls. Each cell had clear, translucent walls, presumably made of the same glass-like material that had partitioned the flyer, and its occupants were completely visible.

I was suddenly aware that my heart was racing. The cells were small and far from enjoyable. They seemed impervious to any attempts at escape, and knowing we were helpless brought a fleeting moment of extreme anxiety. I took a few deep breaths, trying to remember that Demtrius was still free, and he would surely fight to get us released.

Our Dotaran escort brought us to one of the larger empty cells, shining a small laser at the clear barrier. An instant later, part of the wall shifted, creating an opening for us to pass through. I blinked, surprised by what I saw. It seemed different than the Scynthians' technology. Instead of combining matter and making it more dense, this one simply re-arranged the material into a different configuration.

The Dotaran then pushed a few buttons on his compact mattertron, and our party of four floated gently into the cell. When we were all inside, the Dotaran closed the portal, and we were immediately in control of our movements again, free to move around the cell while we waited for judgement.

Demtrius visited our cell a few hours later with a look of defeat written upon his face.

"Things have indeed changed a great deal since I was last here," he said, vexed. "There is a new leadership now, and, though I have vouched for you all, they have denied my request to free you until a proper assessment can be made. Once they've made a decision, whether to free you or not, the judgment will be final. I am sorry there isn't more I could do."

"This is ludicrous!" Pharon exclaimed. "This is your ship, is it not? Retake your command and do away with these absurd impediments!"

"It is not that simple," Demtrius explained. "There are new powers and new loyalties to consider. Yes, I have a rightful claim to the captain's seat, but that was with the old system of hierarchy. With the way things are now, I'm afraid my claim wouldn't be supported by the majority."

"But you are fair and just, and have all the qualities that a good leader should possess," I told him. "I'm sure the crew would follow you again," I said. "What could have changed that would make things so different?"

"For one," Demtrius started, "they do not yet trust me again, which is entirely understandable. I have been gone for months without even an indication of my safety or whereabouts, and then I show up with two Scynthians and news of an army approaching that could soon be at our door step. It is all very suspicious," he said, shaking his head. "Secondly, there is no longer just one captain aboard the Aramis. In my absence, somehow or another, they have decided to take up an oligarchy. Now, there are four captains who share equal power and authority, and they all apparently have their own faithful followers. It has caused some minor conflicts between the factions, but, on the whole, I am told that the crew has been much happier this way. There are those who have stayed neutral in the proceedings, remaining loyal to me, but there aren't many of them."

Demtrius was clearly thinking as he spoke. "It must be their loss of hope," he said in dismay. "We have been here for so long, and we have settled in nicely, but I always maintained strict duties and discipline. Keeping the crew busy is the best way to keep their morale high, but the new leadership has decided to mollify rather than uphold the responsibilities. From what I have observed so far, there is a much more liberal atmosphere aboard the ship, and I fear the crew members are becoming too careless in their duties. None of the new captains would admit it, but I believe that is why we weren't detected out on the ice sooner."

He paused for a moment, letting everything he had just said sink in.

"I do bring some good news, though," he continued. "Since I was their previous captain, they have offered me a position within the new leadership, which means I will hold some authority again. They have placed me on a probationary status of first mate, during which I will be closely monitored and observed, but I will be allowed to sit in on their meetings and speak my mind. In time, I should be able to secure a permanent seat on their council."

"Blasted politics!" Pharon complained.

"So what are we supposed to do in the meantime?" I asked, becoming increasingly concerned. "This was supposed to be our refuge, and you promised me your crew would help get me home."

"I'm sorry," Demtrius said, lowering his head in failure. "I hope you understand I couldn't have foreseen such circumstances."

"Maybe it won't be so bad," I said hesitantly, trying to see things through the eyes of the crew. "Perhaps four Dotarans will be able to rule better than one. You should be able to trust their decisions more now, since they will all need to discuss matters and then agree upon an outcome, thus checking the balance of power."

"You would think so," said Demtrius, "but this only opens up the doors for internal corruption. What if one or more of them is to die and is not immediately replaced, or if one gains leverage on the others? Then one person could control the rest like puppets on strings."

*Isn't that how every government is run?* I thought to myself.

"As long as you have the right people in power, that won't be a problem," said Nadina.

"Yes, but how is one to truly judge another's underlying intentions?" Demtrius questioned.

I thought back to Germany before World War II, and how Hitler had risen to power because the people believed in him, and how Russia's Stalin was able to eliminate Trotsky and any other competition. Both of them turned out to be megalomaniacs and caused the deaths of millions of people each.

"As long as they earn the position fairly, by rising through the ranks based on merit, morality, discipline, skill, and intelligence, there should be no problems," said Nadina. "Or do you not have faith in your own people to choose their leaders?"

"Under normal circumstances, you may be correct," Demtrius admitted, "but not the way things have happened here. It seems it was more of a popularity contest than an election, and done when things were becoming unruly. These aren't the type of decisions to be made in haste."

"Then I guess it's a good thing they've allowed you to rejoin them, even in a diminished capacity," I told him. "Your influence may be instrumental."

"Yes," said a frustrated Demtrius. "I just wish Captain Traeger was still here. He never would have let things go so awry."

"Forget about your Captain Traeger!" Pharon demanded. "You assured me that my daughter and I would be amnestied if we came here with you and the Earthlings, but that was never the case, was it?"

"Please," said a distraught Demtrius. "You must understand the-,"

Pharon interrupted, shouting, "You Dotarans believe you are so special and proper; it sickens me! At least we Scynthians show accountability for our actions!"

"Enough!" Nadina cried with such force and venom that it caused all of us to stop in place. "You know very well that Demtrius has been doing everything he can to help us, so stop venting all your anger and mistrust out on him."

"You would side with him over your own father?" Pharon asked in disbelief.

"There is no side to choose!" she said tersely. "We are all in this together; all trying to accomplish something bigger than ourselves. Jaxon needs to get back home to Earth, the Dotarans to their home world, and we need to somehow find a way to restore order to Scynthia. We can't do any of this until we put aside our differences and let the Dotarans know that we are willing to work with them. They have every reason to mistrust us, so please use some empathy and understanding for once. This will be a difficult transition for everyone, not just you."

Pharon grumbled quietly to himself, unable to argue with his daughter's logic, if only because he was made speechless by her passionate outburst. He may have been a cold, calculating Scynthian council member back on Scynthia, but he still had a weakness for his only offspring; a sentiment he was only just recently beginning to embrace.

Demtrius left the cell soon after that, on his way to meet with the captains and discuss the incoming Tatoran threat. No longer could they simply remain idle.

As Demtrius had said, there are now four captains of more or less equal power aboard the Aramis. The first of these captains is none other than Waylan, the Dotaran that had been clever enough to escape Souza's dungeons and leave directions for any other unlucky Dotarans. He is a war hero among his people, which went a long way in winning him his position, but he is also known for being honorable and trustworthy. Demtrius assured me that, of all the captains, he is the most just, and, frankly, has the best personality too.

Next there's Dolvin, who had been the acting first-mate when Demtrius disappeared. "Dolvin should have become the sole captain of the Aramis at that point," Demtrius explained, "and he did for a time, but he unfortunately proved unable to lead such a large crew and things quickly ran astray." Though he was liked by his peers as the first mate, he was not respected as a commander. In the ensuing weeks after he became the acting-captain, tensions were running especially high aboard the Aramis, and a situation close to mutiny arose in which Dolvin was to be removed from his station for incompetency. That is what eventually led to the new oligarchy being adopted.

When Dolvin was being harassed for his inability to properly manage the ship's affairs, a sly and highly intelligent engineer aboard the ship stepped forward and suggested the new structure of leadership. He was trying to convince the people that Dolvin alone could not manage their operations, but that if he was by Dolvin's side as co-captain, then everything would run better than before Demtrius had gone missing. "Nepalen, however, has very poor social skills," said Demtrius, "and that hurt the amount of confidence the crew had in his ability to command." He apparently speaks awkwardly and more often than not he accidentally turns people away rather than getting them on his side. "He does have some fine ideas on several new and efficient ways to manage the ship, all while keeping this newfound desire for down-time and leisure activities wholly incorporated."

In the end, the equally ambitious Alexitus, a lieutenant on the bridge, was able to convince the crew that they needed a shared leadership. "Alexitus is a utilitarian at heart," Demtrius told me, "all too much like the Scynthians he swears to hate, but he is an effective officer who rose quickly through the ranks because of his ability to delegate and get others to do his bidding." Under normal circumstances, his endorsement of an oligarchy probably wouldn't have been of much influence, but he had struck at the right moment when the system was at its weakest, and the crew, growing more frustrated by the day, believing they would be stuck on Tatora forever, decided they wanted a change.

And that is how the imperial crew of the Aramis created the first Dotaran oligarchy.

Demtrius spoke with the four captains about the imminent attack from Amentus and his Army of the People, so Dotaran emissaries were sent out in a last ditch effort to obtain peace. Alexitus, being a consequentialist in nature, and Nepalen, fearing the "ferocious Tatoran brutes" as he called them, simply wanted to strike first in a grand surprise attack, devastating the Tatoran forces. "Waylan, having been a warrior for decades, agreed that, if it came to it, he would fight," said Demtrius, "but he also emphasized that he saw no pleasure in the onslaught. He reminded them that, though we possess far superior weaponry, if the Tatorans won even a minor victory and any of our technology fell into their hands, the consequences could be dire."

Dolvin, always quick to side with Waylan, added that they had a very limited, non-replenishable crew to consider, and agreed that war would not be good for morale.

When all was said and done, Demtrius was able to convince everyone that peace was in their best interests, so the ambassadors were sent out with Demtrius at their head. It was a dangerous mission, but he needed to prove his loyalty and trustworthiness to the new captains, so off he went.

# Chapter Three
# Demtrius Returns

Demtrius returned from his mission several days later. It had been a long few days for us in the cell with nothing to occupy our time, so when he at last arrived, we were anxiously waiting for him. Unfortunately, he didn't bring any promising news.

"Were you able to achieve peace?" I asked with concern.

"Amentus, and all of his infinite wisdom," said Demtrius in calm sarcasm, "has entirely refused to make peace. He is implacable, and insistent upon our complete annihilation."

"I could have told you as much," Pharon said unhelpfully. "He's a righteous megalomaniac, and there's no reasoning with such a being."

"So what now?" I asked. "Will the Dotarans go to war?"

Demtrius gave a despairing shrug and shook his head. "It is inevitable now," he said, sounding entirely defeated. "We do not want to wage war with the Tatorans, but if they attack, they will leave us no choice but to defend ourselves. The captains won't allow it to come to that, however. They'd rather send a pre-emptive strike to eliminate the threat before our position is compromised. They believe the Aramis' location must remain hidden from the Tatorans at all costs."

"But you'll be fighting against thousands of innocent natives," I said pleadingly, completely off-put by the thought of so many misguided lives being taken. "You can't allow the captains to just attack them indiscriminately. Your relations with the Tatorans will only worsen, and then what? It'd just be another cause for another army to be risen."

Demtrius sighed, "Jaxon, we've already taken all of this into consideration, but something must be done. The captains believe a show of strength will be the best deterrent from future assaults, and I must admit that I don't see any other positive alternatives. What would you have us do?"

"I don't know," I replied. "Leave. Evacuate the ship, or move it if you can. Go someplace where the Tatorans will never find you."

"I wish it were that simple, but a move of that magnitude would undoubtedly attract unwanted attention from the Scynthians."

"And a giant battle wouldn't?" I asked, seriously concerned for the Tatorans. Demtrius and I had spent a great deal of time among them, and we had come to respect and admire many of them. Some had merely been misled by Amentus and his immoral war campaign, while most others had simply been ordered to arms to fight for their War Chief. Now they would all pay dearly for Amentus' ambitions.

Demtrius paused, trying to find the right words. "Believe me, Jaxon, it brings me no pleasure at all to fight against the Tatorans. We've befriended so many of them; Jotus and Jotan, Lorthredo and Montaug, Svix, Ishmae, Marcivul, Carnag, Dwaren, and all the others, but the captains won't entertain a plan that leaves us vulnerable to Amentus or any possibility of a future fight. At least this way we will be able to pick the battleground and have the Tatorans fighting on our terms. It is the only way to ensure the safety of our crew. You must remember, if one of us falls, we cannot simply be replaced like the Tatorans."

"I know," I replied, "but it feels as if you're taking a page straight out of the Scynthians' playbook."

"I'd say they're thinking logically for once," Pharon commented. "Finally ready to do what must be done."

Demtrius ignored the comment. "The attack will be localized to a small portion of their army. We will use our mattertrons to immobilize as many of them as we can, but the mattertrons run on battery packs, and they can only handle so much before we exhaust their energy. With any luck, the nature of our assault will demoralize the rest of the army, causing a full-scale retreat before the need for actual bloodshed. It is a gamble, for sure, but the captains are confident that once Amentus and his army have experienced a taste of our capabilities, they will quickly discontinue their campaign."

"When will this mission be carried out?" I asked with distaste.

"In a matter of hours," Demtrius replied. "Amentus' army is getting close. They are already almost to the frozen tundra, and we must intercept their path before they come any closer. Even our scouting ships have been ordered to make course adjustments, so that they are never flying directly to or from the Aramis. That way, they can't be backtracked to the ship."

Demtrius then sighed, "I must go for now. If all goes to plan, I should arrive back within a week or so. After my return, if we are victorious, then the captains will finally have time to meet with you and pass a judgment."

"Well hurry then," I said to him, "and try not to kill too many Tatorans while you're gone."

Demtrius closed his eyes briefly, heavy with burden, and then left the room.

Demtrius told us it would take roughly a week to deal with Amentus' army, and that was as long as they didn't run into any unexpected problems, but, to our surprise, he returned late on the evening of the third day. I was relieved to see him alive and well, and all of us were long past ready to finally be released from our confinement. We were having severe cabin fever, growing increasingly irritable with one another over the smallest of causes. Our freedom couldn't come fast enough, but that freedom was still subject to the will of the captains. Demtrius told us to have faith in their system, and I was trying, but it was hard to stay positive knowing my fate was once again in the hands of others.

When Demtrius finally arrived at our cell, he looked very troubled.

"How did everything go?" I asked, suddenly concerned by his quick return.

He wiped his hand down his face in anguish. "The

mission was over before it had even begun," he said regretfully. "It was a complete slaughter. Countless Tatorans perished in the battle, and so many more will die in their tents and on the battlefield from their grievous wounds. So many tremendous warriors now dead and gone," he said, shaking his head in guilt. "So many families torn apart by the tragedy, and all for Amentus' illegitimate cause."

"How many Dotarans did you lose?" I asked hesitantly. I had feared for this outcome.

"Not one," he replied to our surprise. "We weren't even involved in the battle."

"I don't understand," I said in confusion. "Who attacked the army then?"

"They attacked themselves," he replied, shaking his head in apparent disbelief.

"Of course they did," Pharon interjected. "In large numbers the Tatorans are completely incohesive, especially with the different faiths between the clans. Amentus was a fool to try and bring them together under one banner. They can't help but fight and feud with one another. Their culture is just too primal."

"Why do you have such contempt for them?" I asked in disgust. "After all we've been through, and all the Tatorans that have helped us along the way, I thought your perspective on them might have changed, but of course not. You're still just the same ignorant and intolerant Scynthian I first met."

"I am what I am," Pharon replied disdainfully, "and I am not ashamed of anything."

Nadina cut in, "Demtrius, please, can you tell us what happened out there?"

"Nothing good," he replied remorsefully. "When we arrived, the light of the new day was just beginning to peak above the horizon, but the war camp was still shrouded in darkness. We approached from the sky with the sun at our backs to mask our advance, but as we came into view, we noticed far too much commotion on the field below. I ordered the fleet to halt, and that's when we saw them; shadowy figures, hundreds of them, moving about the camp stealthily in the gray morning light."

Demtrius was silent for a moment, reliving the horrific tragedy. "The figures suddenly began plunging into tent after tent, and, even from our elevated vantage point, we could hear the screams of the dying and the roars of the defiant. The camp suddenly sprang to life, awakened by the unexpected commotion and calls of distress. They emerged from their tents snarling and with weapons drawn, lunging straight into the melee without a moment's hesitation. Many of them stopped short upon seeing our flyers in the sky, and must have assumed we were besieging the camp. Unfortunately, they realized too late that the attack came from within their own ranks, and many Tatorans died at the foot of their tents, completely unaware of the true enemy."

I sat flabbergasted, literally speechless. Mya had thrown her hand over her gaping mouth in shock and dismay, while Nadina took in the information silently with closed eyes. Pharon just shook his head in genuine amusement, as was his way with tragedies that weren't his own.

"Daylight had finally illuminated the surroundings," Demtrius continued, "and now we could see the sun glaring off of the ruby accouterments of the Dracothian soldiers as they systematically scoured the northern section on the camp in their treacherous onslaught. They attacked with such ferocity and coordination that none of their initial victims even had a chance to defend themselves. The allied clans were instantly thrown in disarray, and most were just trying to make sense of the whole situation. Major and minor chiefs shouted to their warriors, ordering them to form a defensive line, but the Dracothians' unanticipated betrayal had landed such a devastating blow that the resistance dissolved into dozens of separate smaller fights that eventually fizzled themselves out. The Dracothians then moved on to find other victims, while their cavalry waited on the outskirts of the camp to intercept any possible retreat."

"My goodness," said Nadina, her eyes still closed and her webbed fingers tightly interlocked.

"Worse yet," Demtrius proceeded, "when the Arkinian warriors caught wind of the treachery, they abandoned the fight altogether and fled south in their covered wagons, and the Dracothian cavalry let them right through their blockade! They must have made a deal with the Dracothians, and left the Sapphire and Emerald clansmen to fend for themselves!" Demtrius sounded exasperated. "By this point, most of the camp was finally apprised of the dreadful turn of events and they were beginning to rally under the banner of a lone Tatoran warrior. He ordered them to withdraw from the immediate fight, where the grass was slick with blood and littered with bodies, and had them flee east, almost directly toward us. It was a desperate move, but the cavalry blockade was surrounding them, mounted on fresh quadrupedal war-rapts, trained just for this purpose. They closed on the retreating clans, swinging their blades widely and crushing warriors mercilessly under the feet of their rapts. It all seemed lost, but, somehow, the retreating clansmen held on and managed to assemble their archers. Arrow after arrow hurtled through the air, impaling rapts and warriors indiscriminately, and suddenly a path was cleared through the blockade. The retreat was salvaged, for the moment at least, and they continued east, blinding their attackers in the rising sun. War-rapts and draft dugaan were scattered about, wandering aimlessly. The dead and dying covered the battle camp, and the defenders stumbled over their fallen comrades in their hasty retreat. Some were able to mount their own rapts to make for a quicker escape, pulling ahead of their companions and trampling over those unfortunate enough to be in their way. It was mayhem, complete mayhem." I had never seen Demtrius like this, both angered and sad at the same time, and almost without control over his emotions. "The Dracothian cavalry, scorned by their enemy's easy escape through their lines, looked for revenge now. They swarmed after the retreating clansmen, followed by the Dracothian infantry, who, seeing this collapse and fueled by their early victory, were caught up in the blood-lust and chased after the retreating warriors to finish them off completely."

"Wasn't there something you could do?" I interjected quickly. "Distract them with your flyers, or immobilize them with your mattertrons?"

"That was precisely my instinct," Demtrius said, "but the captains had issued new orders not to engage with the enemy. I tried to explain that saving them from civil war would surely have won us favor with the Tatorans, at least some of the clans at any rate, but they thought that route was far too risky. They would have the enemy defeat itself, as it were, simultaneously eliminating the immediate threat and assuring that no animosity was directed toward us for any deaths."

"Your captains made the appropriate decision," Pharon commented. "They are finally doing what they need to do to keep the rest of you alive."

"So you just let the massacre continue?" I asked in horror. "No, I can't believe it, not from you, Demtrius."

Demtrius shook his head. "My ship was the first to break formation, and dozens followed my lead, but we were only a fraction of the fleet and there were simply too many warriors to contain. Normally, just the sight of our ships in the sky would cause a great commotion by lingering there as we had, but in their blind rage and blood-lust, the Tatorans were ignoring our presence almost entirely. The only attention we received came when we began swooping down in front of the Dracothian ranks to send them scattering, but it was only a momentary setback. They jeered at us, cursing us foully I'm sure, but then it was back to the fight. Our menial efforts were hopeless, and even our mattertrons were unable to staunch the flow of attackers."

"A decisive victory for the Dracothians," Pharon commented dryly.

"Not quite," Demtrius retorted with distaste. "We all know how tenacious the Tatorans can be, and the Emerald and Sapphire warriors were no different this day. Though they had been hit hard by casualties, their remaining forces retreated down through a narrow gorge and somehow managed to regroup at the top of its far end to form a ragged defensive line. They stood fast, waiting to receive the charging Dracothian cavalry and infantry, while their rearmost ranks began splitting off and circling around either side of the gorge's rim, unbeknownst to the pursuing Dracothians. Warriors kept trickling in to add to the strength of the defenders, and all the while the Dracothians just kept charging blindly. The bait was taken, and then came the revenge slaughter. One massive volley of arrows was unleashed on the tightly grouped Ruby warriors, killing rapt and warrior alike. Dozens lay dead and countless more injured. Those who could fled back to the fallen camp, harassed by the jeering Emerald and Sapphire clansmen as a constant stream of arrows rained upon their backs."

"The tide of battle then turned," Demtrius continued, "and it was the Emerald and Sapphire clans running after the broken Dracothian horde. Now on the offensive, and led by the mysterious fighting Tatoran, they chased the Dracothians far away, killing any of the enemy's wounded and stragglers as they proceeded. With the immediate threat neutralized, they turned back to the battlefield and began sorting through the dead. The fight had only lasted a bit over half an hour, but the scene below us depicted nothing but horror. That was when we decided to land."

"Why did you do that?" I asked. "With the army broken and in disarray, your mission was already a success, so why chance the unnecessary risk?"

"I couldn't fly home knowing so many Tatorans needed our help," Demtrius explained. "I thought that, perhaps, with all that had just happened, peace with them might finally be achievable after all. I believed if we came to their aid, then they might be gracious for it."

"Were they?" I asked anxiously.

"Hardly," he said in despair. "The moment we landed, we were surrounded by the Emerald and Sapphire clansmen. They were very suspicious of our arrival and ultimately untrusting of our intentions. The mysterious commander of their troops stepped forward to speak to us then. His name was Pyrus, and he told us to turn around and go home. He did not show any anger or hatred toward us, but his voice wasn't very welcoming either. That was when Amentus finally appeared with not a scratch on him or sign of any involvement in the fighting whatsoever. He shouted to the archers furiously, ordering them to send a volley of arrows on our ships. The warrior that had spoken first, Pyrus, nodded dutifully, and then reluctantly called for his warriors to obey. The hail-storm of thehn-fletched shafts came raining down on top of us, but they were easy enough to stop using our mattertrons. It was obvious, however, that none of the Tatorans wanted our help, and so we closed our doors and departed." He finished with heavy sentiment.

"I'm sorry things ended the way they did," I said lamely.

"So, too, am I," Demtrius replied. "It was very unfortunate for them, but, all things considered, I can't say it isn't within our best interests. The Tatorans are now far too weak and disorganized to pose a viable threat at present, though I was hoping dearly that peace could be achieved."

"I guess at least the Aramis and its crew are safe," I reassured him.

"Yes," said Demtrius. "That is what I have been trying to focus on. Now we can move on to other, more important, matters."

"Like releasing us from this unnecessary confinement," Pharon commented derisively.

"Precisely," Demtrius replied. "As a matter of fact, the four captains will be ready to see you shortly."

This piqued all of our interests. We had waited for days, and now it was finally almost time for the captains to pass judgment over us; a judgment I was both anxious and nervous to hear. There was no avoiding it though, so there we remained, patiently waiting to learn our fates.

# Chapter Four
# A Judgment Is Made

Mya, Nadina, Pharon, and I were led through a series of hallways by a slim Dotaran who remained silent for the extent of the escort. We followed a purple line on the floor, which eventually brought us to a grand set of chamber doors with benches on either side, where we were made to sit and wait.

One by one, we were summoned into the room to be seen by the four captains, but no one came out through the door we entered. I was the last to be called in, and the anticipation was unnerving. I thought I would enter a large courtroom, like on Earth, but when I entered the room I was surprised to see how humble and confining it was. The room was barely able to contain the small circular table placed in its center. Sitting around the table were four Dotarans, presumably the captains; Waylan, Dolvin, Alexitus, and Nepalen. They were all facing me, faces stoic and giving away not even the slightest inclination of their thoughts or feelings. I suddenly had the sense of being in trouble at the principal's office. I wished Demtrius could have been there with me.

"You may have a seat," said the Dotaran on the far left of the table, motioning for me to take the empty seat beside him. I would soon learn this was Waylan, the infamous Dotaran who had escaped Souza's dungeons single-handedly. He spoke with confidence and authority, and was sized to match, as his muscles and chest bulged through his jumpsuit. I knew he was a war hero, but he seemed like he should have been a king. As he spoke, his words were translated into English by a multi-purpose utility device at the center of the table, which I was sure was recording our conversation as well.

I took my seat at the table, and the Dotaran to my immediate right had his eyes glued to a small computer tablet, searching for something. His name was Nepalen, and Demtrius had apprised me of his vast intellect. He appeared shorter than the rest, if only by an inch or so, and he had a slightly hooked nose. He searched momentarily, and then found the information he sought.

"Name: Jaxon Grey. Species: Human. Planet of Origin: Earth," said Nepalen, and again the words were translated into English. "Is this correct?"

"Yes," I replied in Dotaran, "and the translator won't be necessary."

The entire table stared at me with surprised looks, and then Nepalen turned off the translator.

"Who are you?" asked the Dotaran sitting across the table to my right. He emanated affluence and privilege, and I could sense a shrewd intellect inside of his blue exterior. As I would soon find out, this was Alexitus, and he was accustomed to getting his way.

"He just told you who I am," I replied somewhat irritably, indicating Nepalen.

The Dotaran sitting across from me to my left, whom I deduced must be Dolvin, chuckled lightly at this, and Alexitus gave him a sharp look. They were all now giving me their undivided attention, more serious than ever.

"Speaking plainly," Alexitus began, casting a suspicious eye on me all the while, "we do not know you and we do not trust you. From what we've gathered, you may or may not be an agent of the Scynthian scum, though Demtrius has vouched for you and says you share no particular loyalty to anyone."

"I am my own man," I confirmed.

"Which would make you even more dangerous," Alexitus added unhappily. "One who is subject to no one cannot be trusted, for their actions and decisions remain unpredictable."

"All I want to do is return home to Earth," I said, trying to relate to them. "If you help me return, then I will be yours to command until such time. My only stipulation is that I will not be forced to go against my own moral code. I will scrub the floors on every level of this ship, but I will not act dishonorably."

Alexitus sat back in his seat, seemingly satisfied.

Waylan smiled, "Maybe you are more predictable than we thought."

"Demtrius has told us his entire tale," said Dolvin to the table, "and, from what he says, Jaxon is as trustworthy as any Dotaran. We both have the same goal in mind, anyhow, don't we?"

"What do you mean?" I asked.

"We also wish to go home," said Waylan. "We have been exiled here for too many years, and we all have family back on Dotara that we wish to see again. There is something we need from you though, Jaxon."

"What might that be?" I asked. I couldn't imagine them needing anything from me, and I was interested to know what it was.

"We need your help with the Scynthians; Pharon and Nadina," he replied. "They could hold the key to everything, if they are willing to help. We have already spoken with Nadina, and she has vowed to assist us where she can, but she does not possess the information we seek. Pharon, however, was a high ranking member of the Scynthian Council, and he may prove invaluable to us, if he will only cooperate."

"So what am I to do?" I asked.

"When we tried to speak with him, he refused to say even a word to us," said Waylan. "We've already asked Nadina to help, but we need you to speak to him as well. Make him understand our situation, and convince him to work with us. This will be for your benefit as much as it is for ours. So, will you help us?"

They all leaned forward, anxiously awaiting my response.

"I will try," I said sincerely, "but Pharon shares as much friendship with me as he does with you. I'm not sure I will have any luck with him." It wasn't what I wanted to say, and the discouragement was clearly written upon each of their faces. I thought for a second, "There might be a way to get him to cooperate. He is the type who would be much more apt to assist if he has something to gain from it all."

Alexitus crossed his arms and looked at me

suspiciously, as did Nepalen. Waylan seemed to have expected such a response, and Dolvin just seemed bored with the proceedings.

"Very well," said Alexitus. "See what he wants, and, if it is reasonable, we will do what we can. Do we have a deal then?"

"Yes, we have a deal," I replied.

"Excellent," he said, and I could see that the others were pleased as well.

"We will require one more thing from you," said Alexitus.

"Of course you will," I replied with slight cynicism.

"We appreciate you speaking candidly, but it has not put all of our worries to rest," he said, pausing for a moment and staring at me. "We have here a device, which is implanted just below the surface of the skin. It will allow us to track your location, monitor your vital signs, and will record any conversations you may have. We will release you from your captivity only under the condition that you let us install this device on your person. The injection is virtually painless and will only take a second."

"The others agreed to this?" I asked skeptically. I wasn't inclined to accept such a request, and I found it entirely invasive to my own privacy.

"Both of the females were kind enough to oblige," Waylan explained, "but Pharon has remained stubborn, so he was brought back to his cell until he changes his mind."

I thought about their request for a moment, but I quickly realized that sitting in a cell wouldn't help me get home, no matter how invasive their device was. I would have to concede to their wishes if I planned to better my own situation.

"If I must," I replied reluctantly.

With that, Nepalen pulled forth a large syringe with a three-inch needle. I gave him my right arm, the one without the camouflaged cuff, but he pushed away my arm and indicated a spot on my neck. "So that we may record your conversations with more clarity," he explained.

With no other option, I allowed him to implant the

device, and I felt a sudden pinch as the needle entered my skin, but the pain only lasted a second.

Nepalen retracted the needle. "It will itch at first, and you will have a miniscule bump there as long as it is implanted, but the bump will be almost imperceptible to the naked eye, and in a day or two you won't even realize it's there anymore. In time, we will remove the device; that is, so long as you prove yourself to us."

I was then dismissed.

I wasn't quite sure what I thought of the four captains, but they seemed to have a good balance between them. I knew they were only doing what they thought best for their people, but I didn't like being in the center of their surreptitious scheme. What was I to do, though?

I was led from the room through a second door on the other side of the table, where I found Mya, Nadina, and Demtrius waiting for me. None of us spoke, but simply followed Demtrius as he showed us to our rooms, which were located directly adjacent to one another. We passed a multitude of Dotarans, but they shied away from us as if we had the plague.

My room wasn't very large; nothing more than a small compartment off one of the main halls with two alcove beds recessed in the wall, one on top of the other. As I entered, a slim metal panel slid down in the doorway, closing it off from the hall. The compartment contained a small desk, a chair, and storage alcoves, again built directly into the wall, conserving the room's limited space. I also found a Dotaran jumpsuit in one of the alcoves, and assumed it was for me. It was a simple and functional room, though I surmised the Dotarans didn't spend much time in them. I could definitely understand why. Under the new oligarchy, the Dotarans were finding time for recreation rather than performing their duties. All work and no play isn't very good for morale.

"The showers and restrooms are shared communally," Demtrius explained to us, "and yours are just down the hall. Please, get yourselves settled, and I will return to collect you for the evening meal."

Before leaving, he explained to us that navigating through the ship could get very confusing, and that the colored lines on the floors lead to different sections of the ship. On the wall next to my door, he showed us a sign that identified what each color meant. None of us could read Dotaran though, so Demtrius created a small translation key for each of us and stuck them to the wall next to the sign.

After a quick and tremendously refreshing shower, I tried on the skin-tight jumpsuit, and it fit me perfectly. It was slightly discomforting that they already knew my measurements, but I was glad for the change in clothing nonetheless. I then met up with Mya and Nadina, and the three of us left to go see to Pharon. I looked for the orange line on the floor, which I already knew led to the ship's brig.

Even with the colored lines on the floor providing the direction, it took us some time to navigate through the ship, and we gained no help from the Dotarans that we encountered. When we eventually arrived at the brig, we were stopped by sentry guards posted outside of the cell room. I tried speaking to one of them, using Demtrius' name to try and gain admittance to the room, but we still had to wait while they relayed a message to Demtrius for confirmation. It took a few minutes, but he came down personally to escort us inside.

The room contained a lengthy corridor with two levels of cells lining either wall, and the room curved just slightly, contouring to the dimensions of the ship. Demtrius waved to the guards at the other end, and they nodded back in reply.

As we passed the cells, I asked Demtrius about the super strong glass-like panes that closed off each cell. He explained to me that the panes were designed to be nearly indestructible; a synthesized hybrid structure of hexagonal diamond, strengthened by immense compression.

"There are ways to penetrate the material," he had said, "but not for anyone held within the cells, and, even for those equipped, it would be a tiresome task. That is why we use transmutation."

Transmutation is another one of the Dotarans' amazing technologies. I can't explain exactly how it works, but basically they use light waves to alter the molecular configuration of specific materials. When an infrared light is directed at the material, it changes to another programmable shape. Other light waves can change the solid into a liquid, while normal sunlight returns it to its original form. It's an amazing process, but only works for a small number of substances that the Dotarans have created, like their clear-pane cell doors.

We found Pharon in one of the cells on the first level. The guards at the computer station shined a laser from their station at the barrier, and the molecules changed, creating an opening to allow us in. We spoke to Pharon at length, trying to convince him to make the concession and get himself released from the cell, but in the end he remained as stubborn as ever.

"If you let them implant the device, then they will let you out of here," said Nadina, pleading with her father.

"I won't do it," Pharon replied obstinately. "Their fearful suspicion will only lead to grave decisions and paranoid naivety."

"You must be reasonable," I pressed him. "You can't do anything from within this cell."

"I will get out of this cell without having the device implanted," Pharon assured us. "I am not unaware of the Dotarans' situation. I know they need me to further their plans, and that is all the leverage I need."

"And if they decide they don't need you?" I asked, playing the devil's advocate.

"Well then it wouldn't matter either way," he replied, "but they will need me, and continue to need me. I am far too valuable of an asset. They think they can control us and play games with us, but I will not fall victim to their schemes."

"Schemes?" I questioned him.

"Everyone has an agenda," Pharon replied tiredly, as if he shouldn't have to explain such an idea. "You should remember that, for those who are not suspicious of the present will never live to see the future."

The trick, I believe, is being able to read between the lines. One should be able to see and understand what is happening clearly, even that which happens behind the scenes, and then think critically about what it all means. Add up all the information you have and make a decision based on the facts of the matter. Unfortunately, not everyone has the ability to think objectively and critically, and others blatantly choose not to.

"You can tell them," Pharon started, "that I will only help them if they forego the implant, and I want complete autonomy in my work. I know the technology, and I won't have them slowing me down or trying to tell me what is best. Those are my terms."

Pharon knew as well as I that the implants in Mya, Nadina, and me were recording the conversation. The door behind us then slid upwards, causing Pharon to smile. "Someone is always listening."

He then left the cell with us and we made our way back to our sleeping compartments. Demtrius was quartered in a different section of the ship, so he broke off from our group soon after leaving the brig. "Follow the black line on the floor to return to the crew quarters."

It was difficult to find the correct rooms since none of the colored lines went directly to them, and all the hallways looked nearly identical, but eventually we did made it back. I took the high bunk, and Pharon, being too large for the small bunk space, was forced to move his bedding to the floor.

The next day, Pharon and I were awoken by the sound of a loud radio tone, and then the voice of a Dotaran making some kind of morning broadcast. He was just concluding a public announcement from Nepalen about the importance of exercising regularly and was about to start the weather forecast for the day.

"I don't suppose there's an off switch to that dreadful babble?" Pharon asked from the floor.

"Not one that I'm aware of," I replied.

The broadcast was over after a few minutes, and Pharon and I got ready to find the dining hall for some breakfast. I looked to the sign on the wall next to the door and saw that the brown strip on the hallway floors would lead to the cafeteria.

We met with Mya and Nadina for breakfast, which was a salad consisting of leafy green and blue vegetables, some type of dried berries, and mixed nuts, along with a small bowl of diced Dotaran fruit. I was surprised it was all so fresh, but I soon learned that the ship had its own agriculture department where they cultivated their food.

While we were eating, Demtrius found us and sat down beside me. "Care for a duel?" he asked.

He and I used to make it a point to practice when we could, but with all the recent travelling we hadn't been able to as of late, especially after Souza IV had captured us and taken our weapons in Souzul.

"But we don't have our blades," I replied.

"I've had new swords specially crafted for us using Dotaran steel, so they're lighter and stronger than our previous ones."

"Then by all means," I smiled back at him.

After breakfast he took me to a training room, leaving Pharon, Nadina, and Mya on their own. I saw the new swords resting on a rack, and the blades almost glowed with a blue tint. They weren't the same swords as the katana-like blades that had been specially crafted for Demtrius and me in Aanthora, but they were double-edged and just as long as our old weapons.

I picked one up, instantly surprised by how light it was. Demtrius must have seen my concern. "You could break a Tatoran axe with one of these," he said proudly. "It's the strongest steel made on Dotara, and would be more valuable than gold on Tatora."

"Well then, let's give them a whirl," I replied, swinging the blade in my hands with ease.

We sparred, and I was definitely a bit rusty, but I couldn't blame the swords; they were fantastic. It didn't help that Demtrius had such incredibly quick reflexes, and he forced my submission three times within just a few minutes. We were in the midst of our fourth duel when Dolvin and Delfwig came into the room.

"Care for a round?" Demtrius asked them, offering them his blade.

"I was never much use with a sword," said Dolvin, "but I have some skill with a bow. I'd rather just use a mattertron though."

"What about you, Delfwig?" Demtrius asked.

"I haven't practiced since you were still acting captain," Delfwig replied, "but I'll take on the human."

I hoped he would be an easier match than Demtrius, but he was just as quick, although a bit sloppier with his moves. I bested him quickly the first time, but after that he had me decisively beat the second and third times.

I spent a lot of time in the training room that day, and afterward, Dolvin and Demtrius took me to the top of the flight deck for some archery practice. Delfwig had other duties to attend to, though.

"It's really just a hobby, but a fun one at that," Dolvin had said. He had multiple targets set up around the ship, and struck each one with a practiced hand. It took Demtrius and me a few tries before getting the distance down, but soon the three of us were having a contest on who could get closest to the target centers. Demtrius and I did about the same, but Dolvin won easily.

I spent the rest of the day with Pharon, Nadina, and Mya, exploring the ship a bit before heading back to our compartments, but then plans changed on the following morning.

When Pharon and I opened our compartment door to leave for the cafeteria, we found two Dotaran guards waiting for us.

"Human," one of the guards said to me. "Your presence is required on the flight deck."

I looked at Pharon, shrugged, and then stepped out of the room and left with the two guards. We followed the red strip on the hallway floor and made it to our destination in a few minutes, after first taking an elevator to a higher level. Now we were on the flight deck.

I saw three ships waiting to launch. They were larger than the ship that had brought us to the Aramis, and waiting outside each was a two-Dotaran crew ready to board, including Demtrius and Delfwig. They must have been preparing for another mission.

The guards brought me to them, and Demtrius extended his hand toward me in greeting.

"I thought Dotarans didn't greet one another with a hand shake?" I asked.

"We don't," he said, "but you do."

I was honored by the gesture, and shook his hand readily. It suddenly struck me how sad I would be once we finally went our separate ways. I had grown very close to Demtrius, and his friendship rivaled that of any I had back on Earth, aside from yours, of course, but I think what you and I have is more than just a friendship.

"I have just received orders from Waylan that we are to contact the northern Tatorans of the Amethyst clan on the island of Mercer. When the captains found out that I can speak Tatoran fluently now, they came up with another plan to acquire peace in this land," he said. "The Mercerians are isolated on their island, just as we are, but they are halfway across the continent. They are a more peaceful, neutral clan, and will be unaware of the catastrophic events with Amentus' army. The captains believe that we might be able to sway their opinions of us by speaking to them in their own tongue, and since you and I have had history with a Mercerian prince, they believe that might be the perfect cause for an audience."

"Svix," I said, remembering his tragic fate, along with Captain Ellios and most of the original crew aboard the River-Rapt. He was a white-furred sailor that came from the far north, and now I learned he was the son of a chieftain.

"Yes," said Demtrius. "His father is Rengar, High Chieftain of the Mercerians. We are to make contact with him and, if possible, form a treaty."

"Do they really think it could happen?" I asked.

"Yes," he replied, "but only if you and I are present. We were with Svix when he died, and his people will find comfort in knowing how it happened. Knowing we were his friends might just be enough." He turned to the ships, "They are all set for the journey. We are to leave shortly."

"Wait," I said. "We can't leave yet."

Demtrius looked at me in question.

"I have to retrieve Svix's amethyst necklace," I explained. "He made me promise to return it to his father, and I can't fail him."

"Well hurry then," Demtrius replied. "The Captains will not be pleased with the delay."

"I left it with Thiesel for safe keeping," I told him apprehensively.

Thiesel, I'll remind you, is a giant serpent, but more importantly, he is my companion. I have known him since before he hatched from his egg, and once he did hatch, he imprinted on me. Now we share an extra-sensory connection that I can't exactly explain, but Thiesel wasn't welcome on the ship.

Demtrius sighed, "Then we should leave now. Quickly, follow me."

Demtrius ordered one of the crew members aboard his ship to transfer to another vessel so that I could sit next to him in the cockpit for the journey. The large elevator brought our ship to the surface, and the aircraft gently lifted off the ground. It was amazing how the flyers made everything feel smooth and weightless. The ship never had any turbulence and was almost completely silent.

We flew a short distance from the Aramis and then touched down on the frozen ice. I thought hard for Thiesel to appear, but a few minutes passed by and he didn't show. Then I saw his head pop up from behind a small hill of snow and he was speeding toward us. He stopped just short of me, sliding the last ten or fifteen feet before coming to a full halt. He was very pleased to see me and licked my face repeatedly. I rubbed the bridge of his nose tenderly, re-acquainting myself with the magnificent beast.

"I need the necklace," I said to him. He understood me as he was always able to do, and then began regurgitating the necklace from his secondary storage stomach. He coughed up the amethyst necklace and it was covered in slimy mucus. I picked it up, cleaned it off with some snow, and thanked Thiesel for holding onto it for me. I didn't want to leave him again so soon, but Demtrius and I were in a hurry, so I said my farewell and went to board the flyer. Thiesel tried to join me, but, of course, could not fit inside the aircraft. I rubbed the bridge of his nose again, assuring him that we'd be back to see him soon, and then Demtrius and I took flight.

# Chapter Five
# The Mercerians

We spotted the island of Mercer from a great distance, arriving an hour or so after dawn. It was a very large island, though miniscule when compared to the size of the Tatora's mainland, and it was covered in dark evergreen flora that somehow managed to thrive in the frigid climate, as did the Mercerians. The island itself was a rough triangular shape and was the only land so far north to be settled by any of the clans. It held an excellent defensive position, surrounded by nothing but ice and water, and had a major settlement at each of its three corners.

We soon came upon the first and largest of these settlements, and Demtrius told me the city was called Finnis, the capital of Mercer and home to Rengar, the Amethyst clan's High Chieftain. There was no high wall or barrier protecting the small city, which was an oddity from what I had seen on the planet so far. The buildings were made of snow compacted into solid bricks of ice that were then stacked atop one another to form thick, sturdy walls. Timber from the nearby forest crossed this foundation to make the roofing, which had an interesting reddish hue to it.

We circled the small city several times, making sure that the citizens moving around in the early morning light could see us plain and clear. As we got closer, I could see the red hue on the trees was actually long red hairs growing out of the tree trunks and all of the branches. The hairs intertwined with the dark green pine needles to form beautiful designs in the canopy.

Demtrius guided our flyer to a clearing on the outskirts of Finnis and touched down gently, followed closely behind by the other two ships. We then exited our flyer and stood gathered in a small group with the other Dotarans. I noticed one of them carried a long, skinny bag filled with something, but my attention turned to the approaching Finnisians.

A contingent of warriors marched out of the city toward our location, armed for battle. Their fur was as white as snow, just as Svix's fur had been. It was a characteristic unique to this isolated clan, which was one of the reasons they called themselves Mercerians rather than Tatorans. At the head of the procession were two pole-bearers carrying the Amethyst clans' flag; a downward facing triangle containing a gyx, or dragon, with spread-wings.

The warriors stopped short in their march a good twenty yards from where we stood. Other than the sword I now wore buckled on my waist again, our group carried no weapons, though the warriors were fully armed. I knew, of course, that all the Dotarans present had with them the compact mattertron that could immobilize a number of Tatorans with barely the lifting of a finger. At the moment, however, things were calm.

The warriors stepped aside as a large, broad-chested Mercerian moved to the front of the group. His eyes were strikingly blue against his clean, white fur. He carried a large battle ax over his shoulder, which I couldn't hope to be able to wield, and around his neck was an amethyst necklace identical to the one Svix had given me. I knew then that this must be his father, Rengar, High Chieftain of the Amethyst clan and ruler of Mercer.

Demtrius reached into the long, skinny bag brought by his subordinate, revealing two long branches of wood. He held up a branch in each hand and then dropped them to the ground, leaving them there. Delfwig, whom I hadn't notice creep up beside me, whispered into my ear, "The throwing down of the branches of the Simoa tree is an internationally recognized sign of peace and trust upon Tatora, as it symbolizes the laying down of arms. If the branches are picked up by the Mercerians, then peace negotiations will have begun."

For a very tense minute, Rengar stood there without moving. It was frigid, and I had only the skin-tight jumpsuit provided by the Dotarans, but I was in a nervous sweat. I instinctively reached for the hilt of my sword for comfort. I did not draw the blade, but kept my hand on its hilt to be ready at a moment's notice.

Rengar, at last, took a step forward and, to my relief, picked up both of the Simoa branches. He then turned around and held them for his warriors to see. After he did this, he returned his attention to our group, mainly Demtrius though.

"I am Rengar, High Chieftain of the Amethyst clan and ruler of Mercer," he said. "What are you doing here on my land?"

"I am Demtrius, a Dotaran ambassador from the Aramis, my vessel, and this is my crew," he said, indicating the Dotarans behind him, who listened to the conversation with their multi-purpose utility devices since Demtrius was speaking in Tatoran. "And this is Jaxon Grey. He and I were friends with your son, Svix."

One of the warriors in the contingent stepped out of formation, but quickly regained his composure and got back in line.

"You know my son?" asked Rengar, very serious and suspicious.

"We knew your son," Demtrius replied, "but, unfortunately, I must bring you news of his untimely death. He was a great friend, and as skilled a warrior and shipmate as I have ever come across."

Demtrius then motioned for me to step forward, at which point I presented Rengar with the amethyst necklace that Svix had once worn proudly. "It was Svix's dying wish that I promise to return this necklace to you," I told him.

"You were there when he died?" asked Rengar.

"Yes," I replied, "and I am sorry I could not prevent it."

"Tell me," said Rengar, "how did it happen?"

"He was fighting off a horde of pirates that had taken over our ship, the River-Rapt. He and his captain were incredibly outnumbered, but they fought with honor until the very last of them had perished."

"A Mercerian wouldn't have his death any other way," Rengar replied.

I could sense much sadness in his tone, but also that of

tremendous pride.

He returned the conversation back to Demtrius. "We have seen your flyers high in the sky, but never before have they touched down on our lands. We do not like strangers here, but I see that you bring with you the branches of the Simoa tree. Ordinarily, though it is our custom to do so, I would not grant you food and lodging since you are not of my species. However, since you were my son's companions, I will grant you your wish and invite you to stay for the evening. We will be keeping a close eye on all of you though."

"Very well," said Demtrius, "but I vow that we are here as your allies, not your enemies."

"One in my position can never be too careful, especially if I wish to remain in power for long," Rengar replied with a quick smirk. He looked back toward his city, "Sverna won't be too pleased to find out that we have extra mouths to feed tonight, even if they are small mouths such as yours. No sense in delaying the inevitable though." He then addressed his warriors, "Back to the city!"

With that, Rengar turned about, seemingly not the slightest bit worried that he might be attacked from behind. I must admit, there was something about Rengar that I instantly admired, though at the time I barely knew him. It was just a gut feeling, but I had learned to trust my gut, and I followed the party of warriors into the city in good spirits.

The citizens of Finnis were surprisingly welcoming, and by that I mean they weren't outwardly hostile toward us. It was most likely due to the friendship Demtrius and I had once shared with Rengar's son, Svix, but I figured that the Mercerians were likely outsiders on their world too due to their difference in appearance, so perhaps they understood the plight of the Dotarans a little better than the Tatorans on the lower continent. The Mercerians were also greatly intrigued by the Dotaran flyers, which all of them had witnessed at one time or another. The ability to fly was far beyond their technological capabilities, and they insisted on asking what the experience was like and if they could take a ride in the flying ships. Demtrius, disregarding Delfwig's concerns, agreed that at some time in the near future, as long as a peace agreement could be made, he would take each of them on a short flight.

The dinner feast took place in the early afternoon inside a very large cabin with one long table extending down its length. The table was filled on either side by the Finnisian citizens, and there seemed to be no sort of class separation between them. The meal was simple, consisting of smoked scarp, roasted elder, stale bread, and fresh cheese. We washed it down with refreshing spring-water, and I couldn't help but notice that no alcohol was served, which seemed a bit peculiar, but I didn't get around to asking about it.

During the meal, Delfwig and the rest of the Dotaran crew remained mostly silent, listening to the conversations through their translators. Demtrius and I, however, continued speaking to Rengar and his family at length, showing them our fluency in the Tatoran language, as well as sharing fond stories of Svix.

Accompanying Rengar at the dinner feast were his other son, Ricson, and his tzulara, Sverna. I've used the term Tzulara previously in my manuscripts, and, up until meeting the Mercerians, I was ignorant as to its meaning. At the feast, I learned that a tzulara is simply the Tatoran equivalent to the Earth term for wife. It's derived from the word 'tzula', which Svix had once told me meant a lasting friendship. In addition, tzulamor is the Tatoran word for husband, and a Tatoran wedding is known as a Tzulamay, though much more happens than just the uniting of a couple during this annual celebration.

When I first saw Ricson, I realized he had been the warrior in the contingent outside of the city that had stepped out of line when Demtrius first mentioned Svix's name. He was the spitting image of his brother, and seemed to be the most affected by his death.

During the feast, Rengar told me that the Mercerians honor the memory of their dead, and that now Svix was with their ancestors protecting his people, so there was no need to mourn for him. He then went on to explain that Ricson was Svix's younger brother and had looked up to Svix very much. Then Svix had left on his mission of self-discovery, and Ricson had grown up without a brother, feeling very alone. That is, until he was mated to another chieftain's daughter, a Mercerian female named Pinut, with whom Ricson was very much in love. Now, however, after hearing of his older brother's death, he was depressed and feeling lonely again.

"It has been a rough time for Ricson," Rengar told us. "He loved his brother dearly, and he has not seen his love, Pinut, in many weeks, either. Only two days ago did he arrive home from his primadon hunt."

"Primadon?" I asked.

"Yes," said Rengar, with some enthusiasm. "They are hideous creatures with fat snub noses, flesh-tearing teeth, and large curling tusks. They have very long arms and a massive upper body, but with only short stubby legs, so they must use their arms to help support themselves. The terrible beasts live on the continent to the south, but from time to time they do manage to find their way to Mercer. The creatures blend into the environment well with their dirty white fur, so they make for excellent hunting sport, but this particular primadon has been menacing us for months. We finally had enough, so I dispatched Ricson and a squad of young warriors to destroy the beast. It was an excellent learning experience for them."

Rengar then turned to his son. "Ricson," he said proudly, "why don't you delight us with the tale from your hunt?"

"Very well, Father," Ricson replied, though with only the ghost of a smile.

With that, many of the Mercerians at the long table leaned closer to hear the tale. Even several of the Dotarans pressed in, intrigued.

"Well, first, as we do in all hunts, we applied the odorless juices from the amona plant, which masks our scent so that we hunters do not accidentally become the hunted. After that, it was easy enough to find primadon tracks in the fresh snow near a recently slaughtered meer," Ricson started, and everyone was giving him their undivided attention.

A Meer, I should mention, is a type of Tatoran sheep, with a big fluffy coat of brown and black fur. The Mercerians herd these meer for their voluminous coats, their tender meat, and the milk they produced year round for their young.

"We tracked the beast for miles and miles into the uninhabited wilderness, until we eventually discovered its lair dug into the side of the mountain. We waited there, not sure if it was inside since there were many tracks that led to and from the den. The last thing we wanted was to get trapped inside the den with a primadon at its entrance."

Many of the Mercerians nodded their heads in agreement, while others shuddered at the thought.

"We waited there until after daybreak, since the primadon is a nocturnal hunter and would be returning to its lair very soon, if it hadn't already. We watched the den from our place of concealment, and saw nothing approach the entrance or leave from within. At that point, we surmised that the beast had been inside the entire time. Being reasonably sure of this, our group then decided what course of action we should take. The majority of the hunters in my group were young and untested, having never been on a primadon hunt, including myself. There were only two veterans in our group, so we deferred to them to help us decide what to do next." He looked down the table at another Mercerian. "Mreeker, perhaps you would like to tell some of this tale, since you are one of those veterans."

Our entire table turned around to see this Mreeker, who sat with bandages wrapped heavily around his torso. "It would be my pleasure," he replied. "As Ricson was saying, they turned to Hendel and I, and we suggested waiting until the creature was asleep, and then sneaking up on it and slaying it. We had done it before with a team of a similar size. The primadon sleeps during the day, so we didn't have to wait long before we heard it snoring heavily from inside the shallowly-dug lair. Then we crept up in single file as quietly as possible. When we got to the entrance, we saw the massive arms and shoulders of the snub-nosed monster. It was hideous, and smelled worse than anything I have ever smelt before. We circled about the primadon while it snored away, but it was all just a ruse. 'Stay clear of its long arms and claws,' I remember saying as I took a step closer, and then the confounded beast sprang for me with its claws." He pulled up his shirt, "It got me right under my left shoulder blade and hefted me above its head. I still don't know how I survived."

"Barely," Ricson jumped in again. "The moment it reached for you, we began thrusting and jabbing at it with our spears. We must have stabbed the beast a hundred times before it finally stopped moving."

"And how do we know you tell the truth, and that this is not just another story?" someone asked.

"Because everyone from the hunt now carries this," Ricson replied, holding out a large primadon tooth, fresh from the carcass, strung about a length of braided string. Other Finnisians from around the table showed their trophies as well. The rest roared and cheered at the sight. For the time being, they were again free from the primadon's predation.

When the feast was over, Rengar led us to a line of small empty buildings that were built side by side. Demtrius and I stepped inside one of these wood and snow built dwellings, where we found a small fireplace and two large beds covered in meer fur.

Rengar walked in behind us. "I will need time to contact the other cities, Weins and Skudland, so that we may all sit to discuss the peace you seek," Rengar told us. "I will send out the carrier squalms tonight, so we can expect the city leaders to arrive in about a week or so, pending no serious delays. In the meantime, you and your crew may take up these homes. They are usually reserved for Tzulamay and festivals, but we are not currently at festival and Tzulamay does not occur for another half-month."

"If I may," Demtrius suggested, "perhaps we might use our ships to bring them here. It would take less than a day to retrieve both parties, saving us all the time and trouble."

Rengar thought about it for a moment. "I would need to come with you, of course," he said finally. "The others will not step foot inside the flyers unless they see one of their own kind step out, especially one such as their High Chieftain."

"Very well," said Demtrius. "I will leave Delfwig and most of my crew here in Finnis with one ship, leaving us the remaining two."

"Excellent," said Rengar. "We will leave at first light."

# Chapter Six
# Peace Talk

In the morning, Rengar, Demtrius, and I climbed aboard one of the flyers, while two other Dotarans powered the second ship. Ricson also accompanied us, since his soon-to-be tzulara, Pinut, lived in Weins. She was the daughter of the chieftain in Weins, a Mercerian named Grissly, and Rengar thought Ricson might prove instrumental in getting them to join us for peace negotiations.

The trip was short, and we got an excellent view of the island as we passed from above. The dark green pine trees with red trunks covered the entire land. The only area that didn't seem to have them was on a higher plateau at the center of the island. Rengar told us the forest was known as the Thehnwood Forest. The trees were called Thehnwoods, named after the Thehn, a large Tatoran bird with black top feathers and a blood-red underside. The unique thehnwood trees had trunks that bore almost the same color as their namesake, though I'm not sure if any of those predatory birds even live so far north.

Weins lay at the eastern tip of the triangular island, built on a harsh, rocky land. We circled the city, making sure our presence was known, and then landed in a clearing on the outskirts, just as before. The city was much the same as Finnis, consisting of many low, one-level buildings built from compacted snow and timber, but there were also dozens of stone-built structures too. It was much more defensible than Finnis, but the landscape was mostly barren and unyielding.

A group of warriors arrived moments later on bipedal rapts, armed for battle. Even their rapts had armor covering their heads, legs, and flanks. At the lead of the group was a massive Mercerian. He alone rode a quadrupedal rapt, for I doubted the bipedal rapts could withstand his weight.

The group stopped in their tracks when they saw Rengar emerge from within the ship, smiling and holding his arms wide open, with Ricson close behind him. The massive Mercerian riding the quadrupedal rapt dismounted and began walking over toward us.

"Rengar?" asked the giant, not believing his eyes.

"Grissly!" Rengar cheered. "Good to see you, old friend!"

They were now standing face to face. Grissly truly was a giant among Tatorans. Rengar, a considerably large Tatoran himself, was at least a full foot shorter than Grissly. He must have stood over ten feet tall, and I barely stood higher than his waist.

"Let us go into town," said Rengar. "We have much to discuss."

The proceedings in Weins were actually rather short. Grissly was loyal to his high chieftain and would do whatever Rengar asked without question. Pinut, his daughter, also helped, since she wanted nothing more than to be with Ricson again. They were still in the throes of passion, and wouldn't live together until the time of their partnership, at which point Pinut would move to Finnis. Grissly, a widower whose tzulara had passed away during Pinut's birth, would not let her leave until such time. Needless to say, the young couple wanted whatever time they could get with one another.

Proceedings in Skudland didn't go as smoothly. Again we were met outside the city by a group of warriors, but their chieftain, Waulf, was not present among them. His son, Scard, was there in his place. He was a young warrior with a freshly grown mane, probably about the same age as Ricson. He had a narrow face, close set eyes, and a fierce demeanor. I could see him watching Ricson and Pinut with nothing but disgust and hatred, or possibly jealously.

Rengar spoke with Scard, but the Skudlandic heir showed little respect for his high chieftain. It was a good thing that Rengar didn't seem to take offense. After a few words, the group regressed back to Skudland and the rest of us followed.

We met Waulf in his main hall, where he sat upon a small throne next to a young Mercerian female that couldn't have been any older than Ricson or Scard. I was taken aback when I saw Waulf lean over and give her a lick up the side of her neck, causing her to cringe with apparent revulsion. Waulf just laughed and beckoned for us to come closer.

Rengar spoke first, as his status granted him. "It seems you and your soon-to-be tzulara are finally bonding."

"Third time's the charm," Waulf replied with a devilish smile. He had small bones tied into his mane, as did many of the other warriors.

"It kind of defeats the purpose of making them your tzulara if there isn't a lasting relationship," Grissly commented.

Waulf scowled. "What brings the two of you here, and in the company of such unworldly guests? The only time my hall is graced by either of you is at festival or Tzulamay, and it is not time for either."

"There are important matters that need to be discussed," Rengar replied.

Waulf looked first at Demtrius and then at me, scowling the entire time. "These matters pertain to your companions here?"

"Very much so," Rengar answered. "I have called a peace summit in Finnis for tomorrow, and your presence is required."

"Tomorrow?" Waulf asked. "You must have lost your mind if you think we can make it to Finnis by tomorrow. It will take me that long to prepare for the march alone."

"We will not be marching," said Rengar. "We will be flying."

Waulf gave Demtrius and me a suspicious look. "This is their dark magic that you speak of, isn't it?" he asked, seemingly offended.

"It is science," said Rengar, "not magic."

"Call it what you will," Waulf replied, waving his hand dismissively, "but I will not step foot inside one of those contraptions. Mercerians are not meant to fly."

"We just came from the flyers," Grissly told him, "and we are fine. Do not let your superstitions control your decisions."

Waulf growled. "What are you trying to say, Grissly?"

"Well surely you are not afraid to fly, not the great Waulf of Skudland," Grissly said sarcastically.

Waulf looked at him with pure hatred upon his face.

Scard, previously standing unnoticed to the side, suddenly spoke. "My father is never afraid!" he shouted defensively. "How dare you accuse him of such cowardice! He should cut you open for your disrespect!"

"Calm down, Scard," Waulf said tiredly, "and learn to show your elders respect." Waulf then returned his attention to Rengar and Grissly. "We will go," he said. "Scard and I will fly with you."

I saw the female Mercerian sitting next to him breathe a sigh of relief.

"Excellent," said Rengar. "We leave immediately."

By the next afternoon, Rengar, Waulf, and Grissly were all sitting in the hall at Finnis with Demtrius, Delfwig, and myself. We had been there for nearly an hour discussing the peace that Demtrius and Delfwig wished to make. They had been informing the Mercerian leaders of all the events that had taken place throughout Tatora over the past several months, and made sure to explain Amentus' grand army and the Dracothian deception. The Mercerians didn't seem particularly concerned with the affairs of the lower continent, except for Waulf, who wanted nothing to do with the Dotarans from the start.

At first, Delfwig, against Demtrius' advice, urged the Mercerians for a full alliance, asking them to come to our aid in case it came to war with the Tatorans on the mainland. These were the apparent orders from the four captains, Waylan, Dolvin, Alexitus, and Nepalen. Demtrius and I knew the Mercerians wouldn't agree to such terms with an alien race that they hardly knew and had never worked with before, but Delfwig insisted on trying. Luckily, Demtrius was able to salvage the negotiations by changing the terms that Delfwig had set to more reasonable ones.

"We only want peace with your people; that is all," Demtrius told them. "We respect your want for isolation and seclusion from the rest of the world, and we will respect your privacy. All we ask of you is that you never take up arms against us, and of course we will never do so against any of your people either. We will leave you alone if you give us this assurance."

"That does sound reasonable," Rengar commented.

"You traveled so far for a simple assurance?" asked Waulf. "Which we could give, and then simply ignore the agreement and attack you anyway."

"You could," Demtrius admitted, "but it is my understanding that Mercerians are true to their word."

"Of course we are," Rengar interjected. "That is, if we decide to give it. Your words sound good, but how can we trust you when none of the other clans have chosen to do so? It is obvious they consider you a threat, and we would be fools not to inquire into such matters."

"We understand your concern," Demtrius replied, "but you must understand that the other clans have not even given us a chance. Long ago, a Tatoran couple named Jotus and Valadine tried to make peace, but unfortunate circumstances, of which we had no way of foreseeing, led to an end in the peace negotiations."

"Jotus of Aanthora?" Grissly questioned.

"Yes, the one and the same," Demtrius answered. "He wanted peace then, and still does now. Did you know him?"

"I met him once, very long ago," said Grissly, "and if he trusts the Dotarans, perhaps one day the rest of us might too."

"You could be the first to create a truce with us, and I promise that none of you will ever regret it."

"The other clans might not like our agreement," Waulf offered. "They could even become hostile, thinking we have betrayed our people."

"He is right," said Rengar. "Tatorans are prideful people, as are we Mercerians, and they might take it offensively."

"It is a possibility," Demtrius admitted, "but I believe once they see the benefits of such a relationship, they might be more inclined to hear us out and accept our offer of peace."

"What are these benefits you speak of?" asked Rengar.

Demtrius and Delfwig smiled.

"If all of you would please follow me," said Demtrius. "I would be happy to show you."

We all made our way outside and onto the main avenue of the city. Demtrius then signaled to his ship, at which point the cargo hold was opened and out came three Dotarans riding on separate snow vehicles. They sped toward us at an alarming velocity, each carrying a sled with a tarp pulled over it tightly.

They made it to us in seconds, and then came to a controlled stop just feet from where we stood. The Dotarans quickly unhitched the sleds from the strange vehicles and pulled them to the side.

"We have retrofitted three of our cycles for use on the snow covered terrain," Demtrius explained. "These ski-cycles are for you. They do not require fuel of any sort, as they are solar powered and draw their energy from the sun. From a full charge, they will last for two years of continuous use, guaranteed."

The three chieftains eyed the ski-cycles wonderingly.

"How do they move?" asked Grissly.

"They use the solar energy from the sun to turn their treads, so you won't have to do a thing but press your thumb on the accelerator there on the right handle bar," Demtrius explained. "Would you like to take them for a spin?"

Neither Rengar, Grissly, nor Waulf would admit it, but I could see they were all a bit reluctant to try the ski-cycles.

"If they don't, I sure do," Ricson said with excitement, quickly leaping onto the nearest ski-cycle.

"The brake is on the left," Demtrius was able to say before Ricson thumbed the accelerator and sped off.

"Count me in too," said Scard, and he too hopped onto a ski-cycle and sped off after Ricson.

"They go awfully fast," said Sverna. She had been waiting outside for the peace negotiations to end. "They seem very dangerous."

"If you would like, we could decrease the maximum speed to a lower setting, although I think you might come to enjoy the wind blowing in your face," Demtrius replied.

Rengar cringed as his son took a tight turn into an

alleyway. "Perhaps you could lower it for now," he said, "and then maybe readjust it later."

Ricson and Scard were now racing around the city, speeding incredibly fast.

"What is under the tarps?" asked Waulf.

I had almost forgotten about the three sleds.

"Those are your next gifts," said Demtrius.

The Dotarans then pulled the coverings off the sleds, revealing a load of blue tinted metal along with dozens of boxes.

"That is Dotaran steel, and it is unimaginably strong, though surprisingly malleable. Your smiths should have no problems molding it," Demtrius told them. "In the boxes you will find dozens of flashlights that will emit light at the push of a button. They work by using a hand-crank, which charges it for a short time. There are also telescopes as well, ones that will allow you to see further than you can imagine. I think you will find these items very useful."

Ricson and Scard had just circled around a group of buildings and were headed back down the main avenue of the small city, where Finnisians watched them from the surrounding streets. Snow and dirt were ripped up and spit out by the treads on their ski-cycles as they raced neck and neck down the narrow strip.

Ricson took the lead and began to pull away, but had to slow down to avoid hitting a young Mercerian cub, and then Scard had the upper hand. Ricson was able to catch up to Scard, and that's when the stakes were raised. Scard suddenly jerked his ski-cycled and collided with Ricson, sending him flying toward a crowd of Mercerians. Ricson just barely avoided the crowd, and was then back on track.

Scard prepared to strike again, and Ricson hit the brakes, so Scard ended up speeding into a nearby building. He pressed the brakes, but still hit the wall at a good fifteen to twenty miles per hour.

Waulf went running to his son, but, luckily, Scard walked away with only minor bumps and bruises.

"We will need time to consider your offer," Rengar told us. "We will meet again in a half-month for Tzulamay, and then you will have our answer."

I should remind you that a Tatoran month is different from an Earth month. A Tatoran day is approximately twenty six and a quarter Earth hours, and there are ten days in a Tatoran week. Continuing in multitudes of ten, they have ten weeks in a month and ten months in a year, meaning that a Tatoran year is about three Earth years, and their Tatoran months are approximately one hundred nine Earth days. I will continue to speak in Earth terms to make it easier for you though.

"I understand," said Demtrius. "We will return in fifty days."

# Chapter Seven
# Dotaran Revelations

On the flight back to the Aramis, Demtrius and Delfwig sat at the controls, while I sat behind them, entertaining myself with a handheld Dotaran children's game, which was meant to stimulate brain activity. I sped through the challenges, as my mind had become much sharper and more focused since I had come to Tatora. I attributed this to the injection I received on Scynthia, now so long ago, just as I did my increased muscular strength and quick healing abilities.

Occasionally, I still tried to read the minds of those around me, but I was never successful. It was like there was always some sort of protective mental barrier blocking my entry. The closest I ever came was feeling someone's energy and emotions, if you can even call that a telepathic ability. It was helpful in feeling out an individual, like a sort of intuitive sense of someone's intentions, and I was grateful to be able to do that at least.

I finished the series of challenges on the handheld game and then placed the device off to the side. I looked out through the front window of the aircraft, and then my gaze drifted to Demtrius. I began staring back and forth from Demtrius to Delfwig, really noticing for the first time how eerily similar they looked to one another, and to most other Dotarans for that matter.

Delfwig noticed my staring and asked, "What are you looking at, Human?"

"The two of you," I replied. "If I hadn't spent so much time with Demtrius, I don't think I'd be able to tell you two apart. And I don't mean just the two of you either. You both look so much like every other Dotaran, so healthy and ageless, and, to me at least, almost identical."

"We are hardly identical," said Demtrius. "For one, I am dozens of years older than Delfwig."

"Yes, and Demtrius' third eye is at least a quarter of an inch higher on his forehead than mine," Delfwig added.

"Compared to humans, your differences are very subtle," I said. "Your bodies are all the same shape and size, your eyes are spaced the same, your noses and ears are the same size and in the same places. It's almost as if you were clones."

"You must understand," said Demtrius, "that our species is far older than the human race. We are higher beings, and I don't mean that your people aren't, but we have had countless ages for our species to evolve and develop fully, both physically and mentally. Our bodies have adapted perfectly to the environment on Dotara, so we are now highly resistant to minor mutations and deviations in our DNA, which would cause the differences in appearance that you have mentioned. We are at the apex of our evolution, and at this point there is no benefit for us to look different."

"Age isn't really a concern for our race either," Delfwig added, stating it mater-of-factly. "We have evolved to a point where, as long as we maintain good health, time has relatively no bearing on our existence. We have found that our cells continue to replicate and regenerate continuously, leaving us 'seemingly ageless,' as you have pointed out."

"What does that mean, then?" I asked. "You all just live forever?"

"We do, of course, expire eventually," Demtrius replied, "but not from such a simple thing as old age. Physical wounds can be fatal, as well as famine and disease, and those three categories comprise most of the fatalities that we incur, but a Dotaran can also die if he does not take care of himself. Proper diet and exercise, as well as abstaining from using harmful substances and maintaining good mental health have as much to do with our longevity as does our DNA. The better one cares for oneself, the longer they will live."

"That's unbelievable," I commented. "If only humans could be so fortunate."

"It more or less applies to you as much as it does to

us," Demtrius said. "The major difference is in the way our bodies function and utilize energy. The best approximation I can make is that our bodies are like batteries; we live and run at the same level of energy and efficiency, but when the time is upon us, our bodies deteriorate rather quickly, and once that begins there is very little that can be done to reverse the process."

"Still," I replied, "I'd like to live as long as I can, and if just staying healthy made it indefinite, that would be fantastic."

"Give it a few millennia," Delfwig said as if it meant no time at all, "and perhaps your species will reach a similar outcome."

"So for a group like your crew on the Aramis," I assumed, "a natural death doesn't occur very often, does it?"

"Indeed, not often at all, for we are all highly trained and incredibly disciplined," Demtrius replied. "We strive to eat only the most nutritious meals, and exercise is mandated daily. The Aramis also employs several psychologists that provide therapy when needed."

"If it weren't for the aggressive Tatorans," Delfwig interjected, "we could live here forever, though it would continue to be a lonely, unfulfilled existence."

"Why lonely?" I asked. "There are so many Dotarans aboard the Aramis, how could you ever be lonely?"

"It is a different kind of lonely than that," Demtrius replied, and then sighed heavily. "It is more of a longing. You see, we all have family and friends back home on Dotara, and it has been nearly sixty-four Tatoran years since we have seen them." That would be about one hundred ninety-two Earth years. "Delfwig and I have two children apiece that went through the same academy together. This is why we've been working so hard to return. Dotara is our home, and everyone we care about is there. There is nothing for us here."

"That's terrible," I said, empathizing with their situation. "I'm so sorry for all of you. I didn't even know you had a wife and children, Demtrius."

"Children, yes, but I have never had a life-partner," he replied.

"Then how do you have children?" I asked curiously.

Demtrius' eyes suddenly widened, and the wrinkle in his forehead twitched. "Have I never told you before? We Dotarans are asexual beings. I birthed my children on my own, and raised them on my own as well."

"Really?" I asked in disbelief. "So you don't have sex?"

"We don't need sex, we don't desire sex, and we don't even have the organs to have sex," Demtrius replied proudly. "We Dotarans are genderless, and each of us produces our own offspring."

"Before coming to Tatora," Delfwig continued, "intercourse was long thought to be a device of only the lower orders of life, but now we find that we are apparently unique in our gender neutrality."

"Almost," I commented. "The Tatorans have three genders; male, female, and then a class of gender neutrals."

"That is true," Demtrius replied, "but the Tatoran gender neutrals do not reproduce at all, while our species does so asexually."

"This is so strange!" I mused. "To think, I'm having such a casual conversation with two aliens about their reproduction processes! It's all so strange!"

"Strange would be voluntarily mixing your bodily fluids with another person," said Delfwig. "I honestly don't know how you humans can stomach the sexual reproduction process. It's absolutely disgusting."

"If you had ever had an orgasm, you wouldn't think it was so disgusting," I replied.

"Perhaps," said Delfwig, "but I sure am glad that I never have to experience sexual intercourse."

"And I'm glad I've had the pleasure of doing so," I laughed. "You don't know what you're missing."

"The only pleasure Dotarans require is that which we get from the love of our offspring and seeing them grow into mature adults," said Delfwig defensively.

"I think you will see your children again someday," I said more seriously. "I can only just begin to understand what you are going through, but, from what you're telling me, you literally have all the time in the world to figure it out. And, not to sound insensitive, but if all else fails, you could always try to begin a new life and family here on Tatora. Surely you've considered this after all the years you've been stranded here?"

"Unfortunately," Demtrius replied with great sorrow, "that will never happen. Once the last of us dies here, that will be the end of us."

"But why does it have to be that way?" I asked. "Wouldn't your children want you to be happy too? I'm sure their lives have not stopped since your disappearance, so why should all of yours?"

"It's not that some of us wouldn't like to," Demtrius answered. "It's just that Dotarans are only capable of producing two offspring in a lifetime. Our entire crew has already had their children, which is why we were selected for our deep space mission in the first place. If any of us were to perish during our mission, we would have someone to carry on our bloodlines back on Dotara, but once the last of us dies here, that will be it, and no one will know what happened to us."

"But like you said," I reminded him, "you and your crew have the potential to live indefinitely, and with Pharon agreeing to work with you, I'm sure one day soon we will both see our homes again."

"I hope you are right, Jaxon," Demtrius said gloomily.

"Likewise," Delfwig replied.

We returned to the Aramis in the evening, arriving during a change in shift, so Demtrius, Delfwig, and the crew had to connect the flyers to their charging ports without assistance.

"The ships run on a battery charge like the ski-cycles you gifted to the Mercerians?" I asked curiously.

"Indeed," he confirmed. "Each ship is housed with incredibly strong, high-powered batteries that provide power to the mattertron. Our Skivs, the single-passenger ships, operate on just one battery, while the Looners, our medium-class ships, like the one we just disembarked from, have dual batteries. Our largest ships, the Dondobah, are complete with four batteries a piece."

"How long can the batteries last?" I asked.

"The mattertron drive requires significant energy, so our ships are only capable of continuous flight for just under a Tatoran day," he told me. "We haven't been able to explore the entire planet yet because of that."

"What about the Aramis?" I asked. "Does it also run on a battery?"

Delfwig laughed lightly at my question.

"No," Demtrius replied. "The Aramis is far too large a ship to run on any amount of battery. It is a retro-fitted warship, and has its own power core."

"What kind of energy does the Aramis use?" I asked.

"Several types," Demtrius began, "but the main source of power-"

Delfwig quickly interjected, giving Demtrius a stern look. "We are not at liberty to divulge that information."

Demtrius conceded. "My apologies, Jaxon. Delfwig is correct. The captains have placed strict orders of confidentiality."

"Of course they have," I replied. Honestly, it made sense though. I wouldn't trust a stranger with my secrets either.

Soon, Demtrius and Delfwig gave their report of the mission to their captains, describing the events in great detail. All of them seemed pleased with the happenings, except for Alexitus, who would rather have had them make their decision before we left the island.

"They have the leverage now," Alexitus told us.

"We can't push them too hard," Demtrius had said. "That might drive them away completely."

That was the end of the discussion.

Later that night, while I was preparing to sleep in my assigned quarters, Demtrius arrived at my door. "May I come in?" he asked.

"Of course, Demtrius, you are always welcome here."

"Thank you," he replied. "I have new orders for you from the captains."

"Wonderful," I said, sarcastically.

"Tomorrow morning, you are to follow the blue strip on the floor to the Science Department, where you will work with Pharon and a hand-picked crew of Dotaran scientists. Pharon will be in charge, and the rest of you will assist him in assimilating his technology with ours," he explained. "I know it is not your field of expertise, but the captains want you to stay close to Pharon. He does not have our monitoring device implanted under his skin, and the captains don't trust him one bit."

"Understandable, I guess, but I will be like a fish out of water," I replied.

Demtrius smiled, "You will do fine there. And don't forget, I would still like to run some tests on you. Don't think I've forgotten what you told me in that Aanthoran prison cell."

He was referring to when he and I had first met, and I had told him my short tale of leaving Earth, receiving the enhancement injection on Scynthia, and then being banished to Tatora.

"Don't worry, you are not the only one curious about what exactly that injection did to me," I replied. "I must say though, I've never felt better in my life."

"So far," Demtrius cautioned me. "We still don't know if it will have any adverse effects. I'm not saying there will be any, but it is something worth knowing."

"Agreed," I said. "For better or worse."

# Chapter Eight
# We Go To Work; I Am Examined

Pharon and I followed the blue line on the floor of the hallway, making our way to the Science Department. As we walked, Pharon informed me that he had visited the lab while I was away.

"It is of the highest caliber," he said with surprising enthusiasm. "Almost anything we might need is located in that room."

"What tasks have Mya and Nadina been assigned?" I asked. They were quartered in the room adjacent to ours, but I hadn't seen them since before my trip to Mercer.

"They will be working in the Aquaponics Department, but I'm not sure what their specific responsibilities will be."

"Aquaponics?" I asked. "Like hydroponics? Growing plants without using soil?"

"Something of the sort," Pharon replied. "It is where they grow their food."

When we entered the Science Department, we were met by four Dotaran scientists. They looked at us with contempt. I could understand the feeling, I guess. Seeing an inferior human and a remorseless Scynthian brought in to do what they couldn't do in all of their time on the ship must have been embarrassing for them.

Though Pharon was clearly the brains in our duo, the Dotarans still showed the same scorn for me as they did for him, especially since I was high in Demtrius' favor. They probably thought I was getting special treatment, and I guess, in a sense, I was.

The Dotarans did all they could to slow us down that first day. Not once did they follow any of Pharon's directions, and they seemed fully content to continue whatever projects they had already been working on before we arrived. Pharon had one of the Dotaran translators with him, until he turned it off, since it was serving no communicative purpose. The Dotaran scientists either remained quiet or blatantly ignored us, and only spoke to one another under their breath in Dotaran. They didn't know I could understand them, however, and of course soon began to speak badly of Pharon and me.

"If you could speak Dotaran," I told Pharon, "you would not be pleased with the things they have to say about you."

"I'll let you in on a little secret," Pharon whispered. He tapped his marker on the small whiteboard he had been scribbling on, and when I looked down, I saw he had written a message in English. The lettering was crude and unpracticed, but it was legible, saying, "I can speak and write Dotaran fluently, as well as English and many other languages, but it serves my purposes better if these Dotarans remain ignorant of that fact. The work will go much quicker without them constantly asking questions and adding their own opinions and ideas."

I smiled. Pharon was always the tactician.

For the remainder of that first day, we did nothing more than create a list of all the supplies Pharon would need, and then began to requisition the many items. The only problem we ran into was that the Dotarans used their special high-powered, long-lasting batteries to operate their devices, which could be recharged a number of ways. Pharon was more accustomed to using detriminium-powered devices, which would provide a much higher energy output over a span of many years.

"Will you still be able to do your work?" I asked him.

"I'm not sure," he said. "It will take more time than I originally conjectured, but I might be able to boost the output power from the Dotaran batteries. It is a long shot, but I will try. If only we had some detriminium. Then I could have you home in a week!"

At that moment, I noticed the Dotaran scientists eyeing us closely with obvious suspicion, but that didn't bother Pharon or me.

For the next week, I assisted Pharon in his work as best I could. Usually that consisted of retrieving tools and other materials, as well as taking measurements and cleaning everything we used. I hadn't the faintest clue as to what Pharon was actually doing. The many equations that he endlessly scribbled down were all in Scynthian and too complicated for me to understand, even though he explained them from time to time as he went.

The Dotarans, finally taking an interest, started walking around our work station and looking over our shoulders at what we were working on, but they were stumped by the Scynthian language too. Pharon worked like a fiend, and the Dotarans could sense that he was doing something significant. They watched us more closely from then on, though still with scornful suspicion.

At the beginning of our second week in the Science Department, when the captains were satisfied with Pharon's progress, I received new orders. They had, of course, been monitoring our activity in the department via the small implant they had injected under my skin, and now they had determined that Pharon, for the time being, could be left under the supervision of two Dotaran scientists. The other two scientists were to escort me to the examination room, where they would begin a series of tests to determine the overall impact and extent of the Scynthian injection serum. I was not looking forward to the testing, but Demtrius promised me he would be present in the room, so I conceded to the captains' orders.

As I was brought to the examination room, I couldn't help but think back to the medical room on Scynthia. I was suddenly very anxious, and I could sense enjoyment coming from the scientists. They seemed to be very much amused by my apparent discomfort, and it didn't make me feel any more at ease.

Demtrius was already standing in the examination room waiting for me when we got there.

"Are you ready?" he asked.

"As ready as I'll ever be," I replied. "Let's get this over with."

As would any doctor, Demtrius and the two attending scientists checked my vitals and gave me a physical assessment first, during which they discovered the metal cuff that was still invisibly wrapped around my forearm. I had again forgotten about cuff, and now the Dotarans questioned me about the camouflaged device. I told them what I knew about it, which wasn't much, and they were none too pleased.

"Ask Pharon or Nadina," I told them. "It is, after all, a Scynthian device."

Demtrius drew several vials of blood from me and placed them within a machine to be analyzed. About an hour later, the machine finished processing the data, and the Dotaran scientists were very excited by the analysis. One of the attending Dotarans showed me the test results, though I couldn't make heads or tails of what they meant.

Demtrius explained their findings. "The serum was extremely effective, enhancing every cell in your body, which would account for your quick healing abilities, as well as any visual or auditory enhancements. Most importantly, you are now using more of your mind," he told me. "Specifically in the frontal and temporal lobes of your human brain. The enhancement to the temporal lobe is what allows you to understand and speak the many languages that are now within your capabilities, and also increases your memory capacity. In the frontal lobe, the serum has heightened your motor skills and cognition levels, though there does seem to be one adverse side effect with regards to your reasoning skills."

"What does that mean?" I asked, suddenly concerned.

"From my observations, I would say it means that you are more prone to risk-taking behavior," he replied. "It's not necessarily a bad thing, but it is something to be cognizant of."

I breathed a little easier. "I'm not too worried about that. I've always been a bit of an impulsive risk-taker, and it hasn't seemed to be a problem for me yet," I said, smiling. My smile diminished somewhat as I thought how untrue that statement was, at least when it came to you. I never did take the risk of expressing my feelings to you, and I sorely regret that now.

"Just make sure you control your impulses, and not the

other way around," Demtrius cautioned me.

"Duly noted," I replied.

"There are some brain functions that we can't quite understand," he continued, "and we think it has something to do with the device you wear on your forearm."

I shook my arm and looked at it, still amazed by the cuff's camouflage, among its other abilities. "Nadina once told me that the cuff is what allows me to speak multiple languages," I explained. "She said it basically reprograms the mind, making connections where the brain normally can't."

"It must work in conjunction with the serum in some way," Demtrius replied pensively.

"Such amazing technology!" said one of the Dotaran scientists.

"We need to bring our findings to the captains immediately," said the other.

The tests had taken the majority of the day, and when I finally returned to my sleeping quarters, Pharon was already there.

"Where were you today?" he asked.

"Being examined," I told him. "The Dotarans were interested in knowing about the serum your people gave me."

"I'm sure they were," he said. "Like I keep saying, we all have our hidden agendas. You should know they only want to harness the power of the serum and use it to enhance their crew. They are just using you, Jaxon."

"Well between the serum and the metal cuff, they will have their hands full for a while."

"Metal cuff?" he asked.

"The device that got stuck on my arm and brought me to Scynthia in the first place," I told him, as if it was of no consequence. "Nadina never told you about it?"

"No, she didn't, and that device will help us greatly!" he said excitedly. "I can use its components to advance my work ten-fold! We'll need to remove it from your arm right away."

"Wait, what do you mean?"

"There is detriminium in that cuff, and that is what

we've been missing," he said in triumph. "You will be home much sooner than we thought!"

It took a second for Pharon's words to sink in, but then I found myself filled with joy. Home seemed so close. You seemed so close. I quickly calmed myself though; I didn't want to get too excited if things ended up falling through.

The following day, we arrived at the laboratory to find the four Dotaran scientists already hard at work, completely focused on some new and exciting task.

"They are trying to create a Dotaran enhancement serum now," Pharon told me, "but they'll be at it far longer than they think. Your human DNA is much more easily manipulated than Scynthian or Dotaran DNA." He leaned toward me, and said, "You hear that?" speaking to the captains through my implanted monitoring device. "They'll be at it for years before they'll get it right, and they'll face many set-backs between now and then!"

While the Dotarans stayed working on their own task, Pharon turned his attention to the project at hand; removing the metal cuff from my forearm.

He worked on trying to disengage the camouflaging and trying to activate the device, but to no avail. "It is damaged," he said unhappily. "These devices are incredibly strong. What did you do to it?"

"When I was in the Pit of the Gyx, a faoler bit down on the cuff," I explained. "It saved my life."

"Well the device won't respond," he said, clearly irritated.

"Is there another way to get it off?" I asked.

"I can remove it manually, but it will be very painful," he replied.

"But if you can get it off, then that will be all you need to advance your work?"

"It will be enough to get you home," he answered, "but the Dotarans will have to procure much more detriminium if they plan on getting their entire ship home."

"Take it off then," I said.

I was so close to seeing you again. Very soon, things would be back to normal. There was an end in sight.

# Chapter Nine
# The Dracari Tree

"Brace yourself," Pharon said to me as he grabbed the cuff with a locked grip. "This is going to be very painful."

He had spent the morning slowly cutting through the cuff with a special Dotaran laser. It was slow work, for at first the cuff was invisible, but Pharon worked diligently. By this time, the four Dotaran scientists, whose names I never ended up learning, had crowded around the work station to watch.

At first I was worried that I might lose the ability to speak and understand so many languages, since the cuff is what gave me that ability, but Pharon explained that the knowledge was already ingrained in my mind now, so I was even more eager to have the thing removed. It had saved my life and given me the power of communication, but now it was time to go home.

Pharon first began cutting where he believed the camouflaging device was located on the cuff, and, after several attempts, he was able to sever the connection. The cuff suddenly materialized, sputtering before it finally stabilized. The Dotaran scientists were instantly awed by this.

Pharon continued to slowly cut through the metal cuff with the laser, making sure not to graze my skin. After some time, he had cut it into several separate pieces. Then we were ready for the painful part of pulling out the many needles that the cuff had lodged into my forearm to stay secure.

Two of the scientists held me down on the work station as Pharon tried to pry the first piece of the cuff from my flesh. He pulled hard, and my arm was in agony as the needles refused to let go. Sweat dripped down from the crest on Pharon's head. Then, quite suddenly, the piece of cuff came free, causing Pharon to almost fall backwards.

I cringed from the pain, but I was also ecstatic. My arm bled from where the needles had been, but one of the scientists dabbed it with a cloth soaked in disinfectant. The blood stopped a moment later, since my quick healing abilities had already begun to repair the small wounds.

"Should I keep going?" Pharon asked.

I was surprised by his consideration, but nodded that he should. The pain was negligible when all I could think about was what I would do once I returned home, and what I would say to you. You must hate me right now, thinking I just abandoned you there in the cabin, but I will be back soon, and then you will understand everything.

Piece by painful piece, Pharon removed the cuff. By the time he was done, my arm was throbbing with pain. One of the scientists wiped it down with another disinfectant cloth, and then bandaged the arm.

Pharon held the pieces of the cuff together in his hands. "Now the real work can begin." He was so excited; he worked the entire day and throughout the night, but with my arm still healing, I was dismissed for the rest of the day.

"I'm fine, really," I had said.

"Take the day," Pharon urged me. "I would if I were you."

I couldn't argue with that.

Quite unexpectedly, the four Dotaran scientists, who, until now, hadn't lifted a finger to help Pharon in his work, decided to step in. They were extremely interested in the cuff, and wanted to learn all they could from it.

With the day to myself, I decided to take a trip to the Aquaponics Department, where Mya and Nadina would be working. I had only seen them in passing since my return from Mercer and I missed their company.

I followed a green strip on the floor to the Aquaponics Department, which was considerably larger than the Science Department, and about the same size as the flight deck. There were separate sections in the room, on several different levels, containing many varieties of fruits and vegetables. The plants grew inside long rows of troughs that filled the department. I looked inside one of these troughs, and found many strange red fish covered in blue dots swimming around under the vegetation.

"The Dotarans call them Iccythas," Mya said, walking down toward me from one of the higher levels in the department. Her voice repeated in Dotaran on a translator. "Sorry, I can turn that off. It is the only way I can talk to them."

I turned around, and Mya gasped when she saw my bandaged arm. "What happened?"

"Oh, nothing really. Just something that happened in the lab," I replied. "So this is where they've been keeping you?"

"Yes," she said with some enthusiasm. "Nadina and I have been learning all we can about the Aquaponics process. It is really very interesting."

"I've heard of Aquaponics before, but what exactly is it?" I asked. "Growing plants without using soil, right?"

"It's much more than that," she replied. "Look here. See the fish inside the trough? The fish and the plants live in what the Dotarans call a 'symbiotic relationship'. We feed the fish, and in turn they produce waste that is nutritious for the plants, whose roots hang down into the water. The plants absorb the nutrients in the iccythas' waste and filter the water to keep toxicity levels low. We feed the fish, the fish feed the plants, and the plants provide our fruit and vegetables."

"A perfect cycle," I said.

"It is incredibly efficient, but I guess that would be a necessity on a ship meant for deep-space travel." She was smiling. "I didn't think I would enjoy it so much, but I actually find the work very satisfying."

"Yes, fish waste, super fulfilling," I replied sarcastically, and Mya gave me a playful punch on my chest.

We talked for a short time, but then Mya had to return to work.

"Promise me that you'll visit again soon," she said.

"I promise," I replied. "Just don't get into any trouble in the meantime."

"Deal," she said cheerfully.

It was barely afternoon on Tatora and already my arm was feeling much better. I returned to my sleeping quarters and donned the black and blue, skin-tight thermal suit that the Dotarans had issued me. It was incredibly thin, but it was surprisingly warm inside the suit. The material it was made from retained the majority of my body heat, but this part of Tatora was frigid, so I also pulled on a thick hooded windbreaker as well.

With so much light left in the day, I wanted to finally go outside the ship and stretch my legs, and hopefully find Thiesel. Somehow. All I knew was that he was somewhere out on the ice, but I had found him before, so I was sure I could find him again. I packed a bag with some food and supplies, and headed for the exit.

As I walked outside, I followed only my gut feeling and the glimpses I could catch every once in a while through Thiesel's eyes. There was little to go on however, as all I kept seeing was him peering through a thicket of evergreen trees at a herd of ram-like creatures, all of which had massive, curling horns protruding from their skulls.

Eventually I found a grouping of trees that looked similar to the images I was getting from Thiesel. I then started hearing a cracking sound, as if someone were slamming rocks together. I rounded a large boulder and happened upon the same herd of rams that Thiesel had been watching. I watched as two lined up and went charging at each other. Just before their heads were about to strike, they both quickly reared back and then slammed their horns together. The noise of the collision travelled far into the tree-line, though the other rams paid no attention to the altercation.

I looked around for Thiesel, but he was nowhere to be seen. The rams continued knocking their heads together.

I heard a branch snap somewhere far to my right, and a split-second later Thiesel was upon the herd. The rams, startled, ran for their lives, but Thiesel was able to capture one in his jaws and another two within the folds of his sinuous body. He made a quick meal out of the three rams, suffocating them and then swallowing them whole. For a second I thought he might choke on the horns, but the rams slid down his throat without any difficulty.

Thiesel immediately came slithering over to me and licked my face with his long, blue tongue. He was even larger now, and still growing. Soon, he would be at the size his mother was when she died high in the jungle canopy outside of Aanthora, while saving my life I should add.

Without warning, Thiesel wound his tail around me and lifted me onto his back with surprising gentleness. I clung to his neck just behind his head, holding on for dear life. Then he sped off into the brush. He whipped and winded his way around tree after tree, and his body ricocheted between the tree trunks, bending and splintering them as he sped through the evergreen forest. It was amazing.

We soon came to a small rise, where a lone, leafless tree stood, appearing gray and cracked. It was very different from the surrounding trees, rising high and spreading its branches out far. It reminded me of the trees in Aanthora, but this tree had a natural beauty that no one could recreate. I suddenly felt overwhelmed, as if I stood before a force I couldn't comprehend.

Thiesel let me down from his body, and we stayed by the tree for an hour or so. I took out my lunch from my shoulder bag and started eating, enjoying the fresh air. Meanwhile, Thiesel slithered up the tree and wrapped around one of the higher branches, soaking in the sunlight. It was cold, but my suit and windbreaker protected me well.

When I finished my lunch, I laid on my back and looked up at Thiesel, who was gazing at our surroundings like a submarine's periscope. I looked at the tree too, wondering what type of tree it was and how it had sprouted in the forest of evergreens. An instant later, the name *Dracari tree* flashed into my mind, and I saw that Thiesel was now staring at me.

"So this is a Dracari tree," I said aloud. "You like this tree?"

Thiesel wrapped around the limb more, as if he were hugging it. Then he swooped down from the limb and wrapped around my body, gently squeezing me.

"I'll take that as a yes then," I said, and Thiesel licked my face.

The sun was starting to sink below the far-off horizon.

"I think it's time I start heading back," I said. "The walk will take me some time."

In reply, Thiesel picked me up as he had done earlier and plopped me on his back.

"Thanks for the lift," I laughed, and rubbed him on the side of his neck. He then sped off toward the Aramis.

# Chapter Ten
# We Need Detriminium

Thiesel dropped me off at the Aramis just after dusk. The sentries on duty had been confused and on the defensive at first, but then they saw me and relaxed.

I returned to my sleeping quarters, and Pharon still was not there. I wasn't surprised. I'm sure he was lost in his work.

I laid down on my bunk and checked my wound. Already, many of the punctures were almost fully healed, and I would no longer need the bandages.

The door to the room suddenly slid open, and Pharon came walking in. "Good, you've returned. I have both good news and bad news."

"Well, good to see you too," I replied. "What's the news?"

"I was able to successfully dismantle the cuff and re-purpose many of its components. However, the key component, its detriminium power supply, was damaged by the faoler bite. I was only able to salvage a miniscule amount of the detriminium, and I'm not sure if it will be enough to power the new device I am making."

"What does this mean?" I asked.

"When I am finished manufacturing the pieces for the device, we will assemble it and test it," he said, "and let us pray that there is enough detriminium to power the device."

It sounded strange to hear him say that.

"Pray?" I asked. "I didn't know Scynthians prayed."

"It is mostly a figure of speech," he said, "but my very distant ancestors did have their deities at one point, though we've foregone all forms of religion on Scynthia many millennia ago."

What he said was interesting to consider, alluding to the idea that a species can evolve beyond the need for religion. Perhaps all young species of a higher intellect look for something to explain their existence, but it takes a very long time to understand that it is entirely inexplicable. The universe has just always been and always will be. It is one of the terrible conundrums of life, I'm afraid.

A week later, I crowded around the work station with Pharon and the four Dotaran scientists while we prepared to test the new device. Pharon had constructed a flatbed with a gravitensor attached, which would levitate the flatbed a few inches off the ground and allow us to move objects of any weight across the lab with barely the touch of a finger. He used the tiny shards of detriminium from the cuff to power the device, but also created a secondary outlet for the Dotaran battery.

A gravitensor, I should explain, is a high-magnitude gravity generator, which can create gravity in whatever direction is desired, or just in certain specified pockets of space. The Scynthians had invented the device several millennia ago, using it for a number of things, such as weaponry, defense, ship propulsion, ship stabilization, entering and leaving a planet's gravitational pull, etc. That is one reason the Scynthians were so interested in the Dotaran mattertron. The gravitensor wasted massive amounts of energy overcoming friction and other forces. When they stole the Dotarans' mattertron, which creates pockets of space that lay between matter, they created a device that could move objects faster than light. Imagine the force of gravity produced by the Sun's mass concentrated on propelling a small ship through a frictionless void; there is no conceivable limit to how fast the ship can go, assuming you have the energy required. Detriminium possesses an incredible potential energy just waiting to be released.

But all we had were shavings.

Pharon activated the device, and it responded instantly, lifting off the floor and levitating evenly. I stood in awe at the major breakthrough, but then the device started to wobble and fell back to the floor. The gravitensor was smoking, and I could see that a corner of its housing had melted away.

One of the scientists grabbed a long cylindrical tube from on a nearby wall and aimed one end at the small flames that now erupted on the gravitensor. A white paste shot out, smothering and extinguishing the small blaze.

We used our hands to fan away the smoke. I choked for a second, and it burned my eyes and throat.

"What went wrong?" I asked Pharon.

"Not enough detriminium," he said, shaking his head. "I will have to try the Dotaran batteries, but I don't believe the result will be any different. Nonetheless, I will attempt it."

It took some time for him to repair the device, but later the next day we were ready for another attempt. This time, however, we were using the Dotaran batteries.

Pharon wired several of them together, hoping to increase the power output. His idea should have worked, in theory at least, but, when he activated the device, it did nothing more than wobble in place and then went dead.

"There just isn't enough power," Pharon complained. "Even if we wired a hundred of these batteries up, there is no way we could sustain success for more than a few minutes. The batteries just aren't a viable source of energy. We need detriminium. If only Demtrius still had the detriminium ring. Just that small, dense rock would have been more than enough to get you home, Jaxon."

I cursed Souza IV, who had robbed Demtrius of the treasure and thrown us in the dungeons under Souzul. We had escaped, but without the one thing that we now needed most.

"Damn Souza," I said.

"We need detriminium," Pharon said once more, "and I know where we can find some."

# Chapter Eleven
# Mission Plans

I stood just inside the captains' conference room where my limited freedom had recently been decided on. Demtrius stood to my right on the other side of the doorway, both of us having been summoned into the room at Pharon's request. There, we listened to the conversation between Pharon and the four captains, which was constantly interrupted by the sound of a Dotaran translator.

"We have left you to your work," said Alexitus, "and now you tell us that you cannot deliver?"

"Do not talk down to me, Dotaran," Pharon shot back.

"Captain!" Alexitus insisted.

Pharon ignored the comment. "I have tried using your Dotaran batteries, but they are not strong enough." He proceeded to explain some of the design and mechanics of the gravitensor, as well as his failed attempts in the laboratory. "I can deliver," he continued, "but I need detriminium to complete my work."

"Might I remind you," Nepalen interjected, "that we are isolated here in the north. We do not have access to any detriminium. We don't even know where we could obtain any."

"And," said Waylan, ever a Dotaran for the people, "any such venture could result in the loss of valuable Dotaran lives. Our forces cannot just simply be replenished, and we will need them all if the Tatorans decide to mount another attack."

"An attack by them would be foolish at this point," Pharon replied. "They have their own internal issues to deal with now. Besides, your new alliance with the Mercerians will surely deter any such action."

"The Mercerians have not yet responded to our proposal," Alexitus reminded Pharon, "and even if they promise to abstain from any fighting, we would do well to remember the number of Tatorans that still want us gone. We have less than a thousand Dotarans in our crew, and the Tatorans range somewhere in the hundreds of thousands, if not the millions."

"All the more reason for you to assign a contingent of strong, able-bodied Dotarans to find me a source of detriminium," Pharon urged them. "A one-time venture could allow me to make the necessary upgrades to the ship and provide you with all the detriminium you would need for years to come. Jaxon could be returned home to his people, and you could all return home to yours."

"It would be risky," said Dolvin, speaking for the first time.

"But if we are successful," Pharon pointed out, "the reward would be worth the risk, and I am confident that, with your excellent leadership," he offered tactfully, "the mission will proceed without incident."

"If we were to assemble a team," said Nepalen, now beginning to warm to the idea, "how would we locate the detriminium? It is one of the rarest elements in the universe, and our crew could search for years without finding any."

"The Tatorans present a detriminium ring to the winner of their annual Pit of the Gyx tournament," Alexitus mused. "They must have a mine or storehouse of the substance somewhere, perhaps even near their fairgrounds at the base of Mount Xar'roc."

"You might be correct," Waylan replied, "but there could be a closer source. Demtrius did tell us of his imprisonment in Souzul, where Souza IV took the detriminium ring from him. We could send a team out to Souzul to recapture the ring."

"Those are both good ideas," Pharon replied generously, "but they are impractical for the purposes I have in mind. We will need a considerable amount of detriminium, much more than the ring would yield, and more than we can hope to find in any storehouse. The detriminium in the ring alone would do little more than power a single one-person transporter. It could get Jaxon home perhaps, but that would be all."

A look of discouragement appeared unilaterally between the captains.

Pharon continued, "I, however, know where we might find the necessary detriminium deposits."

"Where?" asked Alexitus anxiously.

"Yes, where?" asked Nepalen, just as eager.

"When I was still a member of the Scynthian Council," Pharon explained, "we sent emissaries all over this planet. One of those parties was sent to the Okala Mountains, where they detected deposits of detriminium buried deep beneath the mountains. Mount Guya alone sits atop a rich tract of detriminium that could sustain an entire world for several millennia, and there are many more deposits located throughout the mountains as well. These deposits have not yet been mined, at least not while I was in power, but, of course, I cannot be sure what Thuric has been doing since my banishment. It would be prudent to survey the more remote locations first."

"And you know where these other deposits lay?" Nepalen asked dubiously. "The Okala Mountains stretch for thousands of square miles."

"I am already working on that," Pharon replied.

"Working on it how?" asked Alexitus.

"In anticipation of your approval for this venture, I have begun modifying several of your multi-purpose utility devices," Pharon explained. "Soon, the devices will have the ability to detect detriminium. All you'll need to do is point the utility device in a given direction and wait to see if the sensors detect anything."

"It seems you've taken some liberties with your time," Alexitus said scathingly.

"The agreement was that I'd have complete autonomy in my work," Pharon replied, "and only now have I found it necessary to come to the four of you. The decision is now yours to make."

The captains turned to one another with apprehensive looks. Nepalen wrote something down on his computer tablet and passed it around for the other captains to read. They all nodded to one another, and then returned their attention to

Pharon.

"We will assign a team to locate and procure the detriminium using these new sensors," said Alexitus, "but you will remain here, aboard the Aramis, and continue making your upgrades."

Pharon turned and glanced back at Demtrius and me. "Very well," he said, "on the condition that Demtrius leads the mission, and Jaxon accompanies him."

Demtrius and I were both surprised by the nominations.

"Agreed," said Alexitus, without so much as glancing toward any of the other three captains. "That is, if they would like to go."

"I wouldn't have it any other way," I said from where I stood at the doorway.

"I, too, have no objections," Demtrius added.

"Very well then," said Waylan. "This meeting is adjourned."

# Chapter Twelve
# Metamorphosis

With help from the Dotaran scientists, Pharon was able
to complete his modifications to their multi-purpose utility
devices. He also began work on a detriminium sensor for the
ship, as well as a cloaking device. The captains felt the new
additions might prove useful, especially now. The cloaking
device required a considerable amount of energy though, so
only the Aramis itself would be able to use it continuously. The
smaller ships would be limited by their battery capacities.

The modified utility devices took some time to retrofit,
and, when they were finished, the captains selected a special
team of Dotarans to find and acquire as much detriminium as
they could. Demtrius would lead the team, and Delfwig was his
second in command, like he had been on the mission to Mercer.

As the ships were prepared for the voyage, I took the
time to see Mya in the Aquaponics Department. None of us
knew how long it would take to find and retrieve the
detriminium, so I wanted to see a familiar face before leaving.

When I got there, Mya seemed happier than ever,
which somehow seemed to enhance her already radiant beauty.

"Jaxon!" she exclaimed jubilantly. "It's so good to see
you!"

"It's good to see you too," I replied, "but unfortunately
I can't stay long. Demtrius and I are scheduled to leave this
evening on another mission."

"Another one already?" she asked, clearly
disappointed.

"Yes," I said, "and, if we are successful, then I will be
able to get back home very soon."

Mya looked at me with hurt in her eyes. She quickly
turned away, trying to hide it, and then turned back just as

abruptly. "You still want to go back?" she asked almost accusingly, her demeanor having changed to a more serious tone.

"Yes, of course," I replied, caught up in the thought of returning home, so I didn't immediately recognize her distress. "I just can't believe it's all finally starting to come together. Who would have thought Pharon would be the one to get things back on track?"

Mya was quiet, and had turned away to dip her fingers into one of the water troughs.

"Is something wrong?" I asked her. "I thought you'd be happier for me."

"I am," she replied in a sigh. "It's just-" she stopped before finishing her sentence.

"It's just what?" I asked.

"I thought maybe, with things finally starting to go so well for us, you would want to stay here now."

"But there's nothing here for me, Mya." I instantly regretted it. She turned away from me, obviously hurt by my words. "I didn't mean it like that," I stammered, grabbing her hand and turning her toward me again. "I've loved meeting you, and I will never forget you or all that we've been through. It's just, this place will never be my home. Not without-" but I trailed off, attempting too late to spare her from more hurt.

"You must really love her," she said.

"I do," I admitted feelingly.

"It's not fair!" she suddenly voiced fiercely. Tears were beginning to run down her cheeks.

I cringed, "Mya-."

"Stop. Please," she said, cutting me off.

She started to walk away, and took a turn around one of the water toughs before I caught up with her. "I never meant for this to be difficult for you," I said lamely.

"It's my fault," she quickly replied, wiping the tears from her face. "I'm just Nadina's lowly servant, and you're a free man from Earth. Why would you ever want to be with me?"

She was angry now, but I sensed it was directed at herself, not at me.

"It's not like I haven't thought about it," I admitted, causing her to look up with evident shock. Now I turned away, embarrassed, and let out a deep breath. I wanted to tell her how beautiful she was and how any man would be lucky to have her; I wanted to tell her that I would be lucky to have her, but what good would that do? I was leaving and she was staying, so why give her any more hope for something between us. "I'm sorry," I said instead, placing a consoling arm on her shoulder. "I'm truly sorry."

"I know," she replied in a low and raspy voice. She leaned into my body and laid her head on my chest. "Your Ryane is a fortunate woman to have a man like you so devoted to her."

She made me feel guilty; one, for leading her on as I had, and, two, for not telling her that you weren't even aware of my feelings yet.

But, as I had learned in life, it's usually better to say less, so I just stayed quiet.

A minute or two later, I told her how I had to be leaving, and we made very awkward farewells.

I still had time to spare, so I went to see Thiesel next. This time, however, Demtrius came with me. He noticed how agitated I was, but I didn't think he would understand since Dotarans are asexual beings. They only know the love of a parent for a child, and vice versa, but not the far more intimate love that one person can have for another. When he asked me what was wrong, I just told him I had had a troubling dream, and he let me leave it at that.

We took a two-person flyer and flew to the outskirts of the forest where Thiesel was living. I thought hard for him, but we waited for several minutes and he didn't show. I tried to look through his eyes, as I had always been able to do before, but for some reason I couldn't make the connection.

"Something is wrong," I said to Demtrius.

"Do you think Thiesel is in trouble?" he asked.

"I'm not sure," I replied, "but I can only think of one more place he might be. We should hurry."

We took the flyer a short distance to the Dracari tree. From the sky, it somehow seemed more vibrant and alive than it did on my last visit. Demtrius carefully maneuvered the flyer down to the forest floor, but couldn't avoid brushing against a large tree. The ship was fine though.

I got out of the flyer and ran up to the Dracari tree, shocked that it appeared to be growing again. I looked up into the branches searching for Thiesel, seeing fresh leaves sprouting all over. Then I saw something on one of the higher limbs. It was a large, translucent ball hanging from the branch by a thick mucus-like substance, and there was something inside the ball. It was Thiesel!

"What the hell is happening to him?" I yelled.

I wasn't really expecting an answer, but Demtrius started, "It looks like a cocoon. Perhaps Thiesel had not yet reached adulthood and is now going through some kind of a metamorphosis."

"Just like a caterpillar changes into a butterfly," I thought to myself.

"There isn't much knowledge about the anacari species, as most Tatorans that have come in contact with the serpent have either died or caught only fleeting glances, and my people have found no use in studying the species."

I looked up at the chrysalis, trying to imagine what possible transformation Thiesel could be going through, and the terrible discomfort he must have been experiencing. Everyone always thinks of the beautiful butterfly that comes out, but never about the caterpillar that goes in. Its whole body goes through a rough transformation; its legs fall off and its back splits open so that it can grow wings. It must be an incredibly painful process.

I could vaguely sense Thiesel, and something told me he'd be alright. There was nothing I could do, at any rate, and I could only hope that the creature that emerged would still be the same Thiesel I knew and loved.

With nothing else to do, Demtrius and I got back into the ship and quickly rose into the sky.

I took one last look through the ship's small window at Thiesel inside his chrysalis. "Good bye my friend," I thought to myself. "I guess I will be seeing a different you the next time we meet."

Demtrius pressed the accelerator, and off we went back to the Aramis, back to the mission at hand.

# Chapter Thirteen
# A Scynthian Surprise

Our team was already on the flight deck when we arrived back at the Aramis. They were being briefed on the mission, and Waylan himself was giving the speech.

"Pharon claims that there is detriminium in the Okala Mountain range, somewhere near Mount Guya. We know Mount Guya is the home of the Guyans, the Diamond clan, and that the surrounding mountains are thinly inhabited by a small, hairy humanoid species. You should take great care and caution if you come into contact with either of these races. The Guyans, we will assume, hate us like the rest of the Tatorans, and the humanoids can't be expected to be any friendlier."

This wasn't the first I had heard of a humanoid species living on Tatora. I instantly felt some sort of kinship toward them. I knew it was important to the Dotarans that we avoid them, but I really would have liked to meet them. The fact that they existed on Tatora brought all sorts of questions to mind. But, alas, I was resigned to the fact that I would never get my answers.

Waylan took a step toward the three Dotaran flyers. "Each ship now has its own special sensor that will detect detriminium at considerable depths. All you need do is fly over an area and the sensor will automatically pick up a reading if there is any detriminium below," he explained. "I must emphasize that none of you are to take any risks, other than what's absolutely necessary. We expect this to be an uneventful mission, but we have of course have a contingency plan. Be safe and be well."

With that, he walked off the flight deck, and our team began loading into the flyers. I was just taking my first step onto my ship when small orange lights began flashing all along the walls, and then an extremely loud alarm began sounding from every corner of the ship. I looked to the other crew members, and to Demtrius sitting in the cockpit, but everyone was as confused as I was.

From across the flight deck, I saw one of the Dotaran scientists running toward us as fast as he could, waving a computer tablet in his hand. When he finally made it to our ship, he was out of breath, but we soon had him speaking.

"The detriminium sensors!" he shouted. "Pharon was installing the main sensor for the Aramis inside the control room this morning, and now they are detecting massive quantities of detriminium. The readings are off the charts! Here, take a look!"

He handed the tablet to Demtrius, though I'm not sure even he understood the data.

"What does this mean?" Demtrius asked.

"Pharon believes it means that the Scynthians have mobilized!" the scientist replied frantically. "The sensor detected the detriminium high in the atmosphere, seemingly appearing out of nowhere. Pharon said it could only be a fleet of Scynthian ships come to stop him from giving us their technology. He believes they must have back-tracked the signal from the sensor somehow and are now headed here to annihilate us all!"

"It can't be," Demtrius gasped. "It will be genocide!"

"What do we do?" I asked.

"The four captains are on their way here as we speak," said the scientist. "I think they're going to evacuate the ship!"

"But we have nowhere to go," I replied.

"We have an emergency plan for such an attack," Demtrius told me, "but we hoped we would never have to implement the plan. We will need to act swiftly."

Just then, a rush of Dotarans came pouring onto the flight deck with the four captains at their front. They made it to us quickly, and then Waylan reached out to Demtrius and spoke close to his ear, since the alarm was almost deafening.

"We must evacuate the ship!" Waylan shouted. "We already have dozens of crew members entering the tunnels, but the Scynthians will be upon us in minutes. You and I will need to lead our small fleet against their assault to buy the rest of the crew enough time to escape."

"That would be suicide," said the scientist, still standing nearby. "There are too many Scynthians, and we're no match for their advanced weaponry."

"We will give them as much time as we can," Demtrius told Waylan. He turned to his team, "We are needed in the sky."

"Demtrius..."

"Quickly now!" he ordered, pointedly cutting me off. "If the Scynthians want a fight, then we'll give them one. I can't say I haven't been waiting for the chance!"

"Good luck to you," said Waylan, placing his hand on Demtrius' shoulder. "By the hand of Carnyle, I hope to see you again soon."

"By the hand of Carnyle," said Demtrius, also putting his hand on Waylan's shoulder. He then turned to me. "I need to go now. Find Delfwig, he'll show you where to go."

"Fight like a fiend," I told to him. "Show them some Dotaran fury, and teach them that they can't just do whatever they please."

"They will regret this day," Demtrius replied, "and we will remember it forever."

# Chapter Fourteen
# A Parting Gift

As the evacuation commenced, a ship-wide lock down went into effect, completely sealing off the ship's entrances and exits, save for the opening to the sky on the flight deck and the secret passage to the escape route. The flashing lights on the wall turned from orange to red and the repetitions increased to a very rapid pace, stressing the urgency of the situation. The colored strips of light on the floor had all turned red as well and were flashing in a direction that led everyone toward the flight deck.

There was a flurry of frantic activity as hundreds of Dotarans poured onto the deck. Like clockwork, Dotarans hurtled toward their respective flyers, strapping themselves in and preparing their ships. Others ran for defensive positions around the Aramis to operate powerful electromagnetic pulse cannons. They activated mattertron shields that covered the entire ship, making it possible to intercept and repel any projectiles launched upon the hull. The great majority of the Dotarans, however, headed toward a more secluded section of the flight deck, where the floor had opened up to reveal a secret compartment.

Dolvin and Delfwig stood on either side of the compartment, directing fleeing refugees down a stairwell and into the hidden passage. The new passage, I was told hurriedly before Demtrius took flight, led beneath the ice, where the Dotarans had constructed an emergency escape route. It led hundreds of miles away, to a location undisclosed to most of the Dotaran crew. Only Demtrius, Delfwig, and the four captains knew precisely where it emerged.

Demtrius and Waylan had already taken to the air with the rest of their small fleet, leaving me standing on the flight deck. Now they hovered motionless in the sky, effectively creating a net of ships around the Aramis, ready to intercept an assault coming from any direction. They couldn't rely on their mattertron shields to hold out for long, and they knew they would be taking on heavy casualties against the Scynthians' far-superior weapons of war, but the Dotaran fleet had resigned themselves to their terrible fate in order to buy time for the rest of their crewman to reach safety.

Dotarans continued to pour in from every corner of the ship. I was suddenly sent sprawling onto the floor by a hysterical person that went bolting wildly for the escape passage, knocking over whoever stood in their path. The wave of Dotarans making for the safe haven threatened to swarm over me, and I barely managed to crawl out of their path before being trampled.

I got up quickly, unsure what to do. Then it hit me; I had to make sure the others made it out safely. I searched through the crowds for any sign of Mya, Nadina, or Pharon, who had not yet made it to the flight deck. Suddenly, through the densely packed room, I saw Nadina appear through a doorway, towering over the fleeing Dotarans that scurried past her on either side. Behind her, bobbing through the crowd, I could just make out Mya's hair among the bald-headed Dotarans. She was being pulled roughly through the crowd by Nadina, barely managing to hold on as they struggled to make their way toward me.

I blew out a sigh of relief, and was suddenly aware of how much panic I had felt just a moment before. That panic was subsiding now as I worked my way toward Mya and Nadina, waving my hands so they could find me. Nadina quickly spotted me, and grabbed my hand to pull me close as we struggled to shout over the din of fleeing crewman and sounding alarms.

"We need to get into the escape tunnel!" I shouted to them, pointing to where Dolvin and Delfwig still stood directing their shipmates to safety. "Follow the Dotarans!"

Mya nodded, her eyes wide with panic and confusion. Nadina wore the same look, which was entirely unlike her usual regal and confident expression.

The three of us forced our way through the desperate crowd, slowly making our way to the tunnel.

"It's Thuric, isn't it?" Nadina asked, shouting; the fear was evident on her face.

I nodded in solemn confirmation. "Where's Pharon?" I shouted back.

"We couldn't get to him!" Nadina shouted in dismay. "When the alarm sounded we were forced this way by the crowd. We were hoping he'd already be here!"

By this point, most of the Dotarans had made it into the tunnel, and the remaining few were being helped down below by Dolvin and Delfwig. Nadina, Mya, and I still stood on the flight deck, looking for any sign of Pharon. We could no longer see the sky with the way the aircraft elevator was positioned. For all we knew, the battle could have already commenced.

I was fairly positive I knew where Pharon would be, but I couldn't have Mya and Nadina risk their chance to reach safety. For a second I contemplated just leaving the old stubborn Scynthian to his own devices, but I had grown accustomed to the guy, and I knew Nadina would be devastated if we left without him.

"Get into the tunnel!" I said, shoving them toward Dolvin and Delfwig. "I'll get Pharon!"

Without giving her time to object, I turned and ran past the last of the Dotarans entering the deck. Delfwig and Dolvin shot me confused looks as I ran by.

"The door to this tunnel will seal shut in five minutes!" Delfwig shouted. "It will not wait!"

The ship was suddenly shaken roughly and I was thrown off my feet, but I shot back up quickly and kept running. The battle must have begun.

I made it to the Science Department about a minute or so later, but not without enduring several more blasts to the ship, sending me stumbling each time. I entered the lab quickly, and found Pharon tinkering with a multi-purpose utility device at the work station. He had a pile of other devices stacked to his left as well.

"Pharon, what the hell are you doing?" I shouted from the edge of the doorway. "We have to get out of here!"

"That blasted Thuric and his band of rebels!" he shouted in reply, not even looking up from his work. "They must have detected the signal from the detriminium sensors and traced it back to us here!"

"That doesn't matter now!" I screamed. "We have to get out of here! The battle has already begun outside and we will be trapped if we stay any longer!"

"One more second," he said. "I'm almost done."

I was running toward him now, ready to drag him out myself, when another blast to the hull slammed me into one of the work tables. Pharon somehow stayed upright and resumed tinkering with the device.

I got up and ran to him, grabbing him by the arm and trying to pull him away, but he resisted my help. "Wait, we need to take these with us!" he shouted. "None of them can be traced. I made sure of it!"

"Fine," I yielded, grabbing as many as I could and stuffing them into a bag I took from a nearby table. "Let's go!"

Just then another blast struck the ship, and the whole vessel felt like it jumped in the air. Pharon and I were both thrown across the room. We scrambled to get back up, Pharon still clutching his bag full of devices, and ran as fast as we could for the flight deck. I was hoping with all my will power that the doors had not closed to the tunnel, trapping us within the Aramis. The ship was still holding, but shot after shot was pounding the hull mercilessly and I knew it couldn't survive the torrent of fire power for much longer; and neither could we.

Not a moment after we left the Science Department, the wall at the far end of the lab blew inward in one massive earth-shattering blast, revealing a cubic foot or so of the outside. The blast sent us both flying forward, and Pharon landed hard on top of me. He flattened me, knocking the wind from my lungs, and his bag went flying out of his webbed hands.

"Get the devices!" he shouted, scrambling to pick them up.

I coughed, allowing air back into my lungs. "Leave them!" I said in frustration.

"We can't!" he replied. "They are our only hope now!"

There was no time to argue, so I gritted my teeth and helped him gather the various devices as quickly as I could. Once they were all back in the bag, we finally made our way to the flight deck, where Delfwig and Nadina stood at the tunnel entrance with the door partially closed. They saw us and began to yell for us to hurry. I sprinted with all my speed, pumping my arms fast and pulling slightly ahead of Pharon, encumbered as he was by his bag of devices.

The tunnel was only about ten yards away when I was blinded by a bright bluish-green light, and shots of teal plasma came showering down all around us. Miraculously, none of the plasma hit me. I saw the smoldering metal on the floor of the ship where it had struck and I was extremely relieved not to have experienced the same mutilation.

My relief was short lived, however, as I heard Nadina's ear-piercing scream and saw her jump toward us. "No!" she screamed, running toward me from the tunnel entrance. Delfwig reached for her, but she broke free from his grasp.

I turned around, now expecting the worst, and saw Pharon lying in a pool of his own murky-gray blood. One of his legs had been blown completely off and lay half way across the flight deck, while his stomach had a wide gaping hole in it, showing the floor on the other side. Oddly enough, the plasma shots had cauterized most of the wounds, so he wasn't losing blood as fast as he should have been. I had never seen anything like it, but I barely had time to process it all before Nadina screamed again, "Father!"

More plasma blasts came showering down, but my luck remained as I crouched next to Pharon's body, and not one shot so much as grazed my skin. Some rational part of my brain was screaming at me to get into the tunnel before it closed forever, but I could see Pharon was still breathing, and this was my friend. I looked around hopelessly, thinking desperately for a way to save him; I just had to save him!

"Go!" Pharon struggled to say, coughing up more blood. Nadina was by his side now, tears running down her leathery face. "I love you, Nadina," he said weakly, "but you are foolish to stay with me now. I am done for."

"Don't say that," Nadina cried. "I love you, Father. You

can't go now. I need you!"

"I'm...I'm sorry," Pharon managed to say before coughing up more gray blood. He strained to grasp a fallen utility device and pressed it into Nadina's hand. "You must take them," he said weakly. "They're your only hope now."

"What?" she asked.

Pharon was too weak to respond. He moaned with pain as another plasma burst rocked the ship. Nadina held his hand and looked deep into his tiny black eyes as he blew out a heavy breath, never to take another.

I was instantly stricken with grief, but I couldn't even imagine what Nadina must be going through. All I knew was that if I didn't get her out of there we would both meet the same fate.

"I'm so sorry, Nadina, but we need to move," I said gently, laying a hand on her shoulder. "He's gone; there's nothing we can do."

She looked up at me, as if just noticing I was beside her. It took her a brief moment to focus on me, but then she shook her head and straightened her back. "Grab the devices," she said. "He told us we'll need them."

She gave her father a kiss on his bloody cheek and stood unsteadily as I collected the scattered devices again, stuffing them back into the bag with the others. I took Nadina by the hand and pulled her along as fast as I could toward the tunnel entrance, where Delfwig still stood straining to keep the door from closing. "Hurry!" he kept shouting.

We quickly squeezed past him and went down the stairs into the tunnel. It was dark, and dim lights guided the way. Delfwig finally let the door close over the entrance, and it slammed shut with grim force. He then hit a switch next to the door and two more thick layers of metal slid in place over the door for added protection.

It was like we were in another world at that moment; the sounds of the chaos we were leaving behind were instantly blocked out and the rumbling of the ship now went unfelt. There was no turning back. We needed to hurry. The fleet could only buy us so much time, and that time was already ticking away.

## Chapter Fifteen
## Flight Of The Aramis

Delfwig, Nadina, and I ran through the dimly lit tunnel until we came to a large room filled with dozens of platforms, where bullet-shaped trains levitated above their tracks. They had no wheels, and I would later learn that they ran on some type of magnetic rail. The trains were propelled by magnets as well. This apparently required much less energy than using the mattertron, and the attainable speeds were still considerably high.

There were dozens of platforms for these magnet trains, but only a few still remained at their stations.

"Over there!" cried Delfwig, pointing to the nearest train, where Mya stood waving us over frantically.

We rushed over and clambered inside. It had more than enough room for the four of us. Once inside, Delfwig slammed his hand down on a red button at the front of the car, sealing the door shut.

We quickly sat down on seats along the wall and buckled ourselves in, following what the other Dotarans already on-board had done. The train lurched forward a moment later, and then we were speeding along on the flat, straight track somewhere under the ice of the north.

Delfwig sat at the controls of the train, trying to radio Dolvin, Nepalen, and Alexitus, who had been among the first to enter the escape tunnel. It only took him a minute, and then the three captains were on the loud speaker.

"It is Delfwig. The Aramis has been cleared of the remaining crew. The ship has been completely abandoned."

"Well done," Alexitus replied. "Our quick actions have saved us many lives. As long as Waylan and Demtrius can continue to hold off the Scynthians, we should make it to the first rendezvous point safely. There, we must switch our mode of transportation, for the tunnels are too easily tracked. We will then proceed to the second rendezvous point."

"Yes, Captain," said Delfwig, "I will see you at the first rendezvous point."

Delfwig switched off the radio and we sat in silence for a moment. That's when I noticed Nadina's glazed-over expression. She didn't seem to be registering much of anything. Despite the nature of their relationship, Nadina had truly loved her father. Now she would never talk to, or see him, again.

Mya sat beside her, holding her hand, murmuring to her softly. She must have just learned of Pharon's tragic death, and was now trying to console her friend.

I needed to do something to keep my mind off of the tragedy.

"Delfwig," I said, "is there any way to figure out what's going on above? Perhaps a satellite in orbit, or cameras on the Aramis?"

"Actually," Delfwig mused, "I might be able to access the Aramis' radar. We won't be able to see much, but it will be something."

"Do it," I said. "Please."

Delfwig nodded and quickly began fiddling with the computer. He was as fluent with the technology as Demtrius. It was like second nature to him. Soon, we saw a screen full of blue and green dots on the monitor. Delfwig said the blue dots were the Dotarans and the green dots were the Scynthians. The Scynthians, as it appeared on the screen, had far superior numbers, and were quicker and more agile than the Dotaran flyers. Demtrius and Waylan were keeping their small fleet in a tight formation over the Aramis, trying to protect it as long as they could to help further our escape. It made them easier targets for the Scynthians, however, who came in swarms of ten and fifteen to wreak havoc on every pass. I couldn't help but grow increasingly alarmed as more and more blue dots disappeared from the screen.

"They're getting slaughtered out there!" I whispered to Delfwig so as not to alarm the rest of the train's occupants.

"We still need more time," said Delfwig sadly.

"Demtrius and Waylan will be apprised of our progress through the tunnel and will do all they can to see that we make it out alive. It is their duty."

"How far have we gone?" I asked.

"Not far enough," Delfwig replied.

After a short time, the tight formation could hold no longer, and Demtrius or Waylan gave the order to disperse. The blue dots scattered in every direction. It was time to go on the offensive.

"I can't tell what's going on," I complained anxiously.

"Neither can I," said Delfwig, "but I think I have an idea."

Delfwig turned to a panel under the radar screen and removed it, revealing dozens of colored wires. He ripped some of the wires from the wall and began splicing them together.

"Try the radio," he said, pointing to a button next to a small speakerphone.

I pressed the button, but all we heard was a loud tone. Delfwig then untwisted the wires and connected them in different pairs.

"Try it again," he said.

I pressed the button again, and this time we heard static coming out from the speakerphone.

"Excellent," said Delfwig. "Now turn the dial there to adjust the frequency. We should be able to tune into the radios aboard the ships. We won't be able to speak to them, but we should be able to hear them."

I fiddled with the dial, finding only static at first. Then I passed by a frequency that came in loud and clear, but lost it by accident.

"Go back," Delfwig exclaimed. "That was it!"

I adjusted the dial again and suddenly we were hearing Waylan issuing commands to the rest of the fleet. "Squadron leaders, divert as many Scynthian aircraft as you can from the Aramis. It is time to initiate Phase Two!"

"Phase Two?" I asked Delfwig.

"Momentarily they will go on a full-offensive assault," Delfwig explained. "We must have made it far enough through the tunnel."

"But they are trying to lead the Scynthians away still," I pointed out.

"That is just one part of the overall strategy that Demtrius and Waylan devised," Delfwig told me. "The Scynthians will think they caught us off-guard, and will assume that we don't have a plan. It is our hope that their miscalculation will work in our favor, as they will be less likely to use caution when they think victory is moments away. That is when the real strike will come."

"But how?" I asked, unsatisfied with his answer. "How will they overcome the terrible odds? They would need to unleash some powerfully-destructive weapon that the Scynthians don't yet know about; one that could level the playing field."

"Or a weapon that was hitherto not taken as a viable threat," Delfwig commented.

"Yes," I agreed, "but what?"

"The Aramis," he said simply.

I wasn't sure exactly what he meant, but I had a rough idea, and I worried that it wouldn't fare well for Demtrius or the remaining fleet. Demtrius knew the risks though, and, being the former sole captain of the Aramis, would know what was to come.

As the battle in the sky raged on somewhere far above and behind us, the magnetic train carried us along for hundreds of miles. All the while, we listened to Demtrius and Waylan commanding their small fleet.

Delfwig and I sat at the front of the train, while Mya and Nadina sat behind us in the seats along the walls. Nadina was still in shock; she was almost catatonic. Mya sat next to her, now trembling with uncontrollable fear.

The battle was a dogfight at this point and the Dotarans were still losing ships, though not as fast as before. Now, at least, they were doing some damage to the Scynthians. Blue and greens dots were disappearing from the radar screen every few seconds.

The Dotarans were successful in leading the Scynthian fleet away from the Aramis, if only for a few minutes. The Scynthians, it seemed, thought they had the Dotarans on the run, and were pushing hard to finish them off. This lapse in judgment, however, had provided the Dotarans with a prime opportunity.

While the Dotaran fleet was busy leading the Scynthians away from the ship and engaging them in several isolated air battles, Demtrius and Waylan were able to secretly separate themselves from the fleet. Unnoticed by the Scynthians, they quickly made it back to the Aramis, at which point their blue dots flashed on the radar screen and vanished.

"What are they doing?" I asked. "They can't be abandoning the fleet?"

"Demtrius and Waylan are two of our top flight operators," Delfwig explained, "and the Aramis requires at least two Dotarans to operate its controls."

"What are you saying?" I asked, impatiently.

"Phase Two is well under way," he replied, "and we are about to witness the first flight of the Aramis since we were stranded here."

"You mean the Aramis still has flight capabilities?" I asked, highly intrigued.

"That, and much more," Delfwig, replied. "Facts that needed to be kept secret until an event such as this were to happen. The Aramis is almost fully functional, but the ship lacks the ability to break through Tatora's atmosphere and leave the planet's gravitational field. It can still operate perfectly fine here on the planet, though."

"So then, there is still a chance for Demtrius and Waylan to defeat the Scynthians?" I asked with reinvigorated hope.

"The odds are not in our favor," Delfwig stated grimly, "but if anyone can repel the attack, its Demtrius and Waylan."

I was suddenly wracked with guilt for not being up in the air fighting with the others. Instead I was just running away. To be sure, I was no fighter pilot and wouldn't have been much help, but I still felt guilty all the same.

"But if Demtrius and Waylan cannot cause serious damage to the Scynthian fleet very soon," Delfwig continued quietly, "then it is only a matter of time before we are tracked down and slaughtered in these tunnels."

"The captains might be relying too heavily upon this plan of theirs," I whispered gloomily.

"There was no other viable option," Delfwig replied, equally morose. "Now we must sit and wait for the outcome of the battle, and, by the hand of Carnyle, let us hope Demtrius, Waylan, and the rest of the fleet come through for us."

He was right, of course, and it did not sit well with me.

The screen suddenly flashed, and then a large blue dot appeared on the radar.

"That is the Aramis," Delfwig exclaimed.

I saw three green dots disappear from the screen.

"Why can't we hear them?" I asked.

"They must not have activated their communications," he said. "It is only the two of them. But, with the Aramis, I can do us better."

With that, Delfwig was again surfing through screen after screen on the train's computer. Suddenly, the windshield of our train displayed a video feed from some vantage point in the sky.

"What is this?" I asked.

"We are now seeing through the eyes of the Aramis," Delfwig explained, quite satisfied with himself.

The Dotarans still had the attention of the Scynthians and had drawn them in many different directions. We watched as Demtrius and Waylan came around and attacked each isolated battle, providing much needed relief to the struggling Dotaran flyers. They activated the ship's large electromagnetic pulse cannon, which could take out three Scynthian ships in a single shot.

The Scynthian ships, I should add, didn't appear to be made of any solid materials. Each seemed to be a shining sphere of bluish-green plasma energy, with no windows or identifying markings anywhere. Their motions were very similar to the Dotaran flyers, but with better control, steeper turn radii, and much faster speeds.

The pulse cannons aboard the Aramis, however, were more than sufficient to take them down.

Demtrius and Waylan took out dozens of the spherical Scynthian ships. The Scynthians were quick to realize what was happening though, and turned their fleet upon the Aramis in a coordinated attack. They lined up in front of the Aramis, taking up the entire screen, and then they opened fire. It made me flinch at first because the visual quality was so realistic, but no one in the train noticed.

The Aramis was taking one hell of a pounding from the plasma blasts, but its shields were holding up, for the moment at least.

"They won't be able to hold out much longer," said Delfwig.

Sparks flew across the screen and our visual shook violently, and then cut out completely for a few seconds. We reverted to our original screen for the time being, watching an array of green dots surrounding the Aramis.

Unbeknownst to the Scynthians, the remaining Dotarans had regrouped into two separate squads, each of which came striking down on either side of the Scynthian line in a massive pincer attack. Scores of Scynthian ships vanished from sight as the combined forces of the Dotaran pulse cannons and the Aramis' larger cannon blew them out of the sky from three sides.

The Scynthians kept firing at the Aramis, not even deigning to turn upon the Dotaran flyers until the major threat had been neutralized. The Aramis, of course, returned fire as best it could, but even with the combined forces of the Dotarans' assault, they were still outmatched and outgunned by the Scynthian fleet.

The Aramis suddenly leapt forward from its position, driving straight for the Scynthian ships. They were able to evade the massive ship easy enough, but were forced to cease firing while they maneuvered their ships. The rest of the Dotaran fleet capitalized on this, continuing their assault on the perimeters of the Scynthian formation, but now the Aramis was completely surrounded by enemy ships.

A loud blast exploded somewhere out of sight to the right of the Aramis' windshield. The Scynthians had finally managed to take out its starboard mattertron. The ship drooped to its right, throwing Demtrius and Waylan forward and into our view. They slammed hard into the viewing screen and were slow to rise.

"Get up!" Delfwig shouted. "You can still do it!" He turned to me abruptly, "They need to activate the ships central pulse cannon while the Scynthians are still packed tightly around them! It is a last resort weapon, as it will drain the Aramis of most of its energy, but this is the perfect moment with the Scynthians packed in so close! The pulse will wipe out half of their fleet!"

Demtrius and Waylan had finally risen to their feet and were back at their seats.

Waylan switched on the communications. "Stay clear of the formation! We are activating the central pulse cannon!"

"Are you ready?" Demtrius asked solemnly.

"By the hand of Carnyle," said Waylan, "it has been a pleasure to serve with you, Demtrius."

"Our time is not up yet," Demtrius answered.

He must have activated the EMP cannon then, because the screens turned black and all that came over the radio was static.

"They did it," said Delfwig, "and they may have just saved us all!"

"And they sacrificed themselves to do it," I thought sullenly.

The video and radar screens then flashed back on and the radio static ceased. After Demtrius set off the EMP, the ship must have finally crashed to the ground because now all we could see through its windshield was a slanted view of the sky that was partially blocked by a snow dune.

Within our very limited view, we saw debris raining down from the sky. I looked at the radar again, and saw that the EMP had been very effective, though there was still a commanding number of green dots on the screen. That was when we saw them.

At first it seemed like a glitch on the radar screen, but then Delfwig and I knew. Demtrius and Waylan had somehow managed to make it back to their flyers and took off from the Aramis before it crash landed. Now they spun around one another, spiraling, headed right for a group of Scynthian spheres.

"By the hand of Carnyle!" Waylan shouted over the radio. "Fight!"

They took the group by surprise, finishing them off quickly, and then were off tag-teaming more enemy ships as they passed them by. Many more green dots vanished from the radar.

"How can it be?" I asked. "Shouldn't their flyers have been disabled from the EMP, like the other ships?"

"The Aramis had shielding to block the electromagnetic blast," Delfwig explained. "That way, nothing inside the ship, including the ship itself, would be affected. It would hardly due to have the ship fall from the sky whenever the weapon is utilized."

Demtrius and Waylan managed to reinvigorate the few remaining Dotaran pilots and the battle continued to rage on. They regrouped for one final and desperate assault, and then engaged.

Demtrius and Waylan showed exceptional prowess, which, unfortunately, made them the prime targets of the Scynthians' plasma blasts. They zipped through the air side by side, with at least five enemy ships trailing behind them firing bursts of their plasma ammunition. Now we could see them on the screen that showed us the view through the Aramis' windshield. They were far off, but Delfwig was able to enhance the picture so we could see them closer up.

"Let's give them one last show," Waylan ushered, his words transmitting over the radio as he veered his ship to the right to avoid an incoming plasma blast. Demtrius did likewise, veering to the left, and the two went off in opposite directions.

Two of the Scynthian ships followed closely behind Demtrius, while the other three stayed hot on Waylan's tail. There were still dozens of Scynthian ships scouring the sky, and only a handful of Dotarans left to take them on.

Both Demtrius and Waylan made high backwards loops in the sky, and then rotated their flyers to level out. Now they were on a head-on collision course with one another.

"What are they doing?" I asked.

"Whatever is necessary," said Delfwig.

Demtrius and Waylan were just about to collide. I

didn't want to look, but couldn't take my eyes from the screen. Just when it seemed they were finished, they altered their courses abruptly, just in the nick of time. The Scynthians trailing behind each of them were slow to respond, since Demtrius and Waylan's ships had blocked their view of each other. The five spherical ships then collided and erupted in a massive explosion in the sky.

As soon as they lost those ships, they gained new foes to deal with. Two enemy ships descended upon Demtrius, while a third fired at Waylan from a distance. Demtrius was trying furiously to shake off the two Scynthians, but they had him dead in their sights.

Waylan, seeing this development, hastened to aid Demtrius. He came in from the side, firing his pulse canon. He struck one, and the spherical ship puffed into smoke and sunk to the ground. The other fired at Demtrius. He saw it coming and spun his flyer once to the right to avoid the plasma blast, only to be grazed by another shot from the enemy ship.

Waylan was now coming around for a second pass. He fired his pulse cannon again, and, the moment he did, his flyer burst into flames. Waylan's shot had struck the Scynthian ship behind Demtrius, but the third enemy ship that had been far off had circled around and shot Waylan from behind as he was concentrating his efforts on helping Demtrius.

"No!" I shouted.

"It can't be!" Delfwig protested, slamming his fist down hard on the control board.

Demtrius, caught in guilty fury, set his sights on the Scynthian that had fired the fatal blow. He quickly accelerated his flyer to its maximum velocity. "Dotara!" he shouted, and held it for a long breath.

The Scynthian ship didn't expect this. I don't think they believed Demtrius would actually do it, and when he did it was already too late. The pilot tried to move from Demtrius' path, but Demtrius sliced through the left side of the spherical ship. Both ships sputtered momentarily, and then each fell quickly to the ground.

Several Scynthian ships descended to the ground in front of the Aramis' viewing screen, obstructing our view of the aerial battle, which was now almost over. The Scynthians were just hunting down the two or three remaining Dotarans.

"They'll be coming for us now," said Delfwig, pointing out the obvious. "Let us hope that we make it to the first rendezvous point before they find us."

I just sat in my seat quietly, upset by the terrible defeat and feeling responsible for countless more deaths. If I had never donned that metal cuff in the cave on Earth, none of this would have happened, none of it. Now, Demtrius, who had been my closest and most loyal friend here on Tatora, who had been with me since the very beginning, and who had shared every adventure with me, was gone, and it was all my fault.

# Chapter Sixteen
# Fire & Ice

It was a quiet ride the rest of the way to the rendezvous point. I looked out the rear window of the train, watching it progress further and further along the magnetic rail, running from the destruction wrought by the Scynthians. Every so often, I would see a large wall or gate shut behind us, blocking the tunnel from any Scynthian pursuers. Delfwig, however, said the obstructions would only be a small hindrance to the Scynthians and their advanced weaponry.

It's hard to describe all that I felt in those moments. Anger at the Scynthians for all their terrible crimes. Grief for all of the lives lost, including Waylan and Demtrius; Demtrius, who had been like a brother to me. Hopelessness for our present situation. Fear for what was to come. A roller-coaster of emotions winding its way through me, and all I could do was stew on these dark matters.

It wasn't long before we made it to the rendezvous point. It was another station with many platforms, but, at the very far end of the station, I could see a small lake. In the lake, taking up most of its area, was some kind of Dotaran ship, but it was mostly submerged and much too far away for me to make out any other details.

"What's that thing in the water?" I asked Delfwig.

"That is how we are going to make it to the second rendezvous point," he explained. "The Scynthians will have more difficulty tracking us if we travel under water in the Iccaryn."

"The Iccaryn?" I asked.

"That is the name of the submersible," said Delfwig. "It was once the Aramis' emergency shuttle. It has enough room to accommodate the entire crew, albeit somewhat crowded. We moved it here many years ago in case such a situation as this arose and we needed to move quickly. It was Demtrius' idea, actually."

I frowned at the mention of Demtrius, and Delfwig must have seen this.

"If it wasn't for them," he said reassuringly, "we wouldn't even have this chance."

"I know," I replied sullenly, "but it's not much of a consolation prize." Delfwig grimaced, and I realized I had offended him. "I am glad so many of your people made it out though."

We moved fast toward the Iccaryn and were among the last to board the ship. Delfwig headed straight for the control room, and I followed close behind him. I wanted to know exactly what would happen next.

We entered the control room, where Alexitus, Nepalen, and Dolvin stood. There were several other Dotarans about the room too, sitting at different stations. Everyone looked in our direction when we came through the door, everyone except Alexitus.

I still held the bag of devices that Pharon had fought so hard to save, and I handed it to Nepalen. He opened the bag, saw the devices, and nodded, as if he knew exactly what to do with them.

"Start our descent," Alexitus commanded, and the ship's pilot obeyed instantly.

Nadina and Mya had also come through the doorway, and now stood just behind me.

"Seize her!" Alexitus suddenly shouted, and four Dotarans surrounded her, placing her in cuffs and chaining her to a seat. She gave no resistance, still shaken by her father's death.

"What are you doing?" I asked.

"This was all Pharon's doing!" he yelled. "She could be involved too."

"Pharon is dead!" I shouted back. "Let her go. She didn't do anything!"

"Quiet, Human!" he said angrily. "You have no voice here."

Two Dotarans stepped up beside me, and I took the hint to calm down. Arguing now wouldn't save us.

"Any news of Demtrius and Waylan, or any of the others?" Dolvin asked hopefully.

"They are gone. We saw it happen," said Delfwig. "They both fought honorably,"

"It seems they've provided us with the time we needed," said Dolvin.

"They will receive our highest commendation, of course," Alexitus replied. "If you would all please-" but he was cut off by the sound of a loud explosion somewhere not far off.

"The Scynthians!" Nepalen exclaimed fearfully. "They must be in the tunnels!"

"Ready the explosives to detonate on my mark," Alexitus commanded.

I whispered to Delfwig, "Explosives?"

"The tunnel is lined with explosives," Delfwig told me. "We can hit the Scynthians with one last devastating blow. They will have brought their remaining fleet into the tunnel to finish us off, so we will collapse it right on top of them!"

It was good to hear that we'd get some retribution, but it paled in comparison to the major loss we all felt.

"Bring up the tunnel cameras," said Alexitus. "We need to know when to strike."

Four screens appeared on the windshield of the Iccaryn, showing different sections of the tunnel. The last view showed us just a few hundred yards down the tunnel from where our ship was.

"Once they make it past camera three," said Delfwig, "none of them will be able to escape the blast."

We watched intently, and all the while, the Iccaryn took us further away under the northern sea.

"There they are!" said Nepalen. "On camera two!"

We watched as dozens of spherical orbs sped our way.

"How much longer?" Dolvin asked apprehensively. "What if they get too close?"

"We wait until we see them on camera four," Alexitus responded confidently, "and no sooner. We need to make sure we get every last one of those deplorable wretches."

If Nadina took offense, she showed no sign of it. She just sat chained in her seat, stupefied.

"They just passed camera three!" Dolvin exclaimed, almost shouting.

The seconds dragged as we waited to see them on the fourth camera. For a moment, I thought perhaps they had somehow snuck past the camera and were about to shower us with plasma bursts from behind, but then the first of the orb ships appeared on the screen.

"Now!" shouted Alexitus.

A Dotaran at one of the stations hit the switch, and the charges blew. The cameras suddenly went black and the shock wave was almost immediate, but most of all I remember the noise. It reminded me of when I had been leaving the underground lake near the pirate fortress, and I was sure the damage would be similar as well.

The Iccaryn slipped through the water as debris came crashing down over the lake, sealing off the path behind us. Fire and chunks of dislodged ice filled the chamber that had been our first rendezvous point, and the Scynthian invasion had been thwarted. We couldn't be sure, of course, but the captains and Delfwig were fairly positive that we'd be safe for the time being.

"Now what?" I asked Delfwig.

"Now, we go on to the second rendezvous location," he explained. "And after that, we start to rebuild."

"So much destruction," Nadina said flatly, looking out through a window and staring off into the empty water. She shuddered, "So much death."

We continued on underwater in the Iccaryn for hours, putting as much distance as possible between us and the site of the attack. It must have been the better part of a day before we finally surfaced, and I was glad to get some fresh air.

"Where are we?" I asked Delfwig, as I looked out over a frozen landscape. It looked slightly familiar, but I couldn't place it.

"We are just west of Mercer," he replied. "There is an inlet just a few miles from here, which we will enter and follow downstream. Over the years, we've mapped most of this continent, taking pictures with our ships as we fly overhead. The captains were able to use those images to select a place for our refugee camp, where we will regroup and reorganize. The Iccaryn is too small to accommodate the lot of us for long."

We entered the inlet and proceeded through a long maze of narrow, intertwining rivers, until finally it became one large river. The Dotarans didn't have a name for the waterway, but it was the largest river in the north, and was said to reach all the way to the Okala Mountains. For all anyone knew, it could very well be connected to the Zi River thousands of miles to the south of us, but the Okala Mountains remained a mystery to even the Dotarans. Only the Guyans of the Diamond clan and a small-sized class of humanoid creatures dwelled in the extensive mountain range, and not much was known about either group.

The Iccaryn navigated through the river system for another hour or so, careful to remain in the deeper channels along the riverbed, and then Alexitus ordered for the ship to halt.

"We'll wait down here for the day," said Alexitus, "and then tonight we'll surface and go ashore."

We had finally made it to the second rendezvous location; our refugee camp.

While we were stuck waiting, Dolvin and I decided to play a game of cassa on one of the Iccaryn' computers. The Tatoran game had been digitally created upon Demtrius' return to the Aramis so that he could teach it to his crewmates, and now Dolvin and I faced off in a half-hearted match. Spirits were not especially high at the moment, for obvious reasons. I stared at my faoler piece, considering my next move, but could only think of when I had faced one in the Pit of the Gyx before dueling with Demtrius. I was abruptly drawn from my reminiscing when a radio at one of the ship's stations began spitting out some garbled Dotaran. Nepalen hurried to the station and tuned the radio. Suddenly we heard the Dotaran loud and clear.

"Demtrius to Command," said the voice. I thought I

was imagining it, but then I heard it again, "Demtrius to Command, do you copy?"

"He's alive!" I shouted, completely overjoyed. "Demtrius is alive!"

"Command to Demtrius, we are here," Nepalen replied excitedly.

"Am I glad to hear your voice," Demtrius said, sounding very relieved.

"And we are glad to hear yours," Nepalen replied. "Are you hurt at all? Do you need medical attention?"

"A few bumps and scrapes," Demtrius replied casually, "but I am okay."

"Excellent, very good," Nepalen responded. "We will send an extraction to team come find you as soon as it is safe."

"The sooner the better," Demtrius replied. "My ship is stuck in the ice and I cannot get the hatch open."

"Are there still Scynthians in the area?" Alexitus questioned him.

"The last of them disappeared from my radar hours ago," Demtrius replied.

"To be safe," Alexitus answered, "we will need to wait until tomorrow to send out the extraction team, just in case there are any lingering Scynthians."

"I understand," Demtrius said. "I still have auxiliary power, so I'll stay warm enough, and I have an emergency pack with food and water. I will keep my radio on for now until the battery begins to drain." There was a short pause, "How did we fare?"

"You did well," Alexitus praised him. "Very well."

"Thank you, Captain Alexitus," Demtrius replied. "I only wish more of our brethren could have made it through with me."

"It is a miracle that even you are alive," Dolvin commented.

"I am very aware of that," said Demtrius, "and I am very grateful to still be here."

"As are we," said Dolvin feelingly.

"Get some rest," said Alexitus, "and we will see you tomorrow, if all things permit it."

"Very well," said Demtrius.

The next day, Delfwig and I, accompanied by two other Dotarans, twin brothers named Crispin and Thristin, set forth for the destroyed Aramis on one of their few dondobah ships, the Pothos, only instead of flying, we remained submerged so as to avoid detection. It was a good thing they had designed their craft to be both ships of the sky and water; our small team would have run a much higher risk of detection by flying.

Before we left, Delfwig was pulled aside by the three remaining captains. They spoke to him with very serious expression, but they spoke almost in whispers, and I was only able to hear their last remarks.

"Locate and retrieve Demtrius as quickly as possible," said Alexitus, "and search for any other survivors that might be out there, but do so quickly." Alexitus looked over to me, seeing me watching them. "And don't forget the other task we have asked of you."

"We will make haste," Delfwig replied.

We walked away, and when we were out of earshot, I turned to Delfwig. "What was that about?"

"I cannot discuss that with you at this time," he responded, "but you will find out soon enough, I'm sure."

I didn't appreciate his answer, as I always like to be well informed, but I was content to wait. Knowing Demtrius was alive and required our help was all I needed to know at that time.

The water in this northern sea was astonishingly clear, and we sped through it like a torpedo on our way back to the Aramis, or rather what was left of the Aramis. The trip on the whole was uneventful, save for an almost catastrophic encounter with a massive Tatoran whale. We had become surrounded by a large herd of walrus-like creatures when we passed by Mercer, and they proceeded to follow our craft for some time, racing past us and then coming around again. Suddenly the whole heard scattered, and the huge head of a massive whale came straight for us from beneath, its gaping mouth ready to swallow us whole. Delfwig made a quick evasive maneuver, and our submersible nearly collided with the gigantic sea creature, passing within inches of its enormous head. I was gripping my seat anxiously as we sped past and caught sight of its large, tranquil eye. I could have sworn the creature was staring right back at me, and then it blinked and looked away, apparently uninterested in us.

We made it to the battle site the afternoon of that same day, and then made contact with Demtrius. Our radar detected there were no enemy craft in the area, but we still took caution as we docked the submersible and went ashore. We all wore completely white suits to better conceal us from any eyes that may have been spying from above.

Fortunate for us, the Dotarans had recently installed tracking devices in all of their flyers. They had learned from their past mishap with Demtrius, when neither he nor his flyer could be found after he crash landed on the plains outside of the Aanthoran jungle. If they had already had the trackers installed at that time, then Demtrius would have been rescued immediately and I might never have met him. I can't even imagine what would have become of me if I hadn't met him in that dark cell under Aanthora's lofted city, and it suddenly struck me how so many seemingly unconnected and irrelevant events had come together at the right time, or wrong time, like it had all been designed. Even my presence here on Tatora, I was beginning to believe, was more than just an accident. I don't really know how to explain it any better, just one of my gut intuitions, but it gave me a chilling feeling to potentially be the puppet on someone else's strings. I can only do what comes naturally to me though, strings or no strings, and I am still determined to forge my own path in life.

We found Demtrius in short time. Delfwig led our group, following his handheld tracker, until we finally came upon a deep, narrow hole in the ice, at the bottom of which we could see Demtrius' flyer.

"Are you comfortable down there?" I shouted jokingly.

I heard his muffled reply, "Quite. Would you like to join me?"

"Yeah, be right down," I shouted back.

Crispin, one of the accompanying Dotarans, pulled his

portable mattertron from off his back and activated the device. Demtrius' flyer then slowly rose from the hole and was placed gently on the ice. The flyer was so badly damaged, however, that the hatch wouldn't open automatically, forcing Delfwig, Crispin, and Thristin to use their handy laser pens. It took some time, but eventually they were able to carve an opening and Demtrius was pulled out.

"Have you found any other survivors," Demtrius asked with a heavy concern.

"You are the first," Delfwig replied with equal sorrow, "but, by the hand of Carnyle, you won't be the last."

"I hope you're right," said an exhausted Demtrius.

"I'm guessing your ship is completely inoperable?" Delfwig asked.

"Yes, unfortunately," Demtrius replied. "I've already set the self-destruct sequence."

"Excellent," Delfwig replied. "We'll need to do the same for any other ships that are still intact." He looked at his battered superior, "Perhaps you should return to our ship and begin recuperating?"

"Once we've searched the area for any survivors," Demtrius replied obstinately.

We searched, but, to everyone's dismay, not one Dotaran survivor could be found. Most of the flyers had been completely destroyed by the powerful plasma blasts of the Scynthians, but a few were still almost fully intact, though their pilots had invariably expired. Using their compact mattertrons, Crispin and Thristin removed the dead from their temporary tombs and brought them back to the ship. They would take them to the Iccaryn for a proper Dotaran funeral. We never found Waylan, though.

Meanwhile, Demtrius and Delfwig set the few ships to self-destruct.

"Why do you need to destroy your ships?" I asked them. "It seems risky to stay here any longer than necessary."

"To prevent anyone else from stealing the technology, of course" Delfwig replied. "We can't have the Tatorans learning how to fly, now can we?"

"Then what about the Aramis?" I asked, pointing at the

massive ship buried halfway in the ice.

"A risk the captains are willing to take," Delfwig replied. "They want us to preserve the Aramis as best we can for later repair and reuse."

"They plan to rebuild the ship?" I asked.

"Yes," said Delfwig, "and if not the whole ship, then at least its usable parts, like the rest of the upgraded material that Pharon installed before he was killed."

"Pharon is dead?" Demtrius asked, shocked by the revelation. I had forgotten he was yet unaware of all that had happened since he left in his flyer to defend the ship.

"During the attack," I replied, shaking my head gravely.

"That is very unfortunate," he replied with genuine sorrow. "We may not have agreed on much, but I dare say Pharon was a credit to his race."

We soon boarded the Pothos and Delfwig took to the controls.

"I'm so sorry," I said to Demtrius, who sat beside me. "I can't imagine how you're feeling right now, but I hope you know I'm here for you." It felt inadequate, but I'm not very good in these situations, as I'm sure you know.

"Thank you," he replied. "You are a good man, Jaxon."

"What happens now?" I asked him.

"It's time to start anew," Demtrius replied, speaking to all of us, "and the future is best paved with lessons learned from the past."

I liked the saying, and thought I would probably use it again in the future.

I've written everything I thought pertinent thus far, and as I sit here in the Pothos with Demtrius, Delfwig, and the other two Dotarans, I can't help but think of all the tragedies that have occurred since I came to Tatora. I fear we might be too far gone at this point, but, even though we have all lost so much and find ourselves at our lowest, I still focus on the climb ahead.

I still have you in my sights Ryane, and nothing will stop me from achieving that particular vision. I can only hope that this manuscript finds its way to you as I am somehow sure my last one did. I don't know how I know this; it's just another intuitive gut-feeling that I have. I've said before that I believe you and I share some sort of special extra-sensory connection, as if we could almost subconsciously read one another's minds, and I believe that statement holds true even over the vast expanse of space that separates us. I also believe that this uncanny form of telepathy was greatly enhanced by the Scynthian serum I received. If I am correct in this belief, then I hope this manuscript brings you some semblance of understanding as to what really happened that night in the cabin and every day since. I'm just sorry I'm not there to describe it to you in person, but, hopefully, one day soon I might still be able to.

# Interlogue One
# Ryane's Plan

Ryane finished reading the second journal and closed it, absolutely disgusted and infuriated by what she had read. The Scynthians were indeed despicable, and it made her want to scream, but she thought better of it.

Just then, an idea sprang into her mind on how she might effectuate her escape. She quickly flipped through the pages to the map and ripped it from the book, and then tore the map from the first journal as well.

"I figured it out!" she exclaimed. "I know where to find Jaxon!"

Two human servants came walking in, one of them using the metal cuff on his forearm to open the portal.

"Get Orric!" she yelled at them. "I have the answer he's looking for!"

Before they even turned to leave, Orric appeared in the entryway, quite pleased. "You have some information?"

"Yes, I know where they are," Ryane replied. "I can show you on the map in the book."

"How can you be certain?" Orric asked.

"Jaxon and I used to do this when we were kids," Ryane replied. "We would make a picture and copy it, but then add a small change on the copy, and that is where we would meet."

"Clever for an Earthling," Orric remarked.

"Come here and I'll show you," Ryane encouraged him. She put one map on top of the other and studied them. "See, there!" she pointed.

In the time it took Orric to bend his head down to see the maps, Ryane had launched her desperate plan. She moved quickly, taking Orric and the two human servants completely by surprise. She lunged straight for the weird, gill-like slits behind Orric's small ears. If she had surmised correctly, then that would be a sensitive spot for the Scynthian creature.

Much to Ryane's delight, she found that she had complete control over Orric holding him in this fashion. She was behind him, clawing at the inside of the gills with her fingers. Orric tried to stop her, shouting some unintelligible language, but she was small and he couldn't reach behind himself to capture her. He had to crouch a bit and lean to his side in an awkward position. She was effectively controlling his movements as she held him by the gills, forcing him to move where she wanted him to go.

"Make no moves," she cautioned him, "and if your servants try to stop me, I'll rip out your gills before either of them has the opportunity." She clutched tighter with her fingers, eliciting a small yelp from Orric. "It will be hard to breathe when you're drowning in your own blood!"

"Let go of me this instant!" he demanded, though without much conviction. "You have no hope of making it out of here alive."

Ryane started to squeeze again, and Orric, feeling the pain and realizing the helplessness of his position, told the two human servants to stand down.

"The only way this ends well for you is if you send me home and away from this place!" Ryane threatened him, while simultaneously tightening her grip on his gills even more.

"Yes, yes!" he said in somewhat of a panic. "We will go to the transport room and I will configure the computer for your immediate departure!"

It almost seemed too easy for Ryane to bend him to her will. She expected more resistance. *Perhaps*, she thought, *Orric is not accustomed to this sort of distress and not having full control over the situation.* At any rate, she had the power currently, and she would do what she could while she had it.

First she made the human servants relinquish their metal cuffs, which Ryane had noticed were used to open the portal. Then, together, Orric in front and Ryane trailing from behind with her hands still inside his gills, the two of them left the room. Ryane immediately turned Orric around and made him seal the entryway before they proceeded any further, trapping the human servants inside and thus preventing them from alerting anyone of the situation. Ryane watched as Orric used the metal cuff on his arm to close the portal, and wondered at the hideous creature's awesome technology.

She pushed him down the long white hallway, Orric forced to walk awkwardly in a crouched slant since Ryane was so much shorter. Ryane was very apprehensive, not trusting Orric one bit, and she continuously searched the halls for any sign of reinforcements for the wretched alien. She tried to memorize the layout as best she could in case she was forced to retrace her steps, but it all appeared so bland and similar. Her only option was to let Orric lead the way, so they crept past many blank walls and adjoining hallways, but Orric urged her to continue past all of them.

"It is just up ahead," he kept saying.

Ryane pushed him forward faster.

"Now," she said, "I want some answers."

"Of course," said Orric, surprisingly cooperative, even given the present circumstances. Again Ryane was off-put by how quickly Orric gave in, but she decided he was trying to placate her in hopes of mercy.

"Why do you have those books if they are written for me?" she demanded. "From what I read, no one on Tatora has the ability to transport them, and you claim you don't know where Jaxon is, but those manuscripts are proof that you do! How else could you have obtained them?"

"I actually cannot explain that," he replied calmly. "They just appeared in our transport room, at separate times no less. After we received the first manuscript, we thought perhaps Pharon was still working with us, but that doesn't explain the appearance of the second one, since Pharon was killed before your Jaxon completed it."

"Then who sent them?" she asked.

"We do not know," he replied. "It is a mystery to us, too, but we thought we might use this knowledge to our advantage."

"And you never planned on returning Jaxon or me to Earth, did you? You planned to kill Jax the entire time, and who knows what with me after I had served my purpose!"

"You speak the truth," he admitted.

Ryane tightened her grip again, and Orric hissed in pain.

"We are here!" he said quickly. "We are at the transport room!"

"Open it," she commanded him.

Orric touched a few keys on his cuff's small touch-screen monitor, and the portal opened quickly. Heart pounding, Ryane immediately pushed Orric forward into the room, but she should have looked inside first. To her extreme misfortune, she now found herself in a room full of Scynthians.

"Seize her!" Orric shouted in his own language, and the other Scynthians instantly obeyed.

Ryane had no time to react. Two Scynthians blocked the doorway while several others grabbed her arms and legs so she couldn't move. Ryane thought that if she was going to be caught, she could at least cause Orric the most distress possible before they locked her back up, but before she could do anything, she was thumped on the back of the head by one of the Scynthians and lost her grip on Orric's gills. The pain dazed her, and then Orric turned upon her and slapped her across the face with vicious force. Her head snapped to the side, and she could taste blood. She had failed, and now, she knew, things would be much worse for her. She didn't show any fear in the face of her adversaries though, and continued to struggle against their inhuman strength. She wouldn't make it easy for them. Defiance was all she had left.

"Take her back to her room," Orric told the Scynthians, rubbing his neck and gills gently.

Ryane was brought to her room and the portal was quickly opened by one of the Scynthians, using another one of the metal cuffs. The two human servants were still inside, but quickly exited, smirking at her as they went. Ryane guessed their smugness was due to the futility of her escape efforts, and narrowed her eyes at their retreating forms.

The two Scynthians still holding onto her threw Ryane into the room roughly. She landed hard and half-rolled from the force of their toss, but she was up in an instant, fists clenched and ready for action. The two Scynthians remained stolid and indifferent, blocking the entrance. They suddenly sprang to attention though, and then parted from the entryway, allowing Orric to walk past between them.

The portal to the room snapped shut silently behind him, leaving Ryane alone with the hideous Scynthian creature.

"You're going to wish you never did that," he said, seemingly unperturbed, but his arrogant confidence was now replaced with well-placed caution. He stilled rubbed the area around his gills tenderly. "And, I assure you, another opportunity will not present itself."

Ryane was not one to scare easily, but now she feared for her life. She had been handled by the Scynthians with considerable ease, and her escape attempt had gained her nothing except the anger of the cruel and conniving Orric. Even in her fear, though, she maintained an expressionless face, stealing away any satisfaction Orric might get from her discomfort.

"Do you know why I had you read that manuscript?" Orric asked her civilly, but continued without waiting for her answer. "I wanted to impress upon you the lengths of which my confederates and I are willing to go in order to accomplish our goals. Now that you understand, it's time to move forward with my plans for you."

"Believe what you want," Ryane said in protest, finding her courage once again, "but I'll never help you."

Orric's face became hard and serious. "I will get what I want from you, one way or another. Of that you can be assured!"

He touched the metal cuff on his forearm, and the portal in the wall slid open silently. The two Scynthians that had thrown her in so unceremoniously were still standing guard, and Orric ordered them inside the room. "Restrain her," he commanded them, and they obeyed without hesitation, grabbing Ryane roughly and pinning her to the ground. She didn't even fight them this time; it was pointless.

Orric pulled forth a syringe from within the folds of his cloak, and Ryane eyed the needle fearfully, remembering Jaxon's tale of the Scynthians' enhancement serum. She knew that the serum was given to the human slaves on Scynthia before they were harvested for their organs, and deduced that her own death was not far off. Then she recalled what Orric had just intimated, and she knew he had something far more sinister planned for her.

Orric approached her with the syringe, a devilish grin upon his wrinkled lips, and then he bent down to her. "Make sure she doesn't move," he said to the two Scynthian guards, and then, ignoring Ryane's pointed look of malice, plunged the syringe into her shoulder.

Ryane knew that Orric had won this round, and even though her brain wasn't yet up to forming a new escape plan, she still held on to a little seed of hope. For now though, she could do nothing.

Then, unexpectedly, she was overcome with a sudden explosion of energy, her body feeling instantly revitalized and reinvigorated. Never before had she felt such intense stimulation. It made every cell in her body tingle with a vivified sensation. Her heart was beating faster and stronger, but slowly subsided back to normal as her body accepted the serum's effects.

Ryane had a fleeting thought of renewing her escape efforts, but, even in her enlivened state, she knew she couldn't physically overpower her captors; a fact that was soundly confirmed as she struggled against their weight.

"What the hell did you do to me?" she asked of Orric. "What was in that syringe?"

"A means to an end," Orric replied. At least he hoped so. Now he had to figure out how to spark the connection somehow. Pain would be a good motivator, but Orric had another, less strenuous idea. He would plant the seed and see if it came to fruition. "You see," he continued, "I believe what your Jaxon said about the two of you sharing a primitive telepathic link, and now that you have been enhanced, just as your Jaxon was, I believe that telepathy will grow stronger and more refined; a pleasant gift that I've decided to bestow upon you."

Ryane didn't know how to respond, and so said nothing.

Orric bent over and picked up the pieces of paper that had been tossed and forgotten during Ryane's haphazard escape attempt. He held them up to Ryane, "Your Jaxon is somewhere on this map. Now find him!"

Ryane knew what Orric was trying to do, and she vowed never to give up Jaxon's location, but it is nigh impossible to avoid thinking about a specific topic once it's mentioned. The more she tried to push any thought of Jaxon from her mind, the more she found herself doing the exact opposite. And then suddenly she *knew* his location. She shivered, as if she could actually feel the crisp air where he was. Blurred and distorted images appeared in her mind; she could almost see Jaxon and the Dotarans, but the thought was fleeting and the image wouldn't fully materialize, nor did she want it to.

Meanwhile, in an adjacent room, a solitary Scynthian sat in front of a holographic computer screen, closely monitoring Ryane's brain activity. He was tired, but his beady black eyes opened wide as the computer interpreted the Earth-captive's latest thoughts. He quickly activated his communicator and radioed to Orric.

"We have the location, Sir," said the Scynthian. "The scanner just recorded it."

Orric received the communication through his ear-set and smiled devilishly. "Excellent," he responded, forgetting all about the situation that had occurred only minutes before. He then faced Ryane, still bearing his unsettling grin. "Thank you for your help," he said sarcastically in his fluent English. He turned abruptly and left the room, followed by the two guards, and the portal snapped shut behind them.

Ryane was alone once again.

Too Far Gone

# Part Two

# Chapter Seventeen
# On The Hunt

"There they are," said Delfwig. "An entire family of them."

"Remember," said Demtrius, "we need to capture them alive, all of them."

"Of course, Captain," replied Delfwig, addressing Demtrius with his newly appointed title.

There were five of us in the hunting party; Demtrius, Delfwig, myself, and the two Dotaran twins named Crispin and Thristin. The latter two had been specially selected for the hunt by Demtrius, as they were both cunning, intellectual, and had remained faithful to Demtrius, even during his long absence from the crew. The five of us had been tracking a pack of primadons, the large and hideous beasts of the north. A Dotaran had spotted their tracks while returning to the Iccaryn from sentry duty, and Demtrius had decided to lead our group out to capture them.

We were one of several such hunting parties scouring the area for food. The ration supply aboard the Iccaryn would not last the crew for much longer, and it was already mid-winter, meaning most vegetation and wildlife would be scarce. We tried fishing the great northern river, but the Dotarans, even with all of their advanced technology, were poor fishermen. Indeed, their home-world apparently has no surface water, and the fish that thrive in their extensive underground rivers are easily captured using an ancient trapping system. Demtrius and the rest of the survivors from the Aramis had never needed to catch fish before, and despite my efforts to teach them, I was of little help.

All things considered, we did have some luck fishing, using mattertrons to capture spheres of water and then dropping them into large storage containers. It was a hit or miss practice, and for some reason we mainly caught the bottom-dwelling river feiren; the whiskered, catfish-like scarp of Tatora. They look very similar to the feiren I had eaten while a guest of Ishmae, the High Chieftain of the Sapphire clan, the only difference being the presence of an orange underbelly on the northern feiren. The river feiren were high in mercury, however, and there were too many crewmen to feed, so we couldn't rely solely on the fish for sustenance once the food stores were depleted. These primadons, if nothing else, would help supplement our diet, at least for a little while.

We crouched at the top of a small rise, staring down at the primadon pack. They moved steadily south, toward the far-off Okala Mountain Range, using their massive arms like crutches to swing their dwarfed legs forward. I counted six of them; three adults, an adolescent, and two newborns. The Dotaran scout had only found tracks for four of them, but I now saw that the two newborns hung from the necks of their mothers. They used their long arms to hug their parents, locking their large hands behind the back of their parents' necks and resting their small bodies on the muscular torso of the adult.

The leader of the pack, and also the largest among them, stopped momentarily, putting its face to the southward blowing wind. Steam puffed from its snub-nosed nostrils as it sniffed the cold air. It had finally picked up our scent.

We had tracked the primadons using one of the few ships that the Dotarans still possessed, a dondobah dubbed the Pothos. Some crewman had painted all the ships white, hoping to provide some camouflage on the snowy tundra and keep any prying Scynthian eyes from learning our whereabouts. I wasn't sure how much it would help, but it was better for the crew to stay busy instead of worrying even more. Then, Pharon's cloaking devices had been added, so the smaller ships could move around invisibly, and that made me feel even better.

We had started our hunt where the sentry guard had found the tracks, and then followed them from above, using our flyer's infrared scanners to detect any warm-blooded creatures living in the frozen north. It wasn't long before we found our quarry. We had then deliberately placed ourselves behind the wind, letting our scent be carried down to the pack, taunting them with our fresh meat, as was part of Demtrius' plan.

After the great sky battle between the Scynthians and the Dotarans, during which Captain Waylan and Pharon had sadly perished, the crew held a funeral for their fallen brethren. It wasn't a normal funeral, at least not one I was accustomed to. The bodies were preserved in simiole fluid and flash-frozen in a cryogenic chamber aboard the Iccaryn.

"What will happen to the bodies?" I asked.

"They will be maintained as such until we are able to return to Dotara," Demtrius had told me. "There we have sacred familial burial grounds deep within the planet. That is the only place our dead may rest in peace."

After the funeral, an election was held to replace Waylan as captain. Nepalen and Alexitus would have been content to keep the leadership as it was, but the rest of the crew had petitioned that another captain was needed to keep the delicate balance of power in check. It was Delfwig that came forward, motioning that Demtrius should take Waylan's place as the fourth captain. Crispin and Thristin also put their unwavering support behind Demtrius, as did the majority of the crew, so there was little that the leaders could have done to stop the ascension. Demtrius was the highest qualified Dotaran for the position; he was the former acting-captain of the Aramis, he was a war hero like Waylan had been, and he commanded a lot of respect and influence over the crew. There were crew members that had always remained loyal to Demtrius, like Delfwig, Crispin, and Thristin, and those who had once supported Waylan now deferred to him as well. It was the inevitable outcome, and Dolvin readily accepted the change, though I can't say the same for Nepalen and Alexitus.

Demtrius was sworn into command soon after the election. The ceremony was conducted outside of the Iccaryn in the new refugee camp, and almost every Dotaran was in attendance, save for those on sentry duty and other essential positions. Mya was also present, but Nadina was being kept in the ship's brig. After the Scynthians had attacked, Alexitus didn't trust her, believing she and Pharon were somehow the cause of the attack, even though Pharon perished during the battle. Demtrius, Mya, and I had argued on her behalf, but Dolvin and Nepalen agreed with Alexitus, and so Nadina remained confined to the brig.

Demtrius was brought in front of the three captains, using the ramp of the Iccaryn as their stage so all could see. They welcomed him into his new position and had him recite an official oath of allegiance to the crew, promising to always keep their best interests in mind and swearing to uphold his captaincy to the best of his ability.

The ceremony was over quickly, and now Demtrius led our small group on his first official mission as captain: securing a viable source of food. One adult primadon contained hundreds of pounds of meat, and they bred twice a year. Their young could hopefully be domesticated like cattle, to be raised on scarp and small mammals, and then eventually eaten when they had more meat on their bones. The plan now was to capture the primadons, and that was no easy task, even with the advanced Dotaran technology.

I could see the pack leader growing more and more excited at the prospect of a fresh meal. The other primadons immediately picked up on this, and some of them pounded their chests with their massive fists.

"They know we're here now," I said.

"Well then," said Demtrius with a mischievous smile, "let's go give them a proper greeting."

With that, he stood up from his crouched position and began walking down the steady slope toward the roused predators. Delfwig and I were right behind him, but Crispin and Thristin remained atop the rise and out of sight. Demtrius' plan relied upon getting dangerously close to the primadons, so we would try to approach them, and, most probably, provoke them to attack us. Meanwhile, Crispin and Thristin would circle around the flanks of the primadons, still out of sight, to cut off any possible retreat for the large beasts if they decided to turn and flee from us.

As soon as we began walking down the slope, the

pack-leader ushered a terrific roar, startling me and causing me to slip on the icy surface. I flailed my hands and arms trying to keep my balance, but inevitably fell, landing hard on my backside. It hurt more than I would have thought it would, the ice feeling like solid concrete, and I was slow to get back up. When I did, I noticed a fist-sized rock just barely protruding out of the ground where I had landed.

"You should be more careful, Earthling," Delfwig said sarcastically, grinning. "We don't want you getting hurt."

I tried to stand, but had difficulty keeping my footing on the slippery slope. Demtrius was able to take my arm and steady me, though.

I rubbed my backside, knowing it would probably bruise.

The three of us then continued down the slope together.

The pack-leader, having heard my inelegant fall, immediately swung itself in our direction, placing itself between us and its pack. The other two adult primadons then placed their young on the ground and came up on either side of their leader, so that the newborns and the adolescent were positioned safely behind them.

The leader reared back on its small legs for a moment, and then smashed the frozen ground with its terribly large fists, ushering a ferocious roar that echoed several times off the landscape. The other adults followed their leader's actions, trying to deter us, the unwelcome intruders, from approaching any closer. The year-old mimicked the adults, but it had little force with its growing arms, and its miniature roar was drowned out by the larger, louder primadons. I could feel slight tremors in the ground as they beat their fists on it continuously. I paused for a moment, and when I did I thought I heard a creaking noise.

Delfwig, noticing my hesitation, asked, "Not afraid now, are you, Jaxon?"

"How close do we have to get?" I asked him, trying to make my voice sound as even and unperturbed as I could.

"We will need to be within fifteen paces of them for the mattertrons to be in range," he replied.

I wished that Thiesel could have been there with us. The massive serpent, or anacari as the Tatorans called it, was a fearless predator, and we would have benefitted from his unmatched speed and strength. The last time I had seen Thiesel, however, he had been wrapped in a cocoon near the top of a large Dracari tree. The tree lay not far from the destroyed Dotaran ship, the Aramis, hundreds of miles to the west of our refugee camp. I was afraid I would never see him again.

I returned my attention to the pack, and stared at the leader. Saliva foamed at the side of its mouth, first collecting on its tusks and then dripping down to the snow. It was a hideous creature, to say the least, but I found myself admiring the deadly predator.

We were still moving forward, but our progress stalled when we heard the unmistakable cracking of ice. The crack appeared just under the pack leader, but they were all oblivious to the danger. Instead, noticing our halt, the leader swung himself forward, immediately followed by the other two adults. I was taken aback by the speed of their charge. As they ran, they kept their legs together as one and used their arms like forelegs. The crack in the ice followed in their wake, and branched off in several directions.

"Steady," said Demtrius.

"But the ice!" I said desperately.

"Hold your ground!" he commanded, and I did not move.

The three charging beasts were almost upon us and showed no signs of slowing. They were overtaken by their predatory blood-lust; food was within their grasp.

"Now!" shouted Demtrius.

Delfwig and I activated the compact mattertrons. The attacking primadons were instantly lifted off the ground, suspended in mid-air with their bodies completely immobile, confined by the awe-inspiring power of the mattertron.

The Dotaran mattertron, I should remind you, has the ability to create a vacuum space that is literally between matter. It can create a space of absolute nothingness in the air, as well as a space that still has all its natural gases. It can also reduce friction in water, but fails altogether to work on solid matter. The Dotarans are able to use the mattertron to propel their ships by creating vacuum pockets around the flyer in whatever direction they wish to travel. The ship moves into the dramatically lower pressure of the vacuum and continues to move without being acted upon by any outside forces. In turn, the mattertron is also used to trap objects within this vacuum pocket, as we had just done to the primadons.

"We did it!" I cheered.

With the primadons floating above the ice, the crack stopped spreading and we seemed to be in no present danger of plunging into the freezing water below.

"Jaxon, signal the others," said Demtrius.

With that, I put my fingers in my mouth and whistled loudly, a useful trick that had come in handy more than once since I had been on Tatora. While I could still hear the whistle's echo, Crispin and Thristin sprang from their hiding place on the far side of what we now knew to be a large, frozen lake. They sprinted toward the young primadons, and only the adolescent was cognizant of their approach. Like its elders had done before it, the adolescent began beating the ground with its fists, trying desperately to fend off the approaching pair. The Dotaran siblings suddenly separated, and Demtrius, Delfwig, and I began to fan out, creating a circle around the three young primadons. They had nowhere to go now.

After getting into position, Delfwig, Demtrius, and I remained where we were. We didn't want to disturb the ice any more than was necessary, so Crispin and Thristin began to close in on the young primadons from the far side of the frozen lake.

The adolescent still pounded on the ice, with redoubled effort now. It was scared senseless, acting only off the instinct to protect the younger part of the herd. All of a sudden, the adolescent and newborn primadons were gone, lost, as the ice crumbled beneath them. The adolescent's beating on the lake had finished what its parents had accidentally started.

Crispin and Thristin, standing close by on some yet unbroken ice, inched toward the hole, and I could see one of them activating his mattertron. They looked almost identical, as do most Dotarans, and the fact that they were twin siblings made them even more indistinguishable, but I digress.

The water inside the hole began to churn and bubble, and then the young primadons rose from the water, lifted by the invisible force of the mattertrons. They were still trapped within a large sphere of water, but Crispin, or Thristin, quickly moved them over to the sturdier ice and dropped them to the ground. The water splashed away from the three primadons, showing us they were still alive and kicking. That only lasted a moment, however, and then they were captured in the invisible grasp of the mattertron once again.

The mission was a success; no doubt, the first of many accomplishments that would be made by the newly appointed Captain Demtrius.

It took some time for Crispin and Thristin to navigate their way back around the frozen lake. During that time, Demtrius, Delfwig, and I moved back to the crest of the slope, grateful to be off the unstable ice. Once we were all together again, the five of us returned to our flyer, the Pothos, and began our short journey back to the refugee camp. We flew low to the ground, but our spirits were high. We had just contributed to the survival of the Dotaran race here on Tatora. All in a day's work.

# Chapter Eighteen
# The Conundrum

Dozens of Dotarans greeted us upon our return to the refugee camp, clapping and cheering as we came in for our landing. They could see the primadons suspended just below our flyer, held there by the ship's mattertron, and everyone knew we would not go hungry or have to risk mercury poisoning, at least not in our immediate future.

We dropped off our cargo in a newly-built primadon enclosure, and then Delfwig maneuvered our flyer into the nearby river, where the Iccaryn lay hidden under the water. The ship only surfaced a few times per day, and otherwise was constantly moving throughout the intertwining river channels, just in case the Scynthians managed to find the land camp. We entered the submerged flight deck and the outer door closed behind us. Then we waited for the room to be emptied of the water.

Shortly thereafter, I made my way to my new cramped sleeping quarters aboard the Iccaryn, which I shared with the brothers, Crispin and Thristin, and their cousin, Gilpin. We didn't spend much time in the room, though, other than to sleep. Now that we were confined to the smaller ship, and constantly mobile, the entire crew was required to work on one of the three daily shifts. While two-thirds of the crew performed the various duties, a third of the crew was ordered to rest, and then we would switch. This way we would have fresh, alert crew members, and the ship wouldn't seem so crowded. I, however, was in no mood to sleep at this time. I was busy contemplating a terribly puzzling conundrum.

My second journal, just like the first, had mysteriously vanished from my compartment several days before our hunt. I still hadn't recovered the first leather-bound journal given to me by Jotus, lost at the edge of the great Aanthoran jungle, and now this second journal was gone too. The story I'm transcribing to you now is written in yet another journal, and this one will not leave my person for any reason.

I told Demtrius of the journal's mysterious disappearance, thinking perhaps it had been stolen from my sleeping quarters, but the ship's computer showed that no one had accessed the compartment since I was last there. The journal was just inexplicably missing, and I was very concerned that it was the work of the Scynthians.

After the first journal had disappeared, Demtrius and I had speculated that it must have somehow been the Scynthians, or someone working in league with them. Neither of us knew how they could have done it, but the apparent thievery reeked of Scynthian mischief. At the time, though, we weren't really worried, as we had no real reason to believe that we were in any danger from the Scynthians. Now, however, the fate of the stranded Dotarans hung in the balance.

With my suspicions already attuned to the Scynthians, I went to Demtrius for advice, and together we came up with a plan to deal with the potential threat. We knew the journal would lead the Scynthians to our general location, so the other captains were apprised of the situation.

"By the hand of Carnyle," Alexitus had said. "Why would you write down our whereabouts? Are you daft?"

"I thought the journal would be safe aboard the Iccaryn," I told him.

"It doesn't matter now," Demtrius interjected. "We need to discuss what to do about it."

"With the new cloaking device on our ship almost finished, perhaps the Scynthians won't be able to find us," Dolvin suggested.

"Pharon created those devices," Alexitus said. "We shouldn't trust them."

"They have been tested," Nepalen put in, "and they work effectively."

"Still," Alexitus continued, "if they were to find us, we'd be finished."

Demtrius spoke up again, "I think I have a plan."

Demtrius' plan was simple, albeit laborsome: move the camp, yet make it seem like we still resided at the original camp. We would lure the Scynthians into a trap, and then offer some payback. So that same day, we began preparations to move our recently established refugee camp to a new, undisclosed location.

Sure enough, not long after, our prey was baited and the trap was sprung. It was an ingeniously simple trap, yet the Scynthians, so sure of themselves and their information, had failed to detect it. There were about two dozen of them, and they came raining down from the sky, firing their plasma blasts right into the heart of the false camp, destroying everything they hit. The firestorm continued for several minutes until the camp was nothing more than a smoldering patch of scorched earth. When they finally concluded the aerial assault, the fleet landed on the outskirts of the camp. Surrounding each of their orb-like ships was a greenish-blue glow, but the glow instantly diminished as they exited their crafts, revealing a gyroscopic frame around a single seat. The Scynthians were looking to finish off any surviving Dotarans. Then the tables were turned.

All around the camp, buried just beneath the surface of the snow, were dozens of remotely-controlled mattertrons, and hidden among the trees were several cameras that gave us a good view of the false camp. So, from the safety of the Iccaryn in our real camp, we watched as the Scynthians gathered.

My eyes suddenly went wide, and I cursed. Thuric, the Scynthian that had banished me to Tatora and who had presumably led the assault on the Aramis, was first among them. I thought he might have perished in the escape tunnel under the ice when the explosive charges were detonated, but here he was, all well and good, and leading a new group of attackers.

Thuric was a crafty individual, and he was the only one to surmise that something was amiss, but a split second after he realized that they had fired on an empty camp, every last one of them was stuck, frozen in place.

Demtrius had given the order as soon as the Scynthians were in range, and Delfwig had activated the mattertrons. The Scynthians were locked in the vacuum created by the powerful device, eliciting a grand cheer from the crew aboard the Iccaryn.

We used our newly-developed cloaking devices, courtesy of Pharon, may he rest in peace, to conceal our ships as we approached the camp, making sure no other Scynthians could see us. Thuric and his warriors were then immediately stripped of their belongings and taken back to the ship's brig, but not before being scanned for any tracking implants. As an extra precautionary measure, their cells were configured to block out any signals from the outside, so there was little chance our location could be traced. The prisoners were then interrogated by the captains for any useful information, but Demtrius told me they hadn't provided them with anything of value.

"If only we knew where to find some carnatora," I remarked. "Then we could get them talking."

I was referring to the disinhibiting effects of the plant's alluring aroma, which, when concentrated into a specific dosage, acted like a truth serum. Of course, the only place we knew that it grew was in hostile Emerald clan territory thousands of miles to the southeast.

The question that still lingered in my mind, however, was how the Scynthians had obtained the journal in the first place. They were obviously still ignorant of the actual location of the refugee camp, but that didn't stop them from retrieving the book and leaving no traces behind. It was just another mystery that I feared would never be solved.

As I lay there in bed, I couldn't ignore the considerable amount of pain I was still in from my fall on the ice. A large bruise covered much of my lower backside. The Scynthian serum didn't seem to be quite as effective as it once was. I was usually filled with more energy, and the bruise I had normally would have already healed. *Perhaps its effects aren't permanent*, I thought. The more I pondered the thought, the more stressed and anxious I became, and I had begun to feel a growing void inside myself, as if something were missing.

The serum wasn't something I could control, so I tried to push these distressing thoughts and feelings from my mind. There was no point in worrying about it, but my efforts to ignore my feelings met with little success.

I did eventually sleep, but with my sleep came little rest or relief. Instead, I was forced into a terrifying dream. I found myself strapped to a chair with a hood pulled over my head. Someone was tilting my head backwards, and then pouring water over my face, like some kind of water-boarding. The torture continued until, finally, after what seemed like an eternity, the water stopped and the hood was removed. That was when I saw my torturer for the first time; a Scynthian. I looked at my surroundings and discovered I was inside one of the all-white rooms I had seen on Scynthia. My Scynthian torturer suddenly grabbed me by the hair. That was when I realized how long my hair was, and when strands of it fell over my eyes I could see it was thick, dark, curly hair.

I suddenly felt like I couldn't breathe, and awoke gulping lungsful of air. I was covered in a sheen of sweat, mouth completely dry, with my heart beating out of my chest. I recognized that hair. I had wanted to run my hands through it for so long. It may sound strange, but I think I was dreaming that I was you, and that somehow you were being tortured on Scynthia. The dream felt so vivid and real, and the fear was overwhelming.

I was not looking forward to closing my eyes again, but I did, because I needed to rest, and for the first time since that fateful night so long ago, the distance between us reassured me that at least you were safe.

# Chapter Nineteen
# The Captains' Address

I awoke the next morning to an unfamiliar Dotaran voice speaking over the ship's loud speaker, which was placed just above the compartment's entryway. Every day, twice a day, a new crew member would read the daily reports, so eventually everyone aboard the ship would get a turn. Mya and I, however, were excluded from this task since we could not read Dotaran, and I was grateful for that ineptitude. It must sound funny, but I am absolutely petrified of public speaking. Put me up against the dreaded osolisque, that giant arachnid with a rock-like exoskeleton, demoralizing stinger, and two separate mouths, and I'll be able to keep my nerves relatively in check, but stick me in front of a large crowd with a microphone and I fall to pieces instantly.

I went to roll out of my alcove bed and was jolted by a sudden pain in my backside; the wound left over from my fall on the ice. It was hurting even more now. I got up, gingerly, and looked at the contusion in the reflective wall of the compartment. Normally my body would have healed already due to the enhancement serum, but a bruise remained, yellowish-purple in hue, complete with pain and all. The injury must have been more severe than I had originally assumed.

The Dotaran droned on monotonously over the loud speaker for a few more minutes before concluding the daily report.

"The primadons were recaptured, but their enclosure is in extreme disrepair. Work teams five and seven will attend to mending and strengthening the enclosure, while all other teams will continue with their normally assigned duties."

A loud tone then sounded, which always precipitated a direct order from the captains. "Special Attention," the Dotaran resumed. "There will be a ship-wide briefing outside of the Iccaryn immediately following the morning meal time. Attendance for all active personnel is mandatory. That is all."

I finished slipping on my black and blue uniform, the skin-tight one piece that had amazing insulating abilities. I also donned my Tatoran weapon's harness, rather than the one issued by the Dotarans. The Dotarans used a simple belt to hold their weapons and devices, whereas the Tatorans used a harness with supportive shoulder straps, distributing the weight of my belongings equally across my body.

I left the compartment after dressing and headed toward the cafeteria. There were no colored lines on the floor of the Iccaryn, since the ship was much smaller than the Aramis and easier to traverse. Along the way, I stopped by the communal bathroom to wash my face and relieve myself. I had no need to brush my teeth, however, as a Dotaran foraging party had found a trove of droots growing in the nearby forest. The droot, I should remind you, is a carrot-shaped vegetable, but with the color of a turnip. It is highly nutritious, and famous for its ability to cleanse and protect the teeth while also restoring and strengthening the gums. Nature's medicine, and I would be eating it for breakfast.

The cafeteria wasn't far from my room, and, once there, I quickly found my bunk-mates and sat down next to them with my breakfast. I was becoming fast friends with the sibling Dotarans, Crispin and Thristin, and their cousin, Gilpin. We often gathered together during meal times and traded stories of our homes. They, like the majority of the crew, longed for nothing more than to see their home planet again; a sentiment I shared equally, if only so that I could be with you once more. I, however, had only been stranded here on Tatora a short time compared to them. I couldn't imagine being trapped here for nearly two hundred years, cut off from anyone I had ever known or loved. The thought was entirely depressing.

I learned a lot about their home world, Dotara, during our talks. Thristin and Crispin loved their planet, but, strangely enough, described it as a world vastly different from Tatora, lacking in both life and beauty. The oceans had apparently receded millions of years ago, the atmosphere was harsh and slowly becoming toxic, and the Dotarans had long since retreated to the deep valleys and canyons along the ancient ocean floor where some surface water still lingered.

"Dotara is a dying planet," one of them explained, I think Crispin. They were so close in appearance, as were most of the Dotarans, but their family resemblance made them almost indistinguishable from one another.

"Dying?" I asked. "I don't understand. I thought Dotara was a thriving civilization?"

"The civilization is thriving," said Thristin, I believe, "but the planet has been dying for thousands of years. It is an interminably slow process though, and our race has been able to change and adapt to the drastic climate shifts."

"That's...just incredible," I said, almost speechless from the magnitude of their statements.

"You must understand," said Crispin. "Our species dates back over five billion years, and Dotara is nearly double that age. We are not a young race, like the Tatorans, or you humans for that matter. Our home star has only another billion years or so left before it will begin to supernova, and then the planet will truly be doomed. That is one of the main reasons why we were sent out in the Aramis to begin with; to find new life and a new habitat for when our world is finally extinguished."

This new information was very compelling. I wondered why Demtrius had never told me so much about Dotara and the purpose of the Aramis' original mission. Then again, Demtrius was generally a very stoic person; a listener rather than a talker. Though we had conversed often enough, Demtrius still wasn't very forthcoming with his personal information, that is, if not directly asked about it. It was months before I even learned he had two offspring of his own back on Dotara, and he was both mother and father to them. Dotarans, if you remember, are asexual beings capable of producing two offspring in a lifetime. They can also live almost indefinitely, as they do not necessarily have limited lifetimes, so long as they remain safe and healthy. This being the case, and considering Demtrius' age, his children must already be full grown adults, and each of them probably have adult offspring with children of their own. Needless to say, Dotaran families can become incredibly large over one Dotaran lifespan.

It wasn't much of a breakfast, leaving me still hungry and wanting more when I was done, but there were strict orders from the captains to maintain half-rations. When we finished our meals, we brought our trays to their depository window, and then made our way to the briefing. Most of the crew had already finished eating and were standing in formation outside of the ship, waiting for their captains to arrive. There were murmurs of discontent, and the food shortage, mixed with the recent attack by the Scynthians, was causing tensions to run high as of late. It was a good thing the crew was so disciplined, otherwise who knows what might have happened.

As I walked down the entrance ramp, I saw Mya standing in the crowd on my left. I hadn't seen much of her since the evacuation of the Aramis, now several weeks ago, since she was busy, along with many of the Dotarans, trying to create a new aquaponics facility. It was a slow-going process, however, and they were forced to start from scratch with a very limited amount of supplies.

Mya saw me coming down the ramp and signaled for me to join her, waving her arms vigorously. I quickly made my way over to her, and Mya greeted me with a warm hug.

"What do you think they will tell us," I asked.

"Hopefully news from the salvage crews," Mya responded.

"Salvage crews?" I asked.

"Yes," she replied. "They were sent out to the site of the Aramis to recover any usable material from its remains. We will need all they can find if we ever hope to have another aquaponics department up and running again."

The aquaponics department had grown food using a very sophisticated system that required no soil or any addition of plant nutrients. Instead, the plants received food from the nutrient rich waste excreted by the Dotaran fish, the iccythas, which shared the same water troughs as the plants. For the most part, other than providing the proper light and growing conditions for the plants, all they needed to do was feed the fish and the rest would take care of itself. That nearly autonomous system, however, had been lost with the Aramis, and that was one of the reasons the primadon hunts were commissioned. We desperately needed to increase our dwindling food stores.

"Well, if that's the case, I'll look forward to having a full stomach again soon," I remarked. "Any news on the prisoners?"

"Not that I am aware of," she replied. "Thuric and his band of rebels have been stubbornly silent, and I don't see that changing any time soon."

"Have you seen Nadina yet?" I asked her.

"Yes," she replied. "I see her every day, but I can never stay for long. She still mourns for her father, but she's beginning to be herself again."

"That's good, at least."

Mya continued, "I told her Thuric was captured, but she already knew. She saw him and his rebels being taken into the brig. He saw her too, unfortunately."

I didn't mention it to her then, but Demtrius and the other captains had already agreed to allow me to see Thuric later that day. There were still questions I needed answers for, and I was hoping Thuric would be just arrogant enough to reveal some of them.

Our attention was stolen by a small procession of bridge officers that came walking out of the ship, lining up on either side of the entrance ramp. They were followed by the four first-mates, which was an ill-fitting title if you ask me. Then, finally, came the captains. Dolvin and Demtrius came out first, walking side by side, and directly behind them were Nepalen and Alexitus. They came halfway down the ramp and stopped where everyone would be able to see and hear them clearly. Demtrius and Dolvin then spread apart, allowing Alexitus and Nepalen to step between them, forming a line across the ramp.

Alexitus was the first to step forward. "In light of recent events, we would just like to thank each and every one of you for your continued loyalty and commitment to this crew. We know the recent tragedies haven't been easy on anyone, and we praise you on your perseverance through these tumultuous times. Thanks to all of you, we have never been closer to going home."

Some of the crewmen began to clap, but stopped when Dolvin stepped forward next.

"The salvage crews have finally returned from the Aramis," said Dolvin, "and soon it will be time to move on to the next phase of our plan: finding the detriminium deposits so that we can finish the advancements that Pharon started. We know the deposits are located somewhere within the Okala Mountain Range, but the exact location is still unknown, for now at least. First, however, we have other matters of importance."

Demtrius picked up where Dolvin left off. "It is almost time to meet with the Mercerians again for their answer to our proposed treaty. Though we have Dotara in our sights at last, we can't ignore our current state of affairs. Our food stores have been almost completely depleted, and without the support of the Mercerians, we will not make it through the remainder of the winter months. We need their help now so that we may get home later."

"That being said," Nepalen continued, "the recent attack by the Scynthians has cost us dearly, and we cannot spare two teams with ships and supplies. We, your dutiful captains, have discussed this matter over and over again, and we have finally decided upon what we believe the necessary course of action should be."

"We know you have waited far too long to see Dotara again," said Alexitus, "but the search for the detriminium mines will need to wait until after we meet with the Mercerians. Patience, that is what we ask of you, and, by the hand of Carnyle, we will go home!"

His final words elicited a grand cheer from the crew, and I was cheering with them. We were successfully picking up the pieces after the Scynthians' attack and plans were finally getting back on track. As Alexitus had said, we just needed patience now.

# Chapter Twenty
# Thuric

Not long after the briefing, Demtrius brought me to see Thuric. I wasn't looking forward to questioning him, and I had a debilitating migraine that made me keenly aware of every beat of my heart, as the pain perfectly synchronized to it. I had been having a lot of them lately, coming upon me quickly and without a discernible cause, along with a myriad of other random pains and ailments. It was like I was being tortured from the inside. It affected my days so much at times that I ended up seeing one of the ship's doctors for some type of medication. He reluctantly parted with some of his limited supply, but it was only partially effective, leaving me still frustratingly sensitive to light and sound. All I wanted to do was remain in my bed with the compartment's lights off during these bouts of pain. Now, however, I just had to grin a bear it until we were finished with Thuric.

The brig was located on a lower section in the rear of the ship. The room was isolated from the rest of the vessel by a series of secured doors, the last of which consisted of interlocking bars of blue Dotaran steel. A pair of guards stood at each door, and the first pair initially barred our entrance until they recognized they were in the presence of one of their captains. Demtrius nodded at each of them, presented his access badge, and then patted the compact mattertron he wore on his back. The guards quickly bowed away, allowing us to pass through into the brig.

I rubbed circles on my temples, trying to alleviate some of the pain, but it didn't help much, and my entire head felt like it was going to burst.

It was a long corridor, just like on the Aramis. There were eight cells to each side on the first level, and the same layout for the upper level. The cells were small, rectangular rooms, roughly eight feet deep, six feet across, and perhaps another eight feet in height. They were bare, save for a small metal toilet in one corner and a small bench that hung suspended against the back wall, acting dually as a bed, but every cell we passed on the ground level was vacant; all except one. Nadina laid in her cell, sleeping, so we passed the cell without disturbing her.

"Where are the rest of the prisoners?" I asked.

"Above us," he said, pointing to the second, seemingly unreachable level. "We keep them up there for the added security. The cells are only accessible via the use of a mattertron and transmutation."

"Do the guards not have mattertrons of their own?" I asked.

"Not while on duty here," he replied. "It wouldn't be wise to keep the devices even in the same general vicinity as the brig, so we must bring them in with us when we need to see a prisoner or add a member to one of our cells. Again, for the added security."

"As always, you're very thorough," I remarked.

"We try to be," he replied. He removed the compact mattertron from his back and went to press one of its buttons. He paused just before doing so. "Ready?"

"Ready as I'll ever be."

Before I even realized it, we were floating above the floor, ascending steadily toward one of the lofted cells in the middle of the upper row. The closer we came to the ceiling, the brighter the ceiling lights became, forcing me to squint because of my sensitivity. The pain was dizzying.

We came up under the cell and peered into the space, safe behind the incredibly durable window pane. Inside lay a Scynthian on his bench, twiddling his webbed fingers with closed eyes. His hairless brow raised, and he turned his head just slightly, somehow aware of our presence. He cast a devilish smile, and then rested his head back again.

"You actually believe he will be forthright with you?" Demtrius asked. He and the other captains had already attempted to interrogate the prisoners, but with no success. The

Scynthians remained stubbornly silent and uncooperative, just as Demtrius had expected.

"We won't know unless we try," I replied, again rubbing my temples in small circles. To be sure, I thought my chances of eliciting a truthful response were much higher than the Dotarans. The captains were focused on a different set of concerns. My questions had little to do with the blood feud between the two races, and more to do with my personal predicament.

As I've already tried to explain, I just didn't feel quite like myself anymore. Ever since my fall while hunting the primadon, I felt an insatiable emptiness inside myself; a void that I couldn't figure out how to fill. It was eating at me, tearing me apart bit by bit. This eerie feeling came almost simultaneously with the realization that my body was healing slower than it had been, leading me to believe that the enhancement serum was wearing off. My body had become accustomed to the energizing and rejuvenating effects of the serum, and if my body was craving it, that would explain the feeling I had perfectly. It would even explain the headaches; they would be part of my withdrawal symptoms.

This was, of course, just speculation, so, in addition to my questions regarding the disappearance of my journals, I would inquire more about the serum too. Hopefully Thuric was in a talkative mood.

Demtrius gave a hand signal to the guards at the computer station, and a moment later a laser shot forth from high on the wall, landing on the center of the clear wall. It was one solid pane without any gaps or seams, but the laser instantly altered one section of the crystalline structure, providing us a means of ingress into the cell.

Thuric just stayed lying back, not even deigning to sit up and face us. He was apparently unconcerned by his imprisonment, but his steadfast confidence had an immediate unnerving affect upon me. Did he know something we didn't? Had we overlooked a crucial detail at some point? Nothing came to mind, but Thuric seemed so content and without a care in the world. What I would have given for such assurance.

"I was wondering when you'd come," he said, speaking

in Scynthian, so at present only I could understand him. Demtrius had his utility device to translate, but he hadn't activated it just yet. "The blue bastards have already tried to pry answers from my lips, and you'll have the same luck they did."

"We just came to talk," I replied friendly, but I didn't know how long I could hold it up in my current capacity.

"Of course you did," he said dismissively.

Demtrius had now activated his translator and was able to understand the rest of the conversation.

"Still picking up the pieces from my attack on the Aramis, I presume?" Thuric asked Demtrius, taunting him. He sat up smiling and leaned on an elbow, "Tell me, exactly how many Dotarans died in the attack? I have a wager going with my brother that the death toll was no less than one hundred thirty crewmen. Am I close?" He laughed to himself. "And how is Pharon doing?" he asked in feigned ignorance. "Oh, I'm sorry, you lost him during the attack, didn't you?" He laughed again. "That weak old fool got exactly what he deserved. My only regret is that we allowed him to escape Scynthia with his contemptuous daughter before they received their just deserts. I would have pursued them across the universe if it came to that, but my brother didn't believe the pair would be a threat while on this planet. Orric is more merciful than I am; he's remained isolated on Scynthia for far too long."

Orric; I remembered hearing that name once prior. Before I had left Earth, one of the robed men in the cave beneath my uncle's cabin had said the name. Could this be the same Orric?

"Your brother is your superior then?" I asked, intrigued by this bit of information, though still squinting from the cell's bright lights. My head was throbbing in agonizing pain, and I couldn't remember the last time I had felt so miserable.

Thuric's smile lessened. "Orric and I are equals, my small-minded friend, but it is not just the two of us who oversee operations on Scynthia. We have many supporters that aided us in our revolution, and several of them now serve on the new Council with us."

"But Orric apparently has more influence than you do,"

I remarked. My migraine was almost unbearable, and I was sure Thuric could see my present discomfort, but if he did, he didn't comment on it.

"We are a civilized society," he replied in calm indifference, "and we make decisions based on the overall benefit of Scynthia. In this particular situation, the Council found Orric's plan more favorable."

"What is his plan?" I asked quickly. *Could drawing the information out of Thuric be this easy?* For the sake of my headache, I could only hope it would be.

"To put it simply," Thuric replied, bearing another devilish grin, "the slow-burn is much more satisfactory, though I've always been a fan of an expedient execution."

*So it won't be that easy,* I thought. *Damn.*

"Not that it matters much now," he continued. "Your crew is hopeless and in tatters, and the refuge of this hidden camp will not last for long. Orric will find this place, and then he will take advantage of your weakened state. We'll finally be rid of you all, and our plans can go ahead unimpeded once again."

"What makes you so sure of that?" I asked.

"History!" he exclaimed, now standing up. "History has a tendency to repeat itself, and the Dotarans have never fared well when pit against my people."

"We managed to capture you," Demtrius replied. I could tell he was growing agitated.

"A one-time anomaly," Thuric answered dismissively.

"The Iccaryn will never be found," said Demtrius, but lacking conviction. "Not while I have any authority here."

"And if you honestly believe that," Thuric shot back, "then why are you here with me now? You are desperate, and there's no concealing that. Soon someone on your side will make a costly mistake, and then my people will capitalize."

"You're a cocky bastard, huh?" I asked.

"And you're so naive!" he said enthusiastically. "We know everything about what you have been doing here, and we have planned accordingly! You haven't a hope in the world of escaping Orric's wrath! None of you do!"

"Enough." said Demtrius, cutting Thuric off. He was

standing just behind my right side, and the volume of his voice sent additional pangs of pain coursing through my head. "You are our prisoner, and your paltry threats do not scare us in the least. Now stop wasting our time; that is not what we came here for."

"Of course it isn't," Thuric laughed, "but why pass up the opportunity to rub salt in your wounds?"

Demtrius didn't respond, and was somehow able to remain calm.

"You claim to know an awful lot about us," I said, trying to get the conversation on track. My head had stopped throbbing, and the migraine seemed to be dissipating. "Too much, as it would appear. I'm curious, how have you been gathering your information?"

Thuric looked at me with scrutinizing eyes, judging my intentions. "I know what you are really asking, and I believe you already know the answer to that question."

"Please, if you'll indulge me for just a few minutes," I said. "There are some things that I don't quite understand."

He looked at me tiredly, like it wasn't worth explaining himself to a mere human, but then he shrugged his shoulders. "Not like I'll have company again for a while, eh?" He looked at me with his black, beady eyes.

"We know it was you who took the journals," I told him matter-of-factly. "If you knew how to get to them, then why not just finish us off?"

"Perhaps I wanted you to capture me," he suggested connivingly, grinning slowly. "Perhaps you've done everything I've wanted you to do."

I just didn't have the time or energy for his games. "So if this is your genius plan, what is so important about being aboard this ship?" I asked.

"That is for me to know, and you to worry about," he replied unhelpfully.

My headache suddenly came back in full force, hunching me over in extreme agony.

"You don't look well," Demtrius whispered into my ear. "Perhaps we should come back another time?"

"I'm fine," I lied. In truth, the resurgence of the

migraine came with terrible nausea, and beads of sweat suddenly began running down the sides of my face.

"Interesting," said Thuric, regaining our attention. "It must have been...yes yes, that would be about the right amount of time."

"What are you talking about?" I asked.

"Tell me," he asked, "other than your apparent discomfort, have you been experiencing any other unpleasant sensations? Any sudden illnesses, or perhaps you've noticed you're not healing quite as quickly anymore?"

I just stared at him.

"It's just," he paused, feigning thoughtfulness, "the enhancement serum administered to you on Scynthia should prevent you from experiencing any bodily pains, infections, or diseases." He paused, "If the dose you received is still effective, of course."

"What are you trying to say?" I asked, impatient with concern.

"I've seen these symptoms, innumerous times, with our human subjects back on Scynthia," he said confidently. "It happens when the enhancement serum begins to wear off, and the symptoms only worsen the longer you go without a booster shot. How long has it been?" he asked in delight. "Three, maybe four Tatoran months? I'm surprised you're not already writhing in relentless pain. It will pass eventually, but the withdrawal symptoms will get much worse for you before they begin to get better. Not all of our human subjects make it through the withdrawal stage."

I didn't trust him, but I must admit, Thuric had me fairly concerned. I wasn't about to give him the satisfaction of knowing that he was getting to me though.

"Still," Thuric continued, "your fate will be far better than the one that awaits your woman."

"My woman?" I questioned him. The only woman Thuric could be referring to would be Mya, and I was instantly worried for her safety, but I tried not to betray my feelings to Thuric. "Mya is safe. You are the one whose fate hangs in the balance."

"I'm not talking about Nadina's pitiful servant," Thuric

replied, and his devilish grin slowly re-appeared on his face.

It took me longer than I care to admit to understand his meaning, but when I did my eyes went wide with a dreadful realization. "You son of a bitch!" I shouted at him in English, my head ringing with pain.

"She was right where you left her in the cabin," he said casually. "She put up an admirable resistance, but the chloroform worked well enough."

I don't even remember moving, but suddenly I was being pulled off of him by Demtrius, and Thuric was laughing at me.

"What have you done with her?" I demanded savagely. I took another threatening step toward him, fists clenched, but Demtrius held me back. "If you hurt her in any way, I'll tear your damned gills right out of your wrinkled throat!"

Thuric laughed maniacally, taking extreme pleasure in my hysteria. He had me seething with rage, and I was on the verge of striking the grinning prisoner again, but Demtrius checked my cocked arm before I could land the blow. Dotarans are not keen on prisoner brutality.

I turned away from Thuric, to hide my panic. It felt like I had been punched in the gut. *No. NO. No, no, no, no, no.* I forced myself to breathe. *He's lying. That utter piece of rapt dung is lying.* Scynthians, Nadina possibly being the exception, are manipulative sociopaths who always have ulterior motives. Pharon had reminded me of that enough. He was just saying whatever he knew would rile me up the most. *But what if he wasn't lying? What if the Scynthians had really taken you?*

My migraine was back in full force, and I had started to sweat. I needed to get out of this cell. We had learned at least part of the mystery of the journals, and Thuric wasn't willing to give up any other useful information, so we decided to leave.

I made it out of the brig and several feet down the hall before I lost my composure completely. I had endured everything Tatora had thrown at me up until this point, but the thought of you in the hands of Scynthians proved to be too much for me. I thought back to the nightmare that I had recently, the one that had felt so real, of you being tortured, and the immense anger it brought on overpowered my fear and I was able to steady myself.

Demtrius reached a hand out to pull me up from where I had slid down the wall of the corridor. He hadn't said a word while I had processed all of my emotions, but now he looked me in the eye. "We will find her. If the Scynthians have her, we will get her back." He said it with all the determination I was feeling, and I felt better knowing I had his support. "But we cannot help her, or anyone else, until we recuperate some of our losses. We need to focus on our impending trip to Mercer. You have told me how strong your Earth female is. And we don't even know for sure that Thuric was telling the truth." I knew he was trying to make me feel better, while keeping me on task. I would shift my focus back to our mission, but I also knew this cold, twisting feeling in the pit of my stomach would not go away until I knew you were safe.

He was right, though. Our resources were dangerously low, and soon we would run through the Iccaryn's dwindling food stores. We needed help, but the risk of discovery was far greater than we had anticipated. The Scynthians were playing a devious game, and no one aboard the Iccaryn had even a clue as to what the true nature of their plans might be, save for Thuric and his leather-skinned soldiers, but they were keeping that secret well hidden.

"They have my journal," I said to Demtrius, suddenly immensely aware of the enormity of the situation. "They must know of our plans to return to Mercer..."

"I know," he replied grimly. "The captains will not be pleased to hear of this."

"I'm sorry," I replied guiltily, "for everything. Because of me, Ryane-" I couldn't finish that thought, "And we already had to move the entire Dotaran camp once. I should never have written anything about our journeys. It was so foolish of me."

Demtrius stopped in the hallway and touched me on the shoulder. He turned me about, placing his other hand on my other shoulder, and looked me square in the eyes. "None of this is your fault, Jaxon. This entire mess is all the work of the Scynthians, never forget that. Placing unnecessary blame on yourself is not going to resolve the situation."

"But what do we do?" I asked in anguish. "We can't just go back to Mercer with the Scynthians expecting as much. It'll be suicide. And it will put the Mercerians in danger. They may already be in danger."

"Any course of action we take now will be dangerous," he said, "but we have to go. We have no present alternatives."

"And just step right into a trap?" I asked, desperation creeping into my voice.

"We will have to be very careful," he replied dutifully. "We will, of course, need to take extra pre-cautionary defense measures."

"Extra defense?" I questioned him, curious by what he had in mind.

"We Dotarans still retain a few tricks that we have yet to employ," he replied, and cast a brief reassuring smile at me before continuing down the hall.

# Interlogue Two
# Ryane's Plight

Water splashed onto the metal floor of the all-white, oval room that acted as Ryane's prison cell. She was sitting on a chair, soaking wet, with her head bent backwards. There was a hood over her head, and a new Scynthian poured a constant stream of water over her masked face, which she futilely struggled to withstand. She spat and coughed up water, choking on it, and could do nothing but shake her head back and forth, as her arms and legs were strapped securely to the chair.

It lasted for only a few seconds, but it seemed like much longer to Ryane. She thought she was going to drown; indeed, she felt as if she were drowning. This was the worst torture she had yet to endure.

Finally, the Scynthian finished pouring the contents of the water container, at which point he removed the hood from her face and grasped her by the hair. She winced from the pain. The torturer then snapped at a human servant that knelt close by, uttering something in its strange, unintelligible language, and the servant went hurrying out of the room.

Ryane breathed heavily, her face and hair dripping-wet. "Why?" she managed to ask. "Why are you doing this?"

The hideous Scynthian creature looked at her with a devilish smile. "Because it pleases me."

Ryane was losing hope. She was on the verge of breaking, and she felt like that was exactly what the Scynthians wanted, but she refused to give in to them. She fought them with every fiber of her being, but her spirit could only take so much. She feared the inevitable.

Ever since her failed escape attempt, and the subsequent divulging of Jaxon's location, she had been subjected to many traumas, both physical and psychological.

She had been beaten regularly, shocked with electricity, and the Scynthians had even played with the oxygen and gravity levels inside her room. When she tried to sleep, the room would vibrate with a disorienting tone, giving her restless nights and exhausting days. Most recently, she had been starved. The hunger pains grew with each passing day, and were only made worse by the human servants who came into the room parading delicious meals in front of her, taunting and teasing her helpless captivity. At this point, she suspected, they were just doing it to see how far they could push the human body and mind, for there was no longer any reason to keep her here. She couldn't provide them with any information that they didn't already know.

Eventually, she was allowed to eat, and, famished as she was, she ate the succulent meat ravenously. It was the same sweet tasting meat she had been fed when she first awoke on Scynthia, and it made up a considerable portion of her diet. It was about the only thing she didn't hate on that world.

The female servant came back into the room with a covered tray. Ryane knew what it was, as she had grown accustomed to expecting her meals brought to her in this fashion. The servant placed the tray on a small table in front of Ryane and then unstrapped her hands so she could eat.

The cover was lifted off of the tray, releasing a small cloud of steam. Ryane immediately went for the food and began eating, savoring every bite for but a moment as she shoveled it into her mouth and down her throat.

"I see you like the meat," said the Scynthian, who still stood in the room.

Ryane didn't acknowledge the statement, and just kept eating.

Beside her jailer was another one of the hideous Scynthian creatures. Ryane didn't think she had seen this one before, but she couldn't be sure. Her jailer had often taken others to her room to relish in her anguish, but this one seemed different than the others. He didn't seem to enjoy her discomfort, but neither did he seem particularly unnerved, like it was just another duty for him to oversee.

"Our cattle are of the utmost quality when they go to

slaughter," said her jailer, failing to hold back a smile.

The hair on the back of Ryane's neck suddenly stood on end. A Scynthian smiling was never good.

"I'm surprised you like it so much, though," the jailer continued. "Most intelligent species do not like the taste of their own kind."

Ryane went cold and immediately stilled. She looked at her plate with horror, bile rising in her throat. She leaned over in the chair and vomited, until there was nothing left in her stomach. Tears were streaming down her face, and she barely registered that she was hyperventilating. She could take it no more, and the room began to fade in and out. The ringing in her ears stopped as she fainted, falling limp in her seat.

Sometime later, she awakened, alone and cold on the metal floor. She saw the remnants from her meal still on the ground where she had thrown it, even the vomited meat. She shuddered, closing her eyes at the sight, trying not to remember just how many times she had unwittingly gorged on the flesh of her own species. It made her sick again, but, with no food in her system, all she could do was dry-heave. When she was done, her body glistened with a cool sweat and her abdomen ached severely.

She crawled to a mat they had so *graciously* provided her to sleep on, hoping to find some refuge in her sleep, but knowing there would be none. Instead her nights were filled with replays of the horrors inflicted upon her by day. Her sleep was restless and sporadic, when it came at all, and she often woke up in a terrible panic, her heart beating furiously.

She didn't care about the horrid nightmares now, though. Her body was just too exhausted, and sleep would come whether she liked it or not, so there she lay until, several hours later, she was again awakened by the opening of the door.

Ryane didn't move. If they wanted to torture her some more, they were going to have to pick her up and drag her over. As she cracked an eyelid to look to the door, she was surprised to see a different Scynthian than her usual torturer. She couldn't be sure, as most of the Scynthians were indistinguishable to her, but there was something less malicious in its demeanor. The Scynthian walked over to her, carrying a small medical bag. He placed the bag on the floor near Ryane, and then opened it to her, showing her that it only contained the tools of his trade. Next he went to check Ryane's vitals, but she curled away as he reached out, tucking herself into a ball and clamping her arms tight around her legs.

The Scynthian was patient with her, having witnessed some of the cruelties she was forced to endure. "I'm not here to harm you," he said to her in a soothing voice. He had a thick accent, but his English was even better than the new jailer's. "My name is Illoran."

Ryane looked at this Illoran with nothing but contempt, and he could feel the hatred emanating from her emaciated figure.

Illoran, feeling a bit awkward and somewhat ashamed, unusual feelings for a Scynthian, continued, "I am one of the veterinarians for the humans on this station. Salama'an has sent me in here to determine your health and ensure that you will not die just yet." He paused, and then added remorsefully, "I'm afraid his torment may be far from over." Salama'an must be the name of her torturer, the one who had taken over for Orric after her failed escape attempt. Ryane filed that information away, along with the confirmation that her torture was not over.

Illoran had always been sympathetic to the human cattle on Scynthia. Indeed, he had devoted his youthful studies to learning all he could about the humans, who, to him, were some of the most interesting creatures he had ever laid eyes upon. He admired their unique individual identities, their enthusiasm for life, and, most significantly, their ability to love. Scynthians, his own kind, were taught at a very young age to suppress their emotions, and rarely did they celebrate family. This left an unfulfilled void in his life, one that he had hitherto tried to fill through his studies of this unusual species. He studied both the human cattle that were raised on Scynthia and the free humans on Earth, never ceasing to be amazed. It was with a strange fascination that he observed and treated his human patients, tending to them like he would a Scynthian patient. In his eyes, he was simply a Scynthian of medicine, bound by a code to aid anyone in need of assistance.

Now he had hit an impasse. Illoran, stricken with unintended grief, held tremendous empathy for Ryane, and wished he had some means of aiding her outside of his medical expertise. That, however, could only be done in one of two ways; he could show her Scynthian mercy and end her suffering right now, or he could devise some way to effectuate her escape. The former was all but out of the picture. He could save a life, but never before had he intentionally taken one, not even a human's. This meant, in order to help Ryane, he would have to go against his entire civilization and free her.

But could he really do that? If he were caught...no, he couldn't even think of what would happen to him then. The new Scynthian regime, led by Orric, Thuric, and the new rebel Council, was notorious for executing anyone even suspected of treason, and had already killed or converted the remnants of the old Council.

Illoran looked again upon the helpless human captive before him, taking note of her frail and fragile body. He often marveled at how this species had evolved to become the dominant species on their planet. Their newborns were incredibly weak and prone to deathly illnesses, but it just showed the strength and resilience of the humans, to endure so much yet still rise above the rest.

It was these same qualities that he saw in Ryane.

"I must say," Illoran continued, "I am impressed by your fortitude. I don't know many Scynthians who could have sustained so much."

Ryane lay on her side still, just staring off into empty space. Now that she was awake again, she was thinking about how, because of her, Jaxon was probably dead, killed by these horrible creatures, and she would most likely be next. She thought about how dying might not even be so bad, compared to living through more torture.

Illoran again tried to attend to Ryane, but she kicked out her legs, and he was forced to jump back. Stymied yet again, Illoran grabbed his bag and stood to leave. He would return soon though for another attempt to provide her medical assistance.

"I know nothing I can ever say will convince you of
my sincerity," he said to her quietly, as if fearing he might be
overheard, "but I am truly sorry for what has been done to you.
If it were within my capacity, I would set you free and return
you to your planet, but I am only a doctor." He walked to the
portal, and then turned around one last time, "I just hope you
can find some solace in knowing that Orric failed in his attempt
to root out your human friend and the Dotarans that are aiding
him. It was a trap, and a clever one too, from what I'm told. It
won't make your plight here any better, but you don't have to
feel any guilt or shame. Stay strong, little human."

When Illoran left the room, Ryane could finally
breathe. She had almost been tempted to believe him, hoping
that Jaxon was still alive and well, but she quickly remembered
where she was and the people she was dealing with. *Just
another trick*, she thought. *Just another trick to raise my hopes
and then dash them again.* As she closed her eyes, a tear made
its way over the bridge of her nose and down her other cheek,
but she made no move to wipe it away.

Just then, the ominous and disorienting tone sounded
off inside her room. It would be yet another sleepless night for
Ryane.

# Chapter Twenty-One
# Return To Mercer

Plans were set, the course was charted, and ships were prepared. Then, when the day came, we left for the island-continent of Mercer early in the morning. We took the Pothos, our mid-sized dondobah, carrying six occupants, as well as two single-person skivs. All four captains were in attendance, as well as Crispin, Thristin, and their cousin, Gilpin, but Delfwig stayed behind to watch over the Iccaryn and the crew. Demtrius and I were the most important guests, as we had the best rapport with the Mercerians and both of us could speak their language fluently. Not to mention that we had known Svix, the son of the Mercerian High Chieftain, and had returned his amethyst necklace to his father after his death. This was apparently a gesture of great significance in their culture. The Dotarans had also offered several gifts to the Mercerians, a sort of incentive meant to display the possible benefits of such a treaty. It still seemed clear to most, though, that any peace to be had would be wrought by Demtrius and me.

I sat in the Pothos with Gilpin and the four captains, waiting for the flight deck to finish filling with water. Crispin and Thristin piloted the skivs, while Gilpin piloted the Pothos. They were to keep the crafts submerged until we were just off the Mercerian coast, hoping to keep our presence there a secret. To be sure, the ship was also newly fitted with Pharon's cloaking device, but it would drain the ship's batteries much quicker, so we needed to use it sparingly.

We were acting under the assumption that the Scynthians controlled the skies, and we couldn't afford them finding us or the Iccaryn. I felt bad enough as it was, potentially leading the Scynthians to Mercer with my journal writings. The Mercerians didn't need us bringing our troubles with us, so we tried to be as stealthy as possible, hoping the Scynthians wouldn't see our approach and might stay at bay. It was a relatively short trip up the northern river to Mercer, and only a few hours later, we were passing Skudland at the island-continent's southern tip on our way to the capital. I had taken some medicine from a Dotaran doctor, and I could only hope it was enough to get me through the trip.

While we navigated the waterway, my mind was racing with thoughts of you, I still could not accept what Thuric had said; that you were captured by the Scynthians and imprisoned on their strange world. The mere thought of you in any distress sent a pang of guilt through my body. If it was true, it was all my fault. Why did I have to take you to that cabin? I should have just sold it after my Uncle Deecan disappeared, but no, I had to do some stupid grand scheme to tell you how I felt about you, and I hadn't even done that! My chest felt heavy with fear and anxiety, but I took that feeling and turned it into motivation. We would secure peace with the Mercerians, obtain the needed food, retrieve the detriminium, and then I would find you. I kept telling myself it would be that easy, and that soon I would rescue you from whatever the Scynthians were doing to you.

When we arrived at Finnis, our crafts ascended to the surface and emerged inside a pool of slushy ice water. We were surrounded by a frozen sea filled with dozens of mini icebergs of varying shapes and sizes. It was a foreboding view, but the Dotarans had their magnificent compact mattertrons that Crispin and Thristin carried on their backs. With their aid, we made our way ashore with ease; all of us except Gilpin, who stayed behind to submerge the ships and guard them until our return. The air was considerably colder this far north in the midst of winter, but we were kept warm in our skin-tight jumpsuits and hooded wind-breakers.

Almost immediately, our small group of seven was spotted by a Mercerian fisherman and his cub on the shore, both wrapped in furs, on top of their own fur, due to the frigid temperature. They quickly went running back into the small city to alert their chieftain. Several minutes later, a contingent of white-furred warriors left the city, marching in our direction, led by three Mercerians riding ski-cycles at their front. Though the Mercerians had been expecting our return, it seemed they were taking no chances and came in excessive force.

The Dotaran captains, aside from Demtrius, were concerned by this show of strength.

"What is the meaning of this?" Alexitus demanded. "This is supposed to be a mission of peace."

"It is," Demtrius replied, "but wouldn't you be apprehensive if strange creatures appeared on your shores?"

"This is at their request!" Alexitus protested.

"And?" Demtrius asked. "When I returned to the Aramis with Jaxon and our friends, you had them imprisoned, and even I was put under heavy scrutiny."

"That was a very different situation," grumbled Alexitus. "We didn't know if we could trust your new associates at the time, but they did prove themselves to be useful." He squinted his eyes, "Except for that Pharon fellow."

Demtrius, and I, ignored the latter comment. "Now we must prove to the Mercerians that we can be trusted."

To be sure, Crispin and Thristin each wore a compact mattertron on their backs, so there was no real cause for concern if the Mercerians attacked. I also kept my new double-edged sword strapped to my waist, just in case. I always felt safer just knowing it was there.

As the warriors drew closer, I could see Ricson leading them, wearing the same amethyst necklace that once belonged to his late brother. It had been a Tatoran half-month, or fifty days, since I had last seen Ricson, which is approximately fifty-five Earth days, and now he led the contingent of warriors with the same air of confidence and authority as his father, Rengar. Another young Mercerian warrior rode next to him, while a more distinguished warrior rode on the third ski-cycle. All three stopped just feet from us and powered off their ski-cycles before rising.

"You surprised us," Ricson remarked. "We had our people watching the skies for your return."

"We took a different route this time," Demtrius replied, bowing slightly.

Ricson looked over at me, "Nice to see you again,

Jaxon."

"The pleasure is mine," I replied. "How are you and your soon-to-be tzulara?"

"Pinut and I have never been happier," he replied, unable to restrain himself from smiling. He looked around at the surroundings, and then returned his attention to Demtrius. "I hope you have your flying ships somewhere nearby. I was looking forward to the ride you promised us."

"I hate to dash your hopes," said Demtrius, "but I'm afraid that won't be possible this time around."

Ricson frowned, "Does this have anything to do with the bright lights we saw in the western sky recently?"

Demtrius, somewhat surprised that Ricson had made the connection so easily, nodded, "I will explain everything shortly, but for now I think it is best if we get out of the open and head into the city."

"Very well," Ricson replied cheerfully. "Follow me."

Ricson and his warriors turned to lead us on foot, while another warrior took control of Ricson's ski-cycle to take it back to the city. The rest of us began to follow the marching warriors, but not before Alexitus pulled Demtrius to the side for a few words. He spoke in a low tone, but I could still make out his complaints at not being introduced right away.

"It didn't seem important," Demtrius told him.

"He is their leader," said Alexitus. "We should have been properly introduced."

Demtrius smiled at Alexitus' confusion. "That was Ricson," he said. "Rengar's son. He is bringing us to his father now, and I will be sure to make the proper introductions then."

Finnis looked very different from our last visit. The main avenue was filled with tents and vendors, purple flags hung from every window and post, and people crowded the streets from one end of the city to the other. It was their grand Tzulamay festival, and Mercerians from every corner of the land were there for the yearly celebration. *Just in time for the Scynthians to invade,* I thought worriedly.

I only knew of the holiday by name, and when I asked Ricson about it on our way through the crowds, he looked at me as if I must have been joking. After realizing that I was serious, he spread his arms in front of us and said with enthusiasm, "This is Tzulamay! Every year, in the middle of winter before the long night comes, we hold a grand festival. It was originally meant to boost our spirits during the colder months when food would run scarce, but over the years it has developed into much more; a time of allegiance, of unification, and still, most importantly, a time of enjoyment."

"It seems we've come at a good time then," I said.

"The best of times!" Ricson exclaimed. "Tomorrow the celebrations will begin with an oath swearing ceremony, where all cubs coming of age must swear their life-long loyalty and allegiance to my father, and then to their respective chiefs as well. After this ceremony there is a short reprieve with some food and festivities, and then begins the unification ceremony, where all couples who wish to be united for life come together before my father. It is a communal ceremony of sorts, as Tzulamay is the only time in which unifications are performed, and Pinut and I will be a part of the ceremony this year."

Ricson was gleaming with happiness. "Each of us will make a solemn vow to our significant others, a vow that is punishable by law if violated. Then the real celebrations begin, filled with grogg, wine, and entertainment of all sorts. It is one of the few times that ardent spirits are permitted to be consumed on Mercer, and we do not generally pass up the opportunity." He continued, a bit more serious, "In our city, however, the couples do not get to celebrate in these festivities."

"What do you mean?" I asked. "Why not?"

"We are given an extra task, one meant to test the strength of our relationship. If we cannot successfully complete our task, then our unification becomes void and we must wait until the next Tzulamay to try again, if we can face the embarrassment."

"That sounds pretty nerve-racking," I replied.

"It is," Ricson admitted, "but, for those of us who succeed, it will only make the love stronger, and I have no fear that Pinut and I will fail." He said this with such confidence and determination that I couldn't help but believe him.

We continued through the crowd, passing many food

stands and gaming tents. In one tent, a pair of Mercerians dueled, to the pleasure and applause of dozens of spectators. The fighters wielded blue-tinted swords, which must have been forged fairly recently from the Dotaran steel that we had gifted them. In another tent, I saw a silent crowd standing around two Mercerians, who sat on either side of a cassa board. They both seemed to be in deep thought. The hand-crank flashlights that the Dotarans had given to the Mercerians at the previous meeting were now being used to light the main avenue, many of them projecting different colors of light due to colored lenses placed over the bulbs. Every so often there were stages where bands played their instruments, or where performers put on productions. But when the Mercerians saw our group being led through the crowd, everyone stopped what they were doing and watched us as we passed. They didn't seem angered or upset by our presence, but neither did they display any eagerness or acceptance.

We soon entered Rengar's main hall, where we found the high chieftain sitting at the head of a long table. Sverna, his tzulara, sat beside him, while the other chieftains from Mercer sat at his flanks. On the right was the big and powerful Grissly, a giant among Tatorans, and next to him was his daughter, Pinut. She sprouted a smile when she saw Ricson step into the room, and he took a seat at the corner of the table beside his mother and his betrothed. On the left side of the table sat Waulf, and next to him was his young tzulara, as well as his son, Scard. Waulf and Scard both had tiny bones tied into their manes, as was custom for Skudlandic warriors. There were other minor chieftains from the smaller villages in Mercer as well, for Tzulamay of course, but also for this extremely rare meeting between species.

I noticed that Waulf's young mate had an unnatural fascination with her son-in-law, Scard, and was giggling quite often as Scard boasted about his hunting triumphs. They must have been very close in age, but the young Skudlandic female was his father's tzulara. She hardly seemed so by the way she acted toward Scard, but Waulf seemed to be paying too much attention to his food to notice.

Upon the table was a delicious spread. They had

roasted elder and meer, as well as primadon stew. The primadon they ate was the same one that Ricson had helped hunt and kill before our last visit. They also had several types of cheese, bread still warm from the oven, and even fresh droot and bille. Droot had the fine ability to clean and protect the teeth, while bille was notorious for its ability to preserve and strengthen one's eyesight.

We took our seats around the table, at least I did, along with Demtrius and the captains. Crispin and Thristin, however, remained standing on either side of the entrance.

Demtrius took out his utility device and placed it in the center of the table to translate the conversation between races, as well as record it for later reference. He then made the formal introductions.

"We all know why this gathering has been arranged," Demtrius said in Tatoran, partially to please the Mercerians, but also because he liked to practice the difficult language as often as he could. His voice repeated on the translator in Dotaran, "It is our wish to create a peace treaty with your people, but, before I go any further, there have been some important recent events that need to be disclosed."

Rengar looked to his chieftains, seeing many agitated faces. "We would appreciate your candor."

"Much has transpired since our last meeting," Demtrius began. "It is to our dismay that we must inform you of the great and terrible losses we Dotarans have suffered. Without warning, and without any provocation, we were viciously attacked by a fleet of hostile Scynthians. That was the source of the strange lights in the sky that you probably witnessed recently. We did our best to fend them off, but lost many good Dotarans during the devastating sky battle that ensued. In the end, we were forced to evacuate our ship, which now lies in ruin."

Demtrius paused for a moment, taking the time to judge the reactions of the Mercerians, who, on the whole, weren't very welcoming. He then looked back to his co-captains with a look of apprehension before finally continuing. "In light of these tragic events, we now need your help more than ever. Without it, I'm afraid our people will soon go hungry. We will, of course, compensate you the best we can."

"Better to let you starve," Waulf declared carelessly.

"Waulf!" snapped Rengar.

Waulf growled, but then quieted, for the moment at least.

Alexitus, Nepalen, and Dolvin all seemed shocked by this outward display of aggression, but Demtrius nodded to them that everything was fine.

"It was not our intention to ask for anything more from you than abstaining from war," said Demtrius, "especially in the dead of winter, when I'm sure you'll need whatever food you have to get you through until spring, but we have no other alternative at present. We implore you to find it in your hearts to aid us in this time of need."

"First it was peace, now food. What will it be the next time, warriors to fight your battles? Our homes to house your people?" Waulf questioned him angrily. "There will be no end to your desires if we give in now. Not to mention the present danger you've already put us in just by coming here. You've already caused war with the Tatorans, and for all we know now, the Scynthians could be on their way here right now to finish you off!"

"You need not worry," Demtrius replied calmly. "We have taken good measure to conceal our whereabouts. I assure you, the Scynthians will not find us here."

"How could you possibly know that?" Waulf ask belligerently; mirroring my thoughts.

"Waulf!" Rengar snapped again, but Waulf ignored him this time.

"From what you've just told us, you couldn't even protect the lives of your own people!" Waulf continued. "And the Scynthians wouldn't attack you without good cause, so what did you really do to provoke their wrath?"

"That is enough, Waulf!" commanded Rengar.

"No!" said Waulf. "I've tried to understand your side of things, Rengar, but this alliance will be nothing but trouble for our people. The Tatorans will look on us with disgust, and who knows what the Scynthians will do if they learn we are in league with their enemies. This alliance you are trying to build is reckless, and it is going to put innocent Mercerians in harm's way. Let the Dotarans fend for themselves, and we will do the same!"

"Aye!" said a few of the minor chieftains.

"My comrade," said Alexitus, referring to Demtrius, "assured us that you were capable of hearing reason, and that you were willing to listen to what we have to offer. If that is not the case, then we won't waste any more of our time here."

With that, the three captains began to rise from their seats.

"Do not be so hasty!" Demtrius pleaded with his co-captains.

"Wait," said Rengar. "Please, remain seated. I apologize for Waulf's discourteous remarks, but his statements are not unfounded. We are willing to hear you out, but then, you must understand, we will make the decision that is best for our people."

"What more is there to discuss?" Alexitus questioned the Mercerians. "We are hunted by the Scynthians, yes, and all we ask of you is for a little bit of food and your promise to never take up arms against us or aid those who do. In return, we will provide you with knowledge and technologies that your species cannot even fathom."

Despite Waulf's outburst, I could see this piqued the interest of more than one chieftain.

"We do not want to be on this planet any more than you want us to be," Alexitus continued, "and with your help, you might just be rid of us sooner."

"To help you is to invite the wrath of the Scynthians and hatred from the other clans," said one of the minor chiefs.

"If the Scynthians were going to attack," said Grissly, speaking for the first time, "they probably would have done so by now. And the Tatorans?" he said, shrugging his shoulders. "When have we ever cared what they think?"

"So you think we should aid these Dotarans?" asked the lesser chief, clearly against the idea.

"Helping them seems like the right thing to do," Ricson interjected, "and only cowards would shy away from this ethical responsibility."

There was an awkward pause in the conversation, but Demtrius soon broke the silence. "Change is never easy, and hardly ever immediately accepted, especially a change as monumental as this. The proposed treaty we have before us would be the first in our species' history. It could be the start of a great alliance, and yes, it might hold some risk, but we believe that risk to be minimal, and well worth the reward."

Demtrius then turned to talk directly to Waulf. "You are right; we cannot promise that the Scynthians won't visit you, and that they won't be displeased. We do not control them. However, if it helps you in your decision making, when we leave here today, you will have your compensation, and will most likely not see us again for a long time, if ever."

"What do you mean?" Rengar asked, and many of the other chieftains leaned forward in anticipation of the explanation, even Waulf.

"What I was going to say earlier," said Demtrius, looking directly at Waulf, "before I was interrupted, was that we think we have found a way to leave your planet, once and for all. The Scynthians attacked us because we were close to that goal, but we are still determined to achieve it. Now, what say you?"

Demtrius sat back, waiting for their answer.

"You have given us much to think about," said Rengar, "but please, before we are finished with the conversation, tell us more about this compensation you have offered in return for our services. I know my interest has been piqued by the notion, and I'm sure my comrades are also curious."

Rengar was smart. If anything could nullify their complaints, it would be the major benefits they would reap from assisting us. We didn't have gold, and Rengar may not have known that, but what the Dotarans possessed was worth far more than any amount of money. "Knowledge is where real power lies," Demtrius told me once. "It is the currency of the universe." I thought that most of the Mercerians were also smart enough to see that.

In truth, there was hardly anything to spare back at the Iccaryn, but we were willing to trade what little we had in order to obtain the much needed food. We were stacking all of our eggs in this one basket, because if the Mercerians refused to help us now, there might not be many of us left for later. Demtrius looked to Nepalen, who said, "We've brought you another three tons of Dotaran steel and three more ski-cycles, all of which are still loaded on our ships." He was clearly very nervous around the intimidating size and ferocity of the Mercerians. "We have also brought you many tools that will help you live an easier life here. The most important gift, however, is right here."

With that, Nepalen suddenly shoved his trembling hand inside a pocket on his belt. Some of the Mercerians instinctively reached for their weapons, but realized Nepalen meant no harm when he dropped a pouch onto the table, spilling a variety of plant seeds and bulbs.

"Have any of you ever heard of Aquaponics?" Demtrius asked, the last word repeating over the translator in Dotaran, since there was no equivalent expression in the Tatoran language.

For the next few minutes, Nepalen described the method of aquaponics and how it meant the Mercerians would have a surplus of food year round. They would have to build a facility to house the plants and Dotaran fish from the harsh northern environment, but the work would be manageable, especially with some of the new tools they were being given.

"I will need some time to discuss these proceedings with my chieftains, in private," Rengar had told us, once he'd heard the length of the proposition. "Please, go out and enjoy the pre-Tzulamay festivities. We will meet back here tomorrow morning, before the official start of Tzulamay, and you will have our answer."

"Thank you," said Demtrius. Alexitus, Nepalen, Dolvin, and I said our thanks as well, and then we left the long hall. All we could do now was bide our time until Tzulamay began.

# Chapter Twenty-Two
# Rengar's Decision

The night before Tzulamay, we slept in one of the small houses that Demtrius and I had stayed in during our previous visit to Finnis. It was a tight squeeze with all seven of us in the one building, but, with the influx of Mercerians attending Tzulamay, the rest of the dwellings were already occupied. Our ships had no beds and little room, so lodging there wouldn't work either. I didn't mind. It was only for one night anyway. I had endured far worse conditions on my long and arduous journey to reach the Dotarans.

Alexitus and Nepalen, however, found our housing to be unsatisfactory.

"We are captains," said Alexitus, "and a captain does not sleep in the same quarters as his crew, especially in an inferior dwelling such as this."

"With the Dotaran steel we gave them, you'd think they'd have constructed something more lasting and sophisticated," Nepalen added. "It is little more than an ice hut."

"If you'd rather, the ships are only a short walk away," I suggested.

Nepalen, caught off guard, had no response. I could see Crispin and Thristin smiling to themselves.

"And by the by," said Alexitus, "I thought you said we were dealing with rational creatures, Demtrius? Did you see the way they acted in there, and with their high chieftain no less!"

"Honor and respect are what the Mercerians value," Demtrius replied, "but even they can be fearful of the new and unknown. Resistance to change can only be expected, from any rational life-form."

Alexitus huffed, "I don't like it. We've given them all

of the leverage in this, and now they know how terribly vulnerable we are. How can we be sure they won't just promise one thing and do another?"

"That is the risk we all have to take," Demtrius replied simply.

I was up well before the sun on the morning of Tzulamay, which isn't saying much since the night is very long here at this time of year, but I was anxious to hear the Mercerians' decision. Demtrius was also up early, even before me, and was meditating off to the side as he usually did in the mornings. The others, as far as I could tell, were still sleeping soundly.

I needed to relieve myself, so I got up quietly and made my way outside. It was still dark, but the Tatoran sun was just beginning to emerge over the eastern horizon. A dense blanket of icy fog covered the streets of Finnis and the surrounding woodlands. Off in the distance, I could hear the continuous sloshing of icy waves breaking on the rocky shoreline. It was so calm and relaxing; simple and serene. I could see why the Mercerians didn't venture far from their island-continent too often.

I stood there for several minutes, taking in the wonderful atmosphere, almost forgetting that I came out to relieve myself. I quickly ducked behind a tree, did my business, and then started walking back toward the dwelling. That's when I saw them.

Ten warriors were camped not twenty yards from the dwelling. I quickly noticed Ricson standing among them. Curious, I walked over and asked him what they were doing there.

"My father posted us here last night," he replied, "as a precaution."

"A precaution for what?" I asked. "Did he think we planned to sneak out and start massacring Mercerians?" I was half joking, but also half serious.

Ricson, failing to see any humor in this, replied, "We are here to protect you. My father did not think it was entirely safe for your group; several of the chieftains are disgruntled by your presence here."

This news was somewhat disconcerting. If the warriors hadn't been here to deter them, an unhappy Tatoran could have taken out the entirety of the Dotaran leadership in one swift move. Alas, the night was over now, and no one had attempted to do us any harm.

"Soon the entire city will be bustling with activity," Ricson told me. "Tzulamay is our largest and most celebrated holiday."

"I'm glad we can be here to enjoy it with you," I replied genuinely.

Ricson had a pained expression upon his face, one I had seen on him before.

"When I was but a mere cub," he said, "Svix would take me through the city to show me the different games and events. We would laugh and play, and sometimes he would even let me win a game or two. He was great at everything he did."

I was surprised by this display of emotion, and wasn't quite sure what to say. "You're not so different from your brother," I said at last. "I only knew him for a short time, but we grew close during that time, and I believe it is safe to say that Svix would be very proud of you if he were here today."

"Thank you, Jaxon."

I stayed with Ricson for a little while before seeing Demtrius emerge from the dwelling. The fog had mostly dissipated, so he saw us almost immediately. Like I did before him, Demtrius inquired about the warriors, and Ricson repeated Rengar's concerns of treachery.

"I appreciate the sentiment," Demtrius replied, "but, please, do not let any of the other captains know of this. I believe they might react poorly, and we cannot afford that."

"Very well," Ricson replied indifferently.

We watched the small city spring to life as Mercerians began filling the streets to set up shop for the day. A group of musicians began playing music on one of the stages, with a half-shelled dome behind them to amplify the sound. It reminded me of the amphitheater in Aanthora, where I had been sentenced to fight in the Pit of the Gyx by Amentus and the Aanthoran Council.

My mind drifted to Jotus and Jotan. I wondered if Jotus had ever found his son, or if perhaps he still searched for him. I dared not think of the more terrible possibilities that could have befallen them. I wished I could see them again, but I doubted I would ever get the pleasure.

"I trust Rengar and the other chieftains are in the main hall by now?" asked Demtrius.

"They should be," Ricson replied.

"Then let us wake the others and waste no more time," said Demtrius.

"I will let him know you are on your way," Ricson replied dutifully. With that, he assembled his small contingent of warriors and left the immediate area.

Demtrius turned to me, "I didn't think I'd be this anxious to hear their reply. I hardly slept last night thinking about it."

"You're not the only one," I told him.

It was a short walk to Rengar's main hall, above which hung two flags; one, the Mercerians' downward facing purple triangle depicting a gyx, and the other Rengar's house banner, a rectangular purple flag with the picture of a tree branch crossed by a sword to form an X.

"Does the sword and branch have any significance?" I asked Ricson, who stood outside the hall with his mother and Pinut waiting for us.

"That my family is one of peace," Ricson explained, "but we will fight for what we believe in." Soon we were sitting before the Mercerian chieftains at the long table. Everyone was present from the day before, save for Scard and Waulf's young tzulara. As we took our seats, I looked from chief to chieftain, hoping to get a clue as to whether or not they would support our proposal, but their expressions were utterly indecipherable. Even Waulf, whose countenance generally betrayed his emotions, was unreadable.

When we were all seated, Rengar pushed back his chair and stood up to address the table. "After careful consideration and much deliberation," he started, diving right into it, "I have decided we will honor the terms of your proposed peace agreement, as well as assist you in procuring food for your people."

The captains relaxed in their seats, feeling a sense of relief and accomplishment.

"But," Rengar continued, "before we will do so, my chiefs and chieftains insist upon two additional stipulations that must be met."

The sense of relief instantly turned to apprehension. Alexitus and Nepalen looked to Demtrius for explanation, while Dolvin seemed unsurprised, as if he had been waiting for some hidden agenda to be divulged.

Demtrius raised a hand to steady his co-captains, and then nodded his head for Rengar to continue.

"Word is bond with our people," said Rengar, "and, as my chieftains have dutifully pointed out to me, the same must hold true for you Dotarans as well. That being said, each of you will need to join in the oath-swearing ceremony that will be held this morning. In doing so, you will provide us with some assurance that you can be trusted, and will be held personally accountable for your oaths by all who witness them."

"You want us bound to do your bidding?" Alexitus asked accusingly.

"You need only swear to honor our truce and to never cause any harm to any of my people," Rengar replied.

"And will all of you swear the same oath to us?" asked Alexitus.

"I will make the oath," Rengar replied, "and, as High Chieftain, my word alone will suffice."

"Very well," said Alexitus, leaning back in his seat.

"And this second stipulation?" Demtrius asked.

Rengar looked to each of the captains one by one before continuing. "Simply swearing an oath does not give us complete assurance that you will act accordingly, so there is an additional task that we require from all of you; a Mercerian rite of passage, so to speak. You must complete this task the Mercerian way, without the aid of any Dotaran technology. Succeed and we will consider you all honorary members of the clan, and no one will be able to dispute the validity of our truce, but if you fail, I'm afraid there will be nothing we can do for you."

I noticed Waulf seeming oddly pleased.

Demtrius looked to the other captains, all appearing concerned, and then looked back to Rengar, "What is the task that we must complete?"

"The exact nature of this task will be divulged during the Unification ceremony later today," Rengar replied. "For now, suffice it to say that all Mercerian couples must perform this same task in order to validate their unification and show their unwavering commitment to each other. Likewise, completion of this task will show us your commitment as well."

"And this is the only way to earn your support?" Demtrius asked.

"It is the only way," Rengar confirmed.

"Then I believe we have a deal."

# Chapter Twenty-Three
# Friends Come With Benefits

Immediately following the meeting, we made our way toward the rocky, snow covered shoreline to retrieve the gifts from the Dotaran flyers. They still remained submerged under the icy water, guarded by Gilpin, who would now be signaled to bring the crafts to the surface for unloading. We could only hope that no Scynthian eyes were currently watching from above, but to be on the safe side, the ship's cloaking device would be engaged.

When we exited the hall, Pinut was waiting outside for Ricson, and they began walking together, arm in arm. They seemed like a very happy couple. I must admit, it pained me to see such happiness when you were imprisoned on the Scynthian world. I cursed Thuric and his brother, Orric, for taking you, and I knew I would stop at nothing until you were safe with me again. But would you even want me?

After Thuric told me of your abduction, which I still hope, more than I've hoped anything, is not true, my fear of your rejection had returned. Was I being too presumptuous thinking that you had feelings for me and that we could be together? What if we were finally reconnected and back safely on Earth, only for you to reject and scorn me? Had I not abandoned you in that cabin, all alone in the woods, leaving you to be taken by aliens? The fear stilled me, and I had the momentary thought that perhaps it would have just been better if I had simply moved on with my life and stopped pining over you. Perhaps I should have given up hope of ever having a life with you and let the universe push me in whatever direction it chose. It would have been the easier choice, but I took the path that my heart chose, and now you're a prisoner of the

Scynthians. It's my fault, but I still love you, and though that love has never been substantiated, it has never been truer.

I know I can't give up, not until every last option has been exhausted. I have to continue putting all of my time and effort into finding you and returning home to Earth, otherwise I won't be able to live with myself.

I was pulled from my thoughts by Rengar, whose serious demeanor from the meeting had been replaced by a much jollier mood. He walked between Demtrius and me, throwing an arm around each of our shoulders, with Grissly trailing close behind him.

"What a great way to start the day!" he said. "I think this will be the best Tzulamay we have ever had!"

There was enough of a gap in front of and behind us, allowing for some privacy to speak openly with each other. Alexitus, Nepalen, and Dolvin led the way to the water, while most of the chiefs and chieftains stayed in the rear of the group with Waulf. The Skudlandic chieftain was saying something to the rest of the Mercerians, but I was unable to make out what it was.

"You'll be even happier once you see the gifts we have waiting for you," Demtrius replied.

"An excellent day!" Rengar exclaimed. He then looked down at me, "Jaxon, you were quiet during the meeting."

"It wasn't really my place to have any input," I said, "but I think you made a good choice. The Dotarans will prove to be valuable allies, and you can be sure that their motives are just."

"I never doubted them," he replied, "but, unfortunately, I cannot say the same for some of my chieftains."

"Indeed," Demtrius commented. "Jaxon and I stumbled upon the guards outside our dwelling this morning."

"A measure that may not have been needed, but I hope you understand it was only for your protection," Rengar explained.

"I do understand," said Demtrius, "and I trust your judgment."

"It is sad, really," said Rengar, "so many Mercerians preach about their strength and courageousness, but, in the face of change, of the new and unknown, they show only fear. Fear is what truly threatens society. It breeds stagnation, dilutes reason, and provokes irrational thoughts and behaviors. This is why I like to keep an open mind, and learn all I can about the world around me. Knowledge helps to overcome fear; knowledge is indisputably powerful, so long as one knows how to use it."

"It isn't hard to see why you're the leader of your people," I told him with a smile.

"Thank you for your kind words, Jaxon, but it was not my wits that won me this title, only the luck of a good birth," he laughed. "I just try to be the leader I would want and hope that it is enough for my people." He shot a glance behind us at Waulf and his group of followers, "Alas, there will always be those who cannot look past themselves to see the bigger picture. They threaten everything that our ancestors worked to achieve, and that is all too real and dangerous."

The site of the Dotaran ships surfacing hushed the group's conversations. The three flyers had been submerged underwater, and a small buoy had marked the position of each of them. Crispin had shined some sort of portable laser beam at these buoys, which I could only assume was to signal Gilpin down below somehow, for moments later we all watched as the water began churning and bubbling, and the flyers rose to the surface. They were completely cloaked, however, so when the Pothos' hatch opened, the hull seemed to appear out of nowhere, awing the crowd of spectators.

We proceeded over the ice toward a flat clearing just behind us. There, Gilpin began unloading the cargo.

First came the aforementioned items; three tons of Dotaran steel, as well as three more solar-powered ski-cycles. In addition, the Dotarans were able to provide a sled full of hand-crank flashlights, pen-sized lasers easily capable of cutting through the Dotaran steel, and textbooks of varying concentrations. The textbooks were all translated into Tatoran by a computer aboard the Iccaryn; it was specially calibrated by scanning different Tatoran manuscripts until the entire written language was identified. The writing was very elegant and meticulous, as many of the characters were derived from the many plants and animals unique to the planet. It was a complicated language, as each character represented a word or phrase, rather than a single letter. The print is read from top to bottom, starting on the top left of the page reading downward, and then resuming at the top one space to the right, and it was all completely indecipherable to me.

Demtrius told me that the books detailed the advanced agricultural techniques developed by the Dotarans, as well as several disciplines of mathematics, physics, environmental science, fluid dynamics, medicine and surgery, government and military, psychology, sociology, philosophy, etc. With this information, the Mercerians could become well-armed against both nature and other natives; that is, once they learned how to utilize the information, but that would come in a matter of time.

Personally, I didn't think it was wise to provide them with so much valuable information that would have taken them decades, if not centuries, to discover on their own. What if they weren't ready for this information? Who could foresee the potential repercussions? Indeed, that is the exact reason that the Federation in Star Trek had the Prime Directive. I knew Rengar could be trusted with such information, but I couldn't say the same for most of the other Tatorans I had come across on this planet. I shuddered to think how the Ruby clan, or Amentus, would use this knowledge. As a human I knew all too well what an aggressive species could do with science and technology. In the end, I had somewhat convinced myself that no harm would come from it that wouldn't have eventually occurred anyway. Plus, the Scynthians had provided other types of aid and technology much earlier in Tatoran history, and that had benefitted the Tatorans greatly, so perhaps this would too.

Demtrius took some time to explain how to use the lasers, showing them how to adjust the intensity of the beam. On the low setting, the laser was harmless, and could be used for signaling like Crispin had just done minutes before. On the medium setting, the beam could start fires and roast flesh, while on the highest setting it could cut clean through Dotaran steel like a knife through butter. It was a formidable weapon, and I had already obtained one for myself to go along with my lucky Zippo and my new sword made of the blue-tinted Dotaran steel.

One of the last gifts was a piece of defensive equipment for the Mercerians. It was nicknamed 'the Equalizer' by the Dotarans, and in essence was an extremely powerful mattertron that could be installed in Finnis to protect the entire city. If any objects came from above, the Equalizer would capture the objects and redirect them elsewhere, saving the city from possible destruction, like if the Scynthians sent down drones or missiles. "This should be installed straight away," said Demtrius. "It is good for one use, and then will take time to recharge."

The final gift from the Dotarans was their most coveted; their aquaponics system. They possessed a fraction of their original system from the Aramis, and were now splitting that with the Mercerians. At present, the system was not up and running, so no food could be harvested anytime soon, but it would still help both the Mercerians and the Dotarans in the long run.

Out of the flyer came a third sled containing several solar panels and lighting fixtures. After this sled came what appeared to be a large, metal coffin. Inside were just over two dozen iccythas, the red fish covered in blue dots from Dotara that acted as one half of the aquaponics system, as well as hundreds of seeds for special Dotaran plants that acted as the second half of the system. The metal coffin kept them safely frozen in cryogenic suspension, even the iccythas, as the Dotaran fish had the convenient ability to freeze entirely without dying immediately. Months, even years, could go by while it remained in this cryogenic state, and upon thawing the iccythas would flop to life as if no time had transpired. It reminded me a lot of an Earth frog with a similar ability, allowing it to freeze during the winter months and thaw out in the spring. Evolution surely was an exceptional process.

"You will need to create a structure to house the aquaponics system as soon as possible," Demtrius told them. "The cryogenic chamber that keeps them frozen will have enough energy to last one Tatoran month, but the seeds need to be germinated immediately. We have provided you with many different plant species, but mainly the starchy and fiber-filled ningwa and the thorny, cactus-like socra, which produces a thick, nutritious milk full of vitamins and probiotics. These are all we can offer you, so put them to good use. I suggest creating an underground facility where you can more easily control the climate."

"But if we are underground," asked Grissly, "how would we grow them without any light?"

"You will use artificial light to simulate the sun," Demtrius replied. "Do not worry; I will have advisors sent here to help educate you in the use and understanding of all you see before you."

"My people won't forget the kindness of your gifts," said Rengar. "In time, I know they will come to appreciate what you are doing for us here today."

"And I thank you in advance for the assistance you have promised us," Demtrius replied, bowing slightly. "We can only hope that we have come close to compensating you for it."

"You can rest assured of that," Rengar answered.

Pleased with his new acquisitions, Rengar dispatched three Mercerians to transport the cryogenic chamber and the three sleds full of gifts into the city, which they did with ease by using the fast and powerful ski-cycles.

"We should head back into the city now," said Rengar. "The Fealty ceremony will begin shortly."

# Chapter Twenty-Four
# Tzulamay

Sixteen Mercerian youths lined up at the side of the half-shelled dome upon the main stage in Finnis, all waiting their turn to pledge fealty to Rengar and to the chief or chieftain of whatever settlement they came from. Only these future warriors were usually required to make the pledge, as they were the ones fighting to protect their land and their leaders. Now, however, the Dotarans would make a similar pledge, but instead of pledging to fight for them, they would pledge to never take up arms against them, and Rengar was expected to make the same pledge.

In this group of sixteen, all of whom had received their gender assignments within the past Tatoran year, there were only males.

"At Tzulamay," Ricson told me, "we only induct the young males. The females do have their opportunities to join the ranks, but that is done at a later time once they've grown into their gender role more. Our leaders do not like to waste training on those who may not pan out."

As I've told you before, all Tatoran cubs are born genderless, and they do not begin to grow reproductive organs until they hit puberty; well, most of them anyway. The ones who develop into males typically become a bit larger and stronger with burly manes of fur, while those who develop into females are usually the assumed nurturers and have shorter, better groomed fur. By means of this, the males are generally favored to be warriors, and therefore make up the grand majority of any Tatoran military. It is not unheard of to have a female soldier, and you can be sure that any such females would be elite warriors; otherwise they'd never have been accepted into the ranks in the first place.

There is, of course, the third Tatoran gender, or rather the gender-neutral Tatorans, who, even after puberty, do not develop reproductive organs. These irregular Tatorans have difficulty living within society and tend to isolate themselves due to social differences in attitude, intellect, and what they value. I remember the gender-neutral Tatorans in the lofted city of Aanthora. They were taller and lankier than the average Tatoran, and greatly feared Jotus' more aggressive and commanding personality. They were also the city's most intellectual citizens, as is usually the case with the gender-neutrals.

I think it's important to note that male, female, and gender-neutral, in this sense, refer strictly to the reproductive organs of a person, not in how they identify or behave. Clearly, we humans of Earth are a bit different.

The Mercerian youths climbed the steps to the stage, coming to its center, where they stood shoulder to shoulder and faced their leaders. Rengar, along with Waulf, Grissly, and the other chiefs and chieftains of the land sat in wooden chairs just inside the half-shelled dome. One at a time, each of the youths stepped forward, drew their blue-tinted swords, presented them hilt-first to their respected leader, and swore their oaths of fealty. The chieftain would take the sword and lay its sharp edge upon the youth's neck, but then withdraw the blade and accept the oath. This process was then repeated with Rengar, their High Chieftain. The formal display signified that each Mercerian youth was putting their life in the hands of their superior, and bound them to life-long loyalty and allegiance. In return, their pledge-master was responsible for ensuring their safety and well-being. By also pledging to Rengar, it assured that no chieftain could try to usurp his position by force. Mercerians had a high reputation for keeping their word, and the oath-swearing was just another example of this; there were few and far between who would ever break their solemn vows.

The ceremony did not take long, and then the sworn youths stood side to side facing their rulers again. Rengar, along with the other Mercerian chieftains, rose from their seats and each placed a closed fist to their chest. The youths repeated the gesture, and then walked off the stage in single file, while

Rengar and his subordinates again took their seats.

Next it was our turn, or rather the Dotarans' turn, to make their oaths. Only the four captains were required to do so, while Crispin, Thristin, and I stood close by in the crowd. Gilpin still waited aboard the Pothos, which he had resubmerged under water.

Demtrius, Alexitus, Nepalen, and Dolvin climbed the steps to the stage and stood before the Mercerian rulers. Demtrius held his utility device to translate for his co-captains, and adjusted the volume so that the entire crowd could hear them speak.

Demtrius had prepared their oath on the walk back into Finnis from the shoreline, and now they would each recite it in unison.

"We hereby declare, on oath in front of all to see, that no Dotaran shall interfere with or attempt any malicious acts against our new friends, the Mercerians. We swear to honor the truce established here this morning, and shall assist you when possible in reasonable, peaceful endeavors, while excluding any acts of war and other immoral actions. May this relationship be honest and ongoing, and benefit both parties on the basis of friendship and common interest."

At the conclusion of their oath, they bowed to the Mercerian leaders, and then stood waiting for Rengar to make his. The High Chieftain rose to an absolutely silent crowd, all waiting to hear him utter these historic words.

"By the authority of Mercer," Rengar started, "I hereby proclaim the Dotarans as allies, and they will be treated with the dignity, honor, and respect that we afford our allies."

In retrospect, it was very plain, even anti-climactic.

"Now," he continued, "let us celebrate this newly formed alliance!"

Thus ended the fealty ceremony.

It was only mid-morning by this time, and the Unification ceremony wouldn't begin until later in the afternoon. In the meantime, as Ricson had previously informed me, the city was in full celebration. Although dwarfed in comparison, the style and diversity of the different events reminded me of the annually-held People's Fair at the base of

Mount Xar'roc, where Demtrius and I had once fought in the infamous Pit of the Gyx. These festivities, however, weren't going to end with my life hanging in the balance. At least I hoped not.

I was actually having quite a good time. I had come to really enjoy the fun and festive spirit of the Tatorans. Demtrius, too, seemed to be enjoying himself, as well as Crispin, Thristin, and even Dolvin. Nepalen and Alexitus, as usual, were all serious, but I didn't let that detract from my enjoyment. Presently, I sat in one of the beverage tents with Demtrius, Ricson, and Pinut, listening to Demtrius discussing the different strategies of attack and defense in cassa with Pinut, who was familiar with the popular board game.

"Care to test your strategy?" she asked Demtrius, who gladly accepted the offer. Soon they were set up at a nearby cassa table preparing their pieces.

Meanwhile, Crispin and Thristin had somehow managed to befriend a group of young cubs, who now amused themselves by teaching the Dotaran brothers one of their signature Mercerian dances. Dolvin, with a mug full of grogg, attempted to join in on this dance, but had neither the stability nor coordination to keep up, and eventually fell backwards, spilling his drink all over himself. It provoked a lot of laughter from everyone watching, and I dare say I even saw a smirk creep onto Nepalen's face, though he was quick to hide the sign of pleasure.

Demtrius and Pinut had been playing for a few minutes now. I was never much good when it came to games of strategy like this, but, judging by the number of pieces that remained, it looked as if Demtrius had the advantage. He made his moves thoughtfully and with confidence, but Pinut always had a quick counter move, though Demtrius continued to take her pieces from the field. Pinut didn't seemed worried; she just continued with her strategy patiently, capitalizing on moves when she could, but, on the whole, playing more defense than offense. Compared to other cassa games I had witnessed, theirs was progressing rather quickly.

"Who do you think will win?" Ricson asked.

"Demtrius appears to have more pieces," I replied.

"I wouldn't underestimate Pinut's skill level," said Ricson. "This is all part of her strategy."

"Would you like to place a wager on that?" I asked good-naturedly, but we were interrupted before sealing the deal.

Rengar and Grissly, unannounced, came bursting through the tent flaps, sloshing and spilling the drinks in their hands, causing everyone inside to stop and stare. They each threw an arm around the other's neck and clasped the shoulder, then suddenly broke out into song.

"They're drunk!" Ricson exclaimed in disbelief.

"They're enjoying themselves," I remarked.

Others quickly joined in, and soon our tent and the adjacent tents were filled with singing Mercerians. It was very different from any type of singing on Earth, far more guttural and emotional, consisting of words mixed with sounds, each complimenting the other to form what I thought to be an elegant yet powerful song.

"This is one of the few days out of the year that we are permitted to consume the ardent spirits," Ricson explained, "but always in moderation, always."

"They have much to celebrate," I replied.

"He had better sober up by my unification," Ricson said worriedly. "He's supposed to lead the ceremony!"

The tune was over shortly, ending in a happy cheer. Rengar and Grissly bowed to the crowd and then found their way over to where we were sitting. Demtrius and Pinut resumed their cassa match.

"Jaxon!" Rengar cheered, "I trust you are having a good time?" I went to respond, but Rengar just continued on, "Please, you must come with me to see Grissly's wonderful new invention!"

"What is it?" I asked, but Rengar and Grissly had already moved on to Demtrius' table, greeting him with the same enthusiasm.

I turned to Ricson for an explanation, but he just shrugged his shoulders. "Not a clue, but I would sure like to find out."

"What was he just saying to you?" Alexitus asked from

the other side of the cassa table. I was getting the notion that he was somewhat paranoid or jealous, or both.

"I guess he wants to show us something," I responded.

Rengar was back in front of me, "Come, come! You will not want to miss this! All of you, this way!"

Most of the tent's occupants began making their way outside to the street, even the Dotarans, but I stayed behind with Ricson since Demtrius and Pinut were still playing their game.

"We'll be right outside waiting for you," said Crispin.

Demtrius looked up from his game just in time to see his comrades walking out of the tent "We'll have to finish our game after we see whatever Rengar has to show us," he said.

"No need," said Pinut, as she moved a seemingly insignificant piece to a forward position. "I think we are done here."

Demtrius looked down at the game board, as did the rest of us. Demtrius gasped, seeing the weight of Pinut's last move. It was a subtle blow, but Demtrius was beat. Not yet, exactly, but she had enticed him into a trap that, no matter what he tried, could only lead to his defeat.

He closed his dropped jaw and replaced his shock with a smirk. "A few more moves and I would have had you defeated," he said happily. "That was excellent!"

The four of us laughed, and then exited the tent to see what Grissly had invented.

Outside, we met an attentive, awe-struck crowd staring up at something over our heads. I looked up, following their gaze, and was surprised to see a crudely-designed hot air balloon floating just above. It had a wooden platform suspended below it that was anchored to the roof of the hall. The balloon itself was spherical and made out of purple silk, with the stitch seams sealed by some sort of resin. On its bottom was an opening skirted with more silk, where fuel was hand-fed into a small furnace that directed the hot air into the interior of the balloon. The entire thing was enormous, spanning at least forty yards in diameter, and on one side of the balloon was the Mercerian flag, a white picture of a gyx, the same image on many of the purple flags and banners that filled the streets and windows.

"I've never seen anything like it!" roared a warrior.

"It's amazing!" proclaimed another. "How do they get it to stay floating in the air like that?"

Ricson, too, stood in disbelief, awed by the balloon. "Never did I think my eyes would see something like this," he said, his reaction changing from surprise to joy. He turned to Demtrius, "It seems I won't need that ride in your flyer after all!"

Rengar and Grissly stood on the platform, where they worked the furnace, feeding hot air inside the skirt of the balloon to give it buoyancy. Rengar saw us standing in the crowd and motioned for us to join him. Ricson and Pinut took us to the rear of the hall and up a set of steps to the roof of the building. As we walked, I saw Waulf and several other Mercerians enter a building further down the main avenue, closing the door behind themselves, but at the time I thought nothing of it.

I must admit, I was surprised Grissly could come up with such a monumental invention. I had assumed he was a great warrior because of his size, but never expected that his brains matched his brawn. Now I could see where Pinut got her exceptional reasoning skills from.

"Isn't it magnificent?" boomed Rengar.

"It surely is something," I replied. I then turned to Grissly, "How did you come up with the design?"

"I got the initial idea while observing the unique Aanthoran funeral practice of sending off the deceased's ashes in a small, candle-lit paper lantern," Grissly explained. "In my younger years I used to do a lot of travelling. My father, Kodak, thought it would be good for me to learn about the other clans' cultures. It was then that I met our mutual friend, Jotus, while I was visiting Aanthora. He had lost his tzulara, Valadine, and I met him after the funeral ritual in one of the local taverns. He was understandably distraught and depressed, so I bought him a drink. A good Tatoran that Jotus was. It really was terrible about his tzulara." Grissly continued, "Anyway, I saw the paper lanterns and how they took to the sky with ease. I figured that a larger design would function similarly, so I began to find all of the materials that I needed to start construction. My first design was made out of sail cloth lined with paper on the inside, but it was far too heavy and required a lot of fuel to stay afloat for a relatively short amount of time."

"That's when Grissly came to me," Rengar interjected. "He needed silk for the balloon's new design, and that is a very difficult material to come by this far north."

"It took us a while to acquire everything I needed," Grissly continued, "and even longer to build the contraption and test it, but now we shall be lords of the sky once again!"

"Again?" I asked.

"We may not have your fancy flyers," Rengar replied, "but long ago, my great ancestor, Rarald, flew atop the last surviving gyx. It is said that he was somehow bonded to the creature, and they were able to finally unite the warring Mercerian tribes under one banner, the same banner we use today."

"That's incredible," I thought, finding it hard to believe at first, but after everything else I had seen and learned, I lost all doubt. And then it struck me that, if dragons once roamed the Tatoran skies, perhaps the legends on Earth held some truth after all. A man can only imagine.

"Come, join us on the platform," said Rengar. "The balloon is almost ready for lift off!"

Around the edge of the platform was a small rack filled with bricks of dried rapt dung. Rapt dung is very rich in methane, and, when dried out, burns exceptionally well. Like on Earth, many Tatoran farmers on the great plains, and other areas scarce in woodlands, use dung from various animals for heat and cooking. This animal dung, I should add, if left to dry out in the fields for too long, will make the grazing land unpalatable to the livestock, so collecting the dung has an excellent dual effect for the Tatorans, but again I digress.

Demtrius and I stepped onto the platform, which had a thin railing about neck-high, or waist-high for Rengar and Grissly, and was spacious enough for the four of us to stand in comfortably. Ricson and Pinut stayed on the roof, and Ricson unfastened one of the tethers that secured the balloon to the building. The platform moved slightly under our feet as it gently lifted off the ground. There was an audible gasp from the Mercerian spectators below, who were witnessing the flight of this break-through invention for the first time. They must have been acutely aware that they now would be distinctly set apart from their Tatoran counterparts with a commanding aerial advantage. Isolated all alone up in the wintry north kept them safe enough, but they would now have the means to travel vast distances in a comparably short amount of time. That is, once Grissly and Rengar refined their design. The balloon could also be used for military purposes of course, but, luckily for the mainland Tatorans, the Mercerians cherished peace and would not cause trouble unless provoked.

Grissly added more fuel to the furnace. The balloon continued to rise higher and higher, bringing us well over a hundred feet into the air. The Mercerians in the streets below kept growing smaller until they were nothing but blurry figures moving about on the distant ground. The picturesque view of the surrounding landscape was incredible, and the viewable distance only increased as we continued to rise even higher. A forest of thehnwood trees stretched for miles inland, with their red-haired trunks vivid among the green canopies and snow-covered ground. Near the center of the island-continent's interior was a large plateau, but even at our current height I couldn't see to its top.

I noticed a single rope leading from the balloon that tethered us to the ground, stretching several hundred feet now, and soon we would be at its length.

"Not going far, are we?" I asked, indicating the lengthy rope.

"Not if we plan on making it to the Unification ceremony," Grissly replied. "Unfortunately, I have not yet been able to figure out a way to control the balloon's descent, and steering is all but impossible save for relying on the prevailing winds. Through trial and error, I have been able to determine that the wind generally blows in different directions depending on the altitude, so this helps, but it still leaves us with the problem of how to descend quicker. So, for now at least, we can only go as far as the rope will allow."

"You'll figure it out soon enough," Rengar commented. "Of that I am sure. Look at what you have done so far. I can see halfway to Weins from here!"

It wasn't quite that far, but the distance was still considerable.

Thinking of the hot air balloons I had seen and ridden in when I was younger, I turned to Grissly, "What about a cap?"

"A cap?" Grissly repeated. "What exactly do you mean?"

I didn't want to take away from his proud moment, so I didn't mention the fact that balloons like this had been around for many decades on Earth. Instead, I simply replied, "At the top of the balloons, you could place a cap, or vent, which could then be opened via pull cord to allow the hot air out, and, in return, allow you to descend."

"A cap!" Grissly suddenly exclaimed. "Of course! It will take some time to develop the proper air-tight seal for the cap and a harness to help hold it all in place, but that is the answer. A cap; so simple!"

We were now at the extent of the rope. The basket shifted under the new tension, but remained level.

"Now, for the real reason I brought you both up here," said Rengar, his jolly demeanor replaced by a more serious one.

Demtrius and I looked at one another, and then back to Rengar. He turned to look out over the landscape, placing his hands on the railing. "Times are changing rapidly, and, after much consideration, I think the time has finally come for me and my people to better develop our relationships with our Tatoran counterparts on the lower continent. With the new snow machines and supplies that you've provided us with, it will be much more feasible to travel to the next People's Fair. We may not have much to offer, but our meer fur is highly valued, our primadons provide excellent hunting sport, and palagus meat is a rare delicacy south of the Okala Mountains.

"That's great," I said. "What prompted such a bold decision like this?"

Rengar gave us a warm smile, "I've recently learned

some of the potential benefits that come with having friends and allies." He then patted Grissly on the back, "And I know my people will represent us well in the games, which, hopefully, will garner some immediate respect from the other clans. Others may not be quick to admit it, but we Mercerians, as with most Tatorans, are very prideful people."

"And with good reason, too," Grissly added boastfully.

"Have you told them yet?" asked Demtrius, indicating the mass of blurry figures below us.

He was obviously curious of the Mercerians' response to such a shift, and so was I. Judging by the demeanor of the lesser chieftains during the peace talks, we both knew it most likely wouldn't sit well with the majority of the Mercerian citizens, especially so soon after forming an alliance with the Dotarans.

Rengar shot him a knowing look, "There will always be those who will continue to resist change, but I will not allow us to remain isolated any longer. I already plan to meet with each of the other clan leaders to begin trade negotiations. It will take time to develop reliable and trustworthy relationships with them, but, once I have done so, I will strive to advocate on your behalf."

Demtrius and I were surprised by Rengar's unexpected announcement, and then Demtrius responded, "We thank you for your support and assistance. Please, let me know if there is anything else we can do for you."

Rengar suddenly perked up, "Well, it is not all set in stone yet. First, you must complete your Tzulamay quest."

"Ah, yes," said Grissly. "My favorite part of Tzulamay; the quest for the sacred herb."

"That is the quest?" I asked. "To find an herb?"

"The yume herb is not just any plant," Rengar explained. "It is a most sacred herb that allows us to connect body, mind, and spirit. It can only be found during the midst of our harsh winters atop Mercer's great plateau, where it grows from the bark of the mystical Dracari tree. It only emerges at night, and shines with ever-changing colored lights."

A unique plant, to say the least.

"You will leave tonight, immediately following the Unification ceremony, and you must return to us with the yume before its luminescence diminishes completely, which only gives you a few days after it is harvested. Complete this task and our truce will be sealed," he proclaimed. "And, as promised, we will assist you with procuring nourishment for your people.

"We understand," said Demtrius, "and thank you for the opportunity."

Rengar nodded, "I wish you luck."

"We should begin our descent now if we wish to make it in time for the Unification ceremony," said Grissly. "The sun is already getting low in the sky.

"Very well," said Rengar, cheerfully, "begin the descent! We have a ceremony to attend, and it's not every day that one's own son is to be mated!"

# Chapter Twenty-Five
# The Unification Ceremony

The Unification ceremony started at the beginning of dusk. We sat on a wide crag that jutted out into the sea, giving us an excellent view of the sun setting over the water. It was the middle of winter, so no flowers decorated the scene, and everyone was bundled up in preparation for the harsh night time cold that was already beginning to envelope the land. The Mercerians, having thick coats of fur, generally did not need much, if any, clothing, but even they were unable to deal with the extreme cold of the far north's winter. The Dotarans and I, however, wore our skin-tight jumpsuits and hooded windbreakers, which were somehow more than sufficient to keep us warm.

Almost everyone was in attendance, sitting on benches made from the trunks of felled thehnwood trees, while five couples stood at the head of the crowd on the tip of the crag, silhouetted against the dying sun. To my immediate left sat Demtrius, followed by Crispin, Thristin, Dolvin, Nepalen, and finally Alexitus. We sat with Rengar and Grissly on the bench closest to the couples.

Among the couples were Ricson and Pinut, who faced one another, hand in hand. They looked so happy, and again I found myself saddened by it. I brushed it off quickly though; I needed to be happy for them.

A strong wind blew from the west, biting at my exposed face. It was bitter cold and the winter sun was falling quickly, but Rengar assured us that the proceedings would only take a short time.

"The ceremony starts once the bottom edge of the sun falls below the horizon," he had said, "and is over by the time it is done setting."

Presently, Rengar and Sverna walked up to the first couple and presented them with two items; Rengar offered a golden chalice inlaid with small purple amethysts and Sverna offered a glass vase of pink wine, which I later learned was the expensive Miringa wine often enjoyed by the wealthy and powerful. The first couple took the chalice and the vase, and then thanked their High Chieftain. Rengar and Sverna returned to their seats, and we waited for the sun to fall into position.

No priest or person of authority stood by to conduct the ceremony. Rather, it was conducted by the couples themselves, as they passed around the chalice and pledged themselves to their life-partner.

It's interesting to note that the Mercerians, like the Tatorans of the lower continent, do not have any priests or organized sects of worship. Like all Tatorans, they recognize the Scynthians as real beings, but have never come to worship them as gods like other clans have. Even before the Scynthians visited their world, they didn't practice a religion of any kind. Instead, the Mercerians, being very family-oriented, pay homage and respect to their ancestors. They believe their deceased loved ones watch over them, and they will generally try to honor their family's memory by being the best Mercerians they can possibly be. They spend their days knowing that they will only live once, and this has had an interesting effect on how their civilization, isolated from the other nations, has developed. Their lack of religion has freed them to live their lives the way they see fit, and, over time, allowed them to grow into what I believe is one of the more compassionate and rational cultures on the planet.

Despite their lack of organized religion, they have developed higher standards of morality and codes of honor. They make rational decisions based on logic and reason, on facts and observations, rather than blind faith and superstition. They believe in what they can see, taste, touch, smell, and hear. One might think their atheistic culture would hinder their ability to become better individuals, but contrary to that belief, having no religion provided them with a much better foundation to build upon, for what else is there than what we have now? The Mercerians believe in hard work and patience, and it is incredibly hard to find one who is not willing to help another in need. They are a simple people; a fulfilled people; a happy people.

I watched with interest as each mate bit their companion's index finger, drawing blood with their sharp fangs, and then directed the blood drops into the chalice. Wine was then added to the golden cup and was held up high by the couple, at which point they each recited the same phrase. It was hard to hear them over the gusts of wind, but after the third couple performed the ritual I was able to piece it together. It went something like, "Under the eyes of my ancestors, and in front of all witnesses, I hereby pledge to honor, cherish, love, and protect you from now through eternity. As our blood mixes and becomes one, so shall we, in body and in mind. If ever we are separated, may no distance be too far and no night too dark; I will find you, as I cannot live without my other half."

With that, they would each drink from the chalice in turn until it was empty. The golden cup was then passed to the next couple for the short ritual to be repeated, and the couple would walk down the aisle together to the cheer of the large audience, and then prepare for their journey to retrieve the sacred herb.

Rengar leaned over to me, "The mixing of the blood is not just a symbolic unification; it is a biological unification as well."

"How so?" I asked.

"Every being, whether we are talking about Tatorans or Dotarans, primadons or meer, rapt or palagus, we all produce our own unique scent," Rengar explained. "Even you, Jaxon, although I'm not sure if your nose can identify it. Anyway, as we age, our scents change very little, save for a few select times during our lives. Puberty, of course, when we receive our gender assignments, is one of those times, but love is also a trigger for the scent to change. It is hard to explain further, but new life-mates will soon begin to develop the same scent as one another, adding to their overall identity. A tzulara or tzulamor shall always be able to find their mate then. In addition, the couple's new scent acts as a signal to others, so that one doesn't unintentionally court the mate of another."

"That is all very interesting," I said, thinking that it sounded like super pheromones, "but what does that have to do with mixing and drinking of the blood?"

"Drinking their companion's blood quickens the re-scenting process," he replied, and then winked, nudging me with his elbow. "At least that is what most believe. Me, I am not so sure of this, but it is part of our species' sacred Tzulamay ritual, and I would be hard-pressed to alter such a tradition. At any rate, it's well worth it for the miringa wine."

He smiled, and so too did I. The wine, after all, was quite pleasant.

Now it was Ricson and Pinut's turn with the chalice, which sparkled purple as it was passed to them and was struck by the sun. It was now almost below the horizon, but we still had some time before it would be completely out of sight.

The happy couple added their blood to the chalice and then poured in some of the pink wine. As the four couples before them had, they raised the cup high, uttered the same phrases, and took turns finishing the cup's contents. Everyone's attention was on them, watching them in the fading light. My attention was broken by someone clearing their throat loudly. I turned, seeing Waulf standing in the aisle between the benches with his arms crossed, his face betraying no emotion. He then stood aside, revealing his young mate and his son, Scard, walking up the aisle together.

"We have time for one more couple, eh?" asked Waulf, speaking to no one in particular, and as more of a statement than a question. He then waited for Grissly to make room for him on the end of the bench.

With all eyes now on them, Scard and the young Mercerian female continued up the aisle toward the other couples. It must have been extremely awkward for them, as barely a Tatoran half-month had passed since she sat beside Waulf as his soon-to-be tzulara. To be fair, Scard and the female must have been roughly the same age, and Waulf had already been through two other tzularas before her.

"Well, this is unexpected," Rengar remarked, although I didn't really sense that he found it unexpected at all.

"Bored of Jasala already?" asked Grissly.

Waulf huffed. "Found the two of them together in the skud swamp," he shook his head. "So be it, though. She was a flavorless little sprite anyhow. Maybe Scard will get more out of her than I did."

"I'm surprised you're so calm and understanding," Grissly replied. "It's not in your usual fashion to forgive so easily."

"He is my only son, so what else am I to do? Punish the girl and earn his contempt and loathing?" asked Waulf. "I'll find another mate soon enough anyway," he winked.

"Of that, I have no doubt," said Grissly.

They both smiled. It was rare to see them getting along, but Tzulamay has its effects on everyone I guess.

Scard and Jasala were finishing the ritual now, just as the final sliver of sun dipped below the horizon. In the changing light, both Scard and Jasala seemed to glow with happiness.

Rengar and Sverna stood to retrieve the vase and chalice from the new couple. Scard and Jasala bowed to them, and then exited down the aisle following the other couples, who had already disappeared into the gathering darkness. They were on their own now, about to complete their common quest.

And soon the Dotarans and I would be going on that same journey.

# Interlogue Three
# Ryane's Doctor

How long Ryane remained a captive on Scynthia, she hadn't the faintest clue. Her days blurred together, distinguished only by the varying forms of torture she was subjected to day after day. Her figure grew slim and emaciated, as she refused to eat the human meat provided to her, and therefore ate very little. Scars and burns covered her body by the afternoons, only to be repaired by the experienced hand of Illoran for the next day's session.

With help from the enhancement serum, Ryane had refused Illoran's aid for as long as she could, but, fatigued as she was and covered with afflictions, she had no choice but to succumb to the physician's will eventually. She had regressed to fainting spells, and during one of these spells the well-intentioned Illoran had commenced the much-needed treatment.

When Ryane awoke on her mat, it took her a few seconds to fully realize where she was, and, strangely, she felt much better than she had of late. It was then that she noticed the intravenous line running from her arm to an elevated bag filled with a murky-gray solution, and several other wires connected to her that projected her vitals on a small computer screen. Impulsively, she began ripping the wires from her body, and finally came to the intravenous. With a sudden jerk, she removed it, spraying a thick stream of blood about the room.

As she worked to free herself from the wires and tubes, Illoran, having been in an adjacent room where he monitored Ryane's vitals, came running in to stop her from doing any more damage. *Salama'an is doing a good enough job of that as it is,* he thought to himself bitterly as he raced into the room.

When he approached his unruly patient, she began berating him with shouts and insults, which, to his best efforts, he ignored.

"Don't touch me," Ryane screamed, taking a swipe at Illoran's webbed hands as he attempted to re-insert the intravenous needle. "Get those things away from me!"

Hitherto, Ryane had been far too weak to protest so vehemently, but now, having regained some of her strength, she backed against the wall, wielding the needle threateningly toward the one responsible for her daily recoveries.

To his credit, Illoran remained calm and unperturbed, trying to think how he would feel if their roles had been reversed, but he was unable to rationalize the young Earth female's behavior. *I just don't understand it,* he thought to himself. *I am only trying to help her. Why doesn't she see that?*

Meanwhile, and almost unbeknownst to Ryane, her arm had continued to bleed from where she had ripped out the intravenous, spurting streams of blood as she pumped her arms in front of herself trying to ward off the Scynthian doctor. The warm, viscous liquid dripped down her elbow, covering her sleeping mat in the red, sticky substance. Illoran saw this, and, presently, waited for her to lose consciousness from the blood loss; she would be much less difficult to approach then.

Ryane continued to scream obscenities at the Scynthian doctor, her heart beating rapidly, but she soon began to grow light-headed and the room began to tilt. She paused for a moment, trying to regain her composure, but the blood loss was too much. A moment later, she collapsed in a pool of her own blood. Then Illoran was finally able to resume her treatment.

The next time Ryane awoke, the physician, along with all his equipment, was gone. Ryane was slow to rise, still feeling the aches and pains of her ongoing torment. She was feeling slightly better than the day before, and correctly attributed it to the physician she had so indiscriminately berated earlier for all the crimes done to her by the Scynthians. Surely all that had happened to her was not his fault, and he had helped to abate some of the almost unbearable tortures she experienced, but he was still a Scynthian and was therefore guilty.

Lost in thought, she didn't notice the portal to the room open until the visitor was already through the doorway.

"Hello, my dear," said the skin-crawling voice of the insidious Salama'an, who carried with him a long, slender rod with two metal prongs on its end. "I hope you slept well, for I have a lot in store for you today."

He clicked a button on the rod's handle, and a jolt of blue electricity arced between the two prongs.

Days passed like this; Salama'an tearing her down in the morning and Illoran repairing her in the evening. At first, Ryane continued to refuse Illoran's attempts to aid her, so he commenced to treat her while she slept, filling the room with a gas akin to anesthesia that ensured she remained asleep and docile while he doctored her wounds. It didn't take much work to fix her physical injuries, as the Scynthians had long since perfected the art of medicine and Illoran was well versed in these medical practices. Her mental health was a much trickier puzzle though. One day, she screamed out of nowhere, clutching her chest in pain, yelling for Jaxon, but her chest was fine, though her blood pressure was alarmingly elevated and sweat poured from her body. Sometimes, there is only so much one's mind and body can take.

Using Ryane's DNA, he had synthesized new pieces of flesh, which, when placed over an afflicted area, adhered to the skin and would begin replacing damaged tissue. The process is somewhat like skin grafting, but rather than moving healthy tissue from one part of the body to another, the new genetically-engineered tissue acts as both bandage and antibiotic, and greatly increases the body's own natural regenerative properties. The flesh-bandage then assimilates into the skin tissue, and the wound, in most cases, is healed, so long as the infliction is a superficial wound. For deeper, more extensive injuries, the Scynthians have other healing tactics to utilize.

Using these flesh-bandages, Illoran systematically repaired Ryane's body of any scars, burns, cuts, etc. He had even inadvertently mended a scar on Ryane's hip that she had received years ago in a bicycle accident. When all was said and done, he was proud of his work, but still incredibly concerned for the mental well-being of his patient.

*If only she would just consent to treatment!* he thought, frustrated that he couldn't do more to help her.

Soon, however, Ryane begrudgingly came to trust her Scynthian physician, at least with her medical needs. After realizing that he was, in fact, there to help her heal, and had apparently been attending to her while she slept, she commenced to allow treatment; she didn't have much of a choice, and she would rather she was conscious for the process. It helped that, in all their interactions, Illoran was always very cordial with her, and treated her with dignity and respect. He would even bring her bits of non-meat foods to help supplement her diminished diet, and never failed to continuously apologize for her predicament. Deep down under the fog she was living in, no doubt a defense mechanism due to her circumstances, Illoran's kindness began to shake the cobwebs off long abandoned escape plans.

Illoran's earnest resolve to aid this surprisingly resilient human female was never stronger, especially after Orric, the rebel leader, had informed him of their upcoming plans.

"The Dotarans think they are so clever," said Orric one afternoon, recalling the recent attempt upon the Dotaran refugee camp that had in fact been a trap set just for the Scynthians, "but it is we who will have the final victory!"

"What do you have in mind?" asked Illoran, somewhat reluctant to hear what kind of fresh horrors his superior had planned.

"The Dotarans believe themselves safe and hidden," Orric explained, "and that may be well and true for most of them, but they have forgotten one crucial piece of information."

"And what would that be?" asked Illoran, waiting for Orric to finally divulge his plan.

"We have the male human's journals," Orric replied, "and in it he details that the Dotarans and he will be returning to Mercer to negotiate a peace with the white-furred Tatorans. The Dotaran leadership is sure to be there for such an event, of that we can be reasonably assured. The male human has unwittingly given us all we need to know to cripple the Dotarans once and for all."

Illoran demurred, "How do you know this isn't another one of their deceptions?"

"I don't," Orric replied simply, seemingly assured of his information, "but this time I am taking every precaution. Instead of sending in our valuable soldiers, we will use the expendable humans to do our bidding, alleviating ourselves of unnecessary risk."

Illoran thought about the idea for a second, and, though he found it immoral to use the humans in this capacity, he clearly understood the benefits that Orric described and could hardly object without raising suspicions as to his loyalty. The Scynthians are utilitarian by nature, and will do whatever is required to accomplish their goals.

"What I ask of you," Orric continued, "is for you to accompany the team as their veterinarian."

"You want me to do what?" asked Illoran, fairly discontent at the suggestion. Treating an unruly human was one thing, but descending to savage Tatora was completely outside of his realm of imagination.

"You are our best veterinarian," Orric commended him, "and your talents may be needed on the planet's surface."

*Did he not just say that we Scynthians are too valuable to risk?* Illoran thought to himself. *Now he wants to send me down there! What disrespect is this?*

Orric continued uninterrupted, "The defiant Dotarans and the human, Jaxon, have proven to be much more difficult than we originally anticipated, and we cannot allow for this opportunity to slip past us!"

"Then why not simply hit them with a large plasma-blast and be done with it?" asked an agitated Illoran, though he did well to conceal his agitation.

Illoran's suggestion might sound cold and unforgiving, but any reasonable Scynthian would have asked the same question given the circumstances, and with the rebellion that had so recently swept across Scynthia, Illoran did not want to give his Scynthian brethren any reason to look down on him. Not to mention, Illoran was none too thrilled about having to leave the comfort of Scynthia.

"I have instructed Salama'an to use the plasma-blast only as a last resort, if all of our other efforts fail," Orric replied.

"Why only then?" asked Illoran. "Wouldn't a plasma-blast be more affective and definitive? You said it yourself; we do not want them slipping away once again."

"If you must know," said Orric, "we do not yet know where the Dotaran filth are holding our captured brethren. Thuric is among them, and we cannot proceed with our other plans without him. He holds key information to our operations on Tatora, and replacing him now would set us back months, if not years. He is entirely indispensable to our cause."

"He is also your brother," Illoran pointed out, alluding to the fact that Orric actually cared for his blood-relative.

"That is irrelevant," Orric said, quickly dismissing the claim. "If he were not so valuable, his fate would be of little concern, but, unfortunately, that is not the case. In order to be profitable in our endeavors, we need him back on our side."

"So it will be a rescue mission, too, then?" asked Illoran.

Orric paused, realizing he may have divulged too much to this simple veterinarian. "You needn't concern yourself with the attack plans. Salama'an has everything under control. And, after all, you will be remaining on the ship in case your talents are needed."

"Very well," Illoran replied

"I think you'll be pleased to hear that I've assembled quite a force for this venture," said Orric, boasting now. "To fail will be all but inconceivable, especially with this lovely little device in hand." While he spoke, he had pulled a metal ring from his pocket and fingered its edge, admiring the object.

Illoran couldn't help but take the bait. "What is that?" he asked with curious interest.

"A new tool I've had the dissimulation engineers working on," Orric replied proudly. "We've had the technology for ages, but no one thought to down-size it for covert operations! Just think of all the possibilities!"

"That does sound like quite a contraption you have

there," said Illoran sincerely. "Would you care to demonstrate?"

"Of course," smiled Orric, as he proceeded to place the metal ring atop his head like a crown. As he removed his hands, a red beam of light shone from the ring, and then the device rose from his head autonomously and hovered there, like a red-glowing halo. The light beam then flashed down his body, and a moment later Orric's figure phased out of sight right before Illoran's eyes. It was incredible, and Illoran was unable to hide his astonishment.

Presently, Orric's figure phased into view again, and the device sunk back onto his head.

"Marvelous, isn't it?" he asked, removing the metal ring from his head and giving it to Illoran for a closer inspection.

"Incredible," Illoran agreed, and a plan was already formulating inside his mind. "It works for all light-wave frequencies?" he asked.

"Unfortunately, it does have its limitations," Orric admitted, "but it far exceeds anything else we have for covert operations. It won't be long before the engineers have created one that makes an individual completely undetectable, even to infrared and thermal images."

Illoran finished examining the cloaking ring, and then handed it back to Orric, who placed it safely within the pocket of his robe.

"So," said Orric, getting back on topic, "I am sure I can count on you to accompany Salama'an to the planet. I would be remiss if I neglected to include you in this endeavor."

In truth, Orric was merely placating Illoran, attempting to manipulate him into joining the mission, and Illoran was well aware of this. There were many other physicians on Scynthia of greater talent and value, so the fact that Illoran had been chosen proved that he was now considered expendable. Still an asset, so they would not kill him outright, but expendable nonetheless.

Mulling over this new bit of information, and the existence of Orric's cloaking ring, Illoran started to form a plan. He had always been sympathetic to the plight of humans, but he felt a strange intangible connection to his newest patient, the human Ryane, and Orric was unwittingly handing him the tools he needed to help her. In a single moment, Illoran knew, fully and completely, that he would go against everything he had ever been taught as a Scynthian, and he would risk everything he had worked for to set this plan into motion. He would get this human female out of harm's way, and then, if he survived, he would move on to all the other humans trapped on Scynthia. He just needed to get his hands on one of Orric's cloaking rings.

"Thank you for the offer," Illoran replied, finally responding to Orric. "It would be my pleasure."

"Excellent!" said Orric. "I shall inform Salama'an right away!"

# Chapter Twenty-Six
# From Dusk

It was difficult to make headway through the snow-covered thehnwood forest in the midst of the frigid Tatoran night. It was snowing now and, unfortunately, it did well to cover the tracks of our predecessors, so we were walking blind toward our destination for the most part. Demtrius was wise to begin marking trees with his simiole fluid, making sure that, even in the darkest of nights, we would easily be able to trace our path back the way we came.

At the end of the unification ceremony, Demtrius and I had explained the details of our strange quest to the rest of our group.

"This is ridiculous!" Nepalen complained. "We'll never be able to find our way in these conditions. Six days of darkness, and the snow drifts alone are over our heads already!"

"If the others can, then so can we," Demtrius replied patiently.

"But we are not them," Nepalen protested, "and we don't know this land like they do!"

"We just need to head east and find the plateau," Demtrius reassured him. "Once we reach the summit, the land will be flat for miles, so we will be able to see the glow from the plant with ease."

"This Rengar must be enjoying a splendid joke," Alexitus commented. "A quest through the bitter-cold and interminable dark, all for an herb. It is far too risky and a tremendous waste of our time."

"It is not a waste of time if it solidifies our new relationship with the Mercerians," said Demtrius.

"You continue to take them at their word," said Alexitus, "but of course you would. You, Jaxon, and Rengar had a nice private chat up in that balloon. You are not nearly cautious enough. Remember, the Tatorans want us dead, and these Mercerians are still Tatorans, no matter how isolated they are."

"I don't care if you trust them," said Demtrius. "We need them, so we have to work with them, and since they hold the leverage, we are, for the time being, at their mercy."

Alexitus grunted, Nepalen huffed, and I sighed, rolling my eyes at their incessant whining. I almost couldn't see how they had managed to achieve a captain's rank, but, then again, the Dotarans live a very different life-style in a very different environment. It's interesting how technological advancements can improve a race in some areas yet hinder them in others.

We traversed a narrow trail that gently wound its way inland toward the raised plateau, carrying not even a map or compass for navigation. No, just like Ricson, Pinut, Scard, Jasala, and the others, we needed to find our own way to the distant Dracari tree without any outside assistance. We were relieved of all of our "other-worldly" possessions, as the Mercerians called them. The only weapons we were allowed to bring were those that could be made by the Mercerians, so, fortunately for Demtrius and me, we were allowed to keep our finely-crafted swords made of the incredibly strong and flexible Dotaran steel. Rengar provided Crispin, Thristin, Dolvin, Nepalen, and Alexitus with light-weight swords originally used to help train Mercerian cubs, as the full-sized blades proved to be too heavy for them to wield effectively. Even still, they were untrained in hand-to-hand combat, and the blades would do little against a squad of fully-equipped Scynthians, or disgruntled Mercerians for that matter.

We were not just "thrown to the faolers" though. Rengar thankfully also provided each of us with a thick hooded coat of meer fur, a water-skin, some food rations, and cub-sized snow-shoes to aid us in our journey. This journey wasn't meant to be easy, and with the state of affairs the way they were back at the Iccaryn, we could do little else than abide by the rules of the quest and do our best to complete it; the rest of the Dotarans were counting on us.

Aside from finding the sacred yume herb and bringing it back to Finnis, Rengar also instructed us to provide the Dracari tree with a drop of blood each. "It is our gift to the tree," he explained, "for taking its seeds." He then reached into a pouch on his belt, "And lastly, please take this, and leave it amidst the branches. You brought it back to Finnis, so now you can complete its journey by bringing it to its final resting place."

It was Svix's amethyst necklace, the one I had returned to Rengar following the tragic and untimely death of his eldest son, and the same one Ricson had been wearing just hours earlier. I suddenly felt a pang of grief, but I was also happy to be able to do this for Svix and his father.

We continued on through the cold night for hours and hours, some of us more begrudgingly than others, fighting against the driving snow and furious gusts of wind that had each of us chilled to the bone, even through our skin-tight jumpsuits and the added meer fur. I was trying very hard not to think about how our group, not covered in fur like our Tatoran counterparts, ran a much higher risk of hypothermia.

The forest of thehnwood grew predominately on the long strip of land between Mercer's coast and the plateau that made up the center of the island-continent. Though it was the dead of winter, the thorny branches of the coniferous thehnwoods still held their dark green needle-like leaves, as well as the vibrant red moss that covered their trunks like fur. The red of the moss was an identical hue to the red underside of the predatory Tatoran bird, the thehn; the tree's namesake. The forest gradually rose in elevation the closer we got to the plateau, but the rise was nearly imperceptible to us on the ground with snow drifts as high as our heads.

Navigation became increasingly difficult the further inland we went, as we were not at all familiar with the wintry landscape. At present, all we could do was take note of the red moss growth and use it to provide a rough bearing for north, which then gave us our easterly direction. In northern hemispheres, moss tends to grow on the northern side of trees and rocks, because that side receives less sunshine than the other sides. To enhance our navigational accuracy, we neglected any moss grown near the ground or by sources of water, using only moss that had grown high on the trees, hoping to eventually stumble upon the plateau. From what Rengar said, it wasn't too difficult to locate, but we couldn't just rely on blind luck to see us through.

The night appeared darker than usual with the dense forest canopy engulfing our small group, obscuring the snow-covered ground from reflecting the bright starlight. Just finding our way along the narrow trail was difficult enough, not to mention the various roots and rocks that lay hidden beneath the deepening snow. More than once I stumbled and fell on such impediments, as did the others, but onward we continued.

Walking through the dark woods reminded me of our last night together, as we drove toward my uncle's cabin. Only then, the Aurora Borealis had been bright and magnificent in the northern sky, showcasing beautiful shades of green; and I had made a flirty comment about how it brought out the green in your eyes. If I've been keeping track correctly, I've been without the pleasure of your company for almost a full Earth year, but I still have the lingering image of you lying on your back, gazing at the stars and sky. I wish I could just go back to that time, back to you and all that could have been between us. But no, instead, I am on a strange quest for a sacred herb on a wild planet a million lightyears from Earth, seemingly lost deep within the tenebrous entanglements of this disorienting forest. And who knows where you are or what's happening to you right now.

Before my thoughts went down that dark path, I was snapped back to my surroundings by the creaking of a tree limb off to the left of the trail.

"Did you hear that?" Nepalen hissed, his voice hardly above a whisper. "There is something in the trees!"

"Probably just the wind, Sir," Thristin replied. "Try not to be so jumpy."

His words were followed by the loud and unmistakable snap of a branch.

"That wasn't the wind!" exclaimed Nepalen.

We all froze in place, not quite sure what to expect. Out of the corner of my eye, a dark object came swooping down across our path, flapping its wings furiously.

"We are under attack!" Nepalen squeaked, stumbling into Dolvin and Alexitus in his fearful excitement.

"Calm down," Alexitus commanded of his co-captain. "It is only a bird."

The nocturnal critter was gone in an instant, hooting an owl-like call and leaving feathers floating in its wake.

"It is the forest," said Crispin. "It will be full of life at night."

"Predators hunt at night." Nepalen added.

"That is true," Crispin admitted patiently, "but they won't bother us."

"How can you be so sure?" Nepalen asked with skepticism.

"There are many of us, and we are in full health," Thristin replied for his brother. "Any predators out here will want to find easier prey. Unless, of course, we are being stalked by scudgunum."

"Scudgunum are just a myth!" Nepalen scoffed defensively, trying to convince himself, but failing to do so. "And they wouldn't be here on Tatora!" He paused, "Could they be?"

"They are shadow-walkers," said Thristin, "so I'd suspect they could be any place where there is darkness. Just don't go wandering off from the group. Scudgunum always take the stragglers first."

Crispin stood beside his brother, making a menacing face as he slid his thumb across his throat. Nepalen shuddered, while Crispin and Thristin chuckled at his discomfort.

"Shadow-walker?" I whispered to Demtrius.

"A creature of lore," he replied. "It supposedly lives in the shadows. It is a story that we tell our young to keep them from getting into too much mischief. I don't believe there is any actual evidence of the scudgunum's existence, yet the myth has persisted for ages."

It was interesting that the Dotarans succumbed to superstitions and lore just like us, even with all their technological advancements.

Nepalen was still shaken. "I just think my skills would be better utilized back on the Iccaryn," he muttered.

"Oh have some dignity," Alexitus lashed out at him. "By the hand of Carnyle, you are a captain! Act like one!"

I couldn't have said it better myself, but, to be completely honest, I felt a slight twinge of fear as well. My imagination was beginning to run wild in this forest, and was worsened by Nepalen cowering at every sound. Every crunch of snow became a faoler preparing to pounce, every rustle of thehnwood needles a hungry primadon on the prowl, and every footstep brought us further and further away from the safety of civilization. I could only hope that we found the yume herb quickly and that daylight came soon after.

"Maybe we should stop and make camp," Nepalen suggested. "We can resume the journey when it is light out. At least then we'll be able to see what we're doing."

"Rengar said the yume herb can only be harvested at night," said Dolvin, "and we are going to need all the time we can get. I, for one, don't even know what a Dracari tree looks like."

"I do," I replied. "There was one near the Aramis. I saw it a few times, and I'm sure I could find another."

"See?" said Nepalen. "We can rest now and find the tree later."

"Better to find the tree and make the harvest as quickly as possible," said Alexitus. "The sooner we complete this task, the sooner we can return to the Iccaryn."

"I agree," said Demtrius, "the sooner, the better."

"Indeed," Dolvin agreed.

Nepalen began to protest, "But-."

"But nothing!" Alexitus interjected impatiently. "Three to one; the decision has been made. We push forward."

And so we did.

I'm not sure how much longer we travelled, but the seemingly endless night dragged along at a snail's pace, and none of us were getting any warmer. We had been walking for days it felt like, but, without the guiding hand of a moon, there was no way to gauge how much time had actually elapsed. All we had was the hooting of the dark bird that had crossed our path earlier. It seemed to be following us now, letting us know it still accompanied our group with its low hoot that carried across the frozen landscape. We eventually started passing several pairs of Mercerians, returning from their quests. They gave us a wide berth as they passed and we had no contact with them, but it reassured us somewhat that we were on the right track.

We kept our rest stops to a minimum, wanting to complete the quest as quickly as possible, but our bodies could only take so much. We stopped to sleep four times. Each time we took to digging out a small snow shelter to block out the heavy winds, using thehnwood boughs to layer the floor and also to seal off the narrow entrance. I remembered seeing a wilderness show once where they had made a similar shelter, and they had dug out the floor of their shelter to make it deeper, with a small trench running to the entrance. This way, it would allow the cold air to vent out as the shelter was warmed by body heat.

It took a considerable amount of time to make these snow shelters, and we dug in short turns since none of us wanted to run the risk of sweating too much, which would just speed up hypothermia. Each time we completed a shelter it was better than the previous one, although our sleep was invariably difficult and broken, and all the while we were continually harassed by the incessant hooting of that insidious bird, taunting us from the shadows. I had a flashback to my time traversing the great forest outside of Lake Azizi, home of the Sapphire clan, where another feathered creature called the Maku bird had followed us and annoyed us with its chirping. It had the uncanny ability to mimic Tatoran words, and was trained by the Sapphire clansmen to spy on strangers. It made me somewhat paranoid that this owl-like bird was a similar ally of the Mercerians, but to what end I didn't know. Perhaps to make sure we followed the rules of the quest, but I was just conjecturing.

The path before us started to rise gently in elevation, eventually coming to a steep forty-five degree angle of ascent. At the height of this slope was the western corner of the mountainous inland plateau, which rose vertically for dozens of feet to the cliff's dark precipitous heights. The walls of the plateau split in two directions, one running slightly northeast and the other running roughly southeast, forming a flat, inverted triangle before us. The snow had stopped, but I couldn't see beyond the upper edge of the cliff, obscured in darkness as it was. It must have risen even higher still since the stars were bright in the sky everywhere except beyond that upper edge. What we were seeing was apparently only the first tier of the plateau. Somewhere up in that shroud of darkness though, was the flat summit; we just had to figure out how to make the ascent.

Aided by the now-visible starlight, we made a quick inspection of the surrounding area, but, from what I could see, there didn't appear to be a viable path to the summit, at least not where we stood. We had followed the trail as best we could though, and it had led us to this point, so we were relatively sure there had to be some path nearby that would lead to the top. Unfortunately for us, the intense winter wind, whistling and howling as it swept against the cliffside, was driving snow in every direction and covering any tracks left behind by our Mercerian predecessors.

Our quick search of the surroundings revealed nothing, save for a couple of small waterfalls on the northern-facing wall that fell from the higher level in long, narrow streams of frozen ice. Other than that, the tall, rigid walls of the mountainous plateau went on and on unchanged, occasionally jutting out into the forest or receding back somewhat, but always towering over us and providing no path to the top.

Slightly discouraged, and with no obvious options, we contemplated what to do next, but all signs seemed to point toward making a risky climb up the icy and foreboding precipice, if it was even possible. I must admit, I would have been reluctant in even the brightest and driest conditions.

"Well, who wants to go first?" asked Dolvin, attempting to make it sound easy. "I'll be right behind you."

"Maybe we didn't search far enough," Thristin suggested. "We could split into two groups, each taking a side of the plateau to cover more ground, and then meet back here to report what we find."

"Hold that thought," Demtrius interrupted, holding a cupped hand to his ear.

"What is it?" asked Crispin.

"Quiet," Demtrius ordered, and then lowered his voice. "Just listen for a few seconds."

"Listen for what?" asked Nepalen, afraid that his worst fears were coming true.

"I don't hear anything," Alexitus proclaimed dismissively.

"That's just it," said Demtrius. "I don't hear anything either. The bird isn't hooting anymore."

"So?" asked Alexitus.

Just then, seemingly from the darkness itself, an arrow hissed right passed me, so close I could feel the wind from it on my face. The arrow was immediately followed by several more, aimed to kill. Luckily, the strong winds were still blowing so the projectiles all went wide; more arrows would be coming though. Any reasonably good archer could loose ten to fifteen well-aimed arrows in a minute, and we were caught completely off-guard.

Instinctively, I dropped to the ground, bringing Alexitus with me. He began to protest, but then saw the long, feathered shaft of a Mercerian arrow protruding from the tree it had struck, and he closed his mouth, speechless.

"Take cover!" I shouted, though the others were already seeking refuge from the treacherous bowmen. More arrows went hissing by overhead, one of them striking the hard rock of the plateau and shedding orange-white sparks. It was all happening so quickly; I barely had any time to react. The others had been nearer to the trees and were safe for the moment behind the thick thehnwood trunks, but Alexitus and I were still out in the open, now struggling to crawl down the slope to the tree coverage. Our snow shoes made the crawling difficult, and arrows were landing all around us now. I was surprised that neither of us was hit, but the wind was on our side.

That fact was short lived, however, as Alexitus suddenly yelped in pain when an arrow found his shoulder.

Another arrow pierced the tail end of my furs, getting caught and tangled in the loose hide and failing to penetrate my body. I thought of what would have happened had my body been turned just slightly, and shuddered involuntarily at that grave prospect.

Demtrius, courageous as ever, jumped forth from behind his tree with his sword drawn, putting himself between us and our attackers. He seemed ready to take on all of them at once. Meanwhile, Crispin and Thristin ran to Alexitus and were commencing to pull him to the safety of the trees. It was clumsy work in the snow shoes, but without them none of us could have gotten more than a few feet.

The hidden archers took aim upon Demtrius, but, quick as a flash of lightning, Demtrius dodged the lethal shafts and proceeded to help pull me to the trees before more arrows could be loosed.

For a moment, all was silent, save for Alexitus' moans and the howling wind.

"Stay still," Demtrius told Alexitus. "It will be more painful if you move."

"It's already painful!" Alexitus complained. "Wait-," he started, but before he could say more, Demtrius had begun cutting the fur from around Alexitus' shoulder, baring it to the skin to provide access to the wound. Alexitus yelped again, and his cries were answered by another volley of arrows, all thudding into the opposite side of the trees we were taking cover behind.

"Can you get the arrow out?" Alexitus asked weakly, more concerned than I had ever seen him before.

"It went through to the other side," Demtrius replied with some relief. "I can remove it, but I don't know how extensive the damage is internally. It's not bleeding badly, but if an artery or vein has even been nicked, you could bleed out over time. If only we had something to cauterize the wound..."

"Damn Mercerians," Alexitus said weakly. "Had we been permitted our gear, our lasers could have made quick work of this." He had tears in the corners of his eyes, and winced with each gust of wind. "Do what you can," he said, "and be quick about."

"What's the plan of attack, Captain?" asked Crispin of Demtrius.

"Nothing," said Demtrius, as he snapped off the feathered end of the arrow shaft about an inch above the entry wound, causing another yelp of pain from Alexitus.

"Someone cover his mouth," Demtrius ordered, to which Dolvin hastily obeyed. Demtrius then worked on the arrowhead jutting out of Alexitus' collar bone, which was less exposed. It was hard to get a good grip, and Alexitus made muffled moans of pain while he fiddled with it, but finally Demtrius was able to remove the broken arrow. He then took the scraps of fur he had cut off and put them back over the wound. "Hold this here and keep pressure on it," he said to Alexitus, who nodded in acknowledgement. His face was looking pale and he had beads of sweats running down from his temples.

Another volley of arrows came, most of which thudded harmlessly into the trees, but one managed to punch through the branches and nearly struck Demtrius, though he stood unflinching.

"There must be at least three, maybe four of them with bows, and possibly more without," said Demtrius. "I can't be sure."

"What do we do then?" asked Dolvin.

"We fight!" said Crispin and Thristin simultaneously.

Crispin continued, "We can use the night to our advantage, like scudgunum. We may not be able to see them, but they can't see us either."

"I wouldn't be so sure of that," I replied. "Tatorans can see much better in the dark than we can."

"We need to get out of here," Demtrius replied, his usual calm self, even in this tense situation.

"But to where?" asked Thristin. "For all we know, they could have us surrounded by now."

"Up," Demtrius suggested, pointing at the trees. "We know at least that direction is clear."

"Climb?" asked Dolvin. "We'll be right out in the open, prime targets for their arrows!"

As if in response to his protests, more arrows were

loosed, each making a dull thud as they sank into the trees in consecutive order, the last arrow grazing the side of a tree a dozen feet away and ricocheting off to get lost in the snow. Our attackers were guessing now, not quite sure where we were exactly, but their aim was still too close for comfort, and soon they would follow up on foot with axes and swords. If it was the Mercerians, which the arrows indicated it was, then they would know we wielded only children's blades, and they had the far mightier adult weapons of their race.

"There's no time for protests!" said Demtrius. "If you trust me, then fall in line."

Without another word, Demtrius was off, dodging between trees as quick as he could, heading toward a section of the plateau that jutted out into the forest. Then he jumped up into a tree and started climbing upward.

It wasn't the most ideal plan, but even if we had the time to think further, I'm not sure we could have devised a better one. We at least had the wind to throw off their aim and the darkness to help conceal our movements. Nevertheless, my heart was beating wildly and I was entirely unnerved. They had taken us completely by surprise and had already wounded Alexitus. How much longer could we hold out?

Dolvin went immediately after Demtrius, followed by the injured Alexitus, who clutched his furs over the flesh-wound, struggling to climb because of it.

"Come on!" said Crispin to Nepalen. "We have to move!"

"I-I can't," Nepalen replied stuttering.

"They will kill us if we don't move!" said Thristin, thoroughly irritated with his cowardly captain. "By the hand of Carnyle, get a hold of yourself!"

Nepalen stiffened at the mention of Carnyle, but then just shook his head, debilitated by fear.

"Just pick him up!" said his brother, and with that they each grabbed an arm, dragged him to his feet, and began pushing him forward. Once moving, Nepalen protested less, and finally we were able to leave. I heard more arrows being loosed as we left, but none of them struck home.

When we met up with the others, Dolvin and Demtrius

were helping Alexitus climb one of the larger thehnwood trees, and they were making good headway too. The tree grew beside the plateau, just close enough that its upper branches were within arm's reach of the summit. I don't know how we didn't think of this solution earlier.

Demtrius returned to the base of the tree trunk, and I noticed he wore his snowshoes tied together and slung over his shoulder. He was almost knocked off the tree still ten feet from the ground, however, as Nepalen hurried to shimmy up the trunk and out of danger. He cried out once, pricked by the sharp thorns on the branches, but pushed past the pain in his fright and continued upwards.

"Take your snow shoes off," Demtrius told him. "All of you. Quickly now! We need to climb fast. Our tracks through the snow will be easy enough to follow once they've realized we slipped away."

But they already had.

# Chapter Twenty-Seven
## Till Dawn

"Attack!" roared a voice from down the slope, hidden somewhere within the dense forest. "Kill them all!"

The words were spoken in Tatoran, so only Demtrius and I could understand them, but it wasn't hard to guess their intentions. Our attackers rushed forward, swords and axes drawn high over their heads as they emerged from seemingly nowhere. Their white fur and white hooded cloaks provided camouflage, but as they stepped into the starlight their figures were illuminated against the moss-covered thehnwoods.

We quickened our pace, ignoring the many thorns that slashed and stuck us, hurrying to make the ascent. That's when I heard another snap of a bowstring.

It came from above, not behind, and I knew we were surrounded and that our fate was sealed. The arrows came rapidly, but at the pace of only a single archer, and none of the arrows were even coming close to us. Did they not see us?

I looked up, and atop the cliff, loosing arrow after arrow, was Pinut, wielding a short hunting bow. She was shooting down at our attackers with fierce rapidity, forcing them to retreat further into the forest for cover and thwarting their attack, temporarily at least.

"We don't have all night," Pinut called down to us.

Dolvin and Alexitus were already crawling upon the ledge beside her, with Nepalen right behind them, but the rest of us were still in grave danger. We had to move faster. Pinut continued loosing arrows in rapid succession to cover our ascent, but how many arrows did she have left, and where was her new tzulamor?

As if reading my thoughts, Demtrius, having attained the cliff's height, leapt onto the plateau. "Where is Ricson?"

Pinut loosed another arrow, and then pointed down to the forest. At first I didn't understand, but that's when I heard the first scream. It rang out loud, sound waves echoing off the plateau's steep hillside, and then was deftly cut short mid-cry, followed by shouts of confusion.

She threw Demtrius a spare bow and sack of arrows. He caught them and threw them to Dolvin.

Demtrius swung around just as I was getting onto the ledge and leapt back into the tree.

"Where are you going?" asked Dolvin.

"To help a friend," he said over his shoulder, "so follow Pinut's lead and loose a few arrows." He then proceeded to climb back down the tree.

Crispin and Thristin grinned and began to follow him.

"They'll be killed down there," said Dolvin, aghast.

"Then we'll have to help them," I said, and scarce had the words left my lips than I was on the tree and climbing downward too. I turned back once, looking directly at Dolvin, waiting for him to pick up the bow.

He seemed nervous, but then stood straight and walked up beside Pinut. "We've got you covered." There was work to be done.

I descended to the ground and donned my snow shoes again, tying them quickly in order to not be left behind by Demtrius and the anxious brothers. All three already had their snow shoes on and swords drawn, and were now stalking around the flank of our previous position. I hadn't noticed it, but my sword, too, was in my hand, having already leapt from its sheath in a fraction of a second from muscle memory. Our attackers had stopped loosing arrows, and might have exhausted their supplies, but we couldn't be sure. Now, though, thanks to Ricson and Pinut, we would bring the fight to them.

Pinut and Dolvin sent arrows further ahead into the forest, trying to keep whoever was out there at bay and stuck taking cover.

We hadn't gone more than a dozen paces when we heard the second cry of pain and despair. It was close too. Soon we would be right in their midst. My heart was pounding faster and harder with every step, but, surprisingly, I wasn't filled with fear. Rather, it was a charged feeling of excitement and adrenaline, mixed with Demtrius' calm assertiveness and the joyful enthusiasm of Crispin and Thristin; it propelled me forward, for better or worse.

Pinut and Dolvin had just stopped loosing arrows, and I could only assume they were finally out of projectiles. I just hoped our attackers didn't surmise the same. With Pinut at their front and Ricson at their rear, they were already fighting a battle on two fronts, and now with us coming up on their flanks they wouldn't know which direction to defend from.

"Where are they!" one of them shouted. "I don't see them!"

"They're behind us now!" someone replied.

"No, they're on our flanks!" cried another.

It was all chaos for them.

Without another moment's consideration, Demtrius leapt forward, seizing the opportunity to capitalize on the enemy's confusion.

"Watch out!" one of them screamed as he saw Demtrius' fur-covered figure emerge from behind a tree. Demtrius was fast, exceedingly fast, but his prey met his speed with an almost equally quick parry, deflecting a well-aimed thrust for the heart. Like lightning the Mercerian struck back, and the force of his strike put Demtrius slightly off balance, opening him up for an attack by one of the warrior's comrades. By that time, however, Crispin and Thristin had engaged another attacker and were forcing him backward step by step. Demtrius was quick to recover and had also renewed his attack, but with redoubled effort.

This all happened in just a few seconds, and has taken longer to explain than the actual time that elapsed. I had barely leapt from the coverage of the trees when Demtrius went back on the offensive. He occupied one foe, while Crispin and Thristin occupied another, and now a third came charging toward me, roaring ferociously as he uttered his battle cry. He swung wildly, attempting to cut me in two with one savage blow. I tried to jump out of the blade's path, but the lace on my snow shoe unraveled and I lost my footing, causing me to fall backwards in slow motion.

The cold sting of steel cutting through tissue and flesh blurred my vision. My torso burned with intense pain as I rolled sideways, dropping my sword and clutching the fresh wound with both hands. I was utterly stunned, feeling my own warm blood saturating my furs, and was suddenly all too aware of my mortality. My attacker wasn't quitting either. He intended to kill, and, sensing a quick victory, he lunged forward for the coupe-de-grace.

I closed my eyes in anticipation, unable to defend myself and waiting for the finishing blow to strike home. I heard him expel a grunt as he used his full force, but was surprised when I remained unscathed. Instead, my ears rang with pain as steel struck steel, clanging violently and shedding sparks all around me. When I opened my eyes, I saw Ricson locked in battle with my attacker, pressing him closely. Our attackers had lost their advantage and were now tasting the beginnings of defeat, so, angered by the turn of events, they began retreating further into the forest, abandoning the attack.

Ricson immediately began pursuing them, with Crispin and Thristin hot on his heels.

When I realized the fight was over, and that we had succeeded in turning back our attackers, I was over-joyed. Then, the pain returned, ten-fold. My chest felt like it was on fire and blood steadily seeped from the wound, creating a small pool of dark red on the white snow.

"How severe is it?" asked Demtrius, crouching down to assess me.

"I'll be fine," I replied. Then I smiled, "You did worse to me in the Pit of the Gyx."

"Still," he persisted, "I would like to see."

I let him assess the wound, to which he said, "The cut is deep, but I don't believe any major blood vessels were hit. I would be more worried if not for your ability to heal so quickly."

"Lucky me, huh?" I asked rhetorically. "If only I could block out the pain too."

"I can stitch the wound for you once we make it back to Finnis," Demtrius offered, "but perhaps you and Alexitus should return with Ricson and Pinut. Neither of you are in a condition to travel, and they can defend you better than we can."

"Like I said, I'll be fine," I repeated, cringing at the growing pain.

Ricson came back into view, dragging behind him the corpse of one of the archers. Similarly, Crispin and Thristin emerged carrying another archer, but this one was still alive, albeit badly wounded. He was unconscious, and his left leg hung limp and useless, dripping blood from where his Achilles tendon had been severed. The archer would never be able to walk again.

"Look what we found!" said Crispin. "Ricson's fine handiwork, we presume."

Ricson, of course, couldn't understand, but he looked at the crippled archer and nodded, confirming their assumption.

"I don't think they'll return so soon after that," Crispin grinned.

"A rare fight!" Thristin added cheerfully. "Gilpin will sure be sorry he had to miss it!"

Even through my current pain, it was amusing to see their new Tatoran-like lust for fighting.

Pinut was now joining us, having just finished descending the plateau's steep precipice via the large thehnwood tree and gathering what arrows she could find.

"Looks like Ricson and I found you just in time," she commented, unstringing her small bow as she spoke. She then saw the slash across my chest, "Perhaps not soon enough, though."

"It's nothing, really," I said dismissively. "I've been through worse."

"It is an awfully large cut for one so small," Pinut said with genuine concern. "Please, let me dress the wound for you."

"You have bandages?" I asked.

"Bandages?" she repeated, somewhat amused. "Not out here, but the forest will provide everything we need."

Pinut commenced gathering some red moss from a nearby thehnwood tree, as well as some of the tree's sticky sap.

Meanwhile, Demtrius and Ricson stood over me speaking to one another.

"We are very grateful for your assistance," said Demtrius, "but how did you know where we were, and that we were in danger?"

"We didn't," said Ricson. "We were just making our return from the Dracari tree when we happened to see the lot of you, and it only took a second to understand the trouble you were in."

"Well, thank you," said Demtrius, as did I. Crispin and Thristin, however, with the lack of a translator, had Demtrius convey their thanks, which Ricson accepted with a quick nod.

"We are allies now," said Ricson, "and good allies protect one another when the time calls, no matter what the terms of our arrangement may be."

Pinut returned with the sap and moss. She broke apart the moss until it was the size of the cut and then placed it directly over and partially inside of the wound. With that in place, she then applied the sappy resin to seal the wound.

"There," she said, admiring her makeshift remedy. "That should suffice for the time being. The thehnwood moss will help to stop the bleeding and the sap is excellent at preventing infection. You should still seek medical attention in Finnis, though."

"Will do," I lied, knowing my wound would probably have mostly healed by then. "Thank you."

Ricson bent down and pulled up the surviving archer by his white cloak. "Now, let us see who it is that has attacked you. If my suspicious are correct, then Waulf will have a lot of explaining to do."

"By all means," said Demtrius, stepping in to get a better look at the archer's features in the dark night.

Ricson pulled back the archer's hood, revealing a disheveled, blood-spattered, and unfamiliar face and mane. He turned the face from side to side and then ran his fingers through the burly white mane, feeling around for something. "Damn," he said. "Just like the other one, no bones."

"Bones?" asked Demtrius.

"The Skudlandic warriors wear the finger bones of

those they have defeated in battle tied into their manes," Ricson explained. "It is a symbol of status and shows others how skillful the warrior is. If these archers were to have them, than there would be no doubt of Waulf's involvement, but now I can't be sure. We'll have to bring this traitor back to Finnis for a proper interrogation."

"We should be leaving anyway," said Pinut. "We have remained here for some time, and our yume will soon begin to lose its glow."

She opened her arrow sack to show the brilliant glowing herb, but I was on the ground and did not see much except a dull glow of colorful lights. The herb itself was said to be beautiful and magnificent, constantly changing in swirls of different colors, but I would have to wait until we reached the Dracari tree to see for myself.

"You are right, my love," Ricson replied. He turned back to Demtrius, "The Dracari tree isn't much further; perhaps half a day's walk. Once you head back up to the first tier of the plateau, walk to the right and around the bend, and soon you will find the path to the top. Once there, continue straight across the plateau until you reach the frozen lake, and then follow its bank to the right. You will eventually come to a patch of small trees and shrubbery, and just beyond that you will find the Dracari tree. It will be hard to miss."

"Thank you again," Demtrius replied, placing his closed fist to his chest. Ricson returned the friendly gesture, and then picked up the unconscious archer to resume his journey home.

"What about this one?" asked Pinut, indicating the slain archer.

"Leave him for the faolers," said Ricson. He took one last look at our group, "I'll see you all back in Finnis."

And with that they were gone.

It took some time to climb back up to the plateau's first tier now that no one was shooting arrows at us, and I was significantly slowed by my wound, which seared in pain with every movement. Eventually, though, we finally reunited with Alexitus, Nepalen, and Dolvin on the level ground.

"You're alive!" Dolvin exclaimed in happy disbelief. "By the hand of Carnyle, you're all alive!"

He came over to us immediately, as did Nepalen. Alexitus, however, remained kneeling where he was, gathering snow and packing it on his injured shoulder to help numb the pain.

Following Pinut's example, Demtrius had collected some thehnwood sap and more moss, and presently began dressing Alexitus' wound in much the same way Pinut had done mine.

"What happened down there?" Nepalen asked us.

"Sent them running!" Crispin replied with enthusiasm.

"And Ricson took one of them captive!" said an exalted Thristin. They were both still high off of the adrenaline rush. Thristin continued, "By the time we get back, Rengar will know exactly who sent them."

"As if we even have to guess," said Alexitus. "Wretches, all of them. I knew we never should have trusted them."

"You cannot judge an entire race on the actions of a few," Demtrius replied in defense. He just finished applying the sap. "And if we don't secure their help, our people will suffer. Remember that."

"Always trying to act so righteous," said Alexitus with scorn.

Demtrius ignored the comment. Instead, he quickly scanned our new surroundings, but darkness still reigned so he couldn't have seen much; at least I couldn't at any rate. I could barely make out just a few dozen feet and up a slight slope until more vertical cliffs rose to what I presumed was the plateau's actual summit. According to Ricson, now we needed to proceed to the right and soon we would find our path to the top.

"We should rest for a few minutes and then be on our way again," said Demtrius, "but perhaps only Thristin, Crispin, and I should proceed further."

"What do you mean?" Dolvin asked. "Don't we need to do this together?"

"We've come a long way," Demtrius replied, "but with two of our party injured, we should allow them time to rest and recover. We do not want anyone to suffer further injuries."

"But those assassins," Dolvin said fearfully. "What if they come back to finish us off?"

"They won't be coming back anytime soon," said Crispin. "We made sure of that."

I caught Demtrius' eye. "I'm going," I said firmly.

Demtrius looked me up and down, and then, knowing he couldn't sway my decision, nodded.

Alexitus, however, made no such plea and seemed content to remain where he was. Nepalen, too, feeling more secure on the plateau's shelf, opted to remain, but Dolvin made protests to continue on.

"I was too stricken with fear to help you before," he said, "but I'll be damned if I don't see this thing through with the rest of you!"

Demtrius went up to Dolvin and placed a friendly hand upon his shoulder, taking him into his confidence. "You have nothing to be ashamed of Dolvin, and besides, I need you here, looking after Alexitus and Nepalen. We can't leave them afraid and unprotected, now can we?"

Dolvin thought this over for a second. "I suppose you are right," he said at last, "but what can I do if we are attacked again?"

"You keep a good eye out and hide if you see anyone approaching, even us," Demtrius answered. "You hide until you are certain there is no danger."

"Right," said Dolvin, and then, with more confidence. "Right, hide and protect!"

And with that, we were back on the move.


We followed Ricson's directions without error and were finally rewarded when we came upon an excavated section of the wall about twelve feet from the ground with steps leading up to the precipitous heights above. The wall before us, however, was bare and mostly smooth, providing no footholds or crevices to use for climbing.

Demtrius, as always, was quick to provide a solution. "It's too high to jump, even for a Tatoran," he said, "but three of us can make a pyramid with our bodies, and then the fourth person should be able to reach the landing."

"Then how will the rest of us get up there?" asked Crispin. "Whoever goes up first can probably help to pull the next of us up, but the third and fourth will have the most difficulty."

"Teamwork," Demtrius replied simply.

"If only we still had our mattertrons," Thristin commented. "We'd have been to the top and back a hundred times by now."

Demtrius turned to me, "Jaxon, since you are probably the lightest one here, you should be the first to ascend. How is your wound?"

"Never better," I lied, but Demtrius knew, and knew that I would push past the pain.

Crispin and Thristin knelt before the wall, and Demtrius climbed atop them, placing a knee on each of their backs. I was up next, awkwardly trying to climb atop their Dotaran pyramid, but soon I was up and reaching for the landing's edge. I jumped to cling onto the ledge and quickly managed to pull myself up, and then turned to help the next person.

"Crispin, you're next," said Demtrius, placing his back against the wall and cupping his hands low. Thristin followed in step right beside him. Crispin then placed a foot in each of their cupped hands, and put his hands on their shoulders to steady himself.

"On three," said Demtrius, and at the end of the count they launched Crispin upward to latch on to the ledge. I helped him up from there.

"Two down, two to go," said Crispin as he righted himself on the landing.

"Same idea, Thristin," said Demtrius, again placing his back against the wall. "Just remember to jump."

"Yes, Captain," Thristin replied, and soon he, too, was atop the ledge.

"Now is the tricky part," said Demtrius. "One of you will have to hang down over the ledge face-first while the other two hold his legs. I'm going to get a running start to jump my highest, and, when I do so, whoever is hanging down will have to catch my arms, and then the other two will pull us up."

It took us three tries, but finally Thristin and I pulled back on Crispin's legs and brought them both up.

After that, the climb up the steep steps was easy enough. We quickly made the summit, and then the ground was completely flat.

"Straight across the plateau to the frozen lake, and then follow its right bank," said Demtrius, repeating Ricson's directions.

"I don't understand why we couldn't just ask Ricson and Pinut for some of their yume," said Crispin. "It looked like they had more than enough. No one back in Finnis would have been the wiser."

"Because we need to procure our own," said Demtrius. "Ricson knows that too, which is why he didn't offer. The Mercerians embark on this quest for a reason, and cutting corners does not fulfill that purpose."

"I know," Crispin commented, "still would have been nice though."

Indeed it would have, but at least we were nearing our destination. The ground before us was flat and much more welcoming than the forest, so here we donned our snow shoes again and proceeded with haste.

Presently, we saw two figures approaching us from across the plateau. All four of us drew our swords, preparing for another fight. It was Scard and Jasala, presumably returning from the tree. They saw us from a distance too, but just kept walking toward us. They passed by without a word, looking at us strangely with our weapons drawn, and then they continued on without looking back. I don't believe either of them was aware of what had happened to us.

I shrugged to Demtrius, and then we continued on our way. Before we knew it, we had reached the edge of the frozen lake, marked by the low depression it made in the otherwise plain landscape. A few miles around its edge, we spotted the patch of trees and shrubbery. Sure enough, the Dracari tree was just past the patch, and Ricson was right; it was definitely a spectacle. We must have been a few miles away still, but the myriad of ever-changing colors was bright as day, like a natural

Christmas tree already decorated with lights and ornaments. Red, orange, yellow, green, blue, purple, and even white, all present at the same time, each coursing through the tree in different waves and shades of color. Most stunning of all, there were even streaks of the magnificent color of detriminium, that unmistakable yet impossible-to-describe color not found in Earth's realm. It was a truly majestic sight.

Far across the plateau, however, we could already see the sky showing signs of the coming dawn against the eastern horizon. Time was of the essence.

Exhausted as we were, the four of us began running as we covered the remaining ground, all of us in awe at the sight before us. The closer we got, the larger and brighter the tree became, and soon its enormous size was fully realized. Its trunk was easily thirty feet in diameter and must have risen over a hundred feet into the sky, splitting off into dozens of branches. The branches were covered in tiny leaves, and a swirling array of colors projected from cracks in the bark. It was like the tree was a living, breathing creature and we were seeing glimpses of its inner workings.

The first thing we did was provide a drop of blood each, as Rengar had directed. I pricked my finger, and smeared the blood against the trunk, staring up in wonder.

High in the tree, wrapped and tangled among the higher branches, was a strange object, almost polished white and reflecting the tree's scintillating yume blossoms. I couldn't tell what it was until I was right under it, but then I realized just what I was looking at. It was a skeleton, and a large one at that. Judging by its considerable size and length, I immediately thought of Thiesel, my serpent friend. He had cocooned himself inside a chrysalis on another Dracari tree in the distant west. These skeletal remains, however, seemed to have some extra features; several appendages that could have been arms or legs, and perhaps even a set of wings. I finally concluded that I must have been looking at the remains of the legendary gyx, the mythical dragon of Tatora. Perhaps the legends are true, I thought, and Rengar's ancestor really did ride atop one.

As I gazed up into the tree, Demtrius and the brothers circled it looking for any low-lying branches or knots to use as footholds, but to no avail. The trunk was far too wide to shimmy up and was completely bare for twenty feet or so. The glowing yume, of course, was only on the upper limbs, and day was finally beginning to break. I could already see the shimmering herbs receding back within the cracks of the bark. We were so close, just a few feet from where the herbs lay, but might as well have been miles away still with no way to scale the tree.

I looked around for any overlooked branches or footholds, I couldn't help but notice dozens of sets of claw marks from where previous Mercerian couples had struggled to ascend. They were larger and more adept at climbing, but even with their size and claws they apparently had significant difficulties. If they struggled so much, I feared we might never be able to harvest the herb as lightly equipped as we were. Even just a rope would have sufficed, but all we had were our snow shoes, swords, and furs.

That's when it came to me. "I've got it!"

The other three looked at me impatiently.

It was faster to show them my plan, so I took my sword and drove it into the tree as hard as I could, sinking the tip several inches into the trunk at waist-level. I tested it, and it was stuck in pretty good. Next I removed my furs and began wrapping the blade with them. By this time, the others understood my plan.

I finished wrapping the fur around the sword, shivering as I did so, and then used my sword belt to lash it in place. Luckily, the jumpsuit I wore under the fur kept me warm enough, at least for a few minutes anyway.

"Let's hope it holds," I said, and placed a foot on the sword close to the trunk where it was sturdiest. As I placed my full weight on the blade, I was pleased to find that it held me easily. The others had their swords out and furs ready to give to me so I could repeat the process.

"Only one of us needs to go up," said Demtrius. "If you wouldn't mind, I would like the honor."

I smiled at him and then stepped down, "Of course, my friend." I gave him Svix's amethyst necklace and he tied it to his belt.

It took some time, and the rays of the sun were still creeping over the horizon. I had to pry out the bottom two swords and hand them up to Demtrius so he could finish the ascent. That was the most dangerous task since he wasn't able to jam them into the tree as hard while he wobbled on the thin blades, but, somehow, Demtrius was soon able to make it to the branches, so quick and agile was he. And then he was lost in the foliage.

He was gone from sight for a few minutes, but then finally he returned to the base of the trunk, removing each sword and dropping it to the ground as he did so. Daylight was now reigning in on the landscape.

"Were you able to harvest any?" asked Crispin.

Demtrius just opened a small pouch at his waist and allowed us to peer inside, eliciting smiles all around.

"We had better get moving," he said, proud of our hard work.

We finally had the sacred herb in our possession.

# Interlogue Four
# Ryane's Escape

Ryane slept long into the morning, having been afforded this rare occurrence due to the preparations Salama'an had to make for his impending mission. With no piercing noises or shaking floor, Ryane slept deeply for the first time in a great while. Not even her persistent nightmares disturbed her sleep. This night she enjoyed a dream; a dream of Jaxon and her together once again, safe in the confines of their childhood treehouse, where they had made innumerable memories together.

She welcomed these warm visions brought on by her subconscious, unaware that she was even dreaming. To her, it was entirely real, but, had she been lucid, it would only have acted as another poor reminder of her current hopeless predicament. But she was not lucid, and Ryane dreamt through the Scynthian dawn and on through the morning, a faint smile upon her face.

She had known Jaxon for almost as long as she could remember, and they had spent almost every day together, racing each other to the house she lived in with her mother after school, their backyard treehouse waiting for them and their next adventure. Jaxon's parents had both died when he was young. His uncle, Deecan Grey, had taken him in, but Deecan was not exactly the doting fatherly type, and was constantly out hunting or otherwise preoccupied with one thing or another. To say he was a neglectful guardian, however, was entirely untrue, and Ryane knew that Jaxon had cherished the time he spent with his uncle, learning useful skills and diverse life lessons. He spent much more time with Ryane and her mother, though, and when Uncle Deecan finally decided to move north into Canada, where he remained until his disappearance, a pre-adolescent Jaxon opted to stay behind in his New Jersey hometown after Ryane's mother graciously offered him a room in their house.

But this morning, Ryane dreamt of Jaxon as her younger self never had, and the tantalizing images that entered her mind were the furthest things from her living nightmare.

And then came the rude awakening.

Her mind was slow in transitioning from sleep to wakefulness. She heard someone calling to her, but their voice seemed faint and distant. Her body felt cold and stiff, and she had a fleeting out-of-body experience, as if she were trudging through snow. Her eyelids crept open unwillingly, revealing a blurry light as her eyes strained to adjust. The voice seemed closer now, and the words were almost distinguishable, but still they escaped her understanding. Then, with a sudden start of realization, Ryane felt her body being roughly shaken.

"Please Ryane," said the voice. "We need to hurry! There isn't much time!"

Her vision was finally clear and focused, and standing over her was Illoran, looking frantic and worrisome as he shook her by the shoulder.

"What's going on?" she asked, now fully awake and aware of her surroundings.

"We're leaving," Illoran replied hurriedly. "A window of opportunity has arisen, and I'm going to take you away from this place."

Ryane thought she had heard wrong. "Leaving?" she questioned. "To go where?"

A look of anguish flashed over Illoran's face, but he realized they wouldn't be going anywhere until he explained himself, so he quickly began relaying all the pertinent details of his recent conversation with his superior.

"Orric has just informed me of a new plan that he's formulated to finally rid himself of your Jaxon and his Dotaran allies," he rapidly explained, while Ryane stared back through bloodshot eyes. "He is sending a team of human soldiers, led by Salama'an, down to Tatora, and he has just asked me to accompany the team as the ship's doctor."

"Good for you," Ryane replied tartly, annoyed at being

woken from her nice dream to be told something awful.

"Good for us!" Illoran exclaimed.

Ryane failed to understand what Illoran was alluding to, and, in truth, was unable to even contemplate that one of the wretched Scynthians would do anything to rescue her from her ill-mannered imprisonment.

"Don't you see?" asked Illoran, but he continued without waiting for a response. "Orric has just provided me with the means of effectuating your escape! All we need to do is get you aboard the ship, and then I can reunite you with your Jaxon!"

The significance of Illoran's words took a moment to sink in, but then Ryane's eyes went wide with elation. "You can get me to Jaxon?"

"Yes, yes!" said Illoran, glancing back at the doorway quickly. "But we cannot waste any more time!"

"Okay," Ryane replied excitedly, caught up in the thought of seeing Jaxon again. "Let's do it then." She paused for a moment, wondering how exactly Illoran proposed to sneak her aboard the attack ship, and thus to Tatora.

As if reading her thoughts, Illoran reached into his medical bag and drew forth a cloaking ring, which he had been able to procure from a dissimulation engineer who owed him a long-awaited favor. The engineer had also provided him with a utility cuff, a device that is usually reserved only for soldiers, but for which Illoran knew he'd have many uses for. Illoran kept the cuff in his medical bag with a few other useful tools.

"You'll need this," he said, handing the cloaking ring to Ryane.

"For what?" she asked, seeing no valuable use for the metal ring.

"It is a cloaking device," Illoran explained. "Simply seat the ring on your head, and then it will automatically conceal you from visible sight."

Ryane looked at the metal ring, understanding what Illoran was saying yet wondering how they managed to accomplish such a technological feat.

An idea suddenly sprang into Ryane's mind.

*With this cloaking device*, she thought, *I can elude*

*everyone, even Illoran.* As the significance of the situation dawned on her, Ryane couldn't help but think of abandoning Illoran the moment she was invisible and outside of the room. *Illoran says he's trying to help me,* she thought, *but what if this is just another form of Scynthian torture? What if he isn't leading me to Jaxon? And, if not, then where is he bringing me?*

After all she had been through at the hands of the Scynthians, this was the logical thought process. Ryane struggled with her conflicting feelings, but she quickly came to the realization that abandoning Illoran now wouldn't do her any good in the long run. She would still be stuck prisoner on Scynthia, even if her captors never found her, and Salama'an would still leave for his mission to take Jaxon away from her for good. To be sure, if the Scynthians had the ability to create such a device, they would surely have developed the means to penetrate through the cloak or otherwise circumvent the camouflaging. Indeed, on Scynthia there were many ways to detect an invisible fugitive. Besides infrared and thermal imaging devices, which Ryane was already aware existed, the Scynthians also possessed several tools she hadn't thought of; sensors that detected minute changes in air temperature, room pressurization, and the level of gases in the air, as well as highly-sensitive gravity sensors, motion sensors, and weight sensors. The chances of a prolonged evasion were already slim in her mind, and had she considered any of these other methods of detection, she would have instantly realized hiding on Scynthia was futile.

No, she had only two options; stay in her room of captivity, effectively sealing her fate along with Jaxon's, or throw her lot in with Illoran and hope he remained true to his words. It took only a second for her to make the decision.

Ryane had nothing save for the clothes she was abducted in, so all she needed to do was throw on her red and blue flannel shirt and then they were ready to depart.

At the door to the room they stopped. "Place the cloaking ring on your head now and be sure to remain as quiet as possible," Illoran directed her. "Orric has had guards stationed outside of your room ever since you overtook him in your ill-conceived escape attempt."

Ryane thought back to that moment, how she had plunged her fingers into Orric's gills and bent him to her will. In the end, of course, Orric had been able to recapture her, but it still gave her a small amount of pleasure to think about the discomfort she had put him through.

She donned the ring, and, just like it had done when Orric demonstrated it to Illoran, the red beam flashed down her body. A moment later, Ryane was rendered completely invisible to the naked eye.

"Stay close to me," Illoran cautioned her. He couldn't see her now. He could only hope she didn't do anything rash to get either of them caught, and that the room didn't have surveillance cameras. Illoran hadn't seen any, but they could be imperceptibly small, and Orric had other strange instruments recording Ryane too. *Let's hope no one is paying any attention,* he thought to himself, knowing this was a one-way ticket for him too.

They left the room, and Illoran nodded at the two guards standing watch on either side of the doorway. They went through hallway after hallway, passing Scynthians and humans along the way, Ryane still completely invisible and walking close behind Illoran, and soon he had them at the hangar bay without incident.

They shared a short elevator trip from the hangar bay to the flight deck with two Scynthian pilots, who stepped onto the elevator platform at the last second. Illoran traded small talk with them briefly, while Ryane clung to his side for fear that one of the pilots would accidentally bump into her. Scynthians are large creatures, and the elevator platform wasn't too spacious.

As the elevator rose, Ryane forgot all about her present concern of discovery as a completely new world appeared before her. First, the clear walls of the elevator shaft revealed they were underwater, and she could see for miles through the crystal clear water. She saw literal cities of coral rising high from the sea floor and criss-crossing their way in so many directions, glowing various colors, providing food and shelter, filled with fish, mammals, and amphibians that Ryane had never imagined existed. The Scynthians swam and lived in this water, able to dwell on land and in sea without any difficulty, even under the immense pressure of the ocean.

The elevator rose quickly, and soon it shot out above the water's surface, revealing a star-studded night sky. From her vantage point, she was first able to see the vast expanse of space, full of sparkling stars and glowing cosmic matter, and then Tatora came into view and Ryane gaped, awe-struck by the majestic sight. Not even images of Earth taken from a space telescope could have properly prepared her for that beautiful sight, and she let out an almost imperceptible gasp. She instantly cringed and covered her mouth, aware of the small sound she had made, as was Illoran, but, to their extreme relief, the two pilots failed to notice.

The elevator platform soon came to a rest and Ryane saw the extent of the circular flight deck, seemingly open to space and the darkness therein. There were many ships of varying shapes and sizes, but one caught her eye almost immediately. It was a cigar-shaped ship, a hundred yards in length and at least thirty in height and width, and it lay directly before them in the center of the flight deck. Attached to the ship, running down its length on either side, were a number of spherical compartments, which would be used as escape pods in case the ship had to be evacuated. Ryane, of course, could only speculate as to their purpose, and continued to marvel at the sight before her eyes.

The two pilots had already left the elevator platform and were making their way over to the ship, but, when Illoran dallied at the platform for a moment, waiting for the pilots to be out of earshot so he could make sure Ryane was still with him, one of the pilots turned around abruptly.

"The ship is this way, Doctor," said the pilot good-naturedly.

Illoran just waved them on, and began shuffling through his medical bag as if he'd forgotten something.

Standing in formation just to the side of the ship, patiently waiting to board, was a contingent of human soldiers. A quick count of the rows and columns would reveal one hundred fighting men and women, all under the command of

Salama'an, whom Ryane could see standing at the head of the contingent beside Orric and several other Scynthian overlords. They briefly greeted the two pilots as they boarded the ship, and then continued inspecting the troops while each row began to board in single file.

Ryane was suddenly very nervous. Hitherto, she had been too excited and distracted by her mischievous escape, but now she trembled with angst as she approached the group of Scynthians, especially the dreadful Salama'an. Even the thought of him made her muscles tense, and left a bitter taste in her mouth. She didn't fear him, exactly, but to say he made her very uncomfortable would be a major understatement. Ryane felt Salama'an was the embodiment of evil and immorality, and he had garnered the majority of the hatred and disdain that she felt for the Scynthians.

*You're perfectly safe,* she told herself. *They can't see you, and he can't hurt you anymore; none of them can. They haven't even the faintest clue that you're missing from your room yet. Just keep your distance, move silently, and you'll have nothing to worry about.*

Easier said than done, however.

The closer they got, the more anxious Illoran became as well. He had to fight the urge to look around nervously, and even more not to look over his shoulder when others passed close behind him.

"Ah!" said Orric, while Illoran was still a few yards away. "The last member of your team is finally here, Salama'an."

Salama'an eyed Illoran, subconsciously sensing something slightly off with the physician's demeanor, but not thinking any further on the matter. He nodded to Illoran in acknowledgment, and Illoran returned the gesture.

"It'll be a short trip, Doctor," said Salama'an confidently. "Don't even bother unpacking your bag."

"May your mission be carried out expediently," said Orric. "We await your successful return."

Orric and his entourage then exited the flight deck.

"Come," said Salama'an, gesturing for Illoran to accompany him up the ramp and into the ship, "I'll show you to your room."

Salama'an led the way and Illoran followed, pretending to take great interest in the ship so that Ryane could keep up with them. They made it to Illoran's quarters fairly quickly still, as the ship had only two levels, each with a single hallway running from bow to stern. Illoran's room lay at the rear end of the first floor, adjacent to the medical bay.

"I'm sure you will find everything in order," said Salama'an, and with that he left Illoran to his own devices.

The moment the door was shut, Illoran noticeably relaxed, but still had the presence of mind to wait a second for Salama'an to walk out of hearing distance before addressing Ryane. He locked the door shut, and then, when he was reasonably assured of their total privacy, he gave voice to her.

"You can show yourself now," he said, and then began unpacking his medical bag. He expected Ryane to show herself right away, but when he looked up she was still invisible.

"We are alone," he said, trying to reassure her. "No one will bother us here."

Still she remained invisible, and made no noise.

Illoran felt the first tendrils of panic. Had she somehow gotten separated?

He quickly paced through the room, feeling around for her with outstretched arms, but to no avail. Ryane was gone!

While Illoran spoke with Salama'an and Orric outside of the ship, Ryane stayed back, keeping her distance. She took a moment to watch the human soldiers as they boarded the ship, each so strong and physically capable, yet somehow off. These Scynthian-raised humans moved with acute precision, each bending and twisting, and even breathing to the same unheard rhythm. They looked like an incredibly well-oiled battalion. Ryane had no way of knowing, but these human soldiers were not the by-product of military training, but of extensive biological engineering by the Scynthians.

Ryane looked up, suddenly aware that Illoran was gone! She quickly scoured the flight deck, seeing Orric and his comrades walking away from the ship, but no Illoran, or Salama'an for that matter.

*The ship!* she thought, and went running up the line of human soldiers to catch up with her co-conspirator.

As she stepped inside the ship, she immediately came to a long hallway that stretched to her right and left, and since the flow of soldiers was heading toward the right, Ryane had no choice but to head left to start her search for Illoran.

She rounded the corner quickly, failing to use caution, and almost ran head-first into Salama'an as he came walking back down the hallway. Ryane jumped to the opposite side of the hall, flattening herself against the wall, just narrowly escaping contact with him. The sound she made when striking the wall, however, was unmistakable, and Salama'an stopped in his tracks, turning to look directly at Ryane, or rather, through her.

Ryane froze, not even daring to breathe. It was all she could do. Her heart was beating wildly, and she feared Salama'an could hear the loud thumping in her chest. She could kick herself for her stupidity. In a moment he would discover her, and she lacked the imagination for all the horrible things she knew would come next.

"Captain!" came Illoran's voice from down the hall. He was just leaving his room to go searching for Ryane, but had seen Salama'an seemingly staring at an empty wall. Fearing the worst, he quickly shouted, and then hurried to catch up with him.

"If you don't mind," he said, landing heavy steps as he approached Salama'an, "I'd like to see the bridge. I've never been aboard one of these ships before."

"You have the taste for adventure now?" asked Salama'an in feigned surprise, as he couldn't feel more proud of his occupation and thought everyone should feel the same way. "Of course, Doctor, by all means. Right this way."

Illoran had just done two things: Shown Ryane which room was his, and provided an opportunity for her to slip away from Salama'an's keen senses.

Ryane didn't waste the opportunity. Using Illoran's distraction and loud steps as cover, she was able to slowly move away from Salama'an and skirt by, toward the relative safety of her ally's private quarters.

As Illoran walked with Salama'an toward the bridge, the door to his room silently opened and closed, admitting an unseen visitor.

And there, Ryane waited.

Illoran stayed on the bridge longer than he would have liked, watching the crew tediously going through their preparatory safety checks while Salama'an droned on about one thing or another. He didn't want to excuse himself too early after expressing interest in the ship's operations, even though he was distraught over Ryane's disobedience and disappearance the entire time.

*Why didn't she remain close to me?* he thought as he walked back to his quarters, finally having excused himself for the evening. *Now I have no idea where she is until she presents herself to me.*

Illoran was worried for Ryane's safety, and for his own life. He was taking an astounding risk by placing so much trust in this female. He was fairly confident that she hadn't eluded him on purpose; she was relatively intelligent, for a human, and would know his plan was the only viable option for her. He wiped his hand down his face in tired frustration. *Is helping this Earth female really worth all the trouble, and all the stress?*

He entered his room, and quickly scanned the space for any sign of Ryane. He noticed a sunken depression on his bed, and strained to pick up the subtle sound of her breathing while she slept.

"Where did you go earlier?" he began chiding her. "I told you to stay right behind me. Little mishaps like that can compromise everything we are trying to do here!"

"Don't you think I know that?" Ryane replied, annoyed at being lectured. "Clearly it wasn't my intention to get separated, but we're both fine, aren't we?" She removed the cloaking ring, and her figure suddenly appeared right before Illoran. She continued, "You and I are still the only ones that know I'm here, so no harm has been done."

"Eh-oh!" said Illoran, using his extraordinary vocal cords to produce the strange and wondrous sound that is unique to the Scynthians' defense mechanism. He then continued in English, "You must be more careful!"

Illoran put a hand to his forehead, and the other on the wall. "I'm sorry," he said, realizing just how stressed he actually was. "Please allow me to get some sleep. We'll need to be well rested for tonight anyway."

"What's happening tonight?" asked Ryane.

"Well," Illoran explained, "by morning we'll be inside the planet's atmosphere, so if we plan to throw a wrench into Orric's operations, we'll have to do so tonight."

"What are you going to do?" asked Ryane, filled with equal parts concern and curiosity.

"Either something brilliantly simple or incredibly stupid," Illoran replied, providing Ryane with the least bit of reassurance.


The hour grew late, and, as Illoran slept, Ryane paced around the room. She wasn't tired, not now at least, as she anxiously anticipated the night's coming events. Their ship had already ascended from the landing platform and was following a course for Mercer. The ship's cloaking device would safely conceal their presence until they were ready to carry out their surprise attack. They had yet to enter the planet's atmosphere, but would be doing so very shortly.

Meanwhile, on the ship's bridge, Cypha, one of the two Scynthian pilots that had shared the elevator ride with Ryane and Illoran, received an alert on his flight screen.

Salama'an, standing just behind the pilot, looked over his subordinates shoulder at the blinking message. "Is there a problem?"

"Nothing serious, Commander," Cypha replied. "The ship is picking up a small amount of excess weight near the stern. Most likely just some ice accumulation on the landing gear. Nothing to worry about for now. It should break off and evaporate during entry."

"Very well," said Salama'an. "Be sure to keep an eye on the accumulation, though."

"Yes, Commander" Cypha replied dutifully.

A few minutes later, Ziah, the ship's communications

officer, received a radio transmission from Scynthia Command. It was Orric, and he had an urgent message for Salama'an. "I'll take it in my quarters," he said, walking off.

Once he had more privacy, "What is the urgent news?" Now he was speaking directly to Orric.

"You must have your ship thoroughly searched at once," Orric said quickly. "The Earth woman has escaped her room, and no one here has been able to find her."

"But the guards would have seen..." Salama'an started to say.

"Don't tell me what they would have seen!" Orric snapped, uncharacteristically losing his cool for a moment. He recovered almost instantly, "The girl has escaped, and none of our sensors have been able to pick up any trace of her."

Salama'an immediately recalled what his pilot, Cypha, had just told him, and suddenly feared his ship may be harboring the fugitive.

"The veterinarian was the last one to enter her room," Orric continued, "and we fear he has somehow smuggled her aboard your ship. You must act quickly."

"If she is aboard this ship, then I will find her," he replied, "and anyone else who might be aiding her."

"Just do so quickly," Orric replied, "and notify me the moment you have her back in custody."

"Yes, Councilman Orric," Salama'an replied. "Right away."

Orric clicked off.

Salama'an's face did not portray any of the fury he was feeling that a low ranking veterinarian may have pulled one over on him. He needed to investigate Orric's suspicions quickly and quietly. No one would learn of this incident, and he would do what he needed to keep his reputation intact. He exited the captain's ready room and motioned for two human soldiers to follow him, a male and a female, each armed with a plasma pistol, as was he. It was time to find a fugitive, and root out a traitor.

# Chapter Twenty-Eight
## Day 340

"Hold him still!" said the physician to their attendant, as they poked and prodded into Alexitus' wound, assessing the severity and cutting away the necrotic flesh. The wound had turned septic during our return to Finnis, and was now festering, producing a sour, putrid stench that filled the room.

"Careful!" Alexitus shouted at the physician, though neither they nor their attendant could understand him. "Do you even know what you're doing?" Alexitus was a very vocal combination of drunk and annoyed. He had not wanted to be brought to a Tatoran physician, especially since the Dotarans had more advanced medical technology, but his wound had needed immediate care before he could go any further. The physician's attendant had offered both of us some yume tea or strong Tatoran spirits to drink when we arrived, half in an attempt, I think, to shut Alexitus up, but mainly to reduce the pain. Alexitus chose the spirits, and I chose the yume tea, as I was now familiar with its effects.

The physician, Eirgurt, was a tall Mercerian, almost as tall as Grissly, but with a lean look, as if they'd been malnourished for some time. Eirgurt was one of the gender-neutral Tatorans that make up the third, less populous Tatoran gender. They wore bifocal lenses in large wooden frames, and wielded medical tools with the trained hand of a surgeon. The obvious competence of the physician did not keep Alexitus from wiggling around under the knife and moaning incessantly, however, but Eirgurt remained undeterred.

"Come now, steady!" said Eirgurt to the attendant. "Do not allow him to move so much!"

"What are they saying?" Alexitus asked me. He lay on

a bed of straw and meer fur, and I was in an adjacent bed just across the small room.

"They need you to be still," I responded, finding myself staring as the physician did their work.

"I would if they stopped stabbing at me!" Alexitus replied in exaggerated anguish.

On a nearby table was a bucket of heated water, white cloths and bandages, dozens of surgical instruments, a cup full of maggots, a crucible that the attendant had previously been using to crush yume into an oil-extract, and a jar containing a poultice of honey, charcoal, and the medicinal yume oil. This was the extent of the medical equipment that the Finnisians could provide, and it was far better than doing nothing. There would be superior medical treatment aboard the Iccaryn when we returned as well, as Alexitus kept reminding the patient physician.

Demtrius, Crispin, Thristin, and Dolvin were already off with Rengar, Ricson, and several other Finnisians, loading the food supplies from the Mercerians into the Pothos. They were giving us literal tons of northern palagus, a white walrus-like creature with a very long body that, on average, weighs close to a ton. It's the much larger cousin of the otter-like palagin, with the same three streaks of black running down its back with black spots on either end of the streaks. The palagus, however, is easily distinguishable from its cousin by its massive size, giant flippers, and a single ivory tusk that protrudes from its forehead.

While they had gone to secure our food for the winter, Nepalen had elected to stay behind with us. He had been in and out of our room several times with Pinut, but never stayed for long. The sight of blood invariably made him queasy and nauseous, as did the smell.

I was on the verge of vomiting myself, and couldn't wait to leave the room to get some fresh air; if only the cut on my chest had healed like I had expected it to. It surprised me that the wound showed little signs of significant healing. Pinut's makeshift remedy did well to stop the bleeding, but the wound hadn't closed on its own yet, and it needed to be cleaned and stitched soon or else I, too, would run the risk of infection.

Why wasn't it healing as quickly? Ever since I received the Scynthian's enhancement injection, my body had healed itself incredibly fast. I had even survived a fatal wound in the Pit of the Gyx. Were the effects of the enhancement serum really diminishing like Thuric had told me they would? It sure seemed like it, and I decided that once we returned to the Iccaryn I would have the Dotarans run more diagnostics.

When we had secured the yume herb and left the Dracari tree, we had regrouped with Dolvin, Alexitus, and Nepalen on the first tier of the plateau, and then made our way back to Finnis without further incident, taking advantage of the now available daylight, but we were still delayed by Alexitus' deteriorating condition. His shoulder wound had turned septic rather quickly, and worsened rapidly to the point where we were basically carrying him the last leg of the journey. There was little to be done save quicken our pace in hopes that we could make it back to Finnis before gangrene or some other ailment set in.

We travelled for days, and we weren't making great time, but on the sixth day we were met by a party of Mercerians led by Rengar and Sverna. They saw Alexitus' poor state, and had him immediately taken to the small city's only physician, which was still several miles away. Luckily they were wise enough to bring a ski-cycle, so it wouldn't take them long to reach the city. I was fine for the time being. My wound still needed to be stitched, but it wasn't showing any signs of infection, so I stayed to walk with Demtrius and the rest.

Rengar was the first to greet us, and he wore a grave and troubled look upon his face. "Ricson told me of the ambush and the fight," he said with concern. "I'm sorry I allowed something like that to happen, and I hope you know I had no part in it. I thought once out of Finnis you would be safer, but I was evidently very wrong."

"It is alright," said Demtrius. "We knew going into this that we would be stirring up emotions. I just hope you find those behind the attack."

"We haven't broken our captive yet," Rengar admitted, "but there are only a small number of chieftains who would dare to defy me, Waulf being chief among them."

"But there is nothing to tie him directly to the attempt on our lives?" Demtrius asked.

"Not yet," said Rengar. "I do assure you that we will get to the bottom of this one way or another. If force won't do, then I know of another method for extracting the truth from our captive; one the Aanthorans have used for years."

I thought back to Aanthora, and to the flower that had almost digested Mya, the same one that was used in truth serums there. "The Carnatora?" I asked.

Rengar looked at me, "Always surprising me." He smiled. "Yes, I purchased a small supply of it from a trader named Captain Tarq ages ago."

"Of the Tulipa?" I asked.

He looked at me again, "You do get around, don't you?"

"However you do it," Demtrius replied, "so long as you find the culprits. If they get away with this attack, there will be no end to your troubles with them."

"Agreed," said Rengar, "it does me no good to allow insubordination such as this. It must be dealt with swiftly and those culpable be punished severely, but you do not need to stick around for that if you do not wish."

"Unfortunately," Demtrius replied, "it would be neglectful of me to stay much longer while my people are on the verge of starving, and with Alexitus' wound so grievous. We appreciate your physician's help immensely, but we must get him back to our medical facility soon. We should begin loading the rations aboard our ships immediately."

"It will be done at once," said Rengar, "but the food supplies are still being procured."

"What do you mean?" Demtrius asked, slightly concerned.

"You see," said Rengar, "we Mercerians only take as much as we need from our environment, protecting our food sources for future generations, but with the coldest months still ahead of us and with wildlife and vegetation already becoming scarce, we, too, would run the risk of going hungry if we gave you food out of our own supply. So instead, I sent my hunters to the Ice Islands while you were gone, and they only just returned yesterday. They are still butchering the meat for you. This is, of course, due in part to the promise of food from your aquaponics system, you should know."

"Thank you," said Demtrius. He then presented Rengar with the still-glowing yume herb.

Rengar smiled at the sight of the herb, and embraced Demtrius with open arms. I could see Demtrius cringe at the physical contact, but he said nothing.

"You have done a great deed," said Rengar warmly. "Now come with me and reap some of the benefits of your labors."

Our welcoming party escorted us back to Rengar's hall, where another small feast had been prepared, but only Rengar, Sverna, the new couples, the Dotarans, and myself were permitted to enter. This part was for us alone.

The Mercerians, I must add, showed a splendid change in attitude toward our party. They were much more welcoming and jolly in our presence now, finally seeming to have relaxed around us. It was as if we were one of them now, so to speak, and I guess in a sense we were, united and allied. It was rather enjoyable, and I could only wish you had been there to enjoy it with me, especially for the next part.

Sverna, standing beside Rengar at the head of the table, clapped her hands, and two servants came to retrieve the newly acquired yume. Along the long table were several fire pits, previously used to heat the various meals while we ate, but now were uncovered and pots of water were being placed over each of them. When the water began to bubble, the yume was added, and the smell of the boiling tea began to fill the room. At first it was slightly offensive, but it quickly became a warm and pleasant aroma.

The servers brought each of us horns to drink from, and then used a ladle to pour the tea into the cups. The liquid had, amazingly, taken on the swirling colors of the herb, and I suddenly thought about what it might do to my insides. The Mercerians had been taking part in this ritual for ages however, so I was fairly certain it would be safe. It was steaming, and I had to blow on it at first, but soon I was able to sip it. I was surprised by how quickly its effects took hold.

Never before had I felt as I did then, not even when I tried yume again, chasing the ecstatic high. All my worries and inhibitions suddenly flew out the door, somewhat like the aromatic effects of the carnivorous carnatora plant. Even the pain from my chest wound subsided, at least for the time being. My body soon began to feel like it was tingling, a surprisingly pleasant sensation. I was relaxed and almost giddy, yet still focused and fully cognizant, retaining all proper motor functions. My mind felt like it had transcended to a higher plane of existence, and the entire world suddenly seemed to make perfect sense. It was absolute euphoria, and there didn't appear to be any downside to the psychedelic drug, which I now realize was exactly what it was.

Yume, the sacred herb of the Mercerians.

And I already found myself wanting more.

The physician continued exploring Alexitus' wound for further damage, occasionally removing bits and splinters of wooden arrow shafts. Then, seemingly satisfied, Eirgurt began washing the infected area with the warm water. The attendant dried it, and then Eirgurt commenced to place maggots in the wound, presumably to eat whatever infected or necrotic tissue had been missed.

I almost heaved at the sight, thinking about the larvae feeding and moving around inside Alexitus' wound. It made my skin crawl, but it was the most effective treatment available.

With the wound packed, the physician took the poultice of honey, charcoal, and yume oil and began applying it to either side of the wound. There was plenty left in the jar for later, as they would be cleaning the wound and reapplying the poultice periodically throughout the day.

"Oh, by the hand of Carnyle," said Alexitus, as Eirgurt and the attendant moved on from him to me. "Finally, I can rest and recover."

"That makes one of us," I replied.

The physician and physician's assistant, whose name I hadn't caught, washed their hands in a bucket of fresh water, and then examined the deep cut on my chest briefly. "It seems your attacker did the preparatory work for me. A clean cut!" Eirgurt said cheerfully.

"I'm sorry I don't share your enthusiasm," I replied.

"You should," Eirgurt responded. "You see how the edges of the wound are smooth and come together nicely? If they didn't, I'd have to cut it so that they would, but you've been spared that pain. Now, let's get this stitched up for you, and try not to blubber like your friend over there."

Eirgurt inadvertently motioned in Alexitus' direction, and, seeing this, Alexitus asked, "What are you both saying?"

"Just that your wound should heal up nicely, even without further medical aid," I lied.

"Like I trust their handiwork," said Alexitus. "I will have my own people do a proper job of it when we return to the Iccaryn."

Eirgurt had begun stitching my wound, taking a curved needle and sticking it through near the edge of the cut, making sure not to go too shallow and have the stitch tear out. They tied a small knot on the first stitch, and then made a zig-zag pattern down the cut, finishing with another small knot. The stitching didn't actually hurt that much, albeit the skin at the edge of the cut was mostly numb by this point.

"Not even a wince!" Eirgurt exclaimed. "I like you, boy!"

They didn't stay long after that, and, before leaving, Eirgurt instructed the attendant to make us some more yume tea and alcohol to help with the pain. To be honest, the pain was quite bearable, but I sure wasn't going to pass up an opportunity to feel the herb's powerful yet serene effects.

After Eirgurt's departure, Nepalen and Pinut came into the room to check on us. I cupped my warm tea with two hands, drinking it slowly, but Alexitus had already downed his alcohol to alleviate his shoulder pain.

"Wow!" said Nepalen in astonishment. "Alexitus, you look so much better already!"

"As a matter of fact," said Alexitus, "I feel rather well, too." Alexitus attempted to sit up, but was stricken by sudden shoulder pain. "I guess not that well, though."

"Do not worry," said Nepalen, actually smiling for the

first time since we set foot on Mercer. "We'll be back aboard the Iccaryn before you even know it."

"I'm tired," Alexitus said abruptly, lying back fully. "Wake me when we're ready to leave."

"Of course," Nepalen replied.

"Jaxon, how are you feeling?" asked Pinut. "I knew that cut was worse than you would admit."

"I don't know what you're talking about," I grinned. "Just a scratch."

"A scratch, indeed," Pinut replied smiling. "At least your spirits are up."

"The yume tea makes that very easy," I remarked.

There was a sudden commotion coming from outside the dwelling, and the door to the room burst open. In came Eirgurt's young attendant, half hysterical with fright. "The Scynthians! The Scynthians are coming!"

Without another word, he went running back out of the building.

"What did he just say?" asked Alexitus, roused from his rest. "Scynthians?"

"We are doomed!" Nepalen exclaimed.

I was already on my feet, heading for the door to see for myself what was going on. When I was outside, tasting the fresh yet frigid air, I noticed the entire city was abuzz. Everyone was looking up at a glowing object in the sky, which appeared to be descending rapidly upon our location. I don't know if it was the yume tea or the object itself, but the whole thing seemed ethereal, and like it wasn't actually happened.

"It is them!" cried Nepalen, suddenly appearing behind me, and his words brought me back to reality. "They are going to find us and kill us all!"

"We need to hide," I said, but my words lacked any conviction. I, too, was stricken with fear, as I knew our chances of escaping the wrath of the Scynthians was slim to none.

Demtrius and I had gambled, hoping the Scynthians wouldn't come, but we had lost. Now the Mercerians would suffer just for trying to help us in our hour of need. *What had we done?*

# Interlogue Five
# Ryane's Fight

Illoran's sleep was short, and all too soon he and Ryane left the compartment to execute Illoran's risky plan. He took Ryane to a nearby escape pod further in the rear of the ship, using the cloaking ring to conceal her once again, and left her there while he went on to the detriminium reactor room.

"You'll be much safer here," he had assured her. "Bringing you further would only increase the chance of discovery. Once I've altered the ship's attack coordinates, I'll head straight here, and we'll launch the pod to Tatora."

"Okay," said Ryane, "but how will we find Jaxon?"

"I am setting the pod's destination to be the same as the current attack coordinates, which should bring us as close as possible to Jaxon and the Dotaran's whereabouts. I'm hoping they find us, and ideally before Salama'an realizes he's been crossed."

"But what if we can't find him?" she asked.

"Then we go into hiding temporarily," Illoran replied matter-of-factly. "I've packed a week's worth of rations for us both, a utility cuff, and a pair of plasma pistols, just in case. Once we leave this ship, only death will greet our return, so there will be no turning back."

Ryane heard the carefully concealed feelings behind his words, and for the first time in a long while, she found herself worrying about someone other than Jaxon or herself.

"Are you sure you want to go through with this?" she asked. "You can just leave me the supplies and don't come back once you've changed the ship's coordinates. If Jaxon can survive alone on Tatora, so can I."

"Nonsense!" Illoran declared. "I shall accompany you to the planet and see this thing through. You are not the only

263

one wishing to escape Scynthia, you know." He turned toward the door to leave. "Besides," he said, flashing a smile at Ryane over his shoulder, "I know a good deal of vital information that Jaxon's friends will want to know."

With that, Illoran exited the room, and Ryane anxiously awaited his return. She kept the cloaking ring activated above her head, remaining undetectable to the naked eye, but she still had a bad feeling in the pit of her stomach.

All she could do was wait.

Illoran moved quickly to the detriminium reactor room, where he hoped to gain access to the ship's computer mainframe. He knew there would only be one or two Scynthian engineers in the room, and it would provide the safest place to do his work. He planned to change the attack coordinates, but only slightly, hoping not to arouse immediate suspicion on the bridge. If he could send them far enough away from their target zone, then it would give Jaxon and the Dotarans just enough time to escape, as well as greatly help Ryane and him in their flight.

He used his utility cuff to open a portal into the reactor room, as the room was completely sealed off with no built-in door in order to better protect the important machinery from unauthorized access. The cuff's enhanced mattertron parted the metal wall, condensing the metal into itself to create a space large enough for Illoran to pass through.

Inside, he found a large circular chamber filled with various forms of biomechanical technology; living tissue and organs, all harvested from enhanced human slaves or grown in laboratories for a specific design, running to the different machines spread around the room. Tubes inflated and deflated, pumping blood and nutrients throughout. There was an air hole that breathed oxygen into the machinery, as well as waste receptacle sacs, digestive organs to convert organic material into energy, fluid filters to protect the system from foreign objects and contaminates, and bypass lines in case of a blockage. The enhancing effect of the Scynthian serum slightly alters the DNA of the living tissue, indefinitely prolonging the life and resilience of the living machinery, so long as a booster shot is administered bi-annually. The living human tissue is used all throughout Scynthia, replacing the need for other, less sustainable material. This human material has the ability to autonomously grow and repair itself over time, provided it receives the proper vitamins and nourishment.

Front and center as the room's focal point was the powerful detriminium reactor, which glowed with the magnificent yet indescribable shade of the uniquely colored detriminium, but this wasn't something Illoran hadn't seen before. To him, the color was simply known as Argu, which is a color not even known of on Earth and impossible to describe to someone who hasn't witnessed it first-hand. All the same, it is a beautiful and commanding color, and is a testament to the highly-valued intrinsic worth of the detriminium element.

Illoran scanned the room carefully, but, to his surprise, it was apparently unoccupied, alleviating him of having to explain why he was there. If anyone had been in the room, he was prepared to lie his way through, using a flimsy story that Salama'an had given him permission to explore the ship and its different departments, as this was his first time aboard such a vessel. He also wore the utility cuff, which was generally reserved for soldiers, and, as the engineers had no reason to believe any foul play was afoot, they should take the cuff as confirmation of Salama'an's words.

Illoran took a few steps toward the reactor, scanning the room for its computer terminal, which he quickly spotted on the far side of the room.

"What are you doing here?" came a questioning voice from Illoran's left, startling him and nearly causing him to jump. He looked for the owner of the voice, and saw an engineer stepping out from behind some organic cooling tubes. "We don't get many visitors down here," said the engineer, wiping some oil from his webbed fingers. "To what do I owe the honor?"

Illoran quickly relayed the lie he had prepared, hoping it was enough, yet all the while fingering one of the plasma pistols in his medical bag. To his relief, though, the engineer took him at his word and went back about his business.

"Feel free to look around a bit, but please do not touch

anything," said the engineer before returning to his work behind the cooling tubes, again out of Illoran's view.

With a small sigh of relief, Illoran proceeded to the computer terminal, cautiously circling the room in feigned amazement at the complexity of the reactor. After a few minutes of this, he found himself in front of the computer, out of sight from the engineer. He immediately began moving through the different computer screens, but was completely unfamiliar with the ship's system. It would take him some time to figure out how to change their destination, precious time that even Illoran wasn't fully aware was already ticking away.

Salama'an bored his way through the ship like a demon, systematically searching for the Earth fugitive on his way to Illoran's quarters. He wasn't quite sure why, but the veterinarian's company was far more tolerable than most other Scynthians, so he hoped to find the Earth female anywhere but with Illoran.

He sent the two human soldiers away to search, while he proceeded to Illoran's room, wishing to confront the doctor in private. When he opened the door, however, he found the room empty. Illoran was inexplicably absent.

Whatever reservations Salama'an had regarding Illoran's involvement in the Earth female's escape were instantly washed away. Salama'an cursed. He would make Illoran pay for his deception, and, as is the Scynthian way with traitors, he would pay with his life.

Just then, Salama'an received a transmission through his cuff from Cypha on the bridge.

"Commander," Cypha began, "it appears that Pod Eight was accessed a few moments ago, and the air sensors are now picking up a slight increase in the pod's carbon dioxide levels."

Salama'an pounded the wall, *I cannot let them make it off the ship!* He calmly told Cypha it was probably nothing, and that he would check it out, giving away none of the anger he was feeling.

He went running for the escape pod, hoping to stop it before it detached from the ship. They could track it simply enough, or just blast it into oblivion, but Salama'an wasn't

concerned about the pod's recapture so much as he was about
his status and reputation. If he allowed a fugitive and a traitor
to escape his grasp, even for a short time, then his commission
could easily be revoked and given to someone else the council
deemed more deserving. Salama'an had to continuously prove
his worth to keep his position, and he had already allowed an
unauthorized human aboard his ship, so it was with extreme
haste that he made his way to the escape pod, to stop the
departure and to save his future.

While on his way to the escape pod, he used his cuff to
contact the two human soldiers and have them meet him there,
so they arrived just moments behind him. The humans readied
their plasma pistols, and then leapt into the room as Salama'an
opened the portal, but to their surprise, the room was entirely
empty.

Empty, save for an invisible Ryane crouching against
the far wall in utter terror. When the door had slid open, she
thought it was Illoran returning, and she almost spoke before
the two soldiers rushed into the room. Ryane immediately
broke out in a cold sweat.

*Hopefully they just see an empty room and move on,*
she thought, but, if her unfortunate recent past was of any
indication, luck was not on her side.

"Search the room," ordered Salama'an. He was taking
no chances. "Make sure you cover every inch."

The pod was small, so it took less than a minute to
encompass the entirety of the room. Ryane tried to stay away
from them the best she could, tip-toeing around them and
ducking to avoid contact, but her discovery was inevitable. The
two human soldiers were noticeably bewildered when the
barrel of one of their pistols struck an object where none should
have been. Salama'an knew of Orric's cloaking ring, however,
and was less than surprised by the clever deception.

"Seize her!" he ordered.

Salama'an stood in the doorway, effectively blocking
her only escape route, so, even though she remained unseen,
she was quickly within their strong grasp. She kicked and
punched relentlessly trying to break free, and her invisibility
aided her somewhat, but in her struggle the cloaking ring was

knocked away, instantly rendering her visible again. It was short work after that to subdue her.

Salama'an was very pleased at the Earth female's recapture, but something was still gnawing at him. Illoran was nowhere to be found, and who knew what else the treasonous doctor was up to? Salama'an had to find him, and quickly.

"Where is he?" he demanded of Ryane. "Where is the doctor?"

Ryane looked him straight in his black beady eyes, seemingly staring right into the dark depths of his insidious soul, and then spat full upon his face. "You think I'd tell you?" she asked, almost laughing. "I thought you fish-heads were supposed to be smart?"

Salama'an wiped the spittle from his face, and raised his hand to deliver Ryane a menacing blow. Blood appeared at her ear, but she laughed in his face nonetheless. He didn't have time for this, so he contacted Cypha on the bridge. "Have any other sections of the ship been accessed recently?"

Cypha checked his instruments. "It appears the reactor room was accessed only a few minutes ago."

"Very good," Salama'an replied. *The traitor is still within grasp!*

Illoran was stuck. He had already spent several minutes trying to navigate the ship's computer system, but to no avail, and now he feared that he'd never be able to figure it out. He had grossly underestimated the technical complexity involved in his plan, and now things were falling through. Jaxon and the Dotarans would be decimated by Salama'an's force of human soldiers, leaving his and Ryane's fates up in the air.

"I thought I told you not to touch anything!" came the irritated voice of the engineer.

Illoran was nervous, but Scynthians are excellent at suppressing their emotions, so when he turned to answer the engineer, his demeanor was one of confidence and authority.

"Your screens are incredibly dirty," he lied, thinking as quickly as he could. "You should be sanitizing your stations daily."

"Sanitize?" the engineer repeated with scorn. "I'll have

you know..." He glanced at the screen, seeing Illoran trying to access the ship's controls. "What were you just doing?"

Illoran's silence was answer enough, and they stood staring at one another for a moment in a relative stand-off, but then the engineer went lunging for a nearby wall alarm. He had to make it around a piece of machinery first, while Illoran had a clear path to intercept him, and, just as the engineer's hand was falling on the switch, Illoran slammed into him with full force, sending them both tumbling to the floor. The scuffle that ensued was the first physical altercation Illoran had ever been in, and his inexperience showed. The engineer was not much more experienced, but he had the advantage of size and strength over the doctor, and quickly gained the upper hand.

It didn't last long, however. Illoran, fighting for dear life, was somehow able to break free for a moment, and instantly followed up with a vicious swing at the engineer using the utility cuff on his forearm, dazing his adversary and sending him to the ground once again. It was a scramble after that for his medical bag, which he had discarded during his initial interception.

The engineer was slow to rise, holding his head where he had been struck, but his eyes instantly focused on the plasma pistol now held firmly in Illoran's grasp, aimed level with his chest.

"You should be ashamed of yourself, turning against your own people," said the engineer in disgust. "I hope Salama'an..."

"Forget about Salama'an!" Illoran replied. "Now do as I say and lay down on the floor with your hands behind your back. If you try to make any other movements, I will not hesitate to discharge my weapon."

"Don't be a fool," the engineer cautioned him, clearly very worried. "Think of where we are. One shot and you could compromise the entire ship."

"Then you would do well to heed my instructions," Illoran replied sternly.

The engineer remained as he was, attempting to judge the distance between them. It was about twenty feet. If he could create a small distraction of some sort, it could give him just enough time to bridge the gap and disarm the doctor. Even as he looked at Illoran, he could see the slight tremor in the doctor's hand, and the awkward grip with which he held the pistol. It wouldn't take much to disarm him, if only he had an opening.

"I won't ask again," said Illoran, extending the pistol even further and eyeing his target through its sights.

The engineer conceded to Illoran's command, and slowly got down on his knees before placing his hands behind his back and lying flat on his stomach. He was just at too much of a disadvantage.

Illoran kept the pistol on the engineer while he returned some attention to the computer.

"Whatever it is you are doing," said the engineer, "you will never get away with it."

Illoran suddenly had an idea. "You're right," he said, "but you know this system very well. Quickly, on your feet."

"First get down, now up. Would you make up your mind?" the engineer complained. "I'm not as young as I once was."

Illoran ignored the comment. "You will access the ship's navigation system..."

A portal suddenly opened on the far side of the room, stealing Illoran's attention for just a moment, but in that moment the engineer found his opportunity. In a single motion, the engineer was able to disarm Illoran and turn the gun back on him. "The traitor is over here," he called to the newcomers.

"Well done," Salama'an commended him as he walked over to their position, followed closely behind by Ryane and the two human soldiers, who forced her along with rough prompts from the point of their pistols. Salama'an holstered his plasma pistol. "I'll take it from here."

"Very well," the engineer replied dutifully, relinquishing the confiscated pistol to his superior. "I believe the doctor was attempting to alter the ship's course, Sir, but he was unsuccessful."

"It would have done him no good," Salama'an replied, stroking his webbed fingers through Ryane's hair. "Not with his little prize once again in my possession."

She fought hard to evade his touch, but the human soldiers held her firmly in place.

Salama'an redirected his attention to the traitor. "I must admit, your deceit was clever. Futile, but clever nonetheless. I just can't fathom why you would choose to throw your lot in with this inferior creature. Now you will pay for it dearly."

Ryane watched with dread as Salama'an stepped closer to Illoran, placing his plasma pistol just inches from the doctor's head. She had to do something, and fast, but how could she restrained as she was? They held weapons of untold power, and she was unarmed and obviously outmatched.

"Not in here!" the engineer protested. "It is too dangerous to discharge your weapon this close to the reactor core!"

Salama'an had been about to pull the trigger too, but relaxed his arm after hearing the engineer's logic. "Very well," he replied. "It would have been too quick a death for treasonous slime such as him." He motioned toward one of the human soldiers. "Restraints."

The male human stepped forward to hand his superior the restraints, and that's when Ryane made her move. She caught Illoran's eye just beforehand and gave him a wink, alerting him that she had a plan. Or at least that's what she intended to convey, but she didn't know that Scynthians don't use winks in the same manner that Earthlings do. He did, however, pay closer attention after seeing the peculiar wink, and it was good he did.

Ryane suddenly, and quite unexpectedly, turned on the human female that guarded her, knocking her pistol aside and throwing the woman against one of the room's many machines. Ryane then lunged at her, grabbing for the weapon. The female soldier was caught completely off-guard, but kept her wits about her and fought back vigorously. They were stuck in an evenly matched struggle, with the pistol swaying back and forth over their heads. Everyone's eyes were on the two, giving Illoran the opportunity to charge straight for Salama'an, tackling him into the reactor and sending his pistol flying across the room.

"No!" cried the engineer, as he futilely lunged for the pistol, but it was too late. The firearm struck the metal floor and discharged, sending its lethal shot directly into the engineer's forehead, killing him instantly.

Salama'an cursed at the death. He kneed Illoran in the stomach and then knocked him sideways, sending him sprawling to the ground. "How dare you!" he said in fury, and then kicked Illoran hard in the side. The doctor moaned in agony.

Meanwhile, Ryane and the female soldier continued their struggle. They were both tiring quickly, but Ryane fought with the knowledge that losing meant almost certain death, or, even worse. The male soldier came to aid his comrade, but Ryane fought with a dire vengeance, and sent the male soldier down with one well-placed kick to his face, breaking his nose and sending him reeling back into Salama'an.

"Control her!" Salama'an ordered, catching the male and pushing him back toward Ryane, but the male soldier couldn't see with blood and tears filling his eyes, and went stumbling down face first, out for the count.

"You incompetent fool!" shouted Salama'an. "Do I have to do everything myself?" He took one glance over his shoulder, but went wide-eyed when Illoran was missing from where he had fallen on the floor.

"You won't hurt another soul again!" Illoran shouted, emerging from behind a piece of machinery with the discarded plasma pistol tight in his grip. He charged at Salama'an, discharging the weapon multiple times at Ryane's torturer. Salama'an quickly ducked, but the shots went wide anyway. The first of them cut a hole into the organic tissue that lined a section of the wall, while the remaining shots burst into sparks as they struck the machine that Ryane had the female soldier pressed against. The two women continued fighting though, barely even noticing.

Salama'an drew his pistol from its holster while he crouched and dodged between machinery, but Illoran came for him with a fierce resolve. Salama'an had been reluctant to fire his pistol near the reactor after being cautioned by the engineer, but now he traded shots with Illoran, attempting to stop the doctor before his wild shots did any significant damage. Now it was Illoran who had to hide.

Preoccupied as they were, neither of them saw Ryane finally get the pistol away from the female. She slammed the soldier's arm against the corner of a machine, accidentally discharging the weapon, but then it was hers, and the female soldier was at her mercy.

On the other side of the room, sparks flew as Illoran and Salama'an continued to trade shots. Illoran was surprised that fear hadn't debilitated his efforts, but it no longer mattered when one of Salama'an's near misses stuck a container of pressurized gas, exploding just to the right of Illoran's position. He was partially shielded by a work station, but the result of the explosion sent him flying backwards.

Illoran was down, bleeding murky-gray from dozens of places where shrapnel had pierced his flesh. He wasn't moving, and Ryane, having witnessed the entire scene, knew he must be dead. Her only ally was gone, and it was the last straw.

Rage she didn't even know she had been keeping down, erupted forth. She raised the pistol and began firing rapidly at Salama'an. She screamed at him, failing even to form words, just wild, emotional noises, venting her fury as she emptied the plasma cartridge. An organic tube burst just inches from Salama'an's head, but luck was on his side and he dodged the rest by taking cover behind the reactor.

Ryane took a step forward, ready to hunt him down, but she was blind-sided, knocked straight to the ground, struck by the recovered female soldier.

Salama'an saw this, and saw that Ryane did not get back up.

The unique glow from the detriminium reactor began to oscillate in rapid succession between light and dark, and the organic tubing running to the machine suddenly blew from its housing, sending steaming hot liquid in every direction.

Salama'an cursed, and quickly contacted Cypha on his cuff's communicator. "Evacuate the ship!" he ordered. "The reactor has been compromised! Load the escape pods for a full evacuation!" He turned and ran straight for the portal, leaping over the fallen male soldier in his path. "Move!" he commanded the female soldier.

Without protest, she quickly followed him out of the reactor room, and Salama'an closed the portal behind her, locking in Ryane, the unconscious male soldier, and the two Scynthian corpses. Without further delay, Salama'an and the female soldier made their way to the nearest escape pod, fighting their way through the panicking flow of crewman.

They reached a pod, the same pod they had found Ryane in only minutes before. It was already half-filled with crewmen, so they quickly took their places along the wall. The female soldier strapped herself into a seat, while Salama'an checked the status of the reactor via the pod's onboard computer. The reactor was in a full melt-down. It could blow at any moment.

Salama'an made the decision. He activated the launching sequence, closing and locking the pod door. He could hear banging on the other side, but once the launching sequence was activated, the doors were unable to be reopened until the pod landed.

Salama'an strapped himself into an empty seat, and the pod detached from the main ship, shooting up through the planet's upper atmosphere to remain in space. The ship was set to auto-pilot back to Scynthia in the event of an emergency, so now they all sat back and waited to dock. He breathed a momentary sigh of relief, and then came the explosion.

It rocked the pod and blew it way off course, but the computer would correct that automatically. What wouldn't be easy would be explaining the ship's destruction to Orric. Not to mention the deaths of those still left aboard the attack vessel. Salama'an's survival instincts had overcome his leadership duties and he had launched his pod earlier than the rest. He would have to wait until they were back on Scynthia to see just how many of his crew were able to evacuate. No matter the number of casualties, things would not bode well for Salama'an.

Illoran stirred to consciousness, disoriented and bleeding badly all over the hard metal floor. He couldn't see or hear a thing, and his body felt numb.

His senses slowly began to return, and the first sensation he felt was a grueling pain throughout his entire body. Pain like he had never experienced before. It overwhelmed him for a moment, but then the intensity began to subside somewhat. His sight returned in a hazy fog that slowly began to clear, and he suddenly became aware of an alarm sounding. He tried to sit up, and was actually surprised when he was able to do so, though more shoots of pain coursed through his body.

"The alarm," he thought, trying to place its meaning, but his concussion was making it very difficult to think. After a moment it finally came to him. "The reactor. It must be compromised. I have to get out of here."

He tried to stand, but found difficulty rising all the way up, and used the work station as a crutch. Red lights were flashing all around him, and the oscillating glow from the reactor was wildly out of control. He saw Ryane a few feet away, lying motionless.

He quickly scanned the room for his medical bag, and, upon spotting it, painfully worked his way over to retrieve its contents. Each step made the shrapnel dig in more, but he tried to move through it. As focused as he was, he failed to notice the male soldier lying unconscious on the floor before him and accidentally tripped over him. He came crashing down onto the male, eliciting a groan from the injured soldier. The human was still alive.

Illoran considered leaving him there; he didn't know how long he had been out for, and, judging by the state of the reactor, he knew he had very little time. But his desire to help others got the better of him, and he decided to try to aid the misguided soldier.

He reached the medical bag, and inside were a number of his skin bandages, which he would use to patch himself up with later, but now he pushed these aside to find the tools he needed. He soon found them, and quickly injected himself with a powerful pain medication. He did the same for the unconscious human, and then opened a vial of liquid ammonia under the male's nose. The powerful vapors seeped into the human's lungs, waking the male almost instantly. He was still dazed, but at least he was awake now.

He made it over to Ryane and did the same, causing her to spring up with a start. He grabbed her by the shoulder, "We need to get to an escape pod! The reactor has destabilized!"

The human soldier was fully awake and on his feet now. He clearly remembered Illoran from their recent encounter, but now, as he took in the present situation, he knew he had been left behind by his shipmates. He did not harbor any ill-will toward his captain or any of the other crewmen, as he was raised with the same consequentialist values that the Scynthians hold dear, but he still did not want to die. In that same moment, he made the decision to throw his lot in with this traitorous, strangely compassionate Scynthian.

"I'm with you," said the soldier.

Illoran nodded, and promptly collapsed again, having driven the shrapnel further into his body from all the movement. His wounds were very serious, but he would have to wait to do anything about that until they were safely on their way in the escape pod.

They were trapped in the room without Illoran to open the portal, so Ryane and the soldier strenuously helped the doctor to his feet, and, together, they made their way from the reactor room. Illoran used his utility cuff to open the portal in the wall, and left it open as they limped down the hallway. Human soldiers were still running to the various pods, but one after the other was launching prematurely with vacant seats still available. The hall was full of panic and chaos.

*Where is the order?* thought Illoran, placing his hand on the wall to take a short rest. *Where are the other Scynthians?*

But the few Scynthians had been the first to launch their pods, not caring about the humans aboard and not wanting to be anywhere near the ship when the reactor blew.

The entire vessel began to shake and rumble, throwing the ship's occupants every which way. A large fissure suddenly opened up in the wall, making a sharp cracking noise and bringing the ceiling down, blocking off the remaining crew

members from the pods. Illoran heard their shouts and pleas for
assistance, but there was nothing he could do to get to them
now, especially not in his current condition. He cursed the
situation, frustrated that all of his life's work in medicine was
for naught in this unfortunate tragedy.

"What are you waiting for?" shouted the male human,
who stood by tugging on the doctor's robe. Blood and tears ran
down the soldier's swollen face, but he held his composure
admirably. "We need to hurry!"

Ryane, too, was urging Illoran to move, and he finally
regained his wits, allowing the humans to assist him into a
nearby pod. They quickly took their seats and strapped
themselves in beside three other human soldiers who sat with
frightened looks upon their faces.

The portal to the pod slid shut, and the small life-vessel
detached from the ship, jettisoning outward on its way back to
Scynthia. Illoran quickly remembered this, and was hurrying to
unstrap himself from his seat.

"What are you doing?" asked the male soldier, but
Illoran ignored his question. He stood, with difficulty, and
approached the pod's onboard computer system. This system
was much more user friendly than the computer in the reactor
room, and he was quickly able to input new coordinates for the
life-vessel.

"You can't do that," said the male soldier, unstrapping
himself now so that he could intervene, but, just then, the pod's
mother-ship erupted into a fury of flames and debris, sending a
pulse wave of energy in every direction. The pod was struck
and sent careening off-kilter, causing both Illoran and the male
human to launch forward into the wall, destroying the
computer screen. The energy wave overloaded the vessel's
circuitry, and sparks flew from the walls momentarily before
the pod lost all power, leaving it on an unalterable course for
Tatora.

Too Far Gone

# Chapter Twenty-Nine
# Kismet

I stared hopelessly up into the sky, watching the glowing orb of light, I noticed several smaller objects suddenly eject from the craft, shooting away in quick succession. Not long after, the Scynthian vessel spontaneously broke apart in one violent explosion, showering flames and debris in every direction. The brilliant sight elicited many awe-filled gasps from Tatoran spectators, but I simply stood and stared, dumbfounded.

"It's a miracle!" Nepalen exclaimed. "By the hand of Carnyle, we are saved!"

"I'm not quite sure of that," I said pessimistically. "Not while the Scynthians know we're here."

No sooner had I uttered the sentence than more shouts of terror came from the watching spectators.

"A piece of the vessel!" Nepalen exclaimed, pointing up into the sky. "It's headed right for us!"

I wheeled about, seeing the object hurtling straight toward the city, covered in bright flames. It sped through the sky at tremendous speeds, remaining intact the entire way. The citizens went running for shelter, but their small homes would provide no protection against such an impact. It was pointless to try and tell them that though.

I watched in horror as the object approached the city. At that moment, I hadn't a doubt in my mind that it was some kind of massive Scynthian missile, and, with their superior weaponry, probably capable of decimating all of Mercer in one devastating blow.

"What have I done?" I asked aloud, but to no one in particular. To be sure, there was no one left to even answer, as Nepalen had also futilely sought shelter inside with Alexitus.

278

Pinut, too, was absent, but I didn't see which way she had gone.

I didn't even try to run. I'd rather watch until that final moment came.

I had just come to terms with my most probable death when the missile was just overhead, booming as it broke the sound barrier. I could see now that its trajectory had changed slightly, and it would touch down somewhere right outside the city in the thehnwood forest, but the distance wouldn't be enough to save us. Scynthians were thorough creatures, and soon it would all be over.

I watched as it passed by overhead, now less than a hundred feet from the ground. Suddenly, it slowed with unnatural abruptness, captured and redirected by the newly-installed Dotaran Equalizer at Finnis' center. It was still traveling at a considerable speed, though, and then sunk below the tree line outside of the city.

The impact rumbled the earth, showering the surrounding forest with dirt, trees, and other debris, but there was no explosion. I waited for a few seconds, my body tensed, bracing for impact, but still nothing. I stood there, completely bemused. I had thought for sure the Scynthians were putting an end to me, the Dotaran captaincy, and our new-found Mercerian allies with one fatal strike, but the fact that I still stood proved my assumptions incorrect. I was entirely grateful to be so wrong.

*But then what was that thing that had fallen from the sky?* I thought. *Just debris from the ship? Its flight path and changing speeds weren't consistent with free-falling debris though, so what was it?* "An escape pod!" I shouted as the answer came to me.

The Finnisians slowly began to stir from their houses, peeking out their doors to make sure everything still stood.

Rengar abruptly rode down the city's main avenue on a fine looking bipedal rapt, with a contingent of warriors following in suit.

"Find the crash site," he ordered his warriors, "but be on the lookout for any danger. As the Dotarans have already made clear, the Scynthians are crafty and deceitful beings, and we don't know what they are capable of."

With that, the warriors, led by Ricson on his ski-cycle, broke off from their high chieftain and entered the forest to investigate. Pinut had taken one of the other ski-cycles to check on Alexitus and me, so I borrowed it to follow after Ricson. I was curious to see if anyone inside the life vessel had survived the crash.

The first sign of the crash site came when we found the beginning of the debris field, where a section of forest had been completely obliterated by the sizeable object, leaving behind stumps of trees and upturned roots along a hundred foot path. At the end of the path was a shallow crater. It must have been fifty feet in diameter, and clouds of smoke billowed out from its center, but the vessel beneath the smoke remained unseen.

We had approached silently, and now Ricson signaled for part of his contingent to flank the crater and surround it from every side. When everyone was in place, Ricson motioned for two of his warriors to follow him down into the crater. They gave each other worried glances, but obeyed the order nonetheless.

They slowly crept down to the base of the crater, stopping before the diminishing billows of smoke. Along with a few other soldiers, I moved in closer out of morbid curiosity. The two chosen warriors looked to their leader. He nodded to them to proceed further, and then turned to me. "Jaxon, you have seen some of the capabilities of the Scynthians, have you not?"

"Not much," I replied, "but yes, I have somewhat of an idea."

"What can my warriors expect to find down here?" he asked.

I had to think for a moment, and then gave Ricson the best answer I could come up with. "I doubt any living creature could have survived a crash like that, but it has to be some kind of life vessel. Probably for survivors from whatever happened up there in the sky."

"It could carry Scynthians?" Ricson asked.

One of the warriors made it to the center of the crater. "We found something, Sir! It's some kind of strange metal ball. It's big, too, but most of it is trapped under the dirt. The smoke is pouring out of a hole in the metal!"

"Be cautious," he said, moving closer toward them.

"Wait," said the warrior. "Something is happening!"

All three of them jumped back from the object as a portal opened at its top. It opened in the same fashion that the rock wall in the cave under my uncle's cabin on Earth had; the metal receded into itself, which I now knew was due to the detriminium-powered mattertrons of the Scynthians.

Nothing emerged through the portal except for a misty vapor, so, after a minute of consternation, Ricson and the two warriors poked their heads inside the opening.

"What do you see?" I asked.

"Bodies," Ricson replied. "One of them is a Scynthian, but the rest are hu-mans like you."

"Humans?" I said in disbelief. I was at the bottom of the crater in a heartbeat.

"Are there any survivors?" I asked, still scrambling.

"I don't think so," said Ricson. "Wait, the Scynthian! Its hand just moved!"

"They're all starting to move!" said one of the other warriors.

I was right behind them now, and Ricson moved over slightly to allow me a space beside him. I peered into the pod, and when I did, my heart skipped a beat. The whole world seemed to go silent and everything came to a stand-still. At the bottom of pod, just opening her beautiful green eyes, was the love of my life. It was you.

# Epilogue

Salama'an tapped his webbed fingers on his arm rest, nervous of what the Council would do about his tremendous failure.

"Something is wrong," said one of the humans sitting next to the pod's only window. "We seem to be heading back toward the Tatoran planet."

Salama'an unbuckled himself and went to the window. *The human is correct.* He quickly ran to the pod's computer, and found that the navigations were set for Mercer. *Illoran*, he thought with hatred. *He must have changed the coordinates when he was trying to flee with the Earth female.*

He began adjusting the coordinates to bring them safely home to Scynthia, but paused mid-way through. *I can't return to Scynthia, not after all that has just happened. Not after so much failure. But if I finish the mission, I'll be welcomed back, and perhaps even granted a seat on the new Council.*

Salama'an looked around the pod, and at its seven human occupants. "We're going down to the planet," he declared. "We're going to carry out the mission."

The pod, however, held very little in terms of weaponry. Tucked away in hidden compartments were food rations, survival supplies, and a pair of plasma pistols. With his own, that gave them three, but there was no larger weaponry stored aboard, and three pistols wouldn't be enough against even a small crowd of armed Mercerians.

An idea settled in his mind, and he knew what they would do. He quickly entered in a new set of coordinates, and the pod rolled slightly, shifting toward its new destination. Salama'an then strode back to his seat.

The pod soared down through the planet's atmosphere, streaking through the sky completely engulfed in flames at first. It punched through a thick cloudscape, and then began to slow its descent. Dense clouds surrounded the pod, obscuring sight of anything through the small window, but the pod was well on course. Soon the spherical vessel entered a brightly-lit tunnel, at the bottom of which it came to a gentle stop inside a large room.

Salama'an used his arm cuff to open the pod's entrance, and was the first to disembark, followed by the rest of his human crew.

Two more Scynthians came in to the room through a nearby door. They both seemed surprised and a bit flustered. "We weren't expecting any arrivals today," one of them said.

"There was no time to notify you," Salama'an replied, "but Orric has sent me on an important mission, and I will need your assistance to carry out our plans."

The new Scynthians nodded their heads in understanding. "Right this way," said one of them.

Salama'an and his humans were led down a hallway and into a massive room with a glass domed-ceiling, while three of the walls had foundations of rock. Along one of the walls was a line of cells recessed into the rock, all empty save for one, which held a strange blue captive; the original captain of the Aramis, Captain Traeger.

**Here ends the third book in *The Jaxon Grey Chronicles*. Jaxon's story will continue in book four, *Here Today, Gone Tomorrow*. For more adventure on Tatora, visit the series website at TheJaxonGreyChronicles.com or check out the Facebook page.**

**The Story So Far....**

Tatora

# <u>Days on Tatora</u>

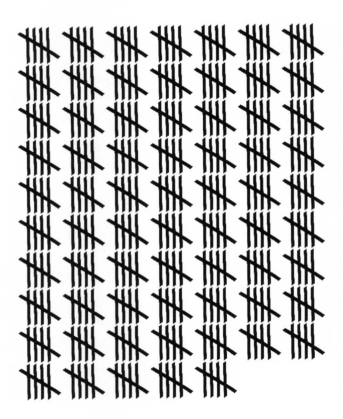

40260780R00170

Made in the USA
Middletown, DE
25 March 2019